COMBA

Author

Brian Elliott

"...Combating Evil portrays an awesome insight into terrorism, and the fight against it...

It is a 'no holds barred', violent thriller, that leaves little to the imagination, and moves along at an incredible, and absorbing pace...

The author graphically depicts action in Northern Ireland and around the world, that leaves the reader absolutely riveted and captivated by the raw brutality of terrorism..."

...Publisher

Help4U Publishing

Copyright: © Brian Elliott 2001.

The right of Brian Elliott to be identified as the author of this work has been asserted in accordance with the Copyright Designs and Patents Act 1988.
All rights reserved. No part of this publication may be reproduced, transcribed, transmitted, stored within a retrieval system, translated into another language in any form or by any means electronic, mechanical, photocopying, recording or otherwise without the prior permission in writing of the publishers.

A catalogue record of this publication is available from the British Library:

First Edition 2001

TRADEMARKS: any product names mentioned within this publication may be trademarks or registered trademarks of their respective companies and are hereby acknowledged.
Although the author has researched the details presented in this book as thoroughly as possible, he assumes no responsibility for any errors, omissions or inaccuracies that may be contained therein. No liability can be accepted for any losses or expenses incurred as a result of relying on any information given therein.

Any similarity between the events and circumstances described and fictitious persons named within, to actual events or circumstances that may or may not have taken place, and to any person or persons, either dead or alive, is purely coincidental.

ISBN   1842740180   Paperback
ISBN   1842740369   eBook - PDF

Printed & bound by Antony Rowe Ltd, Eastbourne

Cover design by Ability   graphics@ability.org

Published in soft back by Help4U Publishing, Preston, UK
.http://www.help4u.net
Visit the Combating Evil Web Site at:
http://www.ewebmarketing.co.uk/combatingevil/index.html

Help4U Publishing

Dedication

**I would like to dedicate this book
To the loving memory of my brother
Gordon
Who was tragically killed**

1942–2001

Citation

"...Warrant Officer Simpson was the Military Intelligence Officer, based in Enniskillen, in the County of Fermanagh. He was the senior Source Handler, recruiting and working with Provisional Irish Republican Army Informants. Although the full details of his work can never be disclosed, it has to be said that his efforts in the fight against terrorism were immeasurable.

Covering a 3-year period, he penetrated 3 Provisional Irish Republican Army Brigades. He personally led 48 Operations, procuring vital information, which was used by Special Forces, in the arrest of terrorists. His driving ability, his dogmatic perseverance, and his forceful character, enabled him to accomplish these operations under the most dangerous, severe and stressful conditions.

His outstanding achievements were paramount in him being placed as one of the most effective and efficient army intelligence operators since the beginning of the Northern Ireland Campaign. He displayed outstanding leadership, fortitude and courage, above the normal call of duty..."

* * *

Regimental Sergeant Major Jack Simpson retired in 1985.
He had served on Operational Tours in Aden, Two in Borneo,
and Six in Northern Ireland.

It was nearly seven years later, that he received a telephone call that would involve him in a harrowing and dramatic Operation.

The Operation was called:

"COMBATING EVIL"

Prologue 1991

Sheer fear and terror was etched on the faces of the two British soldiers. IRA terrorists had captured them; their worst fears realised when Bernadette McGough snarled at them in a most belligerent and menacing voice.

'Move!'

She was head of PIRA's internal security, purposefully formed as interrogators to debrief any member of the PIRA organisation who had been arrested by the security forces. If and when released from custody, after questioning, their terrorist bed-fellows were subjected to more intensive questioning by the PIRA squads. PIRA needed to know whether or not there own security had been compromised, and they were also interested in the security forces interrogation techniques.

Then, as the threat from within grew, PIRA learned to deal with the problem of informers, also known as touts; it had become an enormous issue. In the previous year, the PIRA Army Council estimated that eight out of ten operations in Belfast were compromised because of their own members selling information.

The most experienced, hardened, and ruthless interrogators, were brought in. They dealt with the touts in the most merciless manner. In most cases, victims were severely tortured to death. Their bodies often dumped in full public view, in the republican areas. And there they remained, their own families not even allowed to remove them, until ordered to do so.

* * *

The two soldiers, Lt Jeremy Carver and Sergeant Heather Calvert had been seconded from their parent Regiments to work on covert surveillance operations.

Jeremy was in the first week of his second operations tour in the province; no longer a raw recruit or naive to the perils of the Province. All his young life he had excelled at virtually everything undertaken, had earlier attended University at Newcastle and achieved excellent results. He loved the military way of life, and it was his destiny. He had been training all his life to follow in his father's footsteps, to be special, to be a member of the elite Special Air Service Regiment. Naturally, with a degree under his belt he went off to the military academy at Sandhurst.

He had already mastered four European languages by the age of sixteen, and two years later, along with his normal studies, had become fluent in Arabic and well on the way with Farsi. He was still far behind his father with languages but would catch up, one day.

He was a fitness fanatic and trained extremely hard, and had developed a strong athletic body. He knew what he wanted to do, and had put every effort into achieving his aims, both physically and mentally.

At 23, he'd completed his training and passed out as a second lieutenant. Posted to Aldershot, he joined the Parachute Regiment, and shortly after completing his parachute training his Battalion was sent on a 5-month tour to Northern Ireland.

Most of that tour had been mundane stuff, not a lot happening. He had organised VCP's, these were vehicle check points, set up to dominate a particular area, deterring the movement of terrorists and there weapons, ammunitions, and bombs.

A huge amount of information could be gleaned from a well-briefed VCP, so they were a vital part of the intelligence gathering mechanism. He also, among other things organised foot-patrols, close observation posts and did his share of duty operations officer, and learning all the time. Eventually their tour had ended and they returned to barracks in Aldershot.

After gaining his 'second pip' and being promoted to Lieutenant, he spent some time in his administrative role, still loving the activity, the sports, and the great friendships building amongst high quality people.

Young officers were encouraged to broaden their experience by joining other units for a period of time, while some went off on helicopter pilot's courses, some to be seconded to foreign armies.

As his ambition was to follow in his fathers' footsteps into 22 Special Air Service Regiment, he had decided to gain experience by requesting a secondment to an Intelligence Company. It was a specialist surveillance unit, working in Northern Ireland, and if he succeeded with that role he would be well prepared for a career in the SAS. He'd sailed through the very intensive course and, good or bad, was posted straight back to Northern Ireland.

This was his third day of a week's area familiarisation course with Sergeant Heather Calvert, a pretty and very likeable Geordie, who had confessed to thinking him the most gorgeous man on this earth.

He was tall, dark, and handsome. Pleasant, highly intelligent, and with a humour that knew no bounds, his dirty jokes and the skill that he could deliver them had everyone in stitches. He'd already proved to be tremendous for the morale of the unit and Heather had further admitted to looking forward to working with him. She was now a relatively experienced operator, with 8 months service on her current tour.

They had never been on an operation together, and Jeremy was racking his brain trying to determine why they had been ambushed. Who else was in the car park?

Damn it they were in a country pub near Bangor, in general a good safe area where off duty soldiers with families socialised; a beer garden, children's swings and seesaws. All together an idyllic setting for a wonderful day out with the family.

This did not make sense, but there again this was Ulster. They had only stopped for a few moments to discuss the area that they had been through. Nothing untoward about that, and they had strictly observed all the rules when moving around covertly within the province.

They had not been followed.

Then, all of a sudden, a thought flashed to him. I have it! This could be a training exercise. A very realistic one, and they've certainly achieved their objectives. God they have, and scared the wits out of me.

Please, please let it be a training exercise...

* * *

Heather was thinking of the worst scenario, that maybe they had stumbled into a PIRA operation. This was always a feared hazard. Life was fraught with danger, every single day. Real danger, a danger you could taste, a danger that lingered and festered around every street corner, around every blind turning on any road. It was a perpetual danger, and it was a danger they faced, man or woman engaged in the silent world of the intelligence operators.

PIRA were well known to lay snap illegal vehicle

checkpoints. Anytime, anywhere, anyone could be prone to either being lifted or taken out by this method. These men had scared the daylights out of both of them back at the pub. All three had worn balaclava masks over their faces during the ambush, and that alone was a terrifying sight.

Long after being bundled into the front the van and driven away, it stopped at a lay-by and two of the men got out and started pissing. A female, with an armalite pointed directly at Jeremy, then motioned to Heather with the barrel end of the weapon, and snapped:

'Get out, and get in the front, now, move!' Heather hadn't, and had chosen the security of Jeremy's presence.

One of the men, standing at the back of the vehicle, had jumped in, and had grabbed her right breast. She'd screamed with the viciousness and surprise of the attack. Her assailant had then roared at her, 'Do as you're fucking well told. Now move - and Heather had!

She was now petrified.

* * *

Jeremy's stomach was churning; this was definitely not a training exercise. How could this have happened in his first week, but more importantly, how could he get them both out of this situation? If it was just himself, an opening could lend itself at any time. He felt sure that he could take out two of the men, but that would leave Heather to fend for herself and he couldn't do that.

He knew she must be feeling very uncomfortable in the front of the vehicle, the driver kept touching her leg, and she kept knocking his hand away. The female alongside grabbed the back of her neck, squeezed tightly, and then produced a wickedly shaped knife.

'Touch his hand again, tart, and I'll reshape your fucking face.'

Heather turned white with the sheer menace in the female terrorist's voice. She had known then the deep quandary they were in; knife at her throat, the driver in her pants, and the fingers of his left hand searching, probing; hurting. She had to ease her legs apart; the pain inflicted making her cry out.

Jeremy sensed what was going on; helplessly looking straight into the barrel of a deadly weapon. Then the female eventually yelled at the driver, 'Pack it in, there will be more time for that later on, now get a move on.' He did exactly as he was told. There was no doubt who the leader of the group was.

* * *

They had been driving for some time now, and Heather knew they were running parallel with the border in County Fermanagh, having turned right at Belcoo, heading north. She also knew there were many points where they could turn left and cross the border into the south, but was surprised when they turned right and steered east off the B52 and headed off into the bleak Fermanagh countryside. It was a very rough ride and seemingly endless.

They finally pulled up at a derelict, where she was yanked out and given a vicious kick on the legs and shoved towards the entrance. Jeremy received the same treatment. At all times, one of the terrorists was standing uncomfortably close with an armalite menacingly at their backs.

'Take off your clothes,' yelled the female terrorist.

It was cold, freezing cold, and the biting wind was whistling through the old derelict building. Most of the roof, apart from two cross-members, was missing. The walls had equally taken their toll over the years and had been battered by the incessant high winds and rain, which had caused their slow disintegration over the years.

Despite being pushed to the centre of the derelict, Jeremy bravely shouted at their leader, 'this has gone far enough, we are British citizens, and...'

And, that was as far as he got when the female terrorist stuck the blade of her knife straight into Heathers mouth between her top front teeth and her lip. Heather was up on her toes gasping; blood pouring from her open mouth.

They were yelled at again. 'Take your fucking clothes off, now.' Jeremy was aghast and Heather started to cry both with pain and fear.

'What is this all about? We really are just tourists visiting Northern Ireland.'

'Don't you fucking lie to me, and speak only when I say so. Now, do as I've said and strip.'

Jeremy started to undress, but Heather remained standing and crying.

'Sean, Joe, get her clothes off.'

They launched into Heather. She screamed and yelled at

them, trying to fight, hitting and scratching, but to no avail. They did not take her clothes off, they ripped them off, and where they didn't come off easy the knife helped.

Eventually they were standing, naked, vulnerable, and helpless. Heather was almost breathless; the cold biting into their flesh. They were high up on barren hills, trembling, shocked, horrified, and feeling the cold more than they had ever experienced in their young lives.

'Now, Mr tourist, please enlighten me. Which Regiment are you from?'

Jeremy stood as still as possible and did not answer. The bitch terrorist was right in front of him. He was over six feet tall, which forced her to look up, though she purposefully glanced down at the full mat of hair on his chest and, to further extremities of his well built anatomy. What she saw there was of no interest, other than to make him squeal.

'Well, Mr big man tourist, you do not want to talk do you? Well let's see if this will help.'

She cupped his left testicle and dug hard with her nails and squeezed.

Jeremy gritted his teeth, trying not to let her win, but the pain was agonising, and she would not let go or ease off. She then smiled and did the same to his right testicle. The agony shot right through his body.

'How long have you been talking to your fuckin' tout, my man Mulvenny?'

He remained silent, thinking; I don't believe this. He wanted to scream, you have the wrong people, and if he did, would she believe him - no, he thought, not this one.

She again grabbed his testicles. This time with both hands, squeezing, wrenching, 'Tell me what I want to know? Well Mr bigman tourist, you're going against your own training. Even I know the resistance to interrogation techniques that they fuckin' teach at Ashford.'

The driver of the van, while this was going on, unloaded a large canvas bag and was now lighting a fire in the corner of the building. This was one hell of a bitch, thought Jeremy. What next? Should he tell them who he was?

He was shaking, this kind of treatment during training was far less intimidating, and the cold, the fucking cold was mind numbing. He couldn't dam well think straight. What would his father do in this situation? He was naked, humiliated, hurting like hell, and knew there was more pain to come. Confirmed when his hands were tied together and a rope secured to his bindings. Slung over one of the beams, he was then heaved up, his toes just touching the ground.

'Now strap him,' yelled the bitch.

The men had thick, studded, leather belts, and laid into him until he finally screamed. The force with which they leathered him made resounding smacks that reverberated around the close confines of the derelict.

It went on and on. His aching body, stinging, throbbing, shaking, and despite the freezing cold he was sweating profusely from the heat generated by the beating. With his body heaving on the ropes he gasped and gulped for air, then let out a howl to waken the dead he guessed might be buried nearby. His assailants stepped back, as though shocked, and had at least paused allowing respite to searing welts.

His breathing, along with his assailants, was very loud; rasping, his body bleeding, bruises welling on his back, on his legs, buttocks, arms, and chest. He was racked with pain, his body on fire, but still, the freezing, freezing cold. He could not take this much longer and he could not tell them anything. He didn't know anything!

Then, with a great sigh, Jeremy's resistance snapped, inner resolve unbroken. He screamed out. 'We don't know anything...' He was snivelling, sobbing, hating himself for such weakness... 'You have the wrong people...' He yelled the same thing, time, and time again, his head finally sagging forward onto his chest. He was utterly exhausted.

Bernadette smiled, then spat at him. 'You're a filthy liar and I'll be back. Joe, get the bag.'

She moved slowly toward Heather.

Heather, trying desperately to pull herself together, thought; my god, we've been mistakenly taken for source handlers. Source handlers, to PIRA were equal scums of the earth. They were the ones who recruited informers and then paid or blackmailed the information out of them. They were despised like nothing else, handler and tout alike.

The absurd horror of the situation had hit them both; they were being tortured for information that they knew nothing about. This little vixen was not about to accept that, she knew that the instant Bernadette set to ogling her body. The blood running down her chin, down between her breasts and on down, seemingly amused the other woman...

Heather was dumbstruck. The horror of Jeremy's beating revolving in her mind, still painfully aware of the knife previously thrust into her mouth. Startling reality to their present predicament. As Bernadette moved behind her that frightened her even more, and she cried out quite loudly; a vision of what was going to happen, too vivid, too horrific, a trickle of wee displaying utter fear and further degradation...

Heather stuttered and stammered, 'I need to go... I need to go...please.'

Bernadette grinned and pushed her towards the open entrance and when outside said, 'do your business.'

Heather squatted, naked, freezing cold, with Bernadette looking on. What kind of monster had they come up against? She looked around at vast acres of nothing. Just the type of terrain that normally she would have loved to roam.

But now, reality, what could they do?

She felt the point of Bernadette's knife right down on her lower back. 'Don't even think about it, darling. You're going to tell us all about our man, who by now will be screaming his fucking head off.'

Heather cried again, the female beast caressing her back and bum.

'Now get back in and start talking. When and where did you first turn Mulvenny?'

Heather froze in horror when she looked at the ground in front of Jeremy. The enormity of it, it impacted upon her. Instruments of torture, no, no, surely not, she thought, now looking at pliers, pincers, a portable electric drill, and what looked like iron rods with wooden handles.

Now, both she and Jeremy knew the contents of the canvas bag...

She glanced over at the fire, seeking warmth but didn't find it. What she saw was the fearsome sight of the red-hot glow of iron, a rod already in the fire. Oh my god, she thought. She looked at Jeremy, their eyes meeting in mutual rapport of sufferance to pain, his suffering at present greater than hers. The shites had hurt him bad. Trembling, lips dry and quivering, almost feeling the horrific pain that would be inflicted upon her, her tears flowed and flowed.

Bernadette grinned, the awesome power she held over them perfectly executed, the pathetic sight in front of her obviously pleasing to her and her partisans.

Heather glanced at the knife and pliers that Bernadette held, and although she tried not to, she screamed and screamed.

* * *

Heather Calvert came from a town that lay in a westerly direction 10 miles distant from both Newcastle and Durham, and although not a true Geordie, she prided herself on local accent and origins.

Heather came along late in her parents' marriage, in fact they were amazed that after trying for 13 years, to be finally blessed with a baby. To Gladys and Matt Calvert, both in their early forties, Heather was their miracle, their pride and joy. She was god's gift to them, and they doted on her. They gave her everything, and all through her young life she returned their strong adulation, and the love and devotion, to both.

At eighteen she had needed something out of her life. Her dad had worked down the pits, until at fifty the miner's disease, silicosis, had taken its toll. He was nothing more than an invalid now, spending his various but meagre pensions at the club and the bookies. Her mam had had her hands full with him.

It was time to make a move. At Leadgate, living in her parent's old miners' bungalow, she had lived life as best she could, working in several jobs until her decision to join the army. Her mam and dad were proud of their little girl, but going off to make something of her life in the forces caused some hard swallowing and regret at having to finally let her fly the coop.

She always enjoyed going back home and, taking her parents out to the local. Never any further, for that was what they enjoyed, pints down the club and showing their daughter off to friends and neighbours. 'Yes 'Marra',' her dad would boast, 'she's a corporal now.'

He lived for his daughter, worshipped the ground she walked on and when at home, now, she was his little sergeant. Well, he just about walked on clouds, although he didn't really know what a sergeant was or did, but it had to be very high up. Officer of sorts.

He always cried with happiness for her. Her mam, well she fell in with whatever suited her man that's the way it was up north. But secretly, mam wanted her baby home, she hadn't wanted her to go away in the first place, but thought she had done well.

She was going to marry next year, maybe then she would return with her man and give them their first grandchild. After all, they were not getting any younger.

* * *

Heather had fainted. The boot of one of the men brought her back to reality. Naked and embarrassed, she looked up at the two men standing, grinning, and gawking.

She just lay there in stunned silence recollecting and trying to gather her thoughts together. She started sniffling, her nerves shattered. She couldn't control herself; the freezing cold was on her, in her. All the while Bernadette, mocked her, laughed and then looked to both men, 'well, boys, do you want some fun?'

Both grinned and handed their weapons to the driver. Heather knew her fate. Her eyes pleaded to this thing, this monster, but there was only silent response from the arrogant bitch, disdain of hate in her eyes, followed by a simple nod.

As the men grabbed Heather she became hysterical, begging, pleading, screaming.

'No, Please no, what do you want, what can I do, please no…not this?'

'Tell me about your tout, my man, Mulvenny?' screamed the bitch. 'What is your name, what is your rank?'

'I…we, …do not know him… Please, please…' Heather stammered.

'She is telling the truth for god's sake,' shouted Jeremy.

'Shut your fucking mouth. I told you not to speak… both of you…' she screamed at them… 'Until I say so. Is that fuckin' understood?' she yelled, and then slowly walked over to him. Jeremy froze. This could not be happening. He saw the hostility, the raving lunacy bulging from those demented eyes, and then the vicious swipe with the pliers into his mouth, smashing his teeth, informed him that it was reality; a living nightmare.

'Now fucking shut up,' she retorted, the temper rising in her voice. Confronting Heather again, 'now for the last time, tell me about Mulvenny. What was the last information he gave you?'

There was a dreadful, chilling silence as the brutes dragged Heather over to the corner. Both thugs then removed their trousers. 'No, no… My god, no…' she pleaded, but this seemingly excited them even more.

She was soon being brutalised by two evil and vile men.

They were at her, doing things she had never experienced. They were hurting her like two dogs scrabbling for supremacy over a meaty bone. The hard ground, stones digging in to her flesh, they were biting, hitting, slapping, raping her; in her mouth, grunting and groaning and grinding, changing around... So it went, on...and on... and on...

Jeremy was forced to watch. As if on cue, the men then stopped, resting back against the wall. They were grinning, their victim on her back, on the floor, her legs wide apart; shuddering, sobbing, utterly broken. There was momentary quiet, respite from attack hardly noticeable beneath the manic glare of lecherous intent. The sequence of previous assault was soon repeated with a vengeance, as the men laughed, and finally retreated to put on their trousers.

'Pick her up and bring her here,' raged Bernadette.

The tormentors supported Heather; held her in front of the depraved demon of a woman. 'Are you going to tell me what I want to know?' She yelled.

Heather responded with a loud piecing scream. The depth and fear, generated by the scream, shocked Jeremy, and even in his own agony, he felt distress and sorrow knowing that her mind was deteriorating, very quickly. She then succumbed to intermittent crying and sobbing for her mam, crying for her dad, her sobs making Jeremy cringe and squirm, especially knowing that his turn was next. True to expected form Bernadette nodded.

The men knew what was next, and pulled Heather like a sack of potatoes across in front of Jeremy, kicking their tools out of the way. The fiendish bitch had wanted her standing in front of Jeremy, both feet immediately kicked from under her. She then thudded down on her knees.

Jeremy suddenly realised what they were going to make her do and shouted, 'for mercies sake, you've done enough to her. Let her go.'

'Certainly, bigboy, when you tell me what I want to know.'

Jeremy was in an appalling situation and could only say, with a trembling pain filled voice. 'Please, please believe me, we know nothing of touts, and we're not handlers or whatever you think we might be. Leave her alone, I beg of you...'

Bernadette glared at him, her eyes full of malice, 'we have plenty of time, and you'll break in the end, bigboy. Better now, and save this snivelling wretch any further pain.'

Jeremy was shaking from head to foot; mortified at what they were forcing her to do to him. Christ, what did they expect from him, from Heather? Sexual delirium? Not a chance in hell. Tears ran down his face. He knew his life was going to end, and also that of his sweet, kind and friendly Geordie companion.

They were nearly pulling her hair out with their vile actions.

...And then, at long last...release...then they stopped.

It was not the end for her; they attacked her again, this time with fists, belts and boots. Then pulled back as the female terrorist approached.

Wielding a knife she pointed it at Heather's right breast, said, 'your name and your rank...'

...And to Jeremy's horror, Heather screamed...

'Sergeant Heather Calvert...'

They all turned to face Jeremy...

Bernadette walked up to him, seething, she said, 'you fuckin' liar, you fuckin' liar...now you will tell us about your fuckin' tout!'

Jeremy forlornly shook his head and said, 'we are not tout handlers or whatever you call us...'

She interrupted, 'liar, tell me now about Mulvenny or, she will die.'

Jeremy was swaying on the ropes, devastated, destroyed and couldn't think of anything to protect his young sergeant.

Bernadette nodded at them and the brutes started at her again. They eventually left her beaten, battered and pounded, her face a gory bloody mess, destroyed beyond recognition.

Dead or alive? He couldn't be sure...

Bernadette moved to the fireplace, picked up the red hot rod and felt the heat surge through into the large wooden handle. She moved to stand in front of Jeremy. She then grinned, and held the rod directly in front of his eyes, said, 'you will tell me everything I need to know.'

Then it was moved slowly down, but away from his body, the hairs singeing with the heat. He gasped for breath, the heat from the iron searing him. She moved the rod back up, now getting closer, heat intensely unbearable. 'No, please... No,' he screamed, through shattered teeth.

'Tell me bigboy, tell me.'

She lowered the rod right down, whilst tears streamed down his face as he bellowed the most hideous screaming howl that followed the monstrous and tortuous agony, that she was inflicting upon him.

'Tell me, tell me, tell me...' she screamed at him, her eyes practically bulging out of their sockets.

His sphincter gave way, which was his only response, and then he passed out...

* * *

Chapter One

The telephone call was from the Commanding Officer of Jeremy's Unit. 'Sir, I regret to inform you that your son, Jeremy, is missing in Northern Ireland.'

Brigadier Carver was awaiting a new appointment and was on the holding staff now based in the barracks at Knightsbridge, West London. He was stunned. 'What on earth do you mean, Colonel? My son only joined your unit this week. What the fuck's going on?'

'Your son was on a familiarisation exercise of his area with an operator that he was going to be working with. They pulled into a countryside pub near Bangor, were attacked, and dragged under gunpoint from their vehicle by at least three men. They were driven off by what we believe now to be a PIRA internal security team. A second PIRA team picked up Brendan Mulvenny, who has been an RUC tout for some time. The RUC Special Branch handlers changed their routine and observed the pub, and their tout, through binoculars, watching general movement in the area, assessed the situation, in order to protect their own security. They saw a Ford Escort pull into the car park at 1100 hours. The occupants sat for a few minutes looking at a map. Mulvenny was already in the car park, he got out and headed in the direction of the escort, he then stopped and turned, then tried to run. He never made it, he was taken by two men and was thrown on the floor of a grey Land Rover, and driven away. Another PIRA team was there, in a Bedford van. The RUC handlers had their vehicle parked in woods near the pub and were unable to follow the van. We have not heard anything since. A major hunt is underway, sir.'

Brigadier Carver was shocked, stomach churning, said, 'surely an operation like the RUC were running demanded back-up and the area secured before handlers or touts got there.'

'That has been the case in the past, sir, but budget restrictions... limiting overtime has had all departments running operations on a shoestring. That is why they were taking the precautions they were... Sir, I am required on my other line. I will be in touch immediately I hear anything.'

David immediately called his ex-wife, Sarah, explaining what happened, trying to reassure her that everything that possibly could be done was being done. Carver knew the danger his son was in.

He also knew that Jeremy had very little or no chance of getting out alive from such a bloody unfortunate situation. He felt compelled to get over to the Province, right now. Not that he could do anything; not knowing where his son was or whether he was alive or dead.

He could only pray, shaking, trembling, 'please god, ...not like this, ...no...'

The Chief of Staff, Colonel Harry Windsor, knocked and walked in, saying, 'sir, there's a major incident going on in Ulster. "A Company" has despatched their Lynx helicopters, with four teams aboard. They will be there shortly.' Windsor paused, 'sir, are you all right?' Harry Windsor had known his boss for years and never before had he seen him like this.

'Harry, please sit down,' said Brigadier Carver, his battle hardened face tear-stained. 'A PIRA nutting squad has seized my son.'

'Oh my god, no sir!' replied Harry Windsor.

Regaining a modicum of composure, the Brigadier commanded, 'Harry, get me on the next available shuttle. I'm leaving now for Heathrow. I don't care who has to be taken off it, get me on that flight.'

'Sir, Tom Galloway is up here with a helicopter from Netheravon. He's across at Chelsea Barracks and would get you there much quicker.'

David Carver agreed immediately. 'Get Tom jacked up to leave now, let Netheravon know and ask them to organise a flight plan and refuelling stop at Liverpool. Knowing Tom he will have already refuelled the moment he landed, so he will be ready to move.'

David knew that the flight would take about two hours including stopping for fuel. He also knew he had a very experienced pilot in Tom Galloway, who had served nearly twenty years as a helicopter pilot, twelve of which were with 22 Special Air Service Regiment.

He had first met Tom when he was flying both Scouts and Sioux helicopters in Borneo. He had lost count how many times Tom had extracted himself and his men from forward positions. More so, when in dangerous guerrilla held areas where they probably shouldn't have been in the first place. Pickups were always a very difficult and hazardous task, but Tom just took such heroic acts in his stride.

Trying to take his mind off the immediate predicament of feeling totally helpless, the brigadier watched Tom's skilled hands handling the Gazelle. When David finally boarded the aircraft Tom had already done his pre take off checks and the rotor blades were spinning at full speed. They were biting the air, just waiting for David to strap himself into the five-point harness, which would secure him in the front passenger seat. Then all that Tom had to do would be to raise the collective with his left hand, and the helicopter would begin to rise.

He was only a few feet off the ground, when he used the two-foot pedals to gradually turn the Gazelle 90 degrees to put them on the forward heading that they wanted. Tom did just that and within seconds he climbed to three hundred feet and was following the Thames towards Barnes, talking at the same time with the Air Traffic Controllers at Heathrow. He was soon flying at about one thousand feet, when he was instructed to head north to RAF Northolt. From there he was passed from Heathrow control to London military and headed on a bearing that would take him directly to Liverpool. They were at a top speed of 140 knots, or 150 miles per hour, when Tom made contact with Birmingham Airport.

He was instructed to drop from 4000 feet to 1500 feet and to bypass Birmingham to the north. It was only forty minutes after leaving Chelsea Barracks that Tom swooped into Liverpool Airport. Whilst he was being refuelled, Tom dashed off to the Met office to check on the weather situation. He did not like it. There was a warm front heading across the Irish Sea, which was going to leave him flying through some very wet and miserable weather. Nevertheless, they were soon heading for HQ Lisburn, in Northern Ireland.

It was a very unpleasant journey with Tom flying throughout on instruments. He contacted Air Traffic Control at RAF Aldergrove, which lay about ten miles west of Belfast and requested SRA, which in layman's terms was asking to be guided in by radar.

This was normal procedure when the pilot could not see the ground. He was about five miles out and at about 1500 feet, when he was instructed to drop to 1000 feet. Three miles out he was told to drop to 800 feet, easing the collective down, he still could not see the ground. At 600 feet, still no ground visibility. He had now slowed the aircraft right down to about sixty knots and was again instructed to drop to 400 feet when he was only one mile short of the runway.

At 550 feet he glimpsed the main road, and now that he was beneath the weather front that had caused the awful conditions he over flew the runway and thanked Air Traffic Control and then headed off to HQ Lisburn, which was only a few minutes flying time from Aldergrove.

They landed at 1630 hours, at HQ, Lisburn, in Northern Ireland where Tom was ordered to go to Aldergrove, refuel and return, ready to move as soon as possible.

* * *

The PIRA driver, acting as guard was outside when he saw the headlights in the distance. Shouting to Bernadette, he said, 'we have visitors.'

Bernadette, agitated, replied sharply, 'it'll be our friends. They have obviously had more success than we have.'

She then looked at Jeremy and spat at him. His body, in an atrocious mess, was still swinging silently on the ropes, burnt, battered, and lifeless...

Heather hadn't moved from her position in two hours; the time spent torturing Jeremy to death. Sean pulled her head back by her hair and scoffed, 'she's well dead.'

The car then pulled up outside and it was Pat Maguire. The PIRA ASU commander got out and entered the building. The strong smell of burning flesh and excrement from Jeremy made him cringe. He then said, 'Mulvenny spilled the beans, no problem. We have everything we need to know. He did remark though, before we shot the fucker that his handlers had not turned up. He looked around, smiled, and then sniggered, gestured toward Jeremy and Heather.

'So who the fucking hell are these two?'

* * *

Chapter Two

It was three in the morning when the Puma pilot reported back to the operation room at Lisburn that they had detected a heat source in a derelict south east of the border village of Garrison and, were going down to investigate.

Two of the Lynx from Hereford had just refuelled at the local barracks just north of Enniskillen when they heard the message. They were airborne immediately, the designated heading only a few minutes flying time. The SAS team, lead by a troop commander, ordered the Puma not to land but to hover over the building identifying exactly where the heat source came from. When both Lynx joined up with the Puma, the SAS Captain ordered the second Lynx to scour the area, while he landed with his men, and secured the building.

They searched for booby traps in the immediate area and soon determined that it was safe. The SAS Captain approached the opening and shone his touch, lighting up the horror before him. Pulling himself together, he checked the whole of the building, felt it was safe to enter, and called his team forward.

They gently lowered Jeremy's battered body. Another SAS soldier was already attending to Heather. 'There's a slight pulse here,' he shouted. 'Get the Puma down.'

The doctor on board soon administered oxygen and did what he could to make her comfortable. She was then airlifted in one of the Lynx, their speed far greater than the Puma, their destination Musgrave Park Hospital, Belfast.

David was distraught, sitting in the operations room where he had heard the sitrep from the SAS Captain.

'One female, naked, unconscious, very badly beaten, only a slight pulse, now aboard the Lynx, heading for Musgrave. One male, dead, horrendously tortured. Further details to follow.'

David then had to be helped from the OP's room; mortified and grief stricken. The son he'd worshipped, the son he was so proud of, the son who he had great ambitions for, now taken in this depraved and repulsive manner.

He left for the mortuary sometime during the morning; a

broken man in utter despair. The whole incident was beyond belief. He'd been with his son only five days ago. The mortuary staff had prepared Jeremy's body as best they could. The pathologist begged David to identify his body by the small scar on his brow, seemingly the only untouched part of his body, but given the circumstances of Jeremy's death he needed to see know what had been done to his boy. And, David wanted to see with his own eyes.

'Please leave me.' he commanded...

David spent half an hour with his son. Devastated, and offended at the abhorrent, monstrous treatment that had been inflicted on him; his blood crawled. What had happened was more than outrageous, and he promised his lifeless son... yes, he did... whoever had committed this atrocity, may god help them, because he himself wouldn't...

'Jeremy,' he said, a trembling whisper, 'I swear to you, this day, I will kill the perpetrators who did this. Their suffering will be long and painful, just as yours was.'

Holding Jeremy's hand, kissing it, holding the lifeless body to him, crying, he cried aloud. 'You bastards, you evil, evil fucking bastards.'

He was mortified that he had not been able to help his son in his time of need, a boy who would do anything to help any one else, his son, Jeremy.

He cried and cried, and to hell with manly pride.

The pathologist, after a while, entered and helped David off his knees. He then bestowed to the complete stranger, a compassionate fatherly embrace. Never in his whole medical career had he seen such profound and heartfelt grief?

* * *

Chapter Three

David Carver was born in the Salisbury General Hospital in the spring of 1943. An only child, he was brought up in the Woodford valley, north of Salisbury and educated in the very historic city, at a private school.

He'd enjoyed learning, even more than the mass of sports played. From a very young age he had displayed confidence and enthusiasm in every thing undertaken. His main passion was linguistic studies. He was very ably assisted in this by one of the leading linguists in the country whilst at a private and expensive school; fortunate enough to be taught within a group of ten. It had made an enormous difference, especially in the language department. He'd virtually had the undivided attention of his tutor, the most awkward of words developed by an amazing technique of devouring and retaining the words of each language studied as though his only sustenance.

At seven years of age he could converse fluently in both German and French., and by the time he had finally left school he was equally fluent in Italian, Spanish, and had all but mastered Russian.

Graduating in languages, he proved at Oxford, that he was an outstanding linguist, adding Malay and Chinese to his memory bank. His phenomenal ability allowed him not only to learn a language but also to speak the various dialects and accents of that language.

At University an officer had approached him from MI6 to pursue a career in the foreign department of Britain's Secret Service. He had thought long and hard about this offer but felt that the silent twilight world was not for him, especially at the age of twenty.

His father was very influential in this decision. He was a Professor of Nuclear Physics, based at the atomic site at Aldermaston, and was shortly taking up an appointment as Senior Professor and Director of Operations at the European Laboratory for Particle Physics, an international research centre straddling the French-Swiss border west of Geneva.

David was immensely proud of his father and valued his opinion more than any other person. His mother was a very shy, serene and kind person, who really spent her life doing good for others. All her time was spent working for numerous charities.

She was very wealthy in her own right, having inherited the huge estate where they lived. She had never needed to work, but along with her charity work she chaired virtually every village committee in the Woodford valley. It was her love and joy.

Although he loved and adored his mother, his father was without doubt his mentor. They had spent so many hours together conversing in whatever language took there fancy. He marvelled at the man he was, an eminent Professor, a speaker of six languages, the leading nuclear scientist of his time.

His passion for quantum mechanics, delving into the unknown, devising the techniques for others to follow and learn from, all this together, and being such an intellect was able to pass this knowledge to others, in their own tongue, made him the outstanding man that he was.

They had discussed David's future from about the age of sixteen. David's passion for languages had superseded everything else. He felt that a short term commission in the army or RAF, would get him started and after a three year period he could then make a decision on what he wanted to do.

After all the years of studying he felt he wanted some excitement and eventually chose the army. Following his training at Sandhurst he joined the Parachute Regiment at Aldershot.

He soon realised where he wanted to be and within twelve months was given special dispensation to attend the selection course for the Special Air Service. Normally he would have had to wait at least two years, but his Commanding Officer who had recently been a Squadron Commander in 22 Special Air Service Regiment, saw an outstanding talent.

David had read so much about these soldiers when he was at Sandhurst, he was excited, he wanted to join them, unfortunately the 22 Special Air Service Regiment do not recruit direct from training, a recruit has to be recommended from a military unit, and then attend a selection course.

As fit and strong as he was, the selection period was exceptionally tough. It was his powerful mental strength that gave him his confidence and enthusiasm to go forward, and he quickly followed this up, doing the full SAS course. He loved it. His energies were boundless. The thrill and excitement, the exhilarating challenge, created an abundance of enthusiasm, and how the adrenaline had flowed. His superb fitness, both mental and physical, were an inspiration to the rest of the recruits and more than one in his group benefited by his desire to succeed, it was undoubtedly infectious.

Receiving his SAS beret was a proud day for David Carver, and his parents, who celebrated the day with him, were equally proud of their son.

There was no time for him to relax, with his command of the Malaysian language and its various offshoots; his presence was desperately required in the Far East.

David, over the next twenty years, devoted himself to fighting with the Regiment in all parts of the world. He learned his trade in the hot and humid jungles of Sarawak, Borneo, and his talents, developing as both a fighting soldier and leader. The wealth of experience gained in Borneo held him in great stead when he was seconded to the Australian SAS. He was then attached to the American Special Forces where he served with enormous distinction during the Vietnam War. In all, on three separate occasions he fought against the Viet Cong and the North Vietnamese army for over five years.

He later passed his vast experiences on to fellow colleagues at Hereford. Having served in Oman, throughout the Dhofar campaign his combat skills had evolved through numerous tours in 'bandit country', then in South Armagh, Northern Ireland, the Falklands, and short secondments to South Africa, and South America.

He'd earned his rank to Major, leading his Squadron on many missions. His own team always comprised of Len, Tug, and Jock, who had first served with him in Sarawak, Borneo. He eventually assumed the appointment of Second-in-Command of the Regiment. By now a very senior Major, he achieved his ultimate goal when he was appointed Commanding Officer, 22 Special Air Service Regiment. It was a goal that he had set himself many, many years before, and he was immensely proud to lead this superb Regiment. Given his enormous talent and experience, he proved to be an excellent Commanding Officer.

He personally set the standards for all Special Forces, throughout the world, and showed what could be done...

...Then in February 1991, the telephone call from his son's Commanding Officer, and his world virtually fell apart...

* * *

Chapter Four

Seamus McGough was born in the north, in the county of Armagh, in June 1933. His childhood spent mainly in Armagh and the surrounding areas.

He was fifteen when Ireland withdrew from the Commonwealth in 1948, and then the IRA turned its attention to removing British rule from Northern Ireland and establishing a unified Irish Republic. He had over the last few years become immersed in the republican ideals and was becoming of an age when he felt he had to contribute to the cause.

In 1949 he'd enlisted in the official IRA and very quickly rose through the administration ranks. Alongside his IRA work he'd studied extremely hard and obtained an economics degree at Belfast University.

He met Brenda O'Connell at a Republican rally in Dublin. She was a speaker at the meeting. She'd spoken with a passion and fire, blazed with anger, on the political situation in Ireland, an all-encompassing Ireland. Venomous in her attack on the British Government, she had pulled no punches, and had held them responsible for the Irish civil war of the 20's and for the subsequent division of her beautiful country.

She had studied Irish History at Dublin University and obtained her degree, graduating in 1955.

At the rally, Seamus McGough had liked what he'd seen. Somebody with drive, initiative, young, like himself. Displaying a desire for Ireland, a United Ireland, and an Ireland that integrated the six counties from the north to make the full 32 counties of Ireland.

Speaking with an abundance of confidence, brimming with enthusiasm, both of which produced the zest that belied her tender years. She had the large gathering in her hands, captivated, with not only the skill of her delivery, but the sheer conviction of it. They had been exhilarated one moment, transfixed the next, then excitedly applauding, waiting, and hanging on her every word.

His mind wandered. He had also liked the look of her; tall, slim, dark hair, with a nice pair of breasts. Yes, he'd liked what he'd seen, and what he'd seen he'd wanted, and would have. He'd sought her out after the rally, remembered it well...

'I thought your speech was tremendous, politically correct and delivered most eloquently, very forcibly. Yes, excellent. You certainly have an outstanding way of gripping an audience. Why have we not met before?'

'Thank you for your kind words, Seamus, you may not know me but I am very familiar with you and have listened to you many times in the past. I particularly liked and agreed with your views on an initiative to create a strong financial structure in the movement. It was unfortunate to fall on deaf ears.'

Seamus smiled, at last someone recognised that fanatical faith in the system, does not help to produce an income. Yes, he'd thought, here was someone special. And two hours later, in the Railway Hotel, in Dublin, he'd agreed that he had found someone very special. They'd hardly had time to remove their clothes such was the urgency. They'd made love with intensity, a need to devour; animal lust, demanding, giving, joy, and then fulfilment, a satisfaction that neither had enjoyed before. They'd lain back, both gasping for breath, but only for a short time. They'd cuddled some more. They'd kissed, their tongues probing, and she'd felt his arousal again, and had moved down, kissing his lean taut body, kissing, using her tongue, her mouth, taking it, taking him. She'd pleased him more than he had ever been pleased, on and on, sheer gorgeous pleasure, and he'd loved it...

They met regularly after that. They enjoyed and began to love one another with deep affection. The sex was great, and they were compatible in every sense.

They were both highly intelligent, striving for the same goals and ideals, which ultimately was a United Ireland. They were convinced their collective thoughts, which they endeavoured to communicate to all who would listen, was the answer to the Irish problem.

There had to be a political solution. How could such a beautiful country be split? What were the southern politicians in the 20's thinking of at the time? Michael Collins, yes a one-time guerrilla leader, but an all time betrayer, nothing more in her eyes than a spineless traitor.

He'd left an unpalatable legacy to the people of all Ireland. He'd instigated the settlement with the British, which resulted in a pure and unmitigated disaster, caving in with a disgraceful compromise, which created a nauseous appeasement.

How could he have agreed to two governments, one in the north and one in the south and both unbelievably subordinates to the British Government? It was a recipe for disaster, causing a bitter, cancerous, and on-going conflict, involving all three governments. Saddled with a formula, which proved extremely damaging, creating utter despair, and despondency, especially for the catholic minority in the north, had remained for many, many decades to come.

Meantime, they had both developed their own careers, Seamus having gained Directorship of Finance within a major corporation, based in Dublin, and Brenda teaching at Dublin University.

They'd married at Christmas in 1959 and in October, the following year, Brenda had given birth to a baby girl that they had named, Bernadette...

Seamus and Brenda had settled in to a routine, continuing their normal careers and both working together to achieve their political goals. During the 1960's the IRA conducted a limited campaign in the border areas to the north, which included occasional attacks on army barracks and police stations. Neither Seamus nor Brenda were involved in the violence, they were politically motivated, but did not denounce the violence, as did some of the elder 'officials'.

The ongoing problem that had continually faced the IRA was a total lack of finance and this was an area that eventually had to be addressed, especially if they were to gain the support of the Catholic people.

Seamus and his wife, fearing the strength of the masses of the loyalists, supported by the part-time 'B' Specials and a totally biased and sectarian police force, decided that the movement's financial inactivity had to be addressed once and for all. He'd had a plan and had put it to the Army Council in Dublin.

The meeting had taken place early in February 1969. Seamus with Brenda alongside him had addressed the Council. He had spoken forcibly for two hours, and knew and felt, he had at last, got his message through....

'...In summary, Mr Chairman and members of the Council, our arms, for a prolonged struggle, will not even get us started, they are relics of the past. The weapons that we have to begin a military strategy are nothing more than a joke. Our grand total is twenty-five rusted Thompson sub machine guns, which to my knowledge, were last fired during the troubles in the early twenties. We have a few Lee Enfield .303's and some 9mm sten guns. That is it. Our total funds are currently less than £4,000. We need a team to approach Flannery in America; we need a strategy over there that will generate a good strong and regular income, a constant source that we can rely upon… We need to organise fund raising in the south. And above all we need to motivate the people in the north. I have outlined how we can achieve all these objectives, but it needs time, which is precious, and we need to act now…We must contact other organisations throughout the world that are at this moment fighting oppression. They can help with training and even logistic support to get us started…'

He'd momentarily paused, applause impossible to deny.

'All in this room may not readily know it, but through my office, financed by, unknowingly, the company that I work for, or myself, we have provided assistance to some of these same organisations that I am looking to gain support from.'

This statement had brought startled looks from one or two members and the chairman intervened, saying that he would outline this support at a later time.

'Finally, the oppressed people of Northern Ireland, the Catholics, need us. We will also need them to support our operations. We have to raise finance now in order to ensure our people are not driven back, driven back out of the six counties, out of our rightful inheritance, if we don't act now, then no-one else will. That will be unforgivable and our future generations will not forgive.'

He had then sat down.

The Chairman had taken the floor. He thanked him for his observations and proposals, his dedication to the movement; to his wife also, her contribution to the cause well known by all members. Seamus was told that the meeting would be continuing and he would be called forward at a later date to be informed of the decisions taken.

* * *

Whilst the Army Council were pondering their next moves, the Catholics in Northern Ireland began a forceful campaign for improved economic and political status. They had been subjected to utter and downright misery over the years.

The Catholic people were given the worst houses, the least paid jobs, if any were available. They were downtrodden and revolt was in the air. It was now May 1969, and still no decision from the Council, what bloody old fools they were, the frustrations getting to both Seamus and Brenda.

Towards the end of May, Seamus and Brenda were enjoying the weekend with their daughter, who was home with her friend Kerry, during the long bank holiday break. They were just finishing their evening meal when the doorbell rang. Brenda answered it and Seamus heard the noise of delights of welcome coming from the reception room.

He walked to the door, curiosity getting the better of him, to find out who the visitors were. 'Good evening, sirs,' he said smiling, and walking towards them.

The chairman and deputy of the movement had come to visit him and his wife. This was wonderful. They had both embraced his wife and were now shaking his hand.

The tall one, who was the chairman, said, 'Seamus, we need to speak, are you both alone?'

Seamus replied, 'our daughter and her friend are with us for the weekend, but would understand if they had to remain in their room. We could then retire to the lounge.'

The big man, who both Seamus and Brenda fully respected, although they did not agree with his strong Marxist views, sat down with his friend and started to outline what was happening in the movement.

He talked for some time... a long time... 'And that my friends is why we have not been in contact since your excellent and forthright presentation some five months ago.'

'Well, would you believe that,' Brenda said, 'talk about history repeating itself. A new split.'

'So where do we stand now', remarked Seamus. 'As you have said, the old guard and yourselves have split and now you are calling yourselves the Provisional IRA.'

The chairman remarked, 'as I have said, we have split because collectively we cannot agree on a strategy that we feel will bring a solution to the problem. The Provisional view is that we can only win or even survive, by reverting totally, to the bomb and bullet. History has shown that over the years there has been a marked tendency for successive British governments to withdraw from territories rather than face long and protracted terrorist activities. Not to mention the costs involved. All this being said, the greatest fear and concern to us is that under the current IRA directives, we are unable to give protection to the Catholic peoples of Northern Ireland. Indeed was that not part of your message to the Army Council? We want your support, we want you both to join us in this historic time.'

Seamus smiled. 'At our age I think we lie somewhere between the new and the old. However, our thinking is along your lines, so therefore we are with you. What will be our status?'

The smaller official spoke next, saying, 'we are appointing you both on the new Provisional Irish Republican Army Council.' He held out his hand. 'Welcome aboard.'

They all hugged one another, then the chairman spoke, 'Seamus, you are the Paymaster General, an appointment which gives you total autonomy on all financial Matters. Instigate all proposals that you outlined at the previous meeting. Set up your own team, give me a brief in two months or if you need to speak to either of us at any time, do so as you have direct access...Brenda, we also have an important role for you. We want you to head up and develop our intelligence and security network, they are both fundamental to all our operations. This is a mammoth task, and with your enthusiasm and drive, we know you are the right person for the job. You will have to be ruthless at times...

You both must be present on all major operational briefs and meetings. If this is not possible, then one of you must understudy the other at all times. Although you both have different departments, you will both be responsible for the other in their absence. In due course, you will be informed of the names of Heads of Departments, as they happen. Each department will need funds. Move on this one Seamus, start building the pot by whatever means you feel necessary. You will liase directly with the Chief of Operations, who will be subordinate to you both, tell him what your requirements are and he will organise the military and operational side. He will in effect be responsible for the implementation of your plans.'

He paused for breath, coughed, continued.

'Neither you nor Brenda will be involved in any form of direct contact with the enemy. You must remain above board. We know from the past that neither of you have been involved in violence and we respect that and that is how it will remain. Do you have any questions?'

Apart from swearing dedicated allegiance and loyalty, they had nothing to say and the two officials then left.

A jubilant pair celebrated that night. What they hadn't realised was the deviousness of the two youngsters within their household. The ones, who heard everything that was said, stored in their heads for future reference.

* * *

Chapter Five

Bernadette was educated at a girl's school in Dublin. It was an expensive but excellent boarding school, where people with money sent their children. She, like both her parents, was extremely bright.

She had liked the position of head prefect. This was taken off her after a misdemeanour and Michele Patterson had been given the job. She was livid with this, but knew she would get her own back, in time.

Spending weekends with her parents and weekdays at school, she'd had a good variety to life. She'd got on reasonably well with her parents; learning and following in their republican ways.

They'd indoctrinated her and even as a young teenager she'd proved a fanatic to the cause. Inconceivably, they'd never grasped just how fanatical she had become in virtually all facets of her life.

Anyone who'd disagreed with her at school had made an instant enemy for themselves, sometimes to their utter and dumbfounded regret. Bernadette had tolerated no fools or any one who had not agreed with her beliefs. She'd surrounded herself with a group of like-minded individuals who had ruled the roost; nasty, malicious, corrupt and totally beyond contempt. They'd thought nothing of deliberately causing a total innocent to be severely admonished and even worse. Astonishingly, they'd lied or created a dreadful situation that had often resulted in someone being expelled on the back of a concocted load of nonsense.

When she was fourteen, fully developed and well advanced through puberty, she'd developed into a beautiful young lady, but her callousness, her pure evil, and deceitfulness, had overridden the physical changes taking place throughout her body during the adolescence period.

One Friday evening, late October in 1976, one of their tutors, Maurag Carlisle, a twenty five-year-old from Londonderry, a dedicated and kindly person, had tried to stop their spiteful attack on a prefect, a year older than themselves. The prefect, named Michele Patterson had threatened to expose them for the bullies that they were. Bernadette, in her temper, had said to the young teacher:

'Fuck off and mind your own business.'

Horrified and shaken, never spoken to in that manner before, Maurag had glared at Bernadette, and said, 'you are very evil, and this is not the first time you have spoken like this, I have heard from other teachers of your tendency toward vicious vocal abuse. You just don't care. On Monday, you will be reported and so will your giggling pathetic little group and, if I can get you expelled, rest assured, I will.' Maurag had then led the elder prefect away.

Bernadette, eyes full of hate had stared after the departing pair, and had vowed never to be spoken to with such disdain from a mistress, not in front of her pals, and swore Maurag would regret her action.

The next night, on her rounds, checking that the girls had settled in and that all was well. Maurag had forgotten about the incident the previous day, but Bernadette and her cronies had not.

They had waited for her, and she was destined to pay dearly; yes very dearly, and how…

They had been dreaming and scheming all day. Originally they were only going to frighten her, but as the Saturday had worn on, they had pooled their wicked ideas for retribution, the depth of the punishment more and more severe, and with one trying to out do the other, mostly to impress Bernadette, it would have been a near blood-bath.

However, in the end none of the girls could better Bernadette's scheme. She'd explained it to them in great detail. They'd listened with fascinating glee, in pure admiration and anticipation for the unexpected pleasures that would surely follow. Her plan was brilliant and would be great fun and exciting, and would teach both the cocky bitch and the prefect a lesson that they, the rebels, were not to be messed about with…

It was long after lights out when the girls had snatched Michele Patterson from her room, and with her being a prefect that was easy, as she did not sleep in the dormitory like the rest of the girls. They'd taken her down to the gymnasium and had thrown her quite violently on the rubber mat. Michele, in absolute shock and consternation, with four younger girls standing around her, had said, 'what on earth is going on? Why are you doing this?'

Her long nightdress had risen up and had hardly covered her

lower body. Suddenly having realised she'd grabbed the bottom edges, pulling it down in an attempt to hide and protect herself. They'd all laughed at her; about as humiliating as she'd thought it could be.

'How dare you', she'd seethed, the youngsters standing over her. Then, without warning, they'd leapt on her; she hadn't had a chance. Kerry, Bernadette's best friend had held her in a vice like grip around the neck, the other two had held her arms, and it happened so quickly, Bernadette's voice a chilling factor:

'Now listen to me, Michele Patterson. Make one sound and we'll give you a hiding the like you've never had before, is that clear?' Terrified she'd nodded her head, and had started crying; Bernadette standing with one leg either side of Michele's hips. 'Pull off her nightslip,' she said to the others.

Kerry had immediately released her grip as the other two yanked the nightdress off Michele. It was cold and she had tried to cover herself with hands and arms. Bernadette, had all the while spat at her, and had finally yelled. 'Put your hands down by your side,' which Michele, in her horror, and closing her eyes, had done. They'd all sniggered. Her breasts well rounded, nicely shaped, with large nipples, cold nipples, hard and pointed.

Kerry hadn't been able to resist bending down, and had tweaked them, much to the delight and envy of the others. Michele Patterson, an extremely good-looking teenager had had the body to match. She'd had a huge mound of fair pubic hair, and most definitely the focal point of her body.

Bernadette had pushed her friend away and had said to Michele, a huge grin to increase the humiliation stakes. 'Well madam, you're not so clever now are you. Are you still proposing to expose us for what we are? That's what you said you were going to do?'

The venom in Bernadette's voice, combined with her four evil cronies looking down on Michele's naked body, must have left her feeling absolutely overpowered. In turmoil no doubt, and she had started shaking her head, quite violently, then stopped and had whispered, 'no, please no... don't hurt me. I promise, I do promise, I will never ever say anything, so help me god.'

Bernadette had knelt down beside the elder girl, grabbed her pubic hair with one hand and her right breast with the other. Pulling and caressing both, she had said, 'look at me, Michele Patterson. You will not say anything, because you are going to do something before we let you go, and you'll then definitely keep that promise...'

Bernadette nodded to Kerry, who had then gone and got a Polaroid camera.

'What is she going to do with that?' Michele had said, looking astounded.

'Shut up, and do as I say... Bernadette had snarled...'
'You two, get stripped...'

Michele saw the two smiling faces advancing towards her, both of them undressed. One of them had picked up an object, and she hadn't known what it was.

She soon had, though.

After it was all over, Michele had looked at the photographs, twelve in total, all showing both her face and her intimate private parts. They were devastatingly revealing, especially the last ones, because it looked as if she was enjoying the sequence of events. Her assailants had then taken them off her and Bernadette had said, in the most threatening manner:

'You will now do everything I tell you, or else! Not only will I show them to the school but I will also send them to your mum and dad.'

Michele had pleaded. 'No, please no, give me them back. You have all tricked me, please, please!'

Heartbroken and humiliated, Michele had been defeated and deflated, and had cried more than she ever had in her life, for they were all grinning at her, and their escapade had gone exactly as planned, now they couldn't wait for revenge upon their teacher.

'Please, can I go I am so cold?' Michele had asked, sniffling. Bernadette smiled. 'The night's just starting, sweetheart, and you'll now do as you're told. In fact, Kerry will tell you what you are going to do. Now, sit beside Kerry, and she'll keep you nice and warm...'

Kerry had put an arm around Michele, had cupped Michele's right breast with the other hand. Oh yes, Bernadette and Kerry knew all there was to know about female on female.

Meanwhile, the rest of the girls, all smiling, had retired upstairs to await Maurag Carlisle, but how much could they accomplish the humiliation of a mistress? Compromise, disgrace, and forced resignation? Absolutely, with cunning and a Polaroid camera...

* * *

Chapter Six

David was with friends, back in the Regiment's fold. Some had taken weeks off to help him. They even had a roster at Hereford, so that the only people that could comfort him, understand his suffering, and torment, were there for him.

His best friends were real stalwarts; Peter spent an enormous amount of time with David, and Jane, equally did her very best for Sarah, his ex wife.

He had visited her on his return from Ulster and had given her a very short account of their sons' death. He would never let her know the truth. Sarah had begged David to stay with her, help her through this nightmare, but he hadn't been able to comfort her as well. He'd needed to be on his own, as he had been now for many years. He hadn't meant to be callous, but he also did not want to give false impressions or hopes of reconciliation, when he knew there were none.

He did meet with her when she visited Peter and Jane's house, and all four occasionally went for meals together, but eventually David stopped that, and it was now two months since the tragedy.

It was early May, the funeral coming up shortly, and this, he was dreading. Sarah intended to move back to Wiltshire and try to restart her life and had asked David if he would agree to Jeremy being buried somewhere nearby.

David had thought that there was only one place for Jeremy and that was at Hereford. Jeremy had been brought up there, his ambition to follow his father into the SAS. It hadn't happened, and obviously not meant to be and David eventually succumbed and agreed to Sarah's request. His only stipulation was that the funeral would be at Hereford.

The funeral took place early in the morning, at the local church in Hereford - David's compromise. And Jeremy was buried later that day at the military cemetery on the Wiltshire, Hampshire, border. David and Sarah did comfort one another that day, very ably supported by a young but maturing, Timothy, their younger son. David's parents had joined them at the military cemetery. They had been too broken hearted to travel to Hereford. He'd decided that Sarah had lost the mental strength to hear the truth, and would almost certainly succumb to great depression, and be totally destroyed.

The Regiment mourned that day, and someone, somewhere would pay for what had happened, every man in the unit had made that pledge.

His youngest son had also been devastated, and finding it very difficult to come to terms with his own loss, especially knowing how his brother had met his death. David had decided that he had had a right to know and had told him exactly what had happened.

Jeremy and Timothy were so very, very close, and he was shortly due to commence University, he had been accepted at Winchester, studying the same curriculum as Jeremy. What a terrible tragedy, he would have to work even harder, to dispel visions of Jeremy, from his mind, at this stage of his life.

David Carver told Timothy of the oath he had made and emphasised this again. His bitterness knew no bounds and he again swore to his younger son that his brother's death would be avenged. David Carver also told Timothy that the best that he could do at this stage was to study hard and attain the quality grading of his brother. That would be his epitaph to his elder brother.

* * *

It was now three months after the funeral and David was still grieving for his son. He had returned to his office but the fire, drive, and enthusiasm of the brilliant soldier within had faded to embers of seething hatred. The IRA had devastated his life and his only thoughts were the destruction of the PIRA unit involved in the despicable murder of his son and the horrendous physical and mental infliction's on Heather Calvert.

He suddenly realised that he still hadn't visited her or even contacted her parents. He contacted the military hospital at Woolwich and decided it was time to visit Heather Calvert.

He went by underground to Waterloo Station. Reaching the mainline, he crossed over the footbridge and waited on the platform at Waterloo East for the train to Woolwich. The short journey was cold and miserable. He wished he had travelled by car.

He could have got a taxi up to the military hospital, instead he was prolonging the agony of something he was not looking forward to, but it had to be done, if nothing more than to show her heartbroken parents the respect they deserved.

As he finally walked up the hill towards the Royal Artillery barracks, past the well frequented bars that the 'Gunners' in training used, he turned left at the traffic lights, crossed the road and walked alongside the outer areas of the barracks.

At the top of the hill he turned right and walked across the long frontage that was the home for the Royal Regiment of Artillery. He passed both the Sergeants Mess, and the Officers Mess, both of which, in the past, he had been an honoured guest, on joyous occasions. This time was different, he was not going to enjoy this visit, and he had been well briefed. He walked on and was met at the reception by the Lt Colonel, who was leading the team in their efforts to revive her.

Bill Trefell had spent his life in psychiatry. He had studied the effects of shell shock and other horrendous blows to the mind caused by military operations. He had been prominent throughout the years in the fight to gain justice for the men, who during the First World War were executed for desertion, when in fact they had been badly shell shocked. His frustrations at times boiled over at the sheer callous injustice of what happened.

Bureaucrats, he loathed.

Subsequently, Bill talked with David for two hours outlining the dreadful consequences that had befall Heather, explaining, how her life was totally and utterly destroyed.

'The physical injuries will heal with time, though she will need physiotherapy for years to come.' he said, an anguished expression. 'She was virtually kicked and beaten to death. The only reason she survived, was ironically, where it all happened... in Northern Ireland! The lads in the field had her to hospital in the nick of time before she stopped breathing. The surgeons there, and indeed the rest of the staff, were the most experienced people in the world to deal with these types of injuries. They tended her, soothed her and they cried for her. They're wonderful, wonderful people, doing the job that they do, seeing at first hand, men, women and children maimed, torn apart, by bombs and bullets.'

He shook his head as though disbelieving anyone could be so brutal to a young woman in her prime.

'Their country, throughout the troubles, devastated by

violence, resulting in horrendous injuries all too familiar, but this was one of the most appalling cases for them. They had never seen injuries as bad as this. They knew how, and they knew what had been unmercifully inflicted on her. But what they didn't know was why, and this they could not comprehend. She may never gain her sanity... and will never regain her speech. At this moment in time she's a vegetable. She hasn't uttered a word since the SAS medic tried to revive her. We have tried every known drug, and we will persevere. The system owes her that.'

Bill finally said in a whispered voice, 'she's going to be transferred to a specialist hospital near Southampton in a few weeks time. Would you like to see her?'

David had to; he had to see the damage for himself.

They went in to her room where she was sat looking at the wall. The room looked pleasant enough to him, but fairly basic; simply decorated, nothing special, She was dressed in a hospital gown, and turned to look at the newcomer.

David Carver drew breath. He hadn't expected this, and before he could say anything, she gave out the most horrible scream that David had ever heard. A hideous howling wolf like sound followed that, then silence, utter silence.

Her face was grotesquely disfigured, distorted beyond imagination. One eye had been gouged out; replaced by a black eye patch. There was only slight sight that could be seen from the tiny aperture that was left in the other. All her teeth had been booted out. Her nose was unrecognisable as a nose, and there was merely scarred tissue adjoining to her mouth.

David was stunned and visibly shaken as they quietly left the room. This immense and powerful man, a man of vast military experience, shocked by the sight and action of this now diminutive, forlorn figure that once glowed with pride and passion.

Bill Trefell said, 'David it is worse than what you have seen, there was hardly a bone in her body that was not broken. Even her nipples were bitten off. I will say no more on her injuries, other that I hope the animals who did this fiendish, barbaric, and ferocious attack, will be caught.'

David merely nodded.

He then asked about her parents.

'They, as Heather and Jeremy were, have been badly let down by the system. They have no money, and the community where they live is relatively poor, but they pulled together and a collection was organised. Just enough money for the long bus journey. They visited once. Her father went absolutely berserk here. He couldn't believe that this girl was his beloved Heather, and he destroyed the ward. They haven't been back, simply because they have no money. They were effectively destroyed. Both nearly seventy, you know. It has been a cruel and dreadful blow to them.'

David thought, at least he had tremendous support from his friends, people to help him, but her poor parents, what an appalling situation. Their only child, a once beautiful, caring, thoughtful and loving daughter had been reduced to this.

And the system couldn't even provide a train ticket!

'Bill, I must be off, thank you for your efforts in what you have done and, still doing.' David could plainly see the emotions that Bill Trefell was going through. He said, a hand on his arm. 'I would normally never ever say anything like this Bill, but I'll never rest until I've avenged the death of my son and the brutality that has been inflicted on this poor young lady. There isn't a court in the land that can serve the sort of justice on these bastards that is needed. If they were caught, some idiot in the future would release them. I swore to my son in the mortuary, that his killers would suffer and go through the same kind of hell that he did. And they will.'

* * *

Chapter Seven

Seamus had been preparing and planning for The Provisional Irish Republican Army to seek its own destiny, for many, many years.

He knew the loopholes, and had men in place to exploit every single opportunity. Men in local Government, men in Stormont, men in the Customs and Excise, and even sources very close to the heart of the European Economic Community, in Brussels.

When the call came he would be ready. With his wife achieving the same high office albeit heading up a different department, they could virtually do as they wished. Their control, their knowledge, and above all the power they had been invested with, over a period of time, would leave them in a comparable position, even to that of J Edgar Hoover, of FBI fame.

They both had shown the hierarchy, of which they were now part of, how to advance the movement. And they had, creating one of the most powerful terrorist groups in the world; the Provisional Irish Republican Army, PIRA for short.

Seamus was leading the fight for funds. Heading up protection rackets, he was the brain behind bank robberies, in both the north and south. Tax exemption certificate frauds were in operation, and a gaming machine fraud with every machine in Republican areas paying their profits into PIRA funds. Illegal drinking clubs had helped swell the coffers enormously, too.

Come the moment they would blow up buildings and then only allow PIRA construction companies to rebuild them; massively overestimating the quotes to rebuild what they had destroyed. They couldn't lose He liked to see Government buildings blasted to the ground as it gave him a masochistic and egotistical view that the government was paying for the destruction.

The British government was been drained of taxes from Northern Ireland but still had to pour money in to pay for damages, replacements, increasing both the RUC and the rest of the Security Forces. The economy was seriously becoming destabilised. They would plug one form of illegal operation only for two others to start up. And on it went, the British Government in effect, subsidising PIRA, for the battle against themselves. PIRA were in effect paid to rebuild the damage that they caused. This kept the Catholics in well-paid jobs.

Unstoppable smuggling, using cattle and commodities, heading to the north and then immediately the smugglers crossed the border they returned to the south. It was joked that pigs and other cattle, which travelled daily back and forth over the border to earn EEC subsides, got to know the route so well that they went by themselves! And, sending luxury goods, with a tax difference between the north and south of 20%, to the south was costing both the EEC and the Dublin Government tens of millions.

He organised the destruction of bus depots and buses replacing them with the PIRA's own fleet of taxis all obtained by ill-gotten means. He organised the flow of funds from the United States of America. Under his guidance Noraid was established which provided funds from the American Irish; funds collected from over one hundred cities, the money poured in.

Funds accumulated from sympathisers around the world, were invested, too. He'd enlisted the help and aid from all organisations dedicated to helping the oppressed peoples of the world. Terrorist organisations in Germany, Italy, Libya, and Japan, were but a few of the countries that helped fund, train, and supply logistic support in the early years, when the coffers were dry. And, as the years passed by they were all reimbursed in many different ways, thus retaining massive and continued support.

For the next ten years Seamus and Brenda devoted themselves to the cause. They were both held in high esteem by their peers for their financial commitment and, the success of their initiatives in getting the movement as advanced as it was.

Seamus's business acumen and organisational ability was tremendous. He'd masterminded deals, all illegal, and brought in millions of pounds into the PIRA's coffers. In the first five years the movement had gained over £60,000,000 cash in various banks, throughout Europe, and legal assets in excess of £9,000,000 in the form of businesses and property bought from their illegal operations.

The next five years proved as lucrative. With PIRA running both legitimate businesses and still many illegal ones as long as the cash poured in, the means were immaterial.

His main problem was that of theft from within. Funds that were being collected were not always passed forward. This was discovered on numerous occasions and when caught the culprits were kneecapped. At first, the kneecappings culminated in a shot in the leg, just above the knee, so as not to permanently disable. But as time went on and greed manifested itself, so the punishments became more severe. Bullets were slammed into one knee, and depending on the individual, he might be held up, supported while they repeated the action on the other knee, dooming the thief to a life in a wheel chair.

There was a memorable occasion when an ASU robbed a business in Belfast, and what they hadn't realised was, that they had robbed a Provisional Irish Republican Army owned legitimate business. They had stolen the payroll, and the weekly takings. Seamus knew exactly what had been taken. Internal security was interrogating them and they had owned up to the theft of £20,000. Seamus was in the back of the building and knew they had colluded, as the total missing money amounted to £53,500.

They started on the youngest member and put a shot into both knees, his screams putting fear and alarm straight into the other two. The second one was approached, and standing with his arms, both stretched out, running parallel with the ground he was confronted:

'How much was your cut?'

He whimpered, '£15,000.'

'So you lied to us, when you were given the chance to come clean?'

'Yes, Jimmy told us what to say,' he cried.

'You've been in the movement a long time, so how long have you been thieving?'

'Ever since Jimmy took over from Davie.'

Davie was now in the Maze.

'Where is the money that has been stolen?'

'Spent,' grimaced, Jimmy.

Two bullets tore into each elbow, then two into his knees. He was then thrown down; screaming in agony, joining his friend, and then he heard them start on Jimmy.

Jimmy was petrified, pleading, begging, as he looked at the other two. He had never seen anyone suffer like that. When they told him to take off his clothes, he knew his sufferings were going to get worse.

He was thrown to the ground, and three strong brutes held him down. He looked at the fourth man; the electric drill in his hand enough to loosen any sphincter muscle. His screams rattled Seamus, then the drill and its whirring added to the imminent expectations of pain to be inflicted upon the terrorised victim. Jimmy fainted after the second elbow was drilled, then he was brought to, his ankles next. They completed the six-pack, as they called it, when they shot him in both knees.

The victims were then bundled into the van and thrown out at the Bullring on the Ballymurphy Estate, in West Belfast, a placard over them saying, they stole from you and the movement.

Soon after, the money flowed, as he knew it should...

* * *

Chapter Eight

Brenda, just like her husband, had applied herself to the extraordinary task entrusted to her. Her agile brain produced the early systems that recorded the details of every entrant in to the Provisional Irish Republican Army.

She recorded quite meticulously, every scrap of detail that could be extracted on their enlistment. And over the years she improved methods, bringing in systems that allowed her and her faithful helpers to cross check and analyse every scrap of information.

Wherever possible she validated the information that she was steadfastly building up, collating, and collecting information on their own members. As she very quickly found out, not every one in the cause were as dedicated as Seamus and herself. Such was the power and accuracy of her systems. She had people in the right places. If not, then people who were in the right places were visited at night and recruited, most times against their will... and they were told, as long as they provided what information she wanted, very simply, they would be allowed to live!

She found quite easily the names of all the young colleens who had decided to marry soldiers, and she found it astonishing that Catholics had married Protestant squaddies. They were the ultimate traitors in her book, nothing less. She eventually put out a directive that any Catholic girl found with a soldier would be executed and her mother and sisters would be tarred and feathered for collusion with the enemy.

This happened on many occasions and on one particular time the daughter of a prominent banker had run off with a Senior Non Commissioned Officer and had married him. The banker, who was well known to Seamus, pleaded for the safety of his two other daughters, both teenagers, and his wife. Seamus had told him he would do what he could and would get back to him.

Seamus had then spoken to Brenda on the subject of applying leniency to the family. As they worked phenomenally close to one another and generally, if one asked for what might appear as a favour to the other, it was granted. But this time there was to be no granting of favours. The banker would pay for his collusion, not to the Provisional Irish Republican Army, but to their own private coffers!

Seamus later that night had outlined what he had wanted from the banker. The banker had appeared even more mortified. 'I cannot do that, it is illegal and most unethical, and Seamus, you should know better than to ask me. It would be like committing professional suicide. No, it was out of the question.'

Seamus remarked to him that he admired his professional stance and his outstanding dedication to his employers. He then quietly followed up with a very simple question and statement.

'Tell me sir, which address would you like your married daughters' breasts sent to?' And, he furthered said, 'did he realise that his wife and two teenager daughters would provide an evenings pleasure for the brave Provisional Irish Republican Army soldiers. This always takes place before the horrors of being tied naked to a lamppost, and then there's tarring and feathering…Oh, and one further point sir. It's been decided that fathers should not be excused punishment for their traitorous offspring.' Again, speaking in a very nonchalant casual voice, Seamus ended saying, that he had full admiration for the banker's staunch and ethical stand.

Seamus waited by the telephone for less than 10 seconds before it rang…

He picked up the telephone and said, 'Yes John, I thought that you might want to get straight back to me.'

'Seamus, please be reasonable, I cannot divert dormant account funds into your private account. Auditors would pick that up and they would be down on us like a ton of bricks. Please Seamus, give me a day or two to come up with something and let me get back to you.'

A smirk creased Seamus's face; another one hooked. 'You have forty eight hours, sort it out,' and he put the phone down.

* * *

It was far easier for Brenda to obtain information on the Regiments and Battalions of the British Army.

She purchased with ease Regimental magazines, and placed sleepers in every garrison town, both in the United Kingdom and in Germany. From the information gleaned from these magazines, not only did she know who the next roulement unit was, but from where, and when. It was an incredible lack of security on behalf of the security forces.

As the years progressed she could virtually identify the names of every soldier above Corporal level that eventually served against them in Northern Ireland.

* * *

From the very first day that Bernadette had listened to the men talking with her parents, she always continued with that habit. Both her and Kerry listened and gleaned every scrap of information about the Provisional Irish Republican Army, and indeed, when they had both joined the movement as junior members, at fourteen, they were as knowledgeable about the movement as most senior members.

When they were sixteen, they had missed nothing, knew every member, every dicker, sniper, bomber, bomb maker, anyone of significance, even the members of the elite 'nutting squads'.

What her parents hadn't realised was, that their little daughter had gained access to the large fireproofed safe in the library of their house. The type of safe they had was supposed to be burglar proof, so they would most certainly hadn't expected Bernadette and her friend Kerry, to even think of breaking in.

There were two small blister locks, which were hidden in recesses in one of the beautiful mahogany cabinets. They were about six inches square, both of which held a key. It took two keys to open the huge safe, and each was locked separately within these secure combination blister locks. There was also a combination lock on the safe. But, Bernadette had seen both her parents operating the combinations, so had the opportunity to spy the sequence lock in each combination.

The combination lock was designed for the tumblers to be moved to the right, once through 360-degree turn and set on a certain number. Then two full 360-degrees turn to the left and then again set on a set number. The final movement would be three full 360-degree turns to the right and then set the last number. The only problem the girls had was finding the three groups of numbers for each of the combination locks. They had searched for days, through drawers, cupboards, and any conceivable place that Bernadette's father or mother might have concealed them.

Then Kerry came up with a wonderful idea. 'Let's try your date of birth on one of the blisters,' she quizzically remarked.

Nothing. So they tried it on the other blister. Still nothing. They then tried it on the main safe and still no movement.

Bernadette virtually at giving in point, said, 'that's stupid. Of course we wouldn't be able to open the safe with my date of birth numbers, because even if the numbers were correct, the safe would still require the keys.'

They then tried her father's date of birth numbers in the first blister. No joy!

Last chance, they tried her mothers numbers in the blister, slowly, methodically, turning right a full 360-degrees, then set the first number. Turned back two full revolutions, taking their time, no mistakes, then set the second number. Finally, both praying, then cursing, Bernadette said:

'Fucking well open, you crumby little bastard.' She turned a full three revolutions, set the last number; thirty-three. Bingo. It opened. They both sported huge grins.

They were in.

They now went through the same procedure on the second blister using her father's numbers. They were excited, as they had the two keys. Surely, her date of birth would now, along with the two keys unlock the safe? They placed the keys in the locks and they both turned. With luck, her date of birth would let them enter now and they would have cracked it.

Yes, it did, and they were so proud of themselves. They had access to the most sensitive information about the Provisional Irish Republican Army and other matters. They would soon have power, immense power!

* * *

Chapter Nine

In August, David decided he would have a few days off. It was a spontaneous move, no planning, no preparation, nothing, he just decided there and then that's what he wanted to do.

He knew that this would be the beginning of his long hunt, the search and destruction of the vilest kind of human garbage that walked the earth. Harry Windsor had been brilliant, and David had known that he could totally trust Harry. He'd been a pillar of strength, as had many other colleagues.

Fiddling with his pen he said to Harry, 'I'm going across to Northern Ireland'.

Harry said, 'I've been expecting this. If there's anything I can do, sir, anything...'

David paused, said, 'Yes, there is actually, Harry. Please book me a flight on the 1400 hours shuttle...into the International, for tonight, with a return for, say, late morning. Tomorrow.

David opened his office door to leave, paused, turned, said, 'Harry. Another thing if you don't mind. Could you book a connecting return flight to Newcastle on my return, and a reservation at the Airport Hotel for the evening? Oh... and an Avis car at both airports please.'

For the first time in a long while, David smiled. Harry immediately complied with his boss' requests, ...and then made two further telephone calls.

* * *

David wanted to do a recce. He needed to see and get the feel of Ulster again. He picked up the shuttle at Heathrow and after landing at Aldergrove he went through the strict security and collected his Avis car. He headed for Belfast then picked up the road to Bangor.

His survival drills and instincts were as sharp as ever. No one was following, thank god. What he didn't realise was, that he was indeed being followed and more to the point, he was being protected. Security had known he would be back, and had prepared well in advance for this visit. As soon as they had received the telephone call that he was moving, they were ready to move also. He would not be let down this time or any other time, his son's demise was a hard lesson learned.

David Carver had cried, bitterly cried at times, but so had many SAS soldiers. They were all family. They knew where he was going. What he had to see, and the third SAS team had already secured that area, but with luck he wouldn't see them. A Lynx, at six thousand feet, with an SAS team on board, was ensuring that the car, two miles behind their former Commanding Officer, was well briefed to his exact location.

David pulled into the car park and just sat there. It was a beautiful area; nice enough public house, obviously very old, a romantic setting in differing circumstances, but he would not go inside.

He got out of the car and glanced around the car park, strolled around, just looking out across a field to the woodland beyond. He saw the exact spot that the RUC team would have hidden in, to observe their man.

Now, there were three vehicles in the car park, and just himself a solitary soul.   How could it have happened? The meeting of a tout entailed a military operation. The area comprehensively searched prior to a handler or tout arriving. The handler would also have his own back up in place. If the tout was giving high-level intelligence then there would also be a helicopter in support.

Why, oh fucking well why was their no backup?

Some fucking pen-pushing bureaucrat determined to get his OBE; cutting down on bloody costs.

What a dreadful tragedy, a terrible coincidence having destroyed two young lives. Shaking his head in anguished despair he glanced up; noticed in the distance a Lynx. 'Yes,' he said to himself, 'you should have been here then.'

He strolled to his car, eyes ever alert, and thought how could such a pleasing and enchanting spot like this be the onset of the most heinous crime ever committed to two people. He left, and headed to the place that caused constant nightmares.

He drove steadily, observing the wonderful landscape of the war torn land of the Emerald Isle. He imagined himself following the very same route that been the journey to death for his son and a living hell for Heather. How the two had retained any sense of sanity, obviously knowing what would be in store for them must have been utter purgatory. Hell beyond description.

As he approached the derelict, he shuddered. It was eerie, and he was tense, bodily shaking. He knew he was being watched; inner instincts were honed, his eyes combing the rugged landscape. God pray it be friend not foe. Paranoia was creeping in, but he entered; all evidence of anything horrific having occurred, long since removed.

It was just an old derelict, but how many dark secrets had it witnessed?

He didn't stay long, and would never return to the pub or the derelict again. Before he left, he yelled at the top of his voice, 'you bastards, you bloody rotten fucking bastards. I'll get you.'

Crying bitter tears he walked to his car, then headed back towards the main road. He didn't want to use the same route back so turned right and headed for Belleek, a small border town, part of which was actually in the Republic.

He headed east and pulled up at a lay-by overlooking the vast waterway that was Lower Lough Erne. He thought a place of beauty such as this should never witness the vile hand of terrorism; it should be as it was then, for always, peaceful and serene.

He then noticed, at probably a mile distant, again at around six thousand feet, a helicopter. A Lynx, he thought, and looked again...wondering to himself; why hovering like a shadowy tentative bird of prey?

* * *

David Carver arrived in Belfast and headed straight to his hotel, parking in the underground car park. He had noticed two men whilst driving along level two. One standing by a car, and the other at the exit leading to the hotel reception.

David headed for the reception stairs and the man just seemed to drift away ahead of him. He looked around to see the other man had either vanished into thin air or had ducked out of sight.

David's training automatically swung into effect and he quickly headed for the lift. It was empty. He dived in and immediately pressed the button for reception. The lift stopped and the doors silently opened. Not knowing what to expect, he looked around the wide expanse of this relatively new and magnificent hotel.

He could not imagine an attack on himself would be set in

motion there, in the foyer. Who knew that he was here? And, he had used his vast anti-detection drills from the moment he'd landed in the Province. He had not at any time been followed, or so he had thought. The reception area was crowded.

After booking in and leaving his small luggage case for the porter, he headed for his room. Again he noticed the two men talking together, looking in his direction. He moved very quickly up the two flights of stairs, through the fire door, and crossed the hall to his room. Adrenaline flowed in a rush as he entered the room, closed the door, and completed his personal security checks including checking for bugging devices.

Hearing the fire door open and close he looked out through the external viewing glass. Then he heard a small noise from the room next door. Obviously just another traveller, and he relaxed.

David stayed in his room until about ten, his mind constantly working, but still wandering back to the hated places that he had been to earlier. He decided to have a nightcap and, as he left his room he noticed someone at the far end of the long hallway, dash through the fire door.

Apprehensively, he went down to the bar for a drink.

With a whiskey in hand he was still pondering, trying to work out a strategy yet going in circles. He couldn't exact a starting point. All that was on his mind was revenge, his promise to Jeremy, and how to achieve it.

This was going to be difficult; he was a serving officer, and constantly in demand. He had thought through this particular problem for weeks. Had lived with it, slept with it, and knew that he could never relax until he had destroyed the evil that infested his mind. This was not a place he, as an Englishman, could wander around asking questions. He would have to be patient, and patient he would be.

After driving around today he knew he had a mountainous task. He knew then that it was a task he would never be able to complete on his own. He was also aware that he was taking a tremendous risk being here on his own. Once he got back to his office he would make contact with men of his own calibre, the men he knew, men with equal vast experiences of campaign strategies who would help him achieve his objectives.

But first and foremost, when back with his colleagues he knew that his resignation would shock, but then the preparation and planning for the destruction of PIRA would begin...

* * *

David left Northern Ireland the next morning and as the aircraft climbed, he looked down, and said to himself, I will be back. By god I will be back.

He fought to retain his composure, fighting back the tears, the hurt, the hate, the horrible protracted, lingering soul-destroying desire for vengeance.

He interconnected at Heathrow and headed north. After booking in at the hotel he decided to spend the rest of the day visiting places in Newcastle that Jeremy had constantly referred to in moments of jovial banter.

Dressed in a blazer, grey slacks and polished black shoes. At 39 years of age, he was still a fit looking man and cut a dash with the best the army had to offer, despite having put his body through hell at times. His hair hadn't thinned nor had it turned grey. His shoulders he held high where a lesser man would have been stooping from the weight of a broken heart.

How Jeremy had loved and adored the north east, both the place and the people, and had tried so many times to get his father to visit him when he was at university. Unfortunately, time had never prevailed. Now here he was and regretting, remorsefully, that he had never made the effort.

He visited the home of the 'magpies', St James Park, Newcastle United, where Jeremy, not an avid football supporter, had been initiated. The football club was a religion, a glorious passion, where every one was a great friend.

The brigadier just roamed the city, aimless wandering, exploring. Finally it was eight at night and he noticed a pub that Jeremy had spoken about, often. He entered and ordered a drink.

The place was full of memorabilia, depicting dart matches, football and other sporting team events. Masses of photographs of the individual teams and functions that were held there, adorned the walls as the only form of decoration. He glanced at some of them, and then he saw his son. He looked and looked. Tears welled; no not here he thought, but they were already brimming in his eyes, about to flood. His Jeremy, his son, his boy.

He could see a smiling Jeremy, obviously enjoying himself. He was in a group of about eight people. It seemed quite a rip-roaring evening, clearly depicted within the photograph.

David just stared and stared; dried his eyes, but could feel the tears welling again. Just then a lady came up to him, touched his arm, and said, 'know anyone there? We had a great night.'

David held his emotions in check, replied, 'yes, yes I do. What was the celebration all about?'

She remarked, a tentative smile, 'we had just finished our degrees at the university and we were all going our separate ways the next day.'

'Yes, I imagined something to that effect. My son told me about the hangover he had after his last day up north. He adored it, you know. Up here, and his friends of course.'

The lady asked, 'which one is your son? That's me by the way, amongst these wonderful young people. I was an adult student and by gum, they kept me going. Made me feel young… sorry, I was asking who your son was.'

David's hand shook, as he raised a finger to point out Jeremy.

She looked at him, she had heard that Jeremy had been killed in Northern Ireland. Not how or why, after all, few outside of the military knew the truth.

Her hands came up to her cheeks, over her mouth. 'Oh no, oh no,' she repeated, 'I am so sorry, so very sorry.' David knew she genuinely cared. He felt that immediately, her sincerity and brimming tears displayed utter sympathy and compassion.

'Can I buy you a drink,' was all he could think to say.

'No, thank you, but let me get you one.'

They sat down and introduced themselves.

They talked and talked, and David loved this. He'd met someone who had known his son, and he was finding out more about his son's qualities, his love of people, his desire to help, and oh, how he cared. She'd loved him and so had everyone else.

The bell rang. It was time to leave, but he didn't want the evening to end, and he could've talked well into the night.

'I must go,' she said, 'I have work to do.'

'What at this time of night?' David remarked.

'Yes, I own the pub,' she said, smiling. 'You can stay on if you like, for a night-cap that is.'

Reluctantly, David declined, knowing the importance of his visit the next day, but said to her. 'It has been a long time since I have enjoyed such good company. To talk freely of my son again has been a wonderful moment for me, I thank you for your kindness. I am extremely grateful.'

She smiled, and said, 'anytime, David.' Then bent towards him and gave him the nicest kiss on his lips that he had received in years.

* * *

David was driving to Leadgate the next morning; reflecting on the previous evening.

Angela, at 12 years his junior, had been great company. He felt that she had wanted him to stay and, he also felt it could have been for more than a nightcap.

He'd preferred to savour the talk, and not let anything else interfere with that. When they had parted she was very emotional and given the right time perhaps the evening would have ended differently. But, he had to concede to himself, in that short time together, there was a spark, and for the first time in years.

Now his thoughts were on different matters, and he did not know what reception he may get. He had not spoken to them or, told them of his planned visit. He just knew he had to see them.

He passed through Rowland's Gill and then Medomsley, both probably old mining communities, which had suffered enormously since the demise of the collieries in the mid-sixties and early seventies.

He turned left at a pub called the Hat & Feather, and headed down a hill into Leadgate. Once there he continued on, the road leading up into what he thought would be the main part of the town. He stopped at what appeared to be an old cinema and asked a middle-aged woman for directions to Watling Bungalows.

'Why aye,' she said. 'You have come far too far, hinny. If you turn roond here an' gan back doon the hill, turn right and thems the bungalows.'

David smiled and thanked her very much.

He turned round and headed back, turning right as she had so eloquently put it, found the exact address, and he was now parked outside his intended destination. Opposite, he saw curtains flutter. Neighbours, here, obviously did not miss a trick, he thought.

David felt relatively uncomfortable.

The bungalows must have been built for the miners, when there were still working pits in the locality. He walked past an open gate hanging by one hinge. The small yard he was in had not been cleaned for a long time, and neither had the windows. It had a drab look as though inclement weather from the previous winter had blown the mounting rubbish through the broken gate.

He knocked on the door. An old lady answered it, though barely opened the door, and said, 'yes hinny, what do you want?'

David introduced himself and asked if he could come in. She said she would have to ask her husband and he, David, would have to wait there. She then closed the door.

Eventually, her husband came to the door.

In a low voice he said, 'marra, we don't want any body here, we can manage ourselves.'

David persevered, explaining who he was and, they eventually let him in. They were distressed, long since having retreated into their own little cocoon. The old lady had a tiny pinny on, over a well-worn black dress, the husband a collar-less shirt, unshaven, and baggy trousers kept up by braces.

They were very, very, thin; emaciated. Both gaunt with deep sunken eyes, as if permanently haunted. No television, just an old radio. Seemingly all they wanted - or perhaps, afford! The room had a very dank smell, the smell that of old age, and damp, a damp cold atmosphere that bore the dreadful hallmarks of desperation and poverty.

It was to David the ambience of living in a different world. The husband was sitting on 'his' seat by the fire, an old rocking chair. She was sitting on a hard wooden chair, the only comforts they had.

The husband suddenly said, 'our Heather's coming back soon, when she gets mended and put 'reet'. She's a canny lass is our Heather. A cracking good lass... A sergeant,' he added. 'She'll come back and look after us.'

Gladys, the wife, agreed with him, and went off to make a cup of tea. David followed her, his thoughts on what a devastating tragedy their daughter's hospitalisation had been to them. She told David that Matt hadn't ventured out of the house, and hadn't had a beloved pint since his being told about Heather.

Gladys then said, 'I got this letter the other week and I don't know what to do with it. They're taking us to court?' She started to cry. 'We have always paid our bills, and Matt would never have a pint unless everything was paid.'

David looked at the letter and accompanying invoice. He was astounded. The letter was from a military paymaster, a Major, the letter read...

Ref: Wilful damage to military property...

And finally, should the invoice of £897.65 not be settled within seven days, court action for recovery would immediately follow.

'I'll take this Mrs Calvert. You won't hear again from these people.'

He felt ashamed. It was obviously one thing after another for these poor souls; left to their own meagre devices. He stayed for a short while, desperately trying to think of something that he could do for them. What?

He later toured the area; Consett, straight on through Castleside, straight on, straight on, thinking, just thinking, what could he do? He was out in the country that his son had loved; heather, moors, bracken, the wild, then he saw it, right on top of a hill, The Moorcock Pub. Good, he would have a pint and lunch. The beer was excellent, but it gave him no inspiration, as what to do about the Calvert's.

He headed back, went to the hotel, and booked out. He then decided to go and say farewell to Angela. When he got to the pub, it was as if she was waiting for him.

As he pulled up and parked she came straight out to him. He felt pleased, despite nothing having been arranged beforehand.

She said, 'I am so pleased you came back.'

They drove to the coastal seaside resort of Whitley Bay, parked up, and walked over what she called 'the links', which was a large expanse of grassed area. They then went on down, on to the beach.

It was a summer afternoon, sunny but very breezy.

He looked closely at her, absorbing how gorgeous she was; tall, lithe, a strong body, her dark hair wisping from beneath a quickly applied headscarf, itself whipping in the wind like a pennant. Children were running, happily chasing beach balls that rolled on, and on, in the gusting breeze.

He liked this place just as he had liked the open country, earlier in the day. He felt almost content, as she tucked her arm into his and looked at him. 'Happy?' she inquired.

'I couldn't be any other way with you,' he confessed.

She smiled, looking deeply into his dark blue eyes, and simply said, 'that's nice, David. Thank you.'

They walked and talked.

She had noticeably avoided the subject of Jeremy, but he sensed she dearly wanted to know what had happened, and when they were on their way back, along the now almost deserted beach devoid of laughing children, she tentatively asked what he had dreaded most from her.

There was a long, long pause, and then David stopped walking, and pulled her into him. 'Give me time Angela. We've just become friends, but right now what happened to my son is not something that I want to talk about. All I will say is that I am carrying a burden of overwhelming hatred, and I'm harbouring a terrible bitterness that can only disappear on the death of the evil perpetrators that killed Jeremy...'

She interrupted, placed a finger on his lips, 'I am sorry David it was unkind of me to pry.'

They talked instead of Timothy, who was excelling at languages. 'Just like Jeremy,' he said.

She smiled. 'Yes, Jeremy had the pub in stitches one evening when he had too much to drink. He cracked jokes in five or six languages, and then followed up with singing in those same languages. He had such a unique style, that every one seemed to understand no matter which tongue he chose to perform with.'

They then sat down on one of the many benches on the links, and held one another. It was a beautiful moment for both.

'Why have you never married?' David suddenly asked.

She looked at him in a coy yet provocative manner, then kissed him, and smiled. 'I never found the right man. Besides, nobody has ever asked me.'

They cuddled and kissed, then two giggling children sauntered past.

'Angela,' he suddenly, exclaimed. 'I have to be at the airport in an hour. I must go.'

She looked at him, and said, 'please David, stay with me.

Please...' She was begging. 'I want you to, so very much.' She kissed him, and held him, put her arms around him and drew him close, so close, so very close; several kisses to his cheeks, his lips, and his brow. Hugging, holding, and even in this very short space of time, knowing!

What now, he thought, what now?

This was the man she wanted. She knew in that instant that she loved him. She had loved his son as a friend; a great inspiration, and a loveable young guy who would do anything for any one.

This was the first time in her life that she loved some one. She felt it deep inside; had tasted desire and need.

On that bench, on the links, at Whitley Bay, she had found the man, the man of her dreams. The man that she knew she was going to have to delve into and help, befriend, love, and draw him out of the tormented misery that he was immersed in. He had been horribly hurt. She knew that, and knew that she would have to be patient, and knew that he needed her, even if at first he might deny it.

In her own time and his, she would find out why he was troubled. Only then would she understand the enormity of the burden he'd admitted to. But in the meantime, she would bestow, for the first time in her life the love and affection that she had always wanted to give to a man that she could love, truly love.

David said, 'I have to be in my office tomorrow morning. But well, do you really want me to stay?'

She cuddled into him and murmured, 'yes please.'

* * *

Angela cared; it was evident in her tender love and touch, and he was a total stranger to this kind of loving.

They had returned to the hotel. Never mind the pub. He'd booked in again, and they had showered together. They'd dried each other and she'd told him to lie on the bed, and she'd come to him in naked glory. She'd explored, devoured, and had loved him more than he had ever been loved before...

She asked for nothing in return.

Over the next two months she travelled to London to be with him, and their love for each other was growing deeper by the days. David had discovered that she too, had her moments of heartache and distress in the past, and had battled through. She was a survivor. And he loved her.

Gone were his days of pleading and begging a woman to be reasonable.

Angela was different. On one of her visits, David spoke to her about Heather's parents, and explained his desperation to do something for them. She in turn explained to him the way of the northeast. There was nothing he could do. It was a heartache for them, but they wouldn't want interference at their age, nor 'charity'. They would live with their grief, and unfortunately, would die with it.

* * *

Chapter Ten

Seamus and Brenda were devastated and distraught over the humiliation that Bernadette had brought upon them. They had both come through the same system and hadn't turned out like her, despite their loyalty to the cause.

To Seamus' way of thinking it was all that bloody Kerry's doing that had caused them so much trouble with their daughter. They had both agreed the girls needed to be kept apart, for it appeared that she was turning their daughter into a lesbian. That had to be stopped.

They had decided to speak to Bernadette the next day, but in the meantime, they had other matters to discuss.

'Seamus, we have been working for the movement for many years now, and everyone gets their cut and rake off while we strive to stop them. I think that it is about time that we looked after ourselves. We have put in virtually every penny that we saved in the early years and have not even taken that back. What do you think?'

'Brenda, four years ago I opened three private accounts in our name. Call it insurance against what has been going on, or a nest egg if you like. Since then, I have opened five more in Germany with a small private bank. The laundered money goes straight to our private accounts. Untraceable. We have two Charitable Trusts, again in our names, that are untraceable, and these are in Liechtenstein. We also own properties in Germany, France, and Florida.

I do not like the current thinking, the Marxist views, I listened to the Chairman's speech quite closely and I think that the Government and the people in the South will tremble at the policies that he wants to introduce for a United Ireland.

How can we stop foreign investment, it is the vital lifeblood for any economy? To ban foreign ownership of land and reclaim what is already owned and paid for would effectively destroy our economy. We would lose the confidence of the International Community, and we would become a pariah in these circles; an untouchable, who would invest here? Nobody would, because they would be frightened that we would confiscate what belongs to them.

We have seen that happen in the African continent, with Idi Amin, in Uganda. And believe me it will eventually happen in other states as well. The Chairman wants to make all farms a co-operative, he wants to nationalise all Industries. It would not work and he will turn the people of the South against the movement.'

Seamus paused for breath, continued:

'This is not what we have been fighting for, and it gets worse. He wants us out of the EEC, when over the years, it has been our saviour, it has brought prosperity to the south, and there is more to come in the future. He wants the Government decentralised, with peoples committees, people's courts dishing out their Justice. It would be an end to democracy, as we know it.

Brenda, his policies are doomed. The Catholics in the north would prefer to remain where they are, rather than to be dragged into that quagmire. We must keep planning for the future, our future, and that of Bernadette.'

* * *

It was a bleak wintry morning in Mid February 1991. The meeting was held at a country mansion about ten miles south of Dublin.

The atmosphere was tense, the Army Council was desperately split over a number of issues, and most of the seven members were receiving severe opposition from the immensely powerful General Committee.

The Army Council, the senior element of the Provisional Irish Republican Army, had duty and agenda to set the main policies and the direction that its members would undertake, though there was dissension within the ranks. The Chief of Staff, a very senior member of the Army Council, being the chairman and the voice of the General Committee, it was his responsibility to ensure the Army Council policy is carried throughout the military command.

He headed the ten departments that formed the military and administration command, and those in turn, headed by its own commander.

The whole command structure was flexible, for example, there was overlap. Where an Army Council member may also be Head of a Department, like both Seamus and Brenda, and like the Chief of Staff who also had his own active service unit and, the Derry Brigade Commander.

Reductions of members had forced this policy on them. Nearly two thousand members were in prison, and well over that had been killed. A large number had also just disappeared and given up the cause. Then there were the notorious ones that took money and vanished.

The chairman welcomed every one present, discussed the minutes of the last meeting, and quickly moved on to address the current problems.

Firstly, as always, Seamus was asked to outline the financial position and he rose to speak, and outlined in detail where the money was coming from and where it was being spent. He further emphasised the huge cost of new weapons, new technology, and the costs of maintaining active service unit's both abroad and on the mainland...

'...In summary, comrades, we are a wealthy organisation. Our legitimate businesses are bringing in over twenty million pounds each year, after expenses, and rising. We have given an excellent standard of living to a huge amount of our people, and they have prospered with full employment for many years. Our other activities still generate excellent reserves both in cash terms and favours owed. When I say that, I am referring to our friends abroad, oppressed friends, who at this stage may not have either the equipment or finance to achieve their goals. I have supplied both, at the present time to two organisations. And as confident now as I have been in the past, that our investment in these fledgling organisations will bear tremendous fruits for us in the long term.'

He paused; a moment of deliberate suspense for all.

'We have a huge arsenal of weapons, ammunitions, and bomb making materials. New devices have been ordered and paid for and about to be delivered. I have prepared a balance sheet, and also enclosed the current bank statements of our accounts, copies in the sealed envelopes in front of you. Please open them and I am sure that you will see that the financial department as always has made the necessary funds available for not only the military fight but also the costly political initiatives.'

Seamus McGough paused again, allowing the members to read the statements provided, divulgence and discussion of contents bandied back and forth.

'Seamus,' the chairman said. 'You and Brenda have worked tirelessly for the benefit of our organisation; your joint efforts have been outstanding. Thank you both, so very much.'

He then carried on with the meeting, 'There are a number of points that I want to address. Some of our members are again withholding funds, and this must stop. A few years ago we felt that we had eradicated this problem, so it would appear that maybe we had better start enforcing our justice again.'

The very thought sent cringing ripples of sheer horror through this gathering of hard-core terrorists.

The chairman continued on the same disciplinary theme for some time, then eventually lowered his voice, and said, addressing himself to both Seamus and Brenda. 'I am so sorry that after all you have both done, that we must now deal with the current situation that has been created by your daughter, Bernadette. We would certainly respect your wishes if you felt that you would rather not be present whilst we investigate and discuss this matter.'

'No, Mr Chairman, quite the opposite, all we ask is that Bernadette be given a chance to speak, and explain herself.'

Bernadette was then invited in to the meeting and sat at the end of the long table, opposite the chairman. Her parents were next to her on the right, as she looked down the table. She knew the other members and not only that, she knew all about them and their secrets, too!

The chairman stood up and addressed the meeting for the second time. 'Comrades,' he said, 'we must now discuss the attack on the two army soldiers in Fermanagh earlier this month. Our preliminary investigations were not completed, as Bernadette, the OC of the internal security team that was involved, refused to co-operate. Therefore we have asked her to explain herself here today.

For those that may not be familiar with Bernadette's record since joining, and her progression from junior member to senior, I have decided to briefly outline her achievements...Bernadette left school in 1976 and joined the movement as a junior member in January 1977. She performed with distinction, every task set before her. Year on year, for nearly 16 years she has worked tirelessly behind the scenes, rising to head up her own brigade, which became and still is, the most successful and formidable in our campaign. She has been to training cadres in Libya, South America, Lebanon and Japan, and she is without doubt the most formidable and highly trained guerrilla leader in the Western world. As an individual, she is probably the most dominant, powerful soldier, fighting oppression anywhere in the world.'

He looked to Bernadette, his face expressionless, and his manner adroit whilst returning to the subject at hand.

'Combine all this together, and you will understand why she has destroyed without being destroyed, and indeed is not even known. The security veil that she has effectively thrown around herself has protected her, and has proved her system to be correct. When it is considered, that neither her nor her own active service unit have ever been stopped, apprehended, or even questioned by the security forces, exemplifies her tremendous talent. She has also returned to many countries where experience was gained in assisting individual ongoing training. Her meticulous planning, whether it be bomb making, the planting of bombs, targeting, shooting, whatever the military application, Bernadette, as an individual or as an active service unit commander, and subsequently as a brigade commander, has been head and shoulders above her compatriots. Her fight for the cause has seen few equals, for all these years she has been the greatest thorn in the security forces side.'

For a second it looked as though applause was in the offing, but it never materialised, and he carried on with what appeared to be a dedication speech as opposed to inquisition of past misdeeds.

'...Notwithstanding that, she has made major and significant strides in the advancement of our own internal security. Bernadette's active service unit, when deployed on internal security has always demonstrated its ability to root out the evil within. This is the first time that nothing was gained, but the setbacks from this operation will rebound on us. I will have to answer for what happened, although we have not admitted liability, and in fact, I did put out a statement that it was not our operation. The forces that be know that is untrue. So, where do we go from here because we must never allow a slip like this again, perhaps you can enlighten us, Bernadette?' he said, finally putting her squarely in the firing line.

Bernadette smiled, stood up, and didn't waste any time with overt formality.

'Mr Chairman, I think that we are all going soft in the head.

Who and what is there for you to answer to? What is it that I have done during the course of my duty, to cause set backs, which will have a rebounding effect on the movement?'

The chairman replied, 'Bernadette, you are probably unaware but we are in the political throes of seeking an end to the armed campaign. Negotiations have been underway for some time and the military action went far beyond what we would have liked to help us to achieve these goals, on our terms. You, or a member of your active service unit tortured to death, possibly, two members of the security forces, one being a woman.

'Of course we fucking did,' she shouted back. 'We were after information, and we thought that for once not only had we a fucking tout, but we had the greater prize, that of handlers. And besides that, what has being a woman to do with anything. She was still the fucking enemy and dealt with as such. Furthermore, I am not privy to the information that you have just given. So, that being said Mr Chairman, what do you think I've got, a fucking crystal ball?'

'Bernadette,' he interrupted, standing and raising his voice, he snapped back at her. 'Three points, you do not raise your voice to me, you do not swear in the presence of the Army Council, and you can certainly drop your facetious attitude. Now, do you clearly understand that?'

She was exasperated, and did not apologise but merely nodded, then went on, 'I have been interrogating and executing our own filth for seven years, I have given at least fifty names and descriptions of their handlers to our own security,' she said, looking at her own mother. 'Obviously we do not get their real names, but there are ways and means of finding them. I firmly believe that handlers of touts can be found, not easily, but it can be done.

Unfortunately, on this occasion, I lifted nothing more than what appeared to be a couple of joyriders. But, for god's sake, they were still the enemy, and they were in the vicinity of a tout, in the same car park. If I hadn't lifted them, I might have been here, instead, trying to explain, why not!

Please remember that the intelligence gained from a source handler can be vital, especially a military one. A handler who may have done several tours in that role, with that type of knowledge, cannot be quantified. How many touts could he expose? Think about it. At the risk of hurting or killing two members of the security forces, we could have been in a position to rid ourselves of the scum that has jailed so many of our members. I feel that what I did was well justified.'

She was undaunted by the assembled hierarchy, and intended giving as good as she received.

'My methods may not be pretty, as you are all aware. Our members do not know me, and only those in this room and my team do. But I have put fear in the minds of touts, or any potential touts. The damage that they have done to the organisation is immense. They are a scourge in our midst, have you forgotten how many of our soldiers, men and women, are languishing in prison because of them? Yes, our own soldiers, in prison, yet some of them; the bloody fucking touts are basking on beaches in Hawaii, Bermuda, Pattaya in Thailand, Australia, and New Zealand. And, I am here having to answer to this load of fucking rubbish...'

'Bernadette,' stormed the chairman, exasperated, and again interrupting...but he was shouted down, 'dismiss me if you wish, but I am having my say, Mr Chairman,' and Bernadette continued. 'How many weapons have we lost to these bastards. Hell, we purchase a crate of Armalite's, and by the end of the year nearly all are lost because of touts and their fucking handlers.

Tell me, comrades, what are our active service unit's doing abroad? What has happened for the past two or three years, apart from the odd shooting?'

They looked at one another, her and the chairman locked in eye-to-eye combat.

'I will tell you. Fuck all,' she shouted. 'Have we all forgotten why we have ASU's on the continent and on the mainland?'

Silence.

'Well I haven't. Let me remind you that British soldiers come to yours, and my homeland. They abuse our people, and then they either shoot them or lock them up for a fuckin' long time. And what do they do after that; they go back to their wives in Germany or on the mainland. They have a good fuck, have a good holiday, do some training, then come back, and shoot us again. Yes, that is exactly what happens. Oh! And before I forget, in between their tours here, they sometimes have to return to give bloody concocted evidence in their fuckin' courts against our people, putting them inside to rot for years' at a time. It is perfectly true, so what should we be doing about it?'

She looked around at glum, defiant, glaring faces, and felt the deafening silence.

'We should be devastating them on their home soil...I am a soldier, fighting a just cause. They are the bastards that have branded me a terrorist. Then so fuckin' be it, I act as a terrorist. We all fuckin' should. We should be putting the fear of hell into them, and terrorising the living fuckin' daylights out of their very cosy existence. We should be taking the war to them, not having one minor shooting incident or the occasional car bombing. We should be starting to blast them out of their barracks, and out of their towns. Taking out busloads, or more, not one man in a car. We should be creating destruction, havoc, causing total mayhem, take the bombing to them in a big way, making it fit their crimes, which those bastards have committed over here. We are at war with them for god's sake, and it is time we acted like it, not just here, but also over there.'

She embodied outrage, fanaticism, and utter devotion to her chosen cause...then paused, letting her words sink in, then glaring with menace, just as they had done previously with her, she continued...

'We should be hitting them hard in the cities. London, Sheffield, Leeds, Newcastle, Manchester, and Birmingham. Blast their commercial, industrial, and shopping centres, to oblivion. Also, we should be targeting the financial centres. The major bank headquarters, the Stock Exchange, the large Insurance Institutions. Devastate the infrastructure, and the tourist industry will follow. Cause enough deaths, and destroy enough property, not hundreds of thousands of pounds, but hundreds of millions. That's when it will hurt, and hurt badly.

Then soon, so very soon, we can demolish the will of the people, and they will be the ones to accelerate the demand, they will scream and holler for it. A pull out...

Yes, a pull out of all security forces, from Northern Ireland. That is what is needed, and that has always been the ultimate republican goal.'

She was as good as applauding herself, fist-slamming palm.

'Take Vietnam, yes, yes,' she shouted, 'let's look at what happened there, it was the American people who demanded the end of the war. They'd had enough of the body bags, but worse, they could not understand, why. Their discontentment was shown in every town and every city in America. The whole population was against the war.

Remember all the placards. I was only fifteen then, but I remember. I remember the American population turning against their own soldiers, and when they returned from Vietnam they wouldn't take it any longer, either. It was the first time in American history that its own people turned on its own armies. It had a devastating effect. Soldiers, even veterans, demoralised and disheartened, joined in the demonstrations. President Nixon knew fine well that society was depressed. His military, the fighting men were also depressed. That was a lethal combination.

Then men refused to join the army, preferring to be sent to prison. Young men were fleeing the country, preferring to live in exile in Scandinavian countries, which did not support the war. Despite the political and economical might of the United States of America; these countries would not return the defectors.

That is the atmosphere we have to create. It will be the only way that we will ever achieve the final goal of a United Ireland. I agree that we have to find a political solution, but we must not take a solution that does not include an all Ireland, or we will be defeated, utterly finished. No better than the sell-out seventy years ago...'

The chairman called a halt for a ten-minute break and inwardly despite his vast experience, blew a sigh of relief, his thoughts on how right, how absolutely right she was in everything said.

Her father came up to her and congratulated her, and then whispered, 'I have just found out that it was McAnnally that was after you. He felt that you usurped your powers, and was too pigheaded. He felt that you should be booted out of the organisation.'

'Really!' Was all she said?

During the break, she said to McAnnally, 'could I have a word?'

'Certainly, Let's just walk over there.' He pointed to the corner of the room. 'Now Bernadette, what's your problem?' he said, with a sneer.

'You know what my problem is. You instigated this meeting to destroy me. Why?'

Smiling, so as not to let anyone looking on think they were arguing, he said, 'I think you are nothing but a shite Bernadette. I know of your past and I'll destroy you, as you have others. I do not trust you. I'll see you out, where you belong. And your bombastic verbal attack in there justifies my actions. You have shot yourself in the foot and you are doomed, bitch!' He stepped back grinning at her.

Bernadette equally smiled. 'Well sir, that's very interesting.' She slowly, ever so slowly, whispered to him, 'I also know of your past,' and grinned at him, 'which as you and I both know, is more than very interesting. I'll bring it up in there, what you have been doing, both now, and in the past. It will make my so-called "misdemeanours" pall into insignificance. So, you had better believe me, McAnnally, I'll bring up your past, and then I will not stop talking.

As you know, our leaders despise their own, if they take advantage of their position, and especially when it is for their own sexual gratifications, against children! And, after that, I will see to it that I will be the one to interrogate you. So, just believe me, Mr fucking McAnnally, I will have you strung up to the rafters, not by your wrists, but by your fucking balls, and I will make you scream and scream, till you plead to fucking well die...'

He went sheer white. Terror and shock was written all over his face. The venom in Bernadette's voice went straight to the very core of his existence. He stood shell-shocked, and then fighting his shattered emotions; he tried to speak, with nothing happening, but a slight quivering from his lips...

Bernadette stood, glaring into his face. She had him. She saw that petrified forlorn grimace, the silent pleading of the condemned man before he faces his tormentors and torturers. She knew he would try one last defence; and she also knew that she would walk away, leaving him to stew and fester in the quagmire he had created for himself.

'Bernadette, what do you mean, you know of my past? You have nothing on me.'

'We'll see Mr 'Paedophile' McAnnally,' and she turned and left him.

He was horror struck, he thought, my god, she does know!

'Bernadette, Bernadette,' she ignored him, everyone was looking, 'Bernadette,' he pleaded, as he caught up with her, 'please...'

And just then, the chairman recalled the meeting.

McAnnally was in a daze; the whole of the Army Council and the General Committee knew that he had been screaming for her blood.

The Chairman rose and asked Bernadette if she had anything further to say.

'Not at the moment, although I still have difficulty in trying to understand why I am here.'

'Perhaps Bernadette,' said the chairman, 'Mr McAnnally can shed further light on this matter.' He then sat down.

McAnnally was still distressed, completely and utterly confused, stumbled as he got to his feet; started straightening his collar and tie, put his glasses on then took them off. Then he looked around, shakily opened his notebook...and then closed it. Finally, he looked at Bernadette, who pursed her lips, raised her head slightly, and locked her eyes on him. Those eyes, glaring, staring, fear-provoking, she was intimidating him, and he knew it. He was threatened; and trembled like he had never done in his life, but every one was waiting, when, summoning from his last reserves, said, 'thank you, Mr Chairman.' McAnnally paused. Rubbed his chin, opened his notebook again. He was finding this very difficult, and once again closed his notebook...

His lips and mouth had become so dry, he paused to fill his glass from a water carafe, but when he tried to pick it up, the involuntary shaking allowed him no sustenance, and only delaying the inevitable.

He began to stutter, 'I... I... I... think, ...I ...I think Bernadette has acquitted herself today in the finest traditions of this great movement. I feel that she probably would be better suited to a greater role, broadening her experience, perhaps taking over and motivating all our active service units abroad. While this is being organised I don't think that a hunt for some of our filth abroad, would go amiss...'

'Meeting ended,' the chairman declared. 'Mr McAnnally, remain behind. Thank you Bernadette, as far as I am concerned, the matter is closed, and I will be in touch.'

When they all left the room, the chairman then glared at McAnnally, then shouted. 'What the fucking hell are you playing at? You have brought this meeting to a total and utter fucking charade. I obviously need a new Council Member. You've lost your marbles, now get out...'

* * *

Chapter Eleven

It was December 1991, and David had resigned some months earlier. All that was on his mind was the destruction of PIRA, in particular the ASU that had killed his son. Without doubt he would have gained a Command Appointment within the General Staff, but his tragic loss earlier in the year remained, all desire for service life gone; enough grief still there in a knotted mass of sheer hate and determination.

Any spare time was spent developing a loving relationship with Angela, or the writing of a novel; completed in seven weeks, and compiled from his notes built up over the years. He'd already decided to set up as a consultant, advising Foreign Countries on Special Forces matters. He was soon in constant demand, his fame having spread throughout the world. He knew that Timothy would be spending Christmas with his mother. He himself had been invited, but had declined, and therefore thought he would give Angela a surprise. He had already asked her to get someone to manage the pub over Christmas so that they could spend time together, and she hadn't hesitated, only to say she would have been disappointed if he hadn't.

He telephoned her on the evening of 22nd December, and told her to go to the booking in terminal at Newcastle Airport at 10am the next morning, where her ticket would be waiting for collection for the 11am flight. And as an afterthought he'd said, 'Don't forget your passport.'

She was her normal exuberant self. Absolutely thrilled, and god, he knew how she missed him when he was not around. She loved surprises. 'Where would they be going?' she'd asked, as this had never happened to her before. 'I love you David, I love you, love you,' she'd said. 'Will you be at Heathrow when I get there?'

'No,' he'd said with a grin, 'I'll be in Alaska.' Then offered, 'of course I will be there.'

Little did she know that he would be at Newcastle to meet her!

The next morning he got the first flight up to Newcastle and he was standing there with a huge grin when she arrived for her tickets, spot on ten.

70

During the flight to London he teased her on their final destination. She tried all different resorts, to know avail. 'Give me a clue,' she said. Southampton, my Princess, he said. 'I am still none the wiser, but Southampton will do fine for me.'

Many hours later they were in a taxi driving along the south coast, heading southwest, on the most beautiful Island in the world, and she said, 'David, you cheated on me. How on earth could you say Southampton, as a clue, on the Island of Bermuda.'

'Don't forget, I added the word Princess. My princess,' he beamed. She still looked mystified. 'Look up there to your right.'

She noticed, set back, on the top of a small hill, the most gorgeous hotel in the world.

The driver who had been giving them a wonderful description of everything they had passed, was thrilled to shout, to Angela. 'That there ma'am, is the finest hotel in the whole wide world. It's the Southampton Princess.'

'And where you are now ma'am, is the Parish of Southampton, and believe me, ma'am, I have lived here all my life and I am so proud to say that I am as British as what you are.'

He turned his head round and his great ebullient coloured face beamed, as he flashed the whitest teeth she had ever seen. He must have been in his sixties, but what a flamboyant character, and wearing a decorative, flashy shirt and hat, to match.

'Have a wonderful holiday, and enjoy our friendship, and the hospitality on this, the most romantic island in the world. See you around,' he added, as he drove off, still beaming.

They explored every nook and cranny of the island. They walked miles and miles every day. It was small, tranquil, but elegantly beautiful, just like the people; immaculate, extremely polite, and everywhere was so spotlessly clean. The sky was cloudless, and the sea the deepest blue she had seen, and so many prominent white buildings standing amidst abundance of lush green vegetation.

They visited Hamilton, the capital of the island, where all the men seemed to be dressed impeccably in shorts, tweed jackets and highly-polished shoes, and socks rolled to the knees. As they strolled along, men doffed their hats or nodded with pleasantries. It seemed like an era from the past.

Their hotel, as the driver had said, was the best. They

adored it here; their hotel balcony looked out over the beach, and on to the blue beyond, it was paradise on earth. There was a small golf course to the right of the hotel; well used, even at six in the morning, which was a favourite time for them to stroll hand in hand along the deserted early morning beaches.

They tried the full cuisine of the magnificent array of restaurants and grills, which abounded the hotel complex. Apart from breakfast, they had never eaten in the same place twice, nor had they eaten the same type of meal twice. They had been there ten days now and it had been wonderful. They got on so well, and they could talk all day or they could equally enjoy their own silence. They had kept themselves to themselves apart from the Christmas and New Year festivities, of which they joined in, but a quiet relaxing time was what they had both wanted.

It was the second day of the year. They had just finished breakfast, when David suddenly frowned, as though light years away in thought.

Angela said, 'a penny for them.'

He smiled, drifting out of his thoughts, and said, 'our new breakfast chef, I thought I knew his face from somewhere. I asked him his name when he was serving me, and where he was from, but with his reply I am obviously wrong. He said that he had been brought up, and lived his whole life, apart from now, in Chicago. He was American Irish, although his accent was uncannily in favour of his Irish heritage.'

Angela asked, out of curiosity. 'What was his name?'

David looked at her, and grinned. 'Cornelious McAloon, would you believe?' And they both laughed.

They had decided to spend the morning by the pool, for the first time since they had arrived.

David was reading a book, and Angela, sitting on the sunlounger, glanced around, and generally being a little nosy. Two young ladies who Angela had spoken to the previous day strolled up and asked if the seats beside them were taken?

'No please help yourselves,' she had said.

They settled down, and then introduced themselves. The taller of the two, with the better body, as David had noticed, was Sharon and her friend, was Helen.

David couldn't be bothered with the waffle that started to ensue so went for a swim. When he returned there was a lovely pint of beer for him. Angela knew he would like that, and both girls were also drinking pints. They had said they were on holiday, and had been working as travel representatives in Fuengerolla on the Costa del Sol, in Spain. January, it appeared, was the ideal time for the Spanish reps to take their holidays.

They had, apparently, arrived on New Years Eve, and were at the same party as they themselves had been. They were from Dublin originally, but had spent their entire time since leaving school working in the travel industry, mostly spent in Spain and the Spanish Islands.

David thought he would be clever and duly spoke to them in Spanish, much to their obvious horror. Sharon, red faced and embarrassed, immediately said, 'we have been lazy not learning the language, but with all the lads there, well there just hasn't been the time.'

David felt awful and apologised, 'I am so sorry; I should not have done that. Let me get you another drink,' and he signalled the young waitress. Talk about foot in mouth. Ah well, he was in civvy street now...

The next day he and Angela decided to go round the Island by motor scooters, which was the predominant form of transport for tourists. They were governed to 25mph, which was the island speed limit anyway, so they weren't going anywhere fast. They enjoyed it, and it was something different.

They pulled up at a restaurant for lunch and noticed that they were at a tourist site. It was a bit like the caves at the Cheddar gorge, so they decided to visit. It was eerie. There were not many people about, and they seemed to be going deeper and deeper.

They were in a cavern; a large pool of water, the water being well down. David remarked, that it was most likely connected to the sea, marks along the wall defining where the level of the water had risen to.'

She quite cleverly and in all sincerity, said to David, 'the tide must be out!' He grinned at her, loved her Geordie wisdom, and said, 'I love you.'

They seemed to be deep in the subterranean depths where huge stalagmites and stalactites had formed over many, many centuries. Angela decided to keep her pearls of wisdom to herself this time, but she was dying to ask David why they were here in a hot country.

They started to return and half way up the iron steps, they bumped into the two ladies whom they had met by the swimming pool the day before. They exchanged pleasantries and arranged to meet later that evening at the Pirates Bar on the beachfront, for a drink.

* * *

Chapter Twelve

Bernadette had left the Army Council meeting absolutely furious. She would see that McAnnally would get his just deserts, and how. He was effectively destroyed, or soon would be.

She discussed the matter with Kerry, Joe, Sean and Fred, her active service unit; the four people in her life that would lay down their lives for her at any time.

The next day, the chairman told her McAnnally had waged a war against her. He had been demoted and had lost his seat on the Army Council. He had been very vindictive against her and apologised most sincerely for his actions.

Bernadette simply said, 'I hadn't realised that it was him that caused me the problems. After all, he spoke kindly of me, and recommended me for my new position and tasks!' She also said to the chairman, 'please do not be too hard on him!'

* * *

It was 13.30 pm on the 20 February, three days after the meeting, when the men in hoods lifted him.

The former Army Council member, of the Provisional Irish Republican Army, screamed. But, a solid mahogany baton, belted across his skull, soon shut him up. When he awoke, he was on a mattress, his hands tied behind his back. He had a hood on. He was trembling, already marshalling his thoughts, that his fucking predicament was Bernadette's doing.

'Bernadette!' he yelled. There was no response, nothing, just an unearthly, horrible silence. He screamed again, 'Bernadette, you fucking bitch. Let me go, let me go, or I'll get you for this.'

He was cold. He heard a tap dripping onto something metal. Hour after hour the drip went on, and on, ceaselessly. He even yelled at it to fucking shut up! Then, at last, he heard the door open.

The sound of ...girls...no...surely not? They were coming up to him, their female voices hushed. He tried to get up, but couldn't. 'Who are you, and what do you want? Get this fucking hood off me. Untie me, and turn that fucking tap off.'

'We've come to give you a good time. What's the matter

with you?' They undid his zip. Then they took his trousers and underpants off and slung them in the corner of the cellar.

'Wow,' one of them said.

'Fuck off,' he said. 'Who sent you, and where am I. Turn that fucking tap off, will yuh.'

They remained all day with him, but never took the hood off, nor did they turn the tap off, despite his pleadings. All they did, just before they were leaving, was to loosen the string securing the hood. He was knackered, sexually bruised, and angry.

Then, one of them, with the claws that she sported to protect herself in her trade, drew them down, digging into both sides of his face. He swore and yelled at them, 'you fucking cows. Piss off, and turn that fucking tap off.'

They left the tap dripping, and then left. They handed over the six durex, with the contents, and the scrapings of blood from the nails, and were handed five hundred punts each.

'A taxi will pick you up tomorrow, same time, same place, and the same deal.' They were warned by the coloured girl, ever breathe any of this and you'll be dead meat. They left in the taxi that had just drawn up, grinning from ear to ear. It was the easiest money that they had ever earned, and just for hand jobs too. 'And the same again, with another five hundred smackers, tomorrow!' they were told.

What they hadn't realised was that they would never see a tomorrow!

Kerry drew up in another taxi, and met the coloured prostitute a few moments later. She took the goods, and passed on another five hundred punts then gave the hooker a much stronger warning.

'No need lovey, see you tomorrow,' the hooker said to Kerry. 'Give me a shout anytime.' She would never receive that 'shout', and would be dead and buried within two hours.

Their victim was totally confused. Two girls had played with him all day, and now he was still hooded and disorientated. He didn't know whether it was day or night, and he was thirsty and hungry. And, that fucking tap was driving him mad. Hours and hours went by, or so he thought. Then he heard the door open; heavy boots. At least two, maybe three men and they lifted him into the sitting position. The knot on the hood was being undone. Then it was tightened again, this time under his nose.

'What the fuck are you doing?' he demanded.

Someone grabbed his hair and yanked his head back. He felt a tube or pipe being pushed into his mouth and on down his throat. He was in a state of panic. Shaking his head back and forth, trying to rid this thing stuck inside of him, he felt as if he was going to choke or be sick. He was neither, but wretched. Then he heard the gurgling sound, felt something being poured into him. They were virtually drowning him. Then they stopped, and then poured again. The thing in his mouth was yanked out and he could smell whiskey. His head started to feel the affects of what had been done.

He realised that a funnel had been pushed in his mouth. And had had a bottle of whiskey forced down him. This was fucking stupid; he would have drunk that anyway, as it was he was feeling quite pleasantly drunk. They then left him; had said nothing, absolutely nothing.

He had no idea that it was Sean and Joe who had left him, and were going out on the prowl to fulfil orders from their commander. They stayed out all night and thoroughly enjoyed themselves. Ravishing 'slags' was something they both relished and were good at it!

Reports soon came in that morning that a sexual 'nutter' was on the loose. Two prostitutes had been raped and murdered in Dublin the night before, in the vilest of ways. There appeared to be blood under their nails; one of the first things the detectives noticed, and the forensic scientists would eventually confirm that it was the same man responsible for both killings.

The detectives had assumed this anyway, the vicious slashes around the breasts, and the merciless sexual horrors that had been inflicted pointed to one and the same sadist. He had to be found.

The next day, another two women turned up in the same taxi. As soon as they entered the cellar, their victim yelled at them. 'Turn that fucking tap off.' It was left dripping. On and on, it dripped. The girls followed the instructions and repeated the previous performance, then handed over the goods to the woman who controlled the Belfast prostitutes. Little did she know she would soon suffer the same fate as the coloured girl, as they left in the same taxi; another five hundred punts the richer.

Sean and Joe also paid him another visit. 'Please,' he said, when he heard them enter, 'turn that fucking tap off.' He had been there three days now, and the place stunk. They ignored his pleas. Then they splashed him with the blood that they had carefully taken from both the women killed the previous night. They also stuck a pair of panties in his pockets, which they had stained with his semen.

He then had another bottle of whiskey poured down his throat. They also rubbed his knuckles against the wall, drawing blood, and when Sean and Joe left him he was a gibbering wreck not knowing what in hell was going on or why he was being held there like a dog tethered in a kennel.

That night Sean and Joe visited Belfast. Their attack on the next victims was more vicious than the previous night. But the signs were similar; the killer again, had not only left his semen, but also his blood.

'He would be caught,' the RUC detective had said.

This would be their last visit to the hooded captive. Sean and Joe poured another bottle of whiskey into him. He was drunk, very drunk, gibbering incoherently; filthy, stinking in his own mess. They untied him, handed him his trousers and underpants and told him to put them on. He fell over three times in the process.

'Take this fucking thing off my head and turn that fucking tap off,' he said as he fell over again. The empty bottle was wiped clear of fingerprints. Then it was thrust into his left hand, then the other, and finally it was carefully placed into a bag. Then they drove him to the police station in Dublin, and before he fell out of the car he said in his drunken stupor. 'Turn that fucking tap off.'

It was three in the morning, it was silent, and they'd dumped him against the railings. Sean then drove the car round the corner and as soon as he disappeared, the whiskey bottle was hurled through the police window. Joe then ran to the car and, as he rounded the corner, he heard a policeman yell at the drunk:

'What the fuck are you doing?'

Pandemonium broke out the next day. The first radio announcement said that a staunch republican had been arrested for being drunk and disorderly. The second then said that further investigations were continuing into the behaviour of a prominent Dublin businessman. Then an hour later the press outside the police station had sniffed that something serious was going down, and were gathering in numbers like vultures at carrion.

By nine o'clock that evening, the road outside the police station was blocked completely, the press demanding to know who was inside and what were the charges, if any. The television cameras from RTN were being set up and now, three hours since the first announcement, the whole of the transport system, in and around Dublin was blocked.   People were drifting around the centre of town, saying, 'what's going on? Has the Pope died?'

Inside the police station, it was much more serious. They had been trying to question Padraig McAnnally since 3am, and he was too drunk. When he was dragged in to the station, scratched as he was, blood stained and with a pair of panties in his pocket, detectives were called in immediately. In his replies to earlier questions by police his responses were, 'Fuck off and mind your own business.'

At 4am, the police doctor visited him, and he advised that he was not in a fit state to answer any questions. McAnnally was placed in a cell; his clothing removed, and he was given the customary paper clothed boiler suit to wear.

He was shook and dragged off the bed at 10am by two detectives; and they were told to fuck off. They took him, bedraggled, drunk, unshaven, and in a filthy mess, up to the interview rooms for questioning. Before they started, the doctor sensibly advised that he be given a shower, a drink and something to eat, and maybe then he would be fit to answer questions.

McAnnally was in a state of shock, had a shower, and his brain was trying to burst out of his head. What was he doing there? He was totally and utterly disorientated, and couldn't think, and hadn't realised that apart from three bottles of whiskey he hadn't eaten or had a drink for four days. He was in a world all his own and could remember nothing, absolutely nothing.

It was 6pm before he was in a reasonable state to be questioned, and even then, he kept being sick. All that came up was bile, and he was getting weaker by the minute. He still couldn't remember anything, his mind a complete blank.

Question, questions, bloody incessant questions...

'Mr McAnnally,' the Detective Inspector from the Garda,

said, 'now tell me if I have this right, or am I missing something. I have questioned you for eight hours, and you totally deny having committed murder, or any crime whatsoever?'

'Yes, that's fucking right, and it's about time you chased after your fucking murderers, and leave us decent law-abiding citizens to go home.' McAnnally stood up, and then shouted. 'And that's where I'm fucking going, so bog off the lot of you. I've had enough.'

He turned around only to be faced by another detective. He was very tall, and just shook his head, then with a very menacing voice said, 'sit down, now.'

'I want my solicitor,' he demanded.

The Inspector, at the end of his tether said, 'your solicitor has been here all day, ever since you woke up. Now do you think we can continue.'

'No, I want to go home to bed.'

'Padraig McAnnally, you threw a whiskey bottle through the station window at 3am this morning. You were apprehended by the duty Sergeant, arrested, and then after observing your condition I was called to the station.'

'Yes that's fuckin' right, you twisted bastard,' McAnnally yelled. 'And just because you were got out of your fucking bed, you accuse me of murder. See here, fuck-face, I will sue you for this.'

'Tell him, Mr Solicitor. Anyway, what's your name? I am Padraig McAnnally,' he said, offering his hand, smiling animatedly.

Not accepting the handshake, the solicitor said, 'sit down and listen to the inspector, Mr McAnnally, you are in serious trouble. All blood samples are back and they are positive.'

'I will try again, Mr McAnnally,' said his inquistor. 'Can you tell me where you have been for the last five days?'

'Yes I can,' he yelled, 'I have been here all night and day.' Then he paused and slowly said. 'It's the fuckin' bit before that, which I am having trouble with.'

'Mr McAnnally, you cannot tell me where you have been prior to turning up at the police station. You cannot tell me what you have been doing the past four days prior to coming to the police station. You cannot tell me why you even came to the police station.'

'Yes, I remember that.' He beamed, and then shut up. They were all waiting for him to say something.

'Please, Mr McAnnally, enlighten us?'

He surprised them all then, and said, 'the fucking tap was dripping!'

If it weren't so serious, they might have all erupted in laughter.

'Mr McAnnally, in the last fifteen minutes, as your solicitor has said, we have received confirmed evidence that points directly at you as a murderer, and rapist. Your blood was on both of the murdered girls. Your semen was present in the girls' vaginas, and other orifices of their bodies. Blood was found on your clothes and body, their blood. Your blood was behind one of the girl's fingernails and your face is scratched. Your semen was on one of the girl's knickers, and these were in your pocket. You took them out yourself, and after blowing your nose into them, you handed them to the police sergeant.'

McAnnally turned ashen white; trembling. 'No you have got the wrong man, it wasn't me.' He looked around at the faces, pleading, 'no, it wasn't me. Tell them Mr Solicitor, it wasn't me, for fucks sake.'

'Padraig McAnnally, in the presence of your solicitor, I am charging you with the murder of Miss Annie Cartwright, a female of no known fixed abode. Investigations will continue, where further charges may be brought against you.'

Twenty-four hours later, a terrified, dishevelled Padraig McAnnally was dragged out of the Dublin police station, where a screaming mob was baying for blood.

No woman, despite their profession, should be subjected to what Padraig McAnnally had put those women through...

* * *

Six months later the Supreme Court Judge in sentencing him said, 'this is the vilest of crimes that I have ever had to deal with. You Padraig McAnnally, supposedly a pillar of society, violated these women in a way that suggests that you were totally insane. But medical evidence is very clear that you are not insane. I have evidence here before me that prove you also violated children in the past, and that you are a member of a paedophile club. You are a depraved man, a man that should be removed from society for a long time, a very very long time...Before I sentence you, do you have anything to say?'

'I didn't do anything. I can't remember...' spluttered McAnnally.

'This court sentences you, Padraig McAnnally, to Life Imprisonment, and when it says life, that is exactly what it should mean, in your case. If ever in the future some politician decides to release you, I am sure that another court in the North will try you on the very same charges...Take him away.'

McAnnally was stunned. Then he heard someone quite distinctly call his name from the public gallery; a woman's voice, one that he recognised. He looked up, and saw a smiling Bernadette waving to him. As the attending police attempted to drag him away, he suddenly remembered something; sometime, somewhere, he'd heard someone saying, 'This is Bernadette's doing!'

He looked again to see her clapping, cheering, and then waving at him again.

He screamed at her, 'you fucking evil bitch, you fucking evil bastard, you did this.'

She nodded her head, grinned, and then laughed. He was distraught, and now realised that he had been set up. He was being dragged away, but he was strong, holding back and fighting them, screaming at her, staring at her, horrified by her evil revenge; after all this time...

'It was you, it was fucking you...you fucking rotten, evil bitch,' he yelled.

She nodded in agreement with him, as he was finally led away, screaming his head off.

* * *

Chapter Thirteen

David had spent 1992 building his consultancy business, promoting his hugely successful book, and in between all that his relationship with Angela was developing into something that he had wanted all his life. His love for this beautiful and understanding lady showed no bounds. They had both become devoted and dedicated to each other. But still, there was that one appalling secret he always held back, Jeremy's death.

Angela had never broached the subject since that time on the 'links' at Whitley Bay. She knew the nightmare was still there. After all, she lived and shared David's heartache. But she was patient and knew that David would talk about it when he was ready. Not until they had gone to Washington had she realised what he did. He'd always said that he had an office job with the Ministry of Defence.

She had also accompanied him on his first presentation in America. Collected at the Airport, she'd confessed their transport was the largest limousine that she had ever seen. There was a television, a bar, video, two telephones, and she was taken in by it all. 'This is something else,' she'd said.

They were then met at the hotel, a five-star hotel, by what had appeared to be a reception committee bowing and scraping to David, and addressed her as if she were of royal blood. When they'd gotten to their room she couldn't help but notice that it was the Presidential Suite; the best in the hotel.

She'd remarked to David. 'What's going on?'

He'd smiled, saying, 'only the best for you, Angela.' He'd then picked her up and threw her in the huge sunken whirlpool, clothes and all, and within a few minutes had joined her.'

Later in bed, she'd asked him, 'what are we doing tomorrow,' and he simply replied, after a long pause:

'Oh...tomorrow...we're off to a military presentation.'

She was reading a book and said, as though an afterthought.

'How boring.'

He'd grinned and made no reply.

The next morning Angela had said to him, 'David, why are we getting dressed in evening suit and gown, to go out during the morning?'

He'd laughed and jokingly said. 'The Americans were funny people.'

And again they were picked up by a limousine, and went off to another very posh building; the largest she had ever seen.

When the car had pulled up at a side entrance, they were met by a gathering of not only military people but some in civilian clothes as well.

'Where are we David, I hope that you are not going to leave me on my own, when you go to your meeting?' She looked somewhat flummoxed. 'David, why are these people here?'

'Don't worry, sweetheart, this building is called the Pentagon. It's the largest office building in the world. The home of the American Defence Ministry, just like we have in London.' Then he raised his eyebrows. 'We are here as guests, that's all.'

They went into the building, along a corridor, then up the most decorative staircase that she had seemingly ever seen. Then along another hallway, and apart from about five people, who were in a line, and who they were both introduced to; there was nobody else about.

At the far end of the hall, by a huge set of oak doors were two men standing dressed in livery, similar to what she had seen outside Harrods. David eased Angela's arm through his, and naturally felt her nervous tension as they approached the two men. They nodded to each other, then opened the great doors.

David and Angela went through first.

The roar and clapping engulfed them, as they walked in front of the people they had just met. She turned her head and saw that the people behind were also clapping. There had to be hundreds upon hundreds in the hall, all standing and cheering. She was baffled, and it was too noisy to ask David, why?

He stopped, had noticed someone. 'Please wait a second,' he said in her ear, combating the shouting and cheering. He looked into the audience again, and smiled, raised his arms as if in salute, but it was more than that. An enormous coloured man, with rows and rows of medals, was standing in the front row, crying as he put his arms out to David. In front of every one they embraced. After a few seconds, David moved on but not before Angela heard the man say:

'I love you, sir. See you later.'

There was a dais on the stage to the left, and to the centre there was another man in livery that beckoned them to the seats in the middle, where they promptly sat down. The seats were luxurious to say the least, and there was a selection of drinks by her side, to which Angela noticed no one else had.

She leaned toward David, whispered, 'David, will you please tell me what is going on. We should have got here earlier, then we wouldn't have got mixed up with all the dignitaries, and who was that man that embraced you?'

He smiled, and said, 'you're so wonderfully naive, and I love you. But I feel that you are going to have to share me today.'

'Share you, never.' They smiled to one another, sat back and held hands. As she looked around, she thought, well, we have taken the best seats anyway.

Another man in livery made an announcement. 'Pray silence for the Chief of Staff, of the Armed Forces, General Charles Peter Goodall.'

The man to her left whom she had been introduced to suddenly rose and walked forward to the steps leading directly on to the stage. He then went behind the dais, his voice quietly spoken for such a huge man. He said, 'Mr Secretary of State for Defence, Distinguished, and Honoured Guests, Ladies and Gentlemen, we have waited many years for this moment.

It is certainly the greatest honour that I have had throughout my career, to introduce to you a man that each and every one of you know, or are familiar with, a man who has been decorated by no less than ten different countries. Awarded by the US Congress, our highest military honour, four times, the Congressional Medal of Honour.

He's a soldier of outstanding merit and ability, fluent in eleven languages, and fourteen dialects. It is no secret that many of you would not have been here today had it not been for the outstanding bravery of this English Officer and Gentleman.'

And, at that, the whole assembly stood and the cheering and clapping started all over again, though he waved aside the joyous revelry.

'We, in this hall today, profess to be Special Forces, and are proud of it, but this man, towers above us all. He is Special Forces, in one, so I ask you to stand and please give your friend and mine, and his fiancée, Angela, the warmest of American welcomes.'

The hall erupted!

David stood up, moved forward a pace, and turned to face the generous, thundering applause, from a very special audience. He then pulled a shocked and stunned Angela to her feet, as she tried to say over the deafening roar, 'David, you never told me.'

It started to quieten, and then he said, 'unless you want to join me on the stage you had better sit down.'

Angela didn't sit she just stood in awe and astonished disbelief, as David moved to the rostrum. The General warmly welcomed him with a manly hug. It was fairly obvious they also went back a long way together. The applause and cheering just got louder, and her David was holding centre stage to over 500 serving American officers from specialist forces, from CIA, from FBI, from the DEA, in fact every officer that was available from any USA specialist force or agency attended.

He started talking. Her David.

The hall, crammed full, suddenly fell silent. Every guest in attendance was kept spellbound, enthralled by an educated and outstanding officer of the highest quality. They hung on his every word. The benefits they would gain from his 28 years of virtual continuous military action, was unimaginable. She was flabbergasted, she was thrilled, and she was so proud.

She sat back in her chair, her hands to her mouth, tears trickling down her cheeks. The General next to her handed her a drink. She took it from him, but didn't take her eyes off David. There was a break for lunch, and it was virtually impossible to get anywhere near him.

When the presentation ended, there was a tumultuous uproar. The people behind were patting her on the back also. She had never seen such adulation and it was for her man. It just went on and on and this time she didn't mind sharing her deep love for a man with hundreds of others.

He then called for her to join him on the stage, which she did. She hugged and kissed him, but she still didn't know what had happened to his son, yet she felt that this huge gathering knew, knew of the inner heartache and suffering he'd dealt with in his own way!

The resounding success of his imaginative and forthright three-hour presentation was honoured by an absolute breathtaking eight minute standing applause and, given by probably the most efficient, effective and highly trained fighting force ever assembled under one roof.

Throughout the applause the most senior politician, like the rest, seemed spellbound by what he had heard. Unbeknown to the assembled, he alone though, had made a mental note that would eventually reach his UK counterpart!

The day and night never seemed to end; it was the most joyous of Angela's life. She laughed, she cried, and she loved David so very much and thought what a tragedy that Jeremy couldn't be there.

The big coloured man spoke to her, told her how he had had his legs blown off in Vietnam in a minefield. And he told her with tears in his eyes how David had entered the minefield, dragged him five hundred yards, on all fours, all the while checking for mines, and with him on his back, and under constant fire. He grinned, 'I have three boys and two girls who wouldn't have been here today but for him.'

The stories were endless, but they did eventually make it to their room at about midnight. They shared the whirlpool again, without clothes this time! They then made love, long and passionate, fulfilling each other's desires and needs. Then went back to bed, where they kissed and lay snuggled together, while for the next two hours David outlined the heartbreak of his son's death.

She listened, she cared, and she constantly cried with him. Then they cuddled and kissed some more until he slept, silently. She looked at him and thought. What a wonderful man. She had heard, repeatedly, throughout the day of his courage and bravery. She had spoken with the men whose lives he had saved, this wonderful of wonderful men, and he was hers.

She loved him, loved the hero she had acquired by default of heartbreak and tragedy.

* * *

They returned the next day to the UK and instead of her flying on to Newcastle on her own, he would have none of it. He stayed the night at her pub, which was a first for him.

Watching him playing darts with the locals, she suddenly thought, oh my god, what a contrast to yesterday when they were being treated like gods and he hero-worshipped.

Quite rightly so, but what a come down, and to this.

She felt an awful pain of anguish, but stood up and walked over to him. She kissed him and then walked back and sat down.

He smiled at her, looking a tad thoughtful...

*   *   *

Angela was hopelessly in love with David, and so happy to be with him, but they did have difficulties in meeting with David travelling around the world with his lectures. She also had her pub to run, which was equally demanding. He was so attentive and caring, a great lover too, something that had always been missing in her life before.

For David too, when they made love it always appeared so special, and he would say how wonderful it was and that he had never had that kind of pleasure before.

She would be absolutely distraught if their differing lifestyles got in the way of their relationship. She wanted him, she also knew at thirty-six, she still had hopes for a family, and she wanted desperately to have his child. They hadn't discussed children, and she was frightened to even mention babies.

Last year they had had a wonderful holiday in Bermuda; an idyllic, glorious paradise, yet this year he hadn't mentioned going anywhere. Where was their relationship heading? She had pondered this so many times, then he would ring and they would be having a weekend off somewhere, and her spirits would be high until he was off again.

The last visit he'd brought Timothy and it was a marvellous time. They had stayed at the pub all weekend, and Timothy proved so many times how like his brother he was; the same wonderful generosity, boundless energy, and brimming with confidence. He'd even asked if he could bring his girlfriend up one weekend to stay and she had felt delighted. All three had walked along the beach at Whitley Bay, but now David was out in Australia.

*   *   *

It was a cold, late autumn night, and they were all wrapped up against the elements but it was so relaxing and pleasant to be with Timothy and Vikki. They were a lovely couple, and they were both at the same University and due to graduate in the summer of 1994.

He was a well built young man, just like his brother and father; good looking, and Vikki was a beautiful young woman.

Timothy suddenly remarked, 'Angela I think you have been a brick to my dad. He badly needed someone like you to help him find the old dad we all knew before...before... I can't thank you enough.'

Angela burst into tears, said, wiping her eyes, 'I love him so much. He's the best thing that has happened to me. I miss him dreadfully when he's away.'

'What are you both doing for Christmas this year, he hasn't mentioned anything to me?'

'I don't know, he's so busy,' replied Angela. 'He telephones me every night no matter where he is. Have you and Vikki decided on anything yet?'

'Well we had thought of inviting you and the old man down for Christmas. Would you come?' he asked.

She absolutely beamed, 'just try and stop me. Yes I would love to. Thank you both, so very much.'

They returned to the pub, and Timothy had one person to speak with, before returning with Vikki to Southampton...

* * *

It was a few weeks later that Timothy telephoned Angela and arranged to meet her at Eastleigh Airport, Southampton. It was the week before Christmas, and David would be arriving at Heathrow the next day so she would be able to meet him.

'Bring your passport, you never know with dad, you might end up in Bermuda again.'

'I don't think so this time, Timothy. He has to be in Malaya on the sixth of January to give one of his talks, and I have to be back on twenty-seventh of December to see to the pub.'

Timothy and Vikki met Angela at the tiny Airport, whose main destinations were Guernsey and Jersey. She was delighted to see them and they headed west along the M27 and turned off left at exit 3 heading into the centre of Southampton. They were driving down Mountbatten Way, the main dual carriageway into the city, when Vikki urged Angela to look to their right.

The QE2 was in port.

Timothy said, 'She's being refuelled and replenished with stores, ready for the Christmas voyage to the Caribbean. She's leaving tonight. Would you like a walk around her? They allow visitors on a two hour tour.'

Vikki said with sheer enthusiasm. 'Say yes Angela, please, I've never been aboard.'

Angela grinned. 'Of course, it would be a dream come true for me. I've only seen pictures of her.'

And, off they headed into the dock area. They walked around the ship, enjoying its luxury, its splendour. Then they walked past a sign saying staterooms.

'This is where the toffee-nosed snobs stay on their holidays,' and Timothy opened the first door he came to.

'Are we allowed in?' Angela asked, peering into the spacious room.

'Yes. Why ever not? Lead on.' In the opulent surroundings, Angela just gazed, mesmerised by the richness, and the reality of how the wealthy really indulged themselves.

She then heard a click, turned and the door had closed. She couldn't open it.

'Timothy, Timothy,' she shouted, a sudden rush of panic crossed her normal calm and collective self, 'Timothy, please…'.

Then she heard the voice behind her. 'So, it's my son you want is it?' She turned to see David, a huge grin, arms outstretched. 'I love you,' was all he said.

Angela, wide-eyed, and panic gone, raced to him. 'You're back, you're back, I was going to Heathrow in the morning, to meet you.'

The door reopened and a happy smiling couple walked in. 'It was my turn to trick you,' chirped Timothy. 'Dad did it last year and it was my turn this year. We're all going to the Caribbean.'

Angela was stunned, then said, 'David, I cannot, I promised to be back on the twenty-seventh of December. My staff will go berserk.'

'No they won't,' Timothy said, 'I fixed this up three or four weeks ago when I was up north. You're not due back until the fourth of January. Your staff kept it a secret and sent you a huge Christmas card.'

At that, Vikki produced the card. It was huge; signed by all the pub staff.

'David I don't believe this. I just do not know what to say. It's all too wonderful for words.'

David smiled, adoringly, and said, 'Angela, I love you with all my heart. Will you marry me?'

'Yes, yes, yes…' she cried, hugging and kissing her man.

* * *

Chapter Fourteen

Bernadette had lived with Kerry since they were expelled. Seamus and Brenda had bought them a beautiful house over looking the sea, near Drogheda, in the south. They also had a house in the north near the republican border town of Crossmaglen.

Seamus and Brenda had both got over their fury with their daughter, but they would never forgive her. They accepted the trouble she had got into at school, it was the other business that destroyed their relationship.

No matter what they had said to her, trying to allay her fears, they had tried everything to convince her that they were putting money to one side for her future, it wasn't just for them, but she wouldn't believe them.

And why should she, she had thought. They had tried to persuade her to leave Kerry, and when she stood her ground, they turned viciously on her, threatening to take back the properties and everything else they had given her.

She had screamed at her parents. 'Oh! Will you now, well we will just have to see about that, won't we,' roared Bernadette, sneering at them, 'we'll see, just you fuckin' well watch...'

...To this day, neither could discover how they had gained access to their secure safe.

She was maliciously cruel to them; Seamus and Brenda had lived a nightmare, until at last, they managed an agreement with her. She had blackmailed her own parents. They were threatened with exposure, and certain painful death.

Bernadette had taken copies of their financial misdemeanours, everything that had transpired since they were made members of the Army Council. This included minutes of all meetings, and orders given to the internal security squads. All the information about individual members and, on it went...

She had taken them for virtually every thing they had. All the private accounts on the mainland, all the accounts on the continent, they were left with accounts in the south and in the north. This totalled very little more than what they started with in 1969.

'Don't worry,' she snapped at them, taunting, sneering, 'when you get old, I will look after you! I might even let you rent my house in Drogheda, because soon, I want your mansion here as well.'

The accounts she took were rich, extremely rich. She hauled her father to Germany, to the Munich headquarters of the main bank, and made him sign everything over to her, there and then, every account, every investment. Then she made new arrangements with the banker who her father had been doing 'business' with over the years.

The banker cringed. 'I have been doing honourable business with your father for many years, how can you do this to me.'

'Quite easily, Mr Hofferman, I am a callous, nasty bitch, as my father will tell you. You have three lovely teenage daughters, and if you wish them to stay that way, you will do as I say. And of course, not forgetting you, Mr Hofferman, if you want to keep your balls attached to your body, then at all times, you will always do exactly as I demand.'

Seamus cowered at the verbal abuse she was giving the German banker.

'Now, is that understood?'

She sneered.

Mr Hofferman hesitated, and Bernadette immediately said, 'agree now, you bastard, or I will see you get life, what is it to be?'

'Please, please I will see to your requests, but do not expose me.'

After the visit to Munich, they had then visited Liechtenstein and all the Charitable Trusts were changed into new Trusts, in Bernadette's name.

Although they spoke with their daughter, Seamus and Brenda never visited her, and they would not allow Bernadette into their house again. Thankfully, Bernadette had let them remain in their house, for the time being.

For over ten years, they had perfected the perfect fraud, raking in millions each year, from the systems, which they had devised together, and for what? Their own daughter, their only child, to come along and blackmail them, and finally, to rob them.

How could they have brought into this world such an evil child, they would never ever truly understand.

* * *

Bernadette, Kerry, and the men all left by different routes for London. This was the team, the PIRA active service unit, which outshone all the others. They had killed, maimed, tortured, and operated for fourteen years, with such immense success.

Bernadette always said that their efficiency was down to one person, and that person was Kerry. Bernadette was brilliant at executing the operation and Kerry was the brain behind everything they did.

Sean, Joe, and Fred were dedicated, loyal and no matter what was asked of them, without question they did it. They knew their commander so well, that very often only a nod or a wink was sufficient for them to explode into action. But, they all knew and agreed that without Kerry, they would have been arrested years ago. Leading up to whatever the operation might be, they had followed her instructions implicitly.

Even a simple move to London was executed with great skill and professionalism. It was so designed that their movements would hopefully be untraceable, and if that were the case, at most times they would be undetectable. Irrespective of the inconvenience or cost, they never travelled as a group, especially during an operation. They all had second passports, which effectively doubled their security. Therefore, their only risk was being caught in the act or on leaving. Kerry, always meticulous and painstakingly prepared the finer details. Leaving the scene of an incident was as important to get right as both the lead up to and execution of the operation. So many members had gotten this wrong and wondered why they had ended up in the Maze.

Kerry saw to all of this for them, she never took part in the operation, but was always close by. They knew if they followed her instructions they would be fine. With the execution of any operation, Bernadette the master tactician, the strategist, came into her own. She was the master planner, the expert of implementation.

The design and planting of a bomb, to cause maximum damage and death was the commander's skill. The ambushing of a patrol and the killing of its members, another forte. The capture, the torture, and the extraction of information from the touts, even well after she had what information she wanted, was merely a taster to a brutal finale. She carried on putting her wretched victims through all kinds of hell. Punishing them purely for her own enjoyment, for her demented, despicable and vile satisfaction.

Bernadette was well trained; the organisation had paid thousands of pounds to educate her in these techniques. The chairman at the last meeting had omitted to point out this part in her career, but all present had known. If inflicting pain, as a punishment was required, then Bernadette and her team were tasked.

She had spent time learning her grotesque trade from the military juntas of South America. The Military Regimes that took prisoners for no other reason, than to have 'live torture victims', for their torture training schools. Training schools that had official budgets, staff, training procedures, where their methods were regarded as a science.

There were classes, technical terms, apparatus, pictures of torture, training films, and all that followed up by live demonstrations on prisoners. Men and women that were snatched off the streets, taken away, just disappeared from the face of the earth; used as live guinea pigs for torture, just as the Nazis had victims tortured, supposedly for medical research during Hitler's regime of the Third Reich.

Bernadette had experienced the awesome depraved power of being the torturer, of sexually torturing someone, anyone to death, their lives in her hands. It was the ultimate thrill for her. She would watch others torturing while military officers looked on, and supposedly learning their trade. She'd witnessed soldiers turning up with young students, political activists ordered at gunpoint to throw the bodies of tortured victims onto the back of vehicles, the same means of transport they themselves had just arrived in.

This was part of the discipline of torture, generating fear and instilling horror into the minds of the young. She'd seen petrified faces on those forced to look at mangled, mutilated and horrifically abused bodies, the battered bodies of their friends who had 'vanished' without trace. Stricken, white faced with terror, nothing more than youngsters, they had known their fate lay in her hands.

She fed from her depravity as she travelled throughout these third-world countries. The longer she was there, the more evil she became. If a brother and sister were brought to her, she would put them through a living hell of every sexual deviation and incestual humiliation known to a natural sadist, then execute them as one might a dog in abject pain and no anaesthetic for humane disposal.

When time to depart and return home was a must, she did so most reluctantly. She loved her 'work' in South America, her viciousness in her early twenties even more twisted than through her formidable teenage years.

* * *

Chapter Fifteen

David Carver had spent the morning in Kuala Lumpur, delivering an outstanding presentation to Government Officials and Senior Officers in the Malaysian Army, the content of which had the little fellows absolutely ecstatic; delivered in their native tongue.

They had during the fifties fought the communist insurgence problem with the help of the British Army, and had managed to combat it. They still trained their troops steadfastly and vigorously in order to deter any likelihood of future occurrences of disruption. His vital message to them was to look at what had happened to America in Vietnam. That the mighty US had suffered an inglorious defeat because basically their troops were totally untrained for that type of jungle warfare, more so against a virtually unseen enemy.

His summary for the captive audience was, that they must forever be on their guard against those whom seek to undermine peace and stability, and had shortly afterwards flown on to Singapore.

Now, very comfortable, sipping a large whiskey in the palatial lounge of the world famous Raffles Hotel, he could relax a while in one of the most luxurious places envied by those who had never set foot inside. The hotel essentially catered for the rich and famous, having retained its unique nineteenth century décor and splendour of the long since dead era and atmosphere of British colonial rule.

It crossed his mind to bring Angela out here one day; she would love it, her being such a romantic. The Christmas holiday break seemed so long ago, their family cruise a triumphant coup, and they had been so happy together. What with Timothy and Vikki along as well, the occasion had been so much more worthwhile, a time for getting to know one another, altogether, as a family unit.

When he had proposed to her she had collapsed in his arms, the moment joyous for all concerned. Neither had wanted the holiday to end but, she had returned to her pub and here he was in Singapore. No date had been set for the wedding and that was just as well, especially as he had no idea what was about to happen. He was still on a quest, Jeremy forever in his thoughts.

'Excuse me, sir', said a tiny Chinese waiter, bowing, clasping his hands together as if in prayer. 'Colonel Johnson, from the British Embassy, sends his compliments and requests your kind permission for him to join you.'

A tingle of trepidation zipped through Brigadier David Carver; intuition telling him that this unexpected intrusion could encroach on his now very stable and normal life.

David said. 'Yes, of course,' a sense of apprehension preceding the only directive open to him. 'Please, send him over.'

David glanced around; could not see anyone who looked remotely like a British serving officer. However, a few moments later the waiter returned with a charge in tow.

'My apologies for invading your privacy, sir. I'm Colonel Tony Johnson, the Military Attaché here in Singapore.' A hand bearing an envelope was immediately proffered to David. 'I have been given the enclosed instructions for you. I do know the contents, but not the reasons. Could you kindly read the instructions and I will be able to advise you further.'

The contents were in fact a simple, but effective instruction.

Carver

You are requested to return to London, most urgently.

Johnson will give instructions.

Wilcox

'What in hell is this all about?'

Johnson immediately replied. 'Sir, as I said, I do not know the reasons. My instructions were to contact you and organise your flight to Heathrow, which I have already done. A car will pick you up at reception at 0600 tomorrow morning. Your hotel bill and flight have been seen to. Should you have no further questions, sir, I'll return immediately to the Embassy?'

As the other man remained at attention David Carver thought for a moment or two, then ordered another large whiskey, and tried in vain to comprehend what in hell the note was really telling him. He read the signal again noting the signatory, Wilcox. It gave the message the utmost credence, his mind whirling back to their very long-standing association and deep friendship.

Peter was now Sir Peter Wilcox, former SAS officer, and a very senior Director of MI5 and the Senior Executive of Operations, UK, and Northern Ireland.

David had not met with Peter for some time now, but something in the communique suggested intelligence had a lead for him on a horrendous tragedy that still plagued him with nightmares. Staring ahead, contemplating, yet consciously aware of a continuing presence, he let go a deep sigh, gathered himself, and said, 'thank you Tony. I will see you in the morning.'

If Peter Wilcox wanted to see or speak with David Carver, then he had to go, running if necessary. They went back a long way together, and David Carver had the utmost respect for this very senior civil servant and former commanding officer of the Regiment. He was a man who had been very instrumental in David's own career, dedicated and determined, his relentless energy abounding in everything he embarked upon. Carver had studied the man, his strengths, his powers of leadership, and his will to win at all times. His record in the Regiment was legendary. He was the man who had stood by David during the turmoil and aftermath of Jeremy's untimely demise, when he'd most needed friendship, throughout his darkest hours, the screaming horrors and unfulfilled revenge, even today, aimed at an invisible foe.

* * *

After the long flight from Singapore, David Carver was met at the airport by a Lt Colonel from the 'Ministry' and was taken in a staff car to his overnight stop at the Ritz Hotel.

He was informed that he would be collected at 0900 hours the following morning at the entrance and the scheduled meeting would take place at 1000 hours. Carver knew there would be no point in asking any details about the meeting and just bade his farewells outside the salubrious hotel.

The following morning the driver opened the rear door of the staff car and beckoned David Carver forward. Memories immediately flooded back when Peter Wilcox very warmly greeted him from the confines of limo.

They talked during the short drive, merely minutes from A to

B, on pleasantries and, after they alighted from the car David asked why the brief note for his immediate return? As expected, David was told that he would learn quickly enough and, that after the meeting they would be going straight to Sir Peters' home where they both could talk in private.

The present meeting was being held in one of the small conference rooms in the Ministry building. The building in Whitehall as drab and as uninteresting on the inside as it was on the outside; high ceilings, dull grey décor, not even pictures on the walls to try and brighten the gloom. All the rooms were much the same giving a very lifeless background to the many important and not so important meetings held in abundance within the building.

Coffee and tea was being served in a corner of the room when Sir Peter Wilcox and David Carver, both tall and immaculate in appearance, strode purposefully in. The Parliamentary Private Secretary and a RUC Chief Superintendent were talking together, with their refreshments placed on a large wooden table, which was the central focus of the room.

The PPS moved forward offering his hand to the MI5 officer who completed the formalities of introductions and the group talked preamble, inconsequential waffle, prior to the start of the meeting. Meanwhile a young lady edged around clearing away the cups and saucers, which were obviously needed for some other get-together.

The PPS finally invited the group to take their seats, by saying, 'firstly, may I thank you Brigadier for breaking from your extremely busy schedule and for returning to London for this meeting.'

David looked at him and thought, you fucking hypocrite, I didn't have a pissing choice, and still, after travelling half way round the world, I don't know what all this is about. It had better be good.

He merely nodded in acknowledgement.

'Gentlemen, this meeting and its content, has been agreed at the highest level. What I intend outlining is classified as Top Secret. I will commence with the background to the topic and give the Government's viewpoint.'

Amidst foot shuffling, discreet yawns emitted around him, David listened to the continuing summary...

'...Therefore the Provisional Irish Republican Army's political arm, Sinn Fein has been pressing hard with talks, through the good offices of John Hume, the Independent Democratic Labour Party, Member of Parliament and with direct contact between our MI5 agents, led by Sir Peter Wilcox... The PIRA talks are to appease the majority of the catholic population who most certainly now have a far better quality of life. Major changes have been achieved giving them equality, fairness and a new direction in life. New legislation, anti-discrimination laws, and many other developments have been implemented to afford greater protection for the minority catholic population, both at work and at home...'

The PPS took a brief respite for a quick sip of water, then ploughed on again...

'The communities are slowly integrating again, and old friendships are being restored. As far as they are concerned the objectives of the campaign have been accomplished. They want and are demanding an end to the armed conflict. Whilst The Provisional Irish Republican Army is talking they are also shooting and bombing. They continue to spew death and destruction in order to retain the morale of prisoners who are incarcerated and rotting in the Maze and Magilligan Prisons...Intelligence estimates show that apart from fringe republican elements such as INLA, the active strength of terrorists in Northern Ireland is less than 80, which includes the technicians, trainers and the planners. Actual hard-core terrorists it is estimated that there are less than 30 and they are known, and are under constant surveillance...'

He cleared his throat, glanced around the room and proceeded once more with his present agenda...

'On the mainland, there are approximately 15 known terrorists who are under MI5 surveillance. In the past 18 months PIRA has had limited success with shootings but source's indicate that there is going to be increased bombings on the UK mainland...We are now confident that PIRA has been eliminated in Europe. The special co-operation that we have enjoyed from the major European countries has been phenomenal. These countries have not enjoyed the bombings or shootings by PIRA and indeed as Ian will outline, we have therefore reaped enormous benefits. If we had received the same co-operation from the Dublin Government then the armed conflict could have ended years ago. We must now look to take swift advantage of the depleted PIRA...'

With hoarse voice, he once again took a sip of water.

'The official Government policy or line is that there can be no military solution to the conflict. The end result must be by political means. However, the Cabinet Minister's greatest fears are that we will have an ending to the conflict similar to that of the Gulf war, and that would be totally unacceptable not only to the British Government but also to the British people...Gentlemen, the personal wish of all in government, is for a political solution, but not until we have achieved military success! The resolution of all is solid and they look to the present company to achieve this.'

Brigadier Carver stroked his chin with his right hand, pursed his lips, and about to speak out, Peter Wilcox' gesture of a slightly raised hand precipitated any such action to silent restraint, as they listened to:

'The PM can never accede to assassinations, but he will agree to the constructive use of the intelligence gained from last year's operation.'

David, again stroking his chin, raised his left eyebrow as he glanced at his friend, thought to himself; surely to goodness this twit must know that good intelligence has a very limited life span. Measured at most times in a few hours and on the rare occasion, in days.

The speech went on and on for some considerable time, with bugger all said in typical flowery ministerial jargon...After sufferance of further political drivel the PPS then finally said. 'We will now break for lunch, then Sir Peter Wilcox' brief will follow this.'

During the lunch break, at an opportune time David spoke with Peter and asked him, 'who the hell is that fool?'

Peter grinned, and said. 'Just bear with it, there are developments which I feel, in the long run, will be suitable to yourself, and you will get an opportunity to speak.'

* * *

Chapter Sixteen

Bernadette told them all to travel light. She expected them to be away for some time and she had decided to buy them new outfits.

Fred collected his tickets from a travel agency in Derry. He then hired a car and drove to Waterford in the south, where he handed it back to the rental company. He then travelled by bus to Rosslare Harbour, where he boarded the midday ferry for Pembroke Dock.

After arriving at Pembroke he had a few drinks and left for London on the overnight boat train. The next morning he went to the reception of a hotel in north London, where he had been booked in for the night. He remained there until Kerry contacted him the next day.

The same day that Fred had left Derry; Sean had flown out of Aldergrove at 7am, arriving at Heathrow and took a taxi to a small hotel at Hounslow. His instructions were to remain there for two nights then he would be contacted. Joe left the day after Sean, and took the ferry from Belfast to Stranraer, then a train to Edinburgh where he was booked on the overnight sleeper to London.

Both Bernadette and Kerry had left on separate flights from Aldergrove.

Bernadette had picked up the early morning flight at Aldergrove and after arriving at Heathrow, had interconnected and took a flight to Hurn Airport just outside Bournemouth. A taxi took her to the centre of Bournemouth, where she collected a hire car that Kerry had organised. She then drove to the farmhouse in the New Forest, bought the previous year from ill-gotten funds. There she awaited the arrival of the others.

Kerry had flown to Manchester a little later and had trained it to London; staying the night at the Kings Cross Station Hotel, a planned rendezvous for the next day.

Bernadette's team was the best, a combination now of vast experience in terrorist warfare and self-preservation. She owed them. They were brilliant; a tremendous group. It always appeared that they lived for her. Never once had they questioned her, and never a dispute or a crossword in fourteen years of pure unmitigated violence. They were the polished professionals of terrorism.

Never ever would she have expected Kerry to mature to the degree that she had. Her organisational ability was outstanding. The three men, Sean, Joe, and Fred, had also demonstrated their own sound abilities. It gave Bernadette great confidence knowing that whatever had to be done, would be done with clinical efficiency.

* * *

By midday, they were all at the farmhouse. Elated, wondering what the next tasks were going to be. They had never worked on the UK mainland.

'Before I start, thank you for the efforts you all put in against McAnnally. I have a feeling that he'll not be able to talk himself out of this one. Well gang, back to the present. We're off on new ventures, something totally different. For the next nine months or so we are going hunting.'

Then she paused.

'Hunting!' Sean exclaimed.

'Yes, Sean, tout hunting. How about that?'

Joe remarked, 'where the hell do we start with that.'

Kerry grinned, 'well now, my dear. You are booked on a flight to Kemi a week on Saturday, and as it is early March, you will need very warm clothes, because yesterday it was minus eight over there.'

'Pray tell me, my beloved Kerry,' he joked, 'where the fuck is Kemi?'

She enlightened him. 'It's in Finland, Finnish Lapland to be precise, and at this time of the year you should be able to see that wonderful phenomena, the Northern Lights.'

'How absolutely fucking wonderful. I am thrilled to bits, to be sure, freezing my bollocks off.'

Kerry laughed. 'I don't know anything of that, I am not made that way, what I do know is, your flight is to Helsinki and you connect there to Kemi. I have booked you into the Hotel Merihovi for the night. Your cover is that you are a journalist, covering the European Cup Finals, for slalom skiing. These championships are currently being held on Ounasvaara, which is a hill overlooking Rovaniemi.'

'Very convenient, Kerry, I'll bet you organised that event too,' Joe joked.

'Can you remember Michael Mulcahy?'

'Yes, Kerry, of course I can, my brother is still rotting in the fucking Maze, after being there sixteen years, due that fucking bastard. He was only sixteen years old and it was his first operation. He didn't even have a gun.'

'That is why he is your target.'

'Now we're talking, Kerry. You're a gem.'

'He has a snow mobile business in the Arctic Town of Rovaniemi. He will think he is untouchable, now that he has been settled there for seven years and has married a local girl, plus they have three kids.'

'Sean, you are flying off on the Sunday, the day after Joe. It is a lunch time flight and your destination is Bangkok.'

Sean interrupted. 'Tell me Kerry, am I going after McGurk?'

'Sorry Sean, he hasn't been traced yet, but Bernadette's mother is working on that.'

'Your target is Patrick and Yvonne Murphy.'

'If ever the movement wish to track down and dispose of, as painfully as possible, two fucking heathens, then those two touts have got a be first. They're responsible for hundreds of our soldiers being nicked. In fact, they were great friends of Paddy McGurk, so you may be able to find out from them, where he is.'

Sean smiled, looked at Bernadette, and said, 'I'll find him, and when I do, can I have him?'

'We both will, Sean, yes, we both will... and how.'

Kerry continued. 'The last we heard was that they were both chefs in the Royal Orchid Hotel, in Bangkok. We have contacts with friends in Thailand who will be delighted to help us out. They owe us many favours. I will have details of these contacts before you leave. What you both need to do is to locate your target, I have photographs of them all, but you will still have to verify identification. Yvonne was renowned for a bird tattooed on her backside. Recce the area and watch them. Even if it takes weeks, gain their confidence if possible. Get close to them, find out as much about them, their lifestyles, what they do, where they go, anything you can, then we'll all go out and dispose of them...Both your flights are booked, tickets will be at the respective gates. I will have two thousand pounds cash, each, for you to splash out on them if necessary, they all like money. Make it their downfall, if you need more give me a call.

Please do not try individual action, Bernadette wants to be there at the end.' Kerry emphasised.

Bernadette just remained seated, nodding in agreement.

Fred was looking in anticipation. 'Where am I going,' he asked, virtually pleading with his eyes.

Bernadette spoke to him, 'Fred, you're staying here.'

Gloom was written all over his face, but he knew there would be a reason, and there was...

'You have worked tirelessly without a break for years. You are taking Moiré and the children on a month's holiday to Disneyland in Florida. It's all booked. You'll stay here tonight and meet up with the family at Heathrow tomorrow...Sorry to have dragged you all this way to tell you this, but there is one other thing, your family will not be returning to Belfast. Kerry and me have known that Moiré has hated the place since what happened to you. I am not going to talk of that, but I understand Moiré's feelings...I have bought you a nice house on the outskirts of Bournemouth where you and your family can live in peace. It is time that you had a few settled years together. We will always be here for you, if you want to return to active service.'

Fred was stunned, tears in his eyes. 'You are all my family.' He cried.

Bernadette continued, 'Kerry has set up a bank account for you in Bournemouth. The account will receive £5,000 every month for you to retire on. It will continue to be paid throughout both your lives, so that neither you nor Moiré will have any worries.

Here's the key to the house, go and have a look at it, Sean and Joe can go with you. Tonight we will drink your health.

Tomorrow, the war continues...'

* * *

Chapter Seventeen

Peter Wilcox started his brief, and David knew almost immediately that his former fire and drive was missing but, nevertheless, he would listen.

'The aim of the operation is to produce military success in Northern Ireland prior to enabling politicians to co-ordinate a political solution. This final solution must be acceptable to all paramilitary organisations and political parties both north and south of the border. Selected members of each party are now formulating the political initiative...

The political assumption is that all paramilitaries have instigated an end to all hostilities. To achieve military success the Government has insisted on a number of guidelines, which the planned military operation must strictly adhere to...

A no 'shoot to kill' policy will be in force...

There must be no collusion with loyalist paramilitary forces.'

He glanced at the listeners, then continued.

'In the event of compromise the Government will deny that any such operation ever took place. Within these guidelines we have to formulate a plan to achieve the given objectives. The guidelines are extremely restrictive but I am determined that success must, for the people of Northern Ireland, prevail...Without doubt this is a unique opportunity to shape the course of history and, once and for all, contribute to a final solution to the Irish problem. It is my belief that eight former SAS soldiers and one SAS officer can effectively solve the problem in months.'

David Carver steeled himself and interrupted, 'Sir Peter, I have listened very...'

At that point Peter Wilcox knew exactly what David Carver's objections would be and immediately stopped his old friend in his tracks, by saying, 'David you are here on the strongest recommendation by me. You must hear me out and then we will constructively deal with initial questions prior to formulating the plan.'

Stunned at this rebuke, David nodded in apology and Sir Peter continued.

'As I have indicated, two four man ex-SAS teams, selected

from retired SAS personnel led by a retired SAS officer, could achieve these objectives...The leader would be in direct control with the men on the ground and would liase with Ian and myself for support.'

Like hell, David Carver said to himself.

Turning to David, Sir Peter said, 'you are the most outstanding officer that has served under my command, David. You have the ability to end this campaign of violence and murder. You are my man for the job. Your individual fighting skills will not be required, your major assets to this operation will be your vast organisational skills in this type of operation. Your expertise at disinformation, deception, and downright effrontery, are the key to success...

The GOC, Northern Ireland, and myself have selected you to lead this operation. No other officer has your calibre, and therefore, no other officer has been considered. Your selection, if you accept of course, has already gained the approval at the highest level...I fully realise that you have had no time to consider the concept or even thought of a plan, and what I would require is your agreement in principle. If this is acceptable, then we can start the preparation and planning.'

David Carver thought for a moment or two, and then stood up. He looked to the PPS and then at Ian Walsh. Then he shifted his attention directly at Sir Peter Wilcox, and said. 'Thank you so much for your kind words and most certainly your firm and continued belief in my ability.'

He then averted his gaze to the PPS and as soon as he did this, Sir Peter knew that there was going to be fireworks. The PPS moved with a slight shuffle, noticeably uncomfortable, perhaps wondering what on earth he had done wrong even before Carver started talking.

David spoke slowly, and firmly.

'Sir,' addressing the PPS, 'the Northern Ireland problem has been with us since 1969, and successive Governments have proliferated this horrible, nauseating and lamentable state of affairs...

Politicians, like you, do not listen.

They do what they want in order to further their own pathetic careers. Not caring about the welfare, or giving a damn about the well being of a kind, generous peace seeking community. The people have been left to their own devices, to flounder under the horror of bombs; the bullet, the fear, the absolute trepidation and dread of that late night knock on the door...

Politicians, like you, do not understand...

They cannot feel or taste the terror of 23 years of violence and venom.'

David momentarily paused to get his breath.

'The situation has been provoked and intensified by a total lack of competent political leadership...

Politicians and their so called civil servants, or should I use the correct terminology and say, servants like yourself, who, over the years have exacerbated the problem with a flagrant disregard to honesty...

Yes sir, no sir, I agree sir, three bloody fucking bags full sir, as long as you do not upset the apple cart, then so be it...'

The PPS interjected, 'Carver, how dare you talk to me like this,' David Carver stood his ground, glared, his eyes indicating the anger he felt, as he responded with a raised commanding voice, 'shut up, sir, and for once, listen...'

Again David paused gathering his momentum, and again glaring at the PPS...

'Had the Government of the day, in the early seventies listened, when SAS soldiers were first sent to the Province, and heeded the expert advice of the professional soldiers, the experts, then this campaign of terror would have been over many, many years ago.

The Provo's were in shocked disbelief when they realised that the SAS were going to be their opponents. It virtually paralysed them into a phase of complete inaction until they suddenly grasped that the most efficient fighting force in the world had their hands fucking tied behind their backs...

The Regiment had been restrained by its restricted use; therefore with minimum involvement, it achieved only limited success. Why were the professionals never used to the maximum effect. We have been at war, sir, with the SAS in the Province for nearly 20 years.'

David's anger was evident to all.

'For twenty bloody years we have been told, you will not shoot to kill. Even worse, we virtually have to ask permission to shoot, holding up a fucking yellow card. Don't you think that that is frustrating, that it is undermining the level of competence of the average highly trained soldier, let alone the men of the Special Air Service...?

Soldiers, sir, want to kill terrorists, because that is what they are trained to do. And why the fucking hell not; does PIRA or INLA plant bombs so as not to kill?

No, they bloody well don't, they thrive on murder, flourish on destruction, and then delight with unmitigated pleasure when their terror tactics succeed. W

Let me tell you sir, SAS soldiers are vastly experienced. Individually, they have probably completed two tours of duty in Northern Ireland, or more, with their respective Regiments, prior to enlisting in the SAS regiment. They then have to complete the most gruelling and arduous training course of any fighting force in the world...Once they complete that they are then trained in their respective disciplines to become a highly trained fighting machine for the sole purpose of killing an enemy...'

He paused, the enormity of his verbal assault impacting on his captive audience.

'Then what happens...they are posted to fucking Ulster and are told, you will not shoot to kill, or you will not shoot at all! These men are fighting machines, disciplined, dedicated and highly professional.

Politicians or their fucking servants, obviously feel that we would just wander around shooting all and sundry as if we were on a duck shoot or perhaps after pheasants or grouse....

No sir, we don't, we use our wits to fight, our guile, initiative, and many other traits, and then, as a last resort to protect others or ourselves, we may shoot to kill...

In Ulster we could be charged with a crime if we do that. Tell me how many poor sods are rotting in prison because they have done what they believed was their duty, as soldiers...

There are many, too many.'

He kept going. He had to. It was not just his duty, but also his right, to keep going, keep up this verbal attack on behalf of professional fighting men, who were effectively unable to fight terrorism in the manner they had been trained to do.

'Your masters, with you nodding your head in agreement, want me or some other joker to go and tackle the hard-core element of PIRA that remain. You lay down directives or guidelines on us, which makes the job impossible. We must not shoot to kill. What do you want us to do sir, with the 30 active terrorists? Slap their wrists! And where the hell have you dreamed up the figure of 30.

Let me assure you that recruitment in any terrorist

organisation is self-perpetuating. As soon as a terrorist is captured, or even one that is accidentally killed, there are friends and family who immediately volunteer to take his or her place. Recruitment of terrorists can be likened to a contagious disease, one gets the bug and the rest in the family soon fall foul to the same complaint...

Despite what has been said here, terrorists still have the initiative. There is still bombings and shootings, yet you have said they are all being watched, and you have the audacity to expect us to find a military solution prior to your political initiatives...

Perhaps we should just stand there and shout, "there will be no shooting from now on". Because that is how effective the current campaign has been operated. Do you understand that, sir?'

An ashen-faced PPS trembled; he had never been spoken to like this before. He was visibly stunned by the stark reality of the facts thrown at him. The sheer ferocity of the verbal onslaught had sliced into him like nothing else in his cosseted life. He looked at both the RUC and MI5 officers for some kind of inspiration, but that was a futile gesture.

None was forthcoming.

'And I am not finished,' said David Carver, which caused the PPS's eyes to gape open even wider, and his silent lips to tremble even more. 'I have had soldiers, great soldiers, with families, killed, because of restrictive and diabolical practises and rules placed upon us, by parasites such as yourself...

Yes indeed, and I am sure that you are aware of the death of my own son, killed because of gross political negligence. No sir, not because of any military incompetence on his part, but because some useless oaf, known as a fucking civil servant, decided in his tiny mind that the fight against terrorism could be conducted on a nine till five basis...

You sit there sir, and state that you want an end to the strife and then follow this up by stating that it must be done your way, the political way – a military end governed by political rules. Well let me tell you, sir – it cannot be done. All you will achieve, under these restrictions, is more deaths, more sorrow and sadness. You will prolong the campaign for a further decade or two, until someone comes along, with the guts and balls to say, go out and give me military success, you have total autonomy. Then and only then, will you be in a position to achieve a political solution...'

David was on a roller-coaster, and unwilling to apply the brake, he continued, detailing and denouncing political drivel that in the past had formed the basis of so called military initiatives...

'...And finally gentlemen let me conclude with this. You may feel that PIRA is being brought to its knees, and that maybe so, but look at another scenario...PIRA may feel exactly the same, that they can bring the British Government to its knees.

Why? Because they still have massive power and influence, even if they have depleted numbers. In 1992, they exploded two huge devices, both sadly, with loss of life and devastating affect. The destruction that the two bombs caused, cost more to repair than all the bombings in Ulster put together, since the beginning of the campaign...

Over one billion pounds worth of damage, am I correct, sir? And did you not stand here and say, that the intelligence communities are reporting that there is a growing threat for a continued bombing campaign on the mainland? The danger being, that terrorists still can and will, despite the talking, continue to bomb their way to negotiations in their favour...I have nothing further to say.

Thank you, gentlemen.'

David Carver bent down to retrieve his brief case; a totally distraught PPS looking on. 'With your permission, Sir Peter, I think that would be all for me today and I would wish to return and get on with some constructive work.'

Sir Peter Wilcox casually smiled at David, and said. 'Please David, please sit down for a moment.'

Sir Peter Wilcox addressed the PPS, then said, 'an enormous amount of time and effort had gone into this project. Ian Walsh and myself outlined to you that we needed a free hand without any form of interference...You have now heard the same message again, only this time it was delivered in a more forthright manner...

Go back to your masters and ask them if they have the hidden qualities that Brigadier Carver has outlined, and if they have, then the operation can get underway.'

* * *

During the journey in the staff car, nothing was said about the meeting or indeed any future operation. They talked freely about David's various presentations to military staff officers throughout the world. Especially relating to his address to American Specialist Forces at the Pentagon.

They talked about his highly acclaimed book, "Action", which had, in its first year, made him wealthy beyond his wildest dreams.

They also talked about his secondment to the Australian Special Air Service Regiment. Peter was instrumental in this move, having been his Commanding Officer at the time. At that time David was attached to specialist forces in Vietnam, where his exploits and incredible ventures saved hundreds of lives and made him the most decorated foreign soldier in US military history.

Peter Wilcox referred to his friend's address given at the pentagon, and said, 'it must have been the greatest thrill in the world, to be recognised in such a manner, by such an audience.'

David Carver smiled, said, 'yes, but the real thrill and satisfaction will only come to fruition if political leaders take on board the main message I gave at the end, the message given at all my presentations...

It is absolutely vital that Governments give full and unconditional trust and autonomy to the men specifically trained to deal with terror and terrorists. It is the only way that terrorism can be defeated. It still astounds me that Governments all over the world will spend millions developing the skill of these forces, which are a means unto an end and then totally ignore their advice. Was that not my message today?'

Peter Wilcox did not reply, and merely smiled to himself. He knew that this was not the end; he had seen the note from the American Secretary of State for Defence, which had ultimately ended up on the PM's desk.

* * *

David Carver met Jane Wilcox for the first time since the summer of 1991; the deep affection she held for him portrayed in the welcoming hug, the joy of friendship plain to see.

She was acquainted with the mental persecution and anguish that he had so bravely endured, and his continuing endeavours to make the world a better place.

'David, it's so wonderful to see you again. Still as handsome as ever and looking so well. We both absolutely adore you. Oh, and you're in the same room as before. Dinner will be about an hour, so time enough for you to settle in.'

Peter led David to his room and said they would discuss Northern Ireland after dinner, when Jane would retire early in order for them to talk together, privately.

Dinner passed off fairly quickly with only one reference to the past and when Jane had made it she had realised immediately she had made a mistake. She had said, 'Sarah is still more than fond of you, David... She often telephones for a chat, and very quickly you're the topic of conversation. Your loss David was also her loss. She finds great difficulty in coming to terms with the tragedy, much as yourself. You have to see it from her point of view. After all, you've been able to engross yourself in your work, but Sarah has no such release. She knows that she made a dreadful mistake when she left you. I think she realised that within months, and has had to live with it ever since... Then came the horror of Jeremy's death, and the aftermath. I suppose she hoped, that in the mutual sufferance of the tragedy, that fate would bring you together again. She's still in turmoil, and heartbroken at having lost two of the most important people in her life...'

David stopped Jane, and said, 'I loved Sarah, but she left me, and only two weeks before Jeremy was to start at boarding school. I tried and tried; God only knows how I tried to salvage our marriage, and how I begged her not to leave me. I was prepared to leave the SAS, anything, anything to keep her. But no, she wanted that property developer. He had money. His so-called bloody wealth overpowered any love that Sarah had for me, and if you remember, she took Timothy with her...To be fair...Yes, we had grown apart...'

He paused, why in hell was he feeling a need to justify himself to any one?

'Damn it, my career had me all over the world and Sarah knew that long before we ever got married...

Whatever, I admire your loyalty, Jane, but my life is my own and I am now a different person than Sarah knew. I am sure that in time you will also see that. And in any event, I suppose now is as good a time as any to tell you both, that there is someone new in my life. Her name is Angela and she lives in Newcastle. When time permits I would love to introduce you to her.'

Peter stepped in and changed the subject, 'come on David,

let's not get morbid. The old dragon has work to do in the kitchen and we have much to talk about.'

As David moved from the table he passed Jane who had already started collecting plates. He turned, and gently placed his hand on her shoulder, She faced him and he caressed her cheek, 'I still love you,' and then he kissed her. 'And, your cooking is still as delicious as ever.'

All three smiled, and as her husband of thirty-five years and David headed for the drawing room, she went to the kitchen. In the kitchen, after placing the plates in the sink, Jane put her hands on the worktop and sobbed. It was a cry of deep felt pity for her friend Sarah. She had thought that she could become a matchmaker for her dear friends, Sarah and David. Nothing in this world would make her happier than to see them together again. She naturally pondered what David had meant by 'different person'. Time will tell?

* * *

David and Peter discussed the Northern Ireland situation, especially the tactics that should have been implemented years ago, whilst indulging post-dinner drinks. They reminisced over what had, and could have been, in the strife torn land that was Northern Ireland; had they been given carte blanch to resolve the matter.

Peter excused himself for a few moments and David was left pondering over how he had 'gone to town' against the PPS. Inwardly, he felt that at last the opportunity to avenge his son's death was with him, but he knew that under the restrictions and given rules it would be more likely that he would be killed as well.

Patience had prevailed and his time would come. He had made a promise and it would be a promise he would keep, and how!

When Peter returned, David asked if he had seen the pathologist's report on Jeremy.

'Yes indeed, appalling injuries,' he replied, settling himself in a chair opposite.

The medical report had already provided David with detailed account of what he would be up against, but not as yet, exactly who. DNA tests on Heather showed initially that three men had assaulted her; reduced to two when it was discovered that Jeremy's semen was on one of the swabs that had been taken from inside Heather's mouth. Whereas, a swab of dried spittle found on Jeremy's thighs and stomach; to David's dismay, was determined as coming from another female. In the event that three men were seen to attack them at the public house, the assumption was the female must have been in the van. Only two of the men had sexually attacked Heather, why only two if three were present?

Peter then interrupted David's thought patterns, with, 'I have read many of the medical reports in the past, relating to "nutting" squads and their offensive activities. We understand there is only one group on operation these days. However, a pattern has been detected that one of the men does not get involved in a sexual manner but we have been unable to come up with a satisfactory conclusion. We don't know what relevance there is in that piece of info, if any, or how important it is. Perhaps, only time will tell?'

They both looked somewhat thoughtful for a moment, then all of a sudden the doorbell rang; damn near siren like, both men surprised, and brought back to reality, immediately on their feet as Peter said aloud, 'who the hell... and at this time of night?' He gestured for David to stay put. 'Take a pew again, until I sort this out.'

David glanced around the old house' elegant interior, the most sophisticated security devices on the market discreetly installed exactly as would have expected for the protection of a senior MI5 officer. But could anyone ever be safe, truly safe from harm if, if...?

* * *

Peter viewed a close circuit television monitor and could see the gate at the bottom of his long drive. Outside was a Jaguar car with a man standing, purposefully looking at a partially hidden camera.

'What can I do for you?' said Sir Peter, in not too pleasant tone.

Holding up a Warrant card to identify himself, the man said, 'I apologise for calling on you so late Sir Peter... I have a visitor who must speak with you urgently.'

The electronic gate opened and the car crept quite silently through, and seconds later stopped at the entrance to the house. A Chief Inspector and his driver got out, and both opened respective rear doors, allowing two men in the rear to alight and climb the well-worn steps up to the front of the house.

The door now open, Sir Peter Wilcox stood transfixed at the person in front of him.

'Good evening, Sir Peter', said the Prime Minister. 'May we come in?'

Rarely in his extremely active life had Sir Peter Wilcox been shocked, but this was something else. 'Yes, of course, sir, please do.' The Prime Minister bestowed a smile while Peter Wilcox gathered himself. Then Peter stepped back; ushered the PM into the house.

The PM quickly introduced his companion, Chief Superintendent Flint of the Diplomatic Protection Group. Meanwhile, the driver and the Chief Inspector remained on duty outside the house as the Chief Superintendent and PM moved into the small reception room that housed the CCTV.

'I would hope that your guest is still with you and has not left or retired.'

'No,' replied Sir Peter. 'You could have knocked me for six a few moments ago, and I'm sure he will be as shocked as I was.'

The PM followed Peter Wilcox into the drawing room and saw the near empty glasses and the equally near empty bottle of malt whiskey on the small baize covered table.

David, with his back to the door, was sitting with closed eyes when he heard Peter enter. He turned his head slowly and by this time the two men were almost by his side.

'Good God!' Said an amazed David Carver, 'I don't believe this.'

He stood up, and a hand was thrust out to him, as the Prime Minister said, 'Brigadier, it gives me the greatest pleasure to meet you... I have heard and read so much about you.' He then said to Peter Wilcox, 'well Peter, as I've had the balls to come here and face the flak, perhaps you might like to unearth another bottle of my favourite medication.'

David Carver thought to himself: I like him, and, to coin a phrase, could do business with this man.'

All glasses charged, Sir Peter said, 'I feel something very constructive is about to take place, so may I pre-empt and propose a toast...'

'Gentlemen,' Sir Peter raised his glass, and continued, 'to a successful and peaceful conclusion, ending the troubles in Northern Ireland.'

They repeated the toast and then sat down.

'Well gentlemen, since the return of my PPS, with his tail between his legs, I have spoken with a number of my colleagues. We are of one. There has to be the most strenuous of efforts by us all, so I will be as flexible and as bold as necessary. Our resolve is to terminate the scourge in our society, that is terrorism. This strife must and will end. Tell me, David, what is it that you require? Hold back on nothing. What exactly do you need?'

David grinned. He was elated, and had waited, and waited for this moment...

He spoke for some time, with various interruptions, which he dealt with, to the agreement of all, and finally concluded...

'Sir, under the new guidelines and with the autonomy that I have been given, I am delighted to accept. I will emphasise that nothing in this agreement will come before my mission, to avenge the death of my son. Do you agree?'

'Yes I do, David. I can see that the two missions are inextricably linked... inseparable. The death of your son and the dreadful resulting condition of Sergeant Calvert must be accounted for. The actions of the sadistic killers commands no mercy upon their being successfully hunted down and permanently removed from society...

There can be no other way, an agreement could never be reached in this matter, and if it were, with that type of evil still amongst us, we could never feel secure that it would ever be honoured.

Whatever your requirements, they will receive the highest and immediate priorities...I will brief the Commander of Land Forces, Northern Ireland, personally, and wish you, Sir Peter, to attend. For this mission you will report directly to me and answer to no other official.'

The PM then glanced at his watch, continued.

'David, you have an enormous task, and I want you to know that I have the utmost respect and faith in you. I feel that if this mission can be brought to a successful conclusion, you are the one man with the necessary ability to achieve it.'

The PM then shook David's hand, and said 'Good luck, sir...' and left.

* * *

Chapter Eighteen

David Carver had already set about assembling his team.

They were to meet in one of the secure buildings at Ashford in Kent, the 'home' of Army Intelligence. David Carver had attended numerous courses here in the past, building up his enormous data bank of knowledge, and was now awaiting the arrival of his great friend, the man who had taught him the rudiments of his trade, a man of immense standing in Special Operations. A man that he had worked with in Borneo, Oman, Northern Ireland, and many, many other trouble spots around the globe.

Len Peters had been commissioned in 1976, and achieved the rank of Major, retiring in 1990, having completed 37 years exemplary service. He was a stalwart among men, an achiever through sheer dedication. When his operational role had finished because of age, he had run the training school and applied the same devotion to duty there, as to everything else in his past.

He was the most tenacious man that David had ever met. Nothing would beat him. Len was the man he wanted alongside him when the chips were down. Len had the patience, the unmitigated resolve, and determination to help him destroy, not only the remaining active service units of the PIRA, but foremost to him, the murderers of his son.

Even now, two years on, when he thought about it, the tears were still there, it was so outrageous; a heinous crime beyond words. The horrendous destruction of a young life, his boy at that, had created a terrible void, a vacuum that could never be filled or replaced, not even with Tim in his life. But now, the tide was changing; he was on the move and strike he would, with force.

Len Peters took him out of his reverie the very minute the door was opened. They hugged each other, the attendant Intelligence Corps corporal looking on, amused. Those already present had been briefed that a special type of operation was about to commence, a biggy with freedom and access to anything that they wanted. That had never happened before...

After the manly embrace, Len Looked David full in the face,

then said, 'you were thinking of Jeremy when I came in, weren't you boss?'

'Yes,' David confided.

'You must get it off your mind... Both you and I know we will get them... Have no doubt on that.'

David smiled, 'Len you are looking great...A little greyer than five... or is it six years ago, when we last met. You look as fit as ever.'

'Yes David,' he said, 'I have been preparing for this mission since February 1991.'

'The lads will be here in a minute or two. It's a few years now since we all got together. I had hoped that we would have been able to meet at my farewell from the Regiment, but they were out in Saudi, guarding one of the Princes'. Their joint VIP protection business hit really bad troubles two years ago, and now, instead of employing retired Special Forces people, they have to do it themselves.'

David asked Len, 'Do you know the scale of their troubles?'

'Not fully, I believe what happened was, that they were sold an indemnity insurance policy to cover for anything going wrong. It would appear an incident occurred, and the policy let them down. It had obviously been designed for maximum commission for the salesman, and minimum cover for the business.'

'Considerable debt, then?'

'I hear that they are repaying to their client, at the rate of £3,000 per month, to clear a sum in excess of £300,000.'

'Len, find the name of the client, visit him, and reach an acceptable offer for a one off payment. Most people in this situation would jump at about half, as they must be aware that the lads could just do a runner, or declare bankruptcy at any time. No matter the cost, I'll settle it. Then find where they bank and I'll transfer £50,000 into each account. And that goes for you too.'

Len started to protest, 'If you think that I am accepting payment for doing this job, then you're very much mistaken.'

David said, 'Listen Len, all three of you could be away from your work for a substantial time. I do not intend to stop until I have wiped this scourge off the face of the earth. You all have expenses, mortgages and other commitments, and I do not want monetary worries to affect our aims. Believe me, when I say this Len, in the last year, I have earned after tax, ten times more than I earned in the whole of my military career...I intend once this is over, that my friends will benefit and you and the two lads are top of my list. Oh, and I don't mean this as an afterthought, Len. Could you also sort out accounts for payment for our other two friends, who will be joining us.'

'Yes, if you tell me who they are?'

'In time my friend, in time.' David Carver grinned. 'Anyway Len, you have been retired nearly three years. What have you been up to?'

'I've been operations manager for a security firm and the boredom has just about driven me mad. Once I received your call, I told them where to stuff their job. I cannot believe that some firms exist or survive with the 'tossers' that left are in charge.'

The main door was again flung wide as two men stepped forward, grinning like a pair of Cheshire cats. They were the most likeable men in the world, and tough as they all were, the tears flowed as all took it in turns for rugby style clnches. They had experienced so much together, all on various occasions had saved the other's lives.

They made a great team, one that now faced a tremendous challenge. They were assembled to kill, and kill they would!

'Four more people to turn up,' David informed them. 'Due in fifteen minutes.'

'What facts have we got boss,' Len quizzed, 'and when are we likely to move?' Before David Carver had time to answer, the loud swishing of a Gazelle's rotor blades momentarily drowned the conversation.

Then David Carver, said, 'that's probably our guests arriving in style. Before I brief you, let me just say there will be two other briefs. The first will be from an MI5 officer. Then an officer from the Royal Ulster Constabulary, Chief Superintendent Ian Walsh will give the second brief. He'll bring us up to date with the situation in Northern Ireland...Both these men will be involved with us throughout the operation, and will, in effect, have the immediate powers to demand whatever we require at any time. They are, what you might call, a very high-powered support team.'

And at that, there was a knock on the door, to which Tug said, 'if they came in on that chopper, they must have jumped out over the building!'

The Commanding Officer of the School of Army Intelligence

walked in with his guests Sir Peter Wilcox, and Chief Superintendent Ian Walsh. Len grinned when he saw his former Commanding Officer. Many memories would be shared together. They shook hands, firmly, both glowing with mutual pride and respect.

Sir Peter, now looking the part of a very senior civil servant with shiny silver hair, and Len's considerably grey in colour, both men, although in their mid-fifties were a picture of health and vitality. Tug and Jock, in their mid-forties, both a little grey-tipped, but again, as David had fully expected, as fit as young buck wolves.

Ian Walsh had been through the mill-grind of a tough existence too; shot twice himself, his wife and two policeman brothers killed. He had that haunted look of continued stress and strife having got the better of him; well overweight and prone to a stooping stance.

Surprisingly, David, tall, fair haired, with the constitution of an ox, despite years of action, could still stand out above the rest even in such exalted company. His very presence, no matter what the company, was awe-inspiring. Yet, with some women, like Angela, uncertainty and trepidation played a part in revealing the real person behind the battle-hardened outer defensive shell. He had a soft centre, but few ladies had ever tapped into it...

'Two more to arrive?' Len, Tug, and Jock were discussing and trying to determine who was joining them, then Jock said, 'who else is there, boss?'

Just then, in flying kit, holding a helmet and gloves, six feet tall and still a beanpole, a few remaining scraggly hairs that were salt and peppered, in walked one of the belated to arrive.

'Well I'll be damned,'... 'Strike a light,' and 'Yee god's alive,' was the immediate reaction from Len, Tug, and Jock, who walked up to him, arms wide to hug a good friend and saviour of dozens and dozens of clandestine operations, throughout the world. To them, he was the bravest of the brave. A helicopter pilot, SAS trained, and at fifty-three, Tom Galloway was their hero.

Tom had been with them in Borneo, Oman, Northern Ireland, and many other hotspots throughout the world; always there when needed, waiting, waiting to lift them out of sticky situations or after a successful mission. Very often, especially when it was an emergency extraction, he'd put himself in extreme danger, but always there as promised beforehand.

Jock, still beaming, said, 'Trust you to be bloody flash, Tom. We got here in a bus, and even the boss' arrived in a car. But you, you just had to arrive in your own personal helicopter, din yeh.'

Then moments later, whilst enjoying tea and biscuits, there was a quiet knock on the door. David Carver said, with a huge smile, 'Gentleman, our last member to arrive, and you all know, that in his case, he's definitely last but not least.'

The Commanding Officer rose to his feet, looking on in amazement at the array of very special men and the reception they gave to the last man. They were elite men, probably the most skilled experts of their profession, but the bespectacled, short, overweight man, obviously totally unfit, standing in the doorway a big grin on his face, as good as metaphorically floored the CO.

Ex Regimental Sergeant Major, Jack Simpson had retired nine years earlier, and had settled in the Salisbury area of South Wiltshire. His appearance had always belied the articulate, intelligent and dedicated soldier within. He was a veteran of six operational tours in the province. The last three tours, working in the field of military intelligence gathering, which was highly dangerous work; an operator always in fear of capture.

PIRA were a ruthless enemy, and a source handler's dreaded nightmare scenario of being caught with a tout, all too real at times. All who had attended the training course at Ashford were well warned of the consequences before going it alone.

His unique, individual, and unwavering desire to extract the truth from totally untrustworthy, devious, and evil informants, better known as touts, was paramount in securing the arrest of hundreds of PIRA terrorists. His methods were never discussed at any official level. He produced the goods, and in the climate of terrorist Northern Ireland, that was all that mattered.

On his first tour he had religiously followed the rulebook, but had quickly learned that in this field of operation, the most dangerous and unpredictable, that honesty was not the way ahead. And, the best way to be both successful and to survive was to throw away the rulebook and do it his way. Very unlawfully, very bloody nasty, but highly effective, and it was his methods that changed the course of the intelligence war in the Province!

David Carver was one of the very few who knew how he operated and, admired Jack Simpson for his guts and tenacity. Over the years in Northern Ireland, soldiers from the SAS relied totally on men like Jack Simpson. Men who were at the forefront of the fight against terrorism, whose 'no holds barred' acquisition of information and assessment of that information, not only played a vital part in the arrests of terrorists, but also the safety of those effecting the arrests.

David Carver knew he would need the skills and daring of this man. Although never a member of the Regiment, Jack Simpson, over the latter part of his career had attended many functions at Hereford as an honoured guest. The men in the Regiment knew he was the best, only the best worked for, or with them, and Jack was one of those.

* * *

Sir Peter Wilcox addressed the small assembly. The atmosphere instantly changed from lax and friendly, to that of supercharged concentration.

'Gentlemen, I am honoured to speak with such exalted individuals as yourselves. And it's a thrill for me to speak with old colleagues, great friends from a whole life span, dedicated to the destruction of terrorism...My only regret on this operation is that I cannot lead you in the field. However, I am probably too old, and so you'll be in the very capable hands of David Carver, and I know of no better man to lead an operation of this magnitude...David is in sole command. He has full authority to deal with any situation in whatever manner he thinks fit. Both Ian Walsh and I have agreed with this. It is an unusual operation and as such, demands unusual flexibility. David will have a better feel for what is happening on the ground, and we will be here to pull whatever strings are necessary, to achieve the success that the operation deserves.'

Peter paused, cleared his throat, and continued.

'I will firstly brief you on the background to this operation. In May of last year, MI5 assumed full responsibility for the gathering of intelligence within the United Kingdom. They were replacing Scotland Yard's Special Branch, to counter Provisional Irish Republican Army operations in Britain. The reasons that were stated at the time was due to the demise of the Eastern Block. Many MI5 agents were released to fight terrorism within the UK. Not all agreed with that, and it's well known that it was mostly MI6 who were involved in the foreign spheres of the secret service...

The RUC were very sceptical about this move, and now their worries are real, as MI5 are shortly to assume total control of all counter intelligence operations, Northern Ireland included, and I'll be heading up those operations.'

There was hushed silence all around.

'The biggest problem, in the past few years, has been the reluctance of senior Special Branch officers to disseminate vital information. That will now change, and as you will hear it has already changed for this operation...

The RUC have also been concerned that there has been political manoeuvring by the British Government to gain a settlement on its terms, which might not be acceptable to the RUC...

I was invited to a meeting at Downing Street to discuss the Northern Ireland situation, as on other occasions, but this time it was different. It has been outlined that since 1990, Sinn Fein attended meetings and talks, and had been trying to negotiate a settlement to end the armed campaign. They had, it was believed, had enough of war. These talks, which I have been involved in, were called parallel or dual diplomacy.'

No one interrupted, but there was noticeable shuffling of feet.

'They were good, because the door was always open to find a settlement. At the same time, the Government was able, quite categorically, to deny in Parliament, as they did, that no member of its Government would ever speak with terrorists, not while they were still shooting and bombing.

Apparently, this parallel diplomacy has been going on since 1974, when Willie Whitelaw, had his first talks with Gerry Adams and his associates. It has been going on ever since. Anyway to bring you back to reality. What the Government wanted was a military solution, an end to the fighting, and then they would be in a far better position to negotiate an acceptable deal for all.

In simplified words, they wanted the remainder of the Provo's taken out. Destroyed to the last man! This to me was absolutely overwhelming news, and it was music to my ears.

The room fell absolutely silent; not a cough.

'After one of my meetings with the PM, he asked me to stay behind and to be forthright with him. I did, and then he handed me a note, which he'd thought coincidental. It had been passed from the US Defence Secretary and was a summary of David Carver's first presentation to US Special Forces. The main point that the Secretary had mentioned, was the glowing admiration that these special and brilliant soldiers held for David Carver...

In the note, which was actually addressed to the current British Secretary of State for Defence, it simply said, this man virtually eliminated half the North Vietnamese forces and Viet Cong on his own, so why do you not use him to solve your own Northern Ireland problem?'

Sir Peter laughed. 'Bit "over the top",' he said, grinning to David, but when I handed the note back to the PM, he then said to me, 'this is the same man that you have recommended, right? Do tell me about him.'

Three hours later, the PM said, 'Could he do it?'

The answer was in my grin. I left Downing Street, and immediately got in touch with David.

Then discussions subsequently took place with a selected Parliamentary Private Secretary, who shall remain nameless, and myself. 'Everything I suggested to the PPS to enforce a military solution was, unfortunately, ignored. I was directed by him to implement the proposals and select a team to destroy the Provisional Irish Republican Army, without "a shoot to kill policy in force". In other words, we had the go ahead to destroy the PIRA, without shooting them! I discussed the whole scheme with Ian who found the idea absolutely absurd and appalling.

I went back to the PM but it was in vain; he insisted that we follow the government guidelines as clearly laid down by his PPS.

I then decided I would try to be deceptive, like a friend of mine would be!' he said looking at David Carver.

'I arranged the meeting that the PPS chaired with Ian, David, and myself and nothing having changed, the PPS still assuming his plan was going ahead. I settled back and knew what David's reaction would be. I also knew how keen the PM and others were, to implement a working plan.'

To the joy of all present, David grinned, and then said, 'Sir Peter, you're a devious bastard!'

Peter Wilcox, rallied, 'I know you won't mind me asking this David, but knowing how desperate you were to solve your own problem, did you not take a risk, by initially turning this opportunity down?'

'No not really, I have always said that the time and method

must be right, the timing was perfect, and I knew that the method would also be put right.'

Peter Wilcox chuckled, then paused, a frown showing clearly above his bushy silver eyebrows.

'Why, why was that, David?'

'In the briefing last week, you said it yourself, remember?'

'No... what?'

'I still think I can quote you. "The GOC, Northern Ireland, and myself have selected you to lead this operation. No other officer has your calibre or motivation, and therefore, no other officer has been considered. Your selection, if you accept of course, has already gained the approval of the Prime Minister and is fully endorsed by Ian".'

'You are the devious bastard, Carver,' said Peter, grinning broadly, 'there you have it gentlemen, the background as to why we are here.

As far as I am concerned, the whole of the MI5 department is at your disposal, that includes equipment and anything that is currently in research and development, and ready for trials will be made available. This operation has the highest priority. I will take you around our research and development and our normal issues departments, and you will have freedom to select any equipment whatsoever. Anything that you may feel will help your operation it is yours...

That will happen on Tuesday evening and David will brief you on that. I have a team set up in Northern Ireland who are now working with Ian's team. The collective strengths and efforts, of like-minded individuals can be of tremendous benefit to you extraordinary guys, on the ground...

Finally, I report direct to the Prime Minister, therefore you can understand the credence that has been placed on this operation. I am keeping this short as I am sure Ian will, and David will give the operational brief in detail, which I know will be of more interest.'

David nodded: he would, when given the floor.

'Before I introduce Ian,' said Peter, finalising his brief. 'I would like to give you a brief outline of his background. Ian has worked non-stop since 1969 in the fight against terrorism. He is the most decorated RUC officer in the force. Most of his time has been spent with Special Branch, and, for the past two years he has controlled the TCG(S) which is the Tasking and Coordination Group South based in South Armagh.

Very basically, it means that he is in sole command of the most dangerous area of Northern Ireland, running all covert operations. Ian and I have worked together for so long, we know each other extremely well, and for that reason, he is probably the only Police Officer in Northern Ireland that I would want working on this operation. I cannot recommend him highly enough to you, therefore, without further ado, Ian, the floor is yours.'

Chief Superintendent Ian Walsh stood up and thanked Peter Wilcox for his kind words...'Gentlemen, I cannot express the words of gratitude and satisfaction, that I am to be involved in this operation. I am grateful to my friend, Peter Wilcox, for selecting me, personally. And the satisfaction of working with the most professional of men leaves me in no doubt as to the outcome of this operation. To be part of something that has never been achieved in Northern Ireland, peace in modern times, and without prejudging, I feel in the coming months, that history will be made.'

He glanced at David.

'For the first time in twenty-four years I feel, that at last, we can take the initiative, drive forward and eliminate the cancer of terrorism, that has infested this beautiful land of ours for far too long. For the first time ever, the professionals on the ground are authorised to take the initiative. Make the positive decisions that are necessary, instead of having to abide by a rulebook, that is virtually useless and unchanged since the beginning of the campaign. I have been seconded to this operation, and I want you all to know that I am as dedicated to its success, as are each and everyone of you. The name of this operation has been circulated to every RUC department, and I hasten to add, not the purpose. It is the Chief Constable's directive that at the very mention of the codeword, it assumes immediate priority over any other operation, duty, or task.

He took breath, continued.

'I will have a small, but extremely effective team, working with me 24 hours a day, and this will ensure that at all times, your demands or requests will be met. The men working with me have been personally selected by me. They are immensely experienced within investigative, behind the scene type of work, which may become significant to the ultimate success of the operation. For this operation they have been granted clearance to obtain information from the highest level, which is level seven on the mainframe computer. Never before has this been authorised...

Furthermore, in this direction, through the communications with the Heads of Governments, we are also linked into the CIA network. The information that has been made available to my team is indicative of the extreme importance directed at our operation...'

David couldn't wait to get everything underway, and listened hard to the expertise that was being delivered by this exceptional officer. And the RUC officer continued with such strength of character, that it totally belied his bland and ordinary appearance. But David was nobody's fool. He knew he was reliant upon the pragmatism and dedication, of men like Ian Walsh, to do the delving and seeking, finding and rooting out this scourge; so that he and his men could take the necessary action, and destroy...

'...From today our team in Northern Ireland will collate every piece of information that has been gathered by all agencies, in the previous 24 hours. Along with what we glean from our own resources, it will be condensed into a daily sitrep, four copies of which you will receive at 8am daily. Included in this will be the movement of all known terrorists, and information from Provisional Irish Republican Army informants.

I have prepared a list of terrorists, who are actively involved with either bullets or bombs, but no concrete evidence being available to "nail" them... I have also prepared a list of touts, and their current role, if any, in the Organisation.

And to show the massive weight accorded this operation we have also managed to obtain the names of the source handlers, those who are managing these touts, irrespective of being RUC or Army, and their availability has been made to us. This gentlemen, as I am sure you are aware is without precedence. Every agency in the past has always protected their tout. And in doing this, at most times, it has subsequently eroded the value of the information, and by the time the information is disseminated, it is of little worth or consequence.'

Again feet shuffled, everyone eager to stop the chat and get moving.

'I am delighted to say that with the joint communiqué, from the Chief Constable and the General Officer Commanding, Northern Ireland Security Forces we have achieved immediate and full dissemination of information. We are also in a position for Don, either to accompany a source handler on his operation, or even take over his tout. Where it comes to the gathering of new information, Jack has total autonomy.

There are many other important events that have taken place, which, when pieced together, are relevant to the operation. However, there is already a mountain of information to be divulged, so we will introduce this throughout the week...

I now would like to give you a personal overview, my opinion on what I see as the overall position over the past eighteen months, and how that will affect the future.'

There was a prevailing air of unrest among the fighting men who hated briefs at the best of times, worse when at levels to match a schoolroom lecture.

'I do feel that the time is ripe for a peaceful settlement. It is true that the Provisional Irish Republican Army is a depleted and demoralised force. That being said we can never be complacent, because even a handful of fanatics, especially as well armed as the Provo's, can still cause utter devastation to life, limb and property. There is escalation of the severity of their bombing...

David has already brought this up in a different context at a previous meeting that I have to say, I thoroughly enjoyed. Depleted the enemy may be, but last year they detonated two of their biggest bombs, one, in April, at the Baltic Exchange in the heart of the City. The other, a little later, at the southern end of the motorway leading into London, destroying a major flyover controlling a network of routes...

British Insurers had to pay for this damage, and the cost for repair was enormous, to say the very least. It was far in excess of the whole of the damage in the previous 24 years of terrorism in Northern Ireland...

That gentlemen, is an outrage. Two bombs, causing that amount of damage. It is colossal, and it tells us something. They have new policies and possibly new people in place, to raise their profile. Who and why?'

The faces before him brightened, ears alert.

'Well, I believe I know why, but not who. Three months after these two bombs, a huge haul of explosives was intercepted, and our information was, that it was destined for another attack on the infrastructure, but this time there would have been severe or even massive loss of life.

Again, enhancing my belief that something has drastically

changed. There were other smaller isolated bombings, which indicated to me that these were probably detonated by the long-term bombers in London. Then, finally in 1992, there was the attempt to destroy Canary Wharf.

There was a huge amount of semtex, but it was only the detonator that went off on this occasion. As bad as it was, only one man was killed and the damage was restricted...

The picture is building; present intelligence from other sources suggests that there are massive threats to both life and property throughout 1993...I agree with these sources, the bombing pattern has changed and I also believe, so will the locations and type of targets.'

Ian paused a moment, knew that he had to round off his brief or lose vibrant interest in what he was saying.

'That is my assessment, based on trend. The picture was building, but so was the atmosphere and the tension was creeping in. I interpret these changes as an attempt by the Provisional Irish Republican Army to bomb their way to the negotiating table. They are talking, as Sir Peter has pointed out, and have been for a number of years about a cease-fire.

However, they will only accept that, on their terms, and the increased bombing campaign is their way of achieving their aims. I believe the increased profile on the mainland has been instigated by the South Armagh Provo's. They are the real hard-core element. Both Belfast and Derry are reduced to bit part players, youngsters learning the trade...

What we are finding now is that there is more activity from the Loyalist hard-core paramilitaries. Although, in the main, there has either been sectarian violence and killings, or straight forward none terrorist activities. The maze is starting to fill with "ordinary decent criminals", and especially, young ones.'

Ian Walsh continued with his very constructive brief...

'...And finally gentlemen...as we work together through the coming weeks, we will be able to fit the jigsaw together and coupled with the daily sitreps, a plan of action will emerge. Enough from me now, I suggest a break, and then to David.'

Tea was served and cleared away, everyone wanting to hear David Carver.

He stood up, an air of expectancy descended in a silent hush. The boss was ready, and so were they. David immediately gave his sincere thanks, then said, 'you all know the reason why we are here. Let there be no doubt that first and foremost, I am out to avenge the horrific death of my son, Jeremy. I made that perfectly clear at earlier briefings, and that was accepted. I am aware I would not be able to do this without the tremendous support that all of you have offered. You have put yourselves out, made yourselves available, and for that, I am eternally grateful...

The operation has started from today, and there has been a great deal of pre-planning, as we have all heard... The operation has been given the codename...Operation Combating Evil...

The impact of "Combating Evil" had noticeably registered among his volunteers.

'The object of the operation is to eliminate all PIRA active service units, both in Northern Ireland, and in the UK. In doing so, we should be able to identify the active service unit that I am looking for, and effect its destruction.

The operation does not end until we have achieved all objectives. We have heard the unprecedented support that the operation has been given. But let me make it absolutely clear, it is not going to be easy. Even with this level of support, we must ensure that identification is positive...We will still have to dig, and root out these bastards.

Any elimination must not point at a team such as ours. I firmly believe with careful planning and preparation, we can achieve this goal...It is also vital that we move fast. Ian has outlined that PIRA bombers are on the move. We have to get after them. Lives are imminently at risk. The threat of PIRA is real, with the spate of bombings, they are on a forward momentum, and the only way to stop them is to crush them in their tracks.'

He had absolute attention from all concerned.

'I will deal with how we are going to do this on a final briefing on Saturday, that will take place here at 8am.' David then addressed himself to Peter Wilcox and Ian Walsh, 'I would like both your teams present for the initial brief and introductions to ourselves. Although at most times we will deal direct with you, I think it is important that we know the backroom staff, and indeed, they meet us. Tom can go out and bring them across on Friday evening...

Tom, Peter, Ian, and myself will visit Northern Ireland tomorrow. We will recce two sites that Ian has recommended for our base. Whichever we choose, we must be ready to move with all our personal equipment by 1600 hours on Sunday...

There will be two Lynx and Tom's Gazelle. Only one Lynx will return, leaving a Lynx and a Gazelle for the operation, or for Tom to play with!'

Chuckles ensued.

'We, initially, will be protected and looked after by a Company from the Reserve Battalion. They will provide guards on the site as well as a ring of covert ops in strategic positions about a mile out. They will cook for us and do all our logistics...Our programme for this week is to absorb as much of the background information that we can, and that starts immediately after this brief.'

He looked to Len.

Len, I want you to switch back to being the expert that you are with explosives, especially the IED's, and anything new in the booby trap line that you may find at MI5. Be well familiarised because I have a strong feeling that we will need everything that we can get our hands on...

It also may mean that you will have to have a day at the Regiment for some "live" training, and if you feel that is necessary, then it can be done early next week. I would also like you to sort out the weapons and ammunition requirements. I have prepared a list, but would like it checked and added to it where necessary...

The Quartermaster at Hereford will be collecting what he can and sending it across to our selected site on Sunday morning.'

David had his men hanging on his every word.

'There are eight volunteers from the Regiment who will maintain our equipment and man the operations room throughout this operation. They will be based and housed with us, but will have no operational role on the ground whatsoever. They are the only ones that we speak to on site...They will do all liaisons with the Guard Company.'

He turned to Tug and Jock.

'I want you both to work together on lock picking and other break-in techniques, including anything new from MI5. Once you have brushed up on your techniques, I want you to practice this within these barracks. The Commanding Officer has given permission for you to test the camp security, so have some constructive fun!'

Jack was next.

Don, you will be having first contact with the enemy, as always.

'Once Tug and Jock have sorted their first task out, I would like you to take these pair of thugs under your wing. I think that you will need all the help that we can give you, to get started. Although I don't mean to teach you to suck eggs, if I can broadly outline to you what is basically required, then you can build up on that.'

It was time to generalise a prospective turn of events.

'Familiarise yourself with the names of all touts, their handlers, and look at the quality of information passed. Go back as far as you feel necessary, time permitting. Concentrate on the touts, find out who their friends and relations are. What contact do they have with the terrorists? See where there may be links with Ian's list of active members...

I would like to see a list of the wasters, the money takers that may not have been handled right or have been raking us off. We'll soon put them to good use,' he said with a grin. 'All in all, the touts and their information, is where our starting point is. Delve into them, "live" with them and sort out who we will lift first.

This role is vital to get us off to a good start. Be in constant touch with any handlers that you use, especially following up on the mass of information that will come in. Talk with Ian, there may even be merit in Tom taking you across the water after our visit to MI5, I will leave you to get on with that.

We will have seven cars at our disposal, all of which are armoured and all high powered. BMWs, Mercedes' and Audi', and also a van, to be changed every two days. On occasions, we will be getting the same car, but only when resprayed and different number plates fitted.'

The briefing continued for some time, David finally rounding off with:

'A progress meeting will take place every evening and where possible it will be held at 2200 hours, commencing this evening...

Gentlemen, are there any questions?'

'Yes,' replied Don, 'with respect David, I believe my starting point is the RUC source handlers who were watching their man Mulvenny, prior to him being lifted. I've read their reports and I don't like them. They leave far too much to be desired.'

'I am sure that can be arranged, and yes again, I do agree with you, Don. I felt much the same after reading those reports over a year ago, now. Ian, please arrange this for Jack and I feel that your presence would be greatly appreciated...

Any further points?

No... Good, then let's get cracking...'

** * **

Chapter Nineteen

Sean read on the flight about the former soldiers of the Cambodian Government, who had fled their country in 1975.

At about the same time as North Vietnam seized Saigon, Pol Pot's Regime moved in to Phnom Penh, the capital of Cambodia. Anyone who protested was killed. The regime was despotic. The people were oppressed, mass murder took place, and soldiers of the previous government either fled the country or were executed.

A band of soldiers fled together, heading out into the country, finally reaching the northern province of Phurni Skov. They were a spent force, now totalling about fifty, mentally and physically destroyed, stealing to survive.

Hearing that they were being pursued, they eventually headed further north crossing over the huge mountain belt, the Phnum Dangrek Range, into Thailand.

Settling over the border in the tiny hamlet of Ban Don Ao, there they remained until being moved on by the Thai Authorities.

Some had wanted to return to their homeland, but it was now 1978 and the North Vietnamese had just invaded Cambodia over throwing the regime of Pol Pot.

Being unsure of what they would be returning to, they headed west then south and finally reaching Chanthaburi on the south coast. What they were earning over the years was paid out in bribes to officials.

Still trying to find a place to settle and with there numbers growing, gathering new wives on the move, and the addition of children, they could move no further west or south and settled in the locality of Ban Chak Nok, near the town of Sattahip.

Seamus had heard of their plight many years ago and when they reached Sattahip, he decided to help them.

He visited them; bought them Thai citizenship, and they were eternally grateful. Seamus saw it as an investment for the future, for so little cost.

It was now pay back time…

* * *

When Sean booked into the Royal Orchid, he asked if they cooked a good Irish stew. The receptionists looked at one another. They had never been asked for this before, so one of them rang the kitchen.

'Yes they did,' she had said, and Sean smiled. But that was soon gone when she followed it up with, 'we had an Irish couple that were chefs, but they left nine months ago…Fortunately, they left the recipe.'

Bloody hell, he said to himself, all this fucking way and they've moved. They are probably working in Bournemouth. After dressing, he went down for his lunch. He was quite surprised when he discovered that the commissary was English.

He said to him, 'my cousins are Patrick and Yvonne Murphy. They worked as chefs here until nine months ago, and I am trying to find them. Yvonne's mother has died, I would be very grateful if you could or are able to help me.'

'I am sorry sir,' he said, 'we have had no one with that name here.'

Sean looked at him in amazement. 'Are you absolutely sure, Yvonne's father gave me your fine hotel as their place of work. He will be absolutely devastated if they cannot attend after I have travelled all this way. Can I show you their photographs, please?' he asked.

'Yes indeed,' and the commissary looked, and then smiled. 'That's not Patrick and Yvonne…That's John and JoJo.'

'I don't suppose that you know where they went to?'

'Yes of course, they moved to the Royal Cliff Beach Resort, which is a five star hotel, about five miles south of Pattaya.'

'Sir, you have been most helpful, thank you so very much.' Sean was in raptures, as he walked with a swagger on his way to lunch.

* * *

Once he had located Pattaya he booked a car and headed off on the seventy-mile journey down the coast road. He had decided to leave his current booking in the Royal Orchid and would come back here prior to leaving Thailand.

For now though, he would book in for a week at the Royal Cliff Beach Resort. He had to give his own passport, as his forged one was still with reception at Bangkok. He also decided not to ask any questions here. He didn't need to. He visited Pattaya that night thoroughly enjoying a sauna, massage, and the 'trimmings'.

The next morning at breakfast there was no sign of his prey. In fact, he waited for five days and then he saw Yvonne Murphy. The adrenaline flowed. He could have quite cheerfully walked right up to her and killed her. No, he could not do that. That would be too easy a way out. This bitch, and her man were going to suffer.

He had time enough for revenge, and later at the evening meal she was cooking steaks on a hot plate. Sean sat eyeing her, picturing her without her clothes. Yes, he thought, I'm going to enjoy myself. He decided to have a steak, and she was full of laughter:

'Hullo,' she said, 'just in, are we?'

'No,' Sean replied, 'I've been here for five days, only two to go.'

'That's a nice Derry accent, is it not?'

'It might have been years ago. I've been living in Southampton for the past twenty years. Got a haulage business there and I'm having a well-earned week off.'

'How would you like it?' she asked.

'What?'

'The steak,' she said, a grin.

'Rare, please, I like seeing the blood running across the blade.'

'You're a rare one by the sound of it.'

'So,' Sean inquired, 'are you out here on your own then?'

'No.' She raised her eyebrows at him, nodded into the distance behind her. 'My husband is with me, he works here as well.'

'What's your name, gorgeous, or am I not allowed to know that.'

'It's JoJo, and what might you be called.'

He hadn't planned for this. He was booked in as Sean Heggaty, his own name, yet he couldn't lie here so he simply said. 'Most people have called me "Paddy" all my life, so I won't be arguing with that.'

'Your steak is ready, and it's been nice talking to you.'

He noticed her eyes panning over him; ripe for the taking...

She was at breakfast the next day, cooking the eggs. No sign of Patrick though. Damn, he had to be somewhere. Sean waited until she was free and went up to her.

'Hullo JoJo, remember me?' He grinned; course she did. 'I

waited for your knock on my room door, but none came?'

'You cheeky bugger.' She laughed, a sly glance directed at him. 'I knew you were a rare one when I first saw you.'

'Where's your other half? I thought you said he worked here?'

'He does, but we're on different shifts at the moment. Tonight he starts at six and finishes at eight in the morning after early breakfasts. We've been out here in Thailand for ten years and worked here for eight.

Sean felt like saying, you lying bitch you've been here five years and in this hotel nine months. His eggs were cooked and he went to walk away when she said, 'you didn't say what your room number was?'

'It's 249, but would it not be better where you live?' he asked, 'or do you live in the hotel?'

Someone had walked up to be served, so he didn't get an answer. But right through breakfast he could see that she couldn't take her eyes off him.

His rugged features, thinning hair, the paunch that was beginning to show, made it difficult for her to access his age. Perhaps forty, maybe forty five, and she was only thirty three.

Yes, it would make a nice change to be wanted as a woman, not just as marital baggage. Might this Sean Heggaty be her route out of a living nightmare? He seemed to be well off, a businessman indeed, and nice enough.

Her man was always too tired, or couldn't be bothered with the sensual intimate side of life. She had begun to hate him. He had caused her and her family so much trouble, and she had never wanted to be involved in underhanded goings on in the first place.

* * *

After breakfast Sean lay on his bed and knew that he could not and would not give his body to a fucking tout. He telephoned the kitchen and asked to speak with her. He lied saying, 'I have to go back to the UK tonight instead of tomorrow, which means I have to pack and get up to Bangkok now.'

He then said, 'JoJo, I can't tell you how much I wanted you, maybe we can meet some other time?'

She readily agreed. 'Paddy, you don't know what you're missing. But if you can't stay, will you telephone me?'

Thank you very much he thought, and grinned to himself, 'of course I will, give me your number...'

After making a further telephone call to the small Kampong of Ban Khlot, he left within the hour and instead of driving north, he headed south. He arrived in the town of Sattahip and stood by the car waiting in the bus station car park.

He saw the three men and a woman get out of a Bedford van that had to be at least twenty years old. They in turn spotted him and briskly bridged the gap.

'Mr Sean,' was all one said.

'Yes,' he smiled.

They knew what he wanted; they knew what was expected of them. They would not let anyone down, and Sean said that he would be in touch. He gave them twenty thousand bahts, a fortune to them, then said, 'when the operation is over to our satisfaction, there will be another twenty thousand...'

He arrived at the Royal Orchid, at 8pm. He telephoned JoJo from the outside line at the hotel, 'I don't know where you live?'

'Paddy I am so pleased you rang, I have been thinking of you all day.'

'Quickly, JoJo, my flight has just been called forward. I will try and get out in a months time, do you still want me?'

'Yes, yes I do. Write this down. 18C, Ban Thung Klom Road, Ban Chak Nok, Pattaya. Please hurry back.'

'I will do. Bye gorgeous,' was all he said, and replaced the handset. He then went and enjoyed a huge cocktail in the very elegant lounge of the Royal Orchid.

Well tonight Sean, my boy, you are going to have some fun. A couple of nice teenagers will do lovely, or maybe three!

He showered, dressed casual but immaculate, and then he rang a number in Ban Khlot near Sattahip. He passed on the address and telephone number; delighted with himself. Bangkok was renowned as the official sex capital of the world, and Sean intended checking it out. He wasn't going back yet. Still far too much to do, he chuckled to himself.

Four days later, still at the Royal Orchid, he telephoned from the outside line and contacted Kerry. 'Yes it's going great. I paid our friends but I'm not finished out here, can you send me another two grand?'

'Yes, it will be at your reception first thing in the morning. Have you followed my instructions, to the letter Sean?'

'Of course I have, Kerry.'

And he thought, yes I have...I think...

* * *

Chapter Twenty

Len Peters was in his element. He was in the experimental explosive and technical department of MI5. He had been deluged with new facts, new techniques, new devices, and he was at liberty to take anything he so wished.

He loved the new stun grenade, a little card measuring four inches long and two inches wide. Tear a strip off the end; slide it under a door, and bang, all occupants' totally stunned and disorientated for twenty minutes.

Gone were the days of having to break in and throw in a stun grenade. The risk then was always too great. As soon as a door was touched, the risk of the door being blasted by heavy machine gun fire from within was immense, and many men had died as a consequence.

* * *

Jack Simpson spent the afternoon reading every scrap of material that had been brought across by Chief Superintendent Ian Walsh. He needed to be in Northern Ireland. He had to get out there as soon as possible and his first port of call would be the source handlers who had been observing the tout Mulvenny.

Ian Walsh had arranged for them to be at the police station at Enniskillen at 2000 hours on Wednesday. He felt frustrated with the wait, however one handler had already left the RUC and two had been demoted, the fourth member was now a Chief Inspector, but employed in traffic as opposed to Special Branch. Jack had been warned that they were not very co-operative, so he shouldn't expect too gain much from them.

We'll see he thought.

Jack had done his homework on these guys, and had already had reams of paperwork faxed to him. Tug and Jock had worked through the night with him. They had gone over the reports compiled by the men, time after time, and still could not comprehend the inaccuracies and their lack of preparation for such an operation. These were very experienced police officers.

He decided that he would leave earlier on the Wednesday and would arrive at 1200 hours. He spent three hours reading up on everything related to the death of Jeremy and he shuddered at the shocking depravity that the youngster had suffered...

How on earth had his good friend, David, the mental energy to retain his own sanity, after seeing what his own beloved son had gone through? Drifting back to reality, he was in his element to help his friend, because right now, this was the best place to be.

He was in the collators' office in Enniskillen police station. The murder of Jeremy had taken place on their patch, and most of the investigations had taken place from there. Three collators helped him with the crosschecking, and the digging out of further information.

By the time of the planned meeting with the RUC source handlers, who had been on that case, Jack Simpson had read everything available, including their own police records. Ian Walsh who had come across with him had had other business to attend to and arrived just before the RUC officers.

Chief Superintendent Ian Walsh introduced himself and Jack to the three who turned up. The officer that had retired, who had in fact been in charge, decided for whatever reason, not to attend.

It was blatantly obvious that the others had attended against their will. Their faces spoke volumes. The interview room was sparse, the only furniture in there was a small table, four chairs, with the three men sitting opposite, and facing Jack Simpson.

'Gentlemen,' Jack Simpson said, 'I am here working on Operation Combating Evil, and in connection with that operation I have reason to question you all on a specific operation that took place here in February 1991, which I believe you were all a part of. Do you all understand what I am referring to?'

They all nodded. The eldest of the three then suddenly spoke out, 'and who the fuck might you be?'

Chief Superintendent Ian Walsh spoke from the back of the room, where he was standing, only a few feet behind Don, 'it is of no consequence who this man is. You all know who I am, and as police officers you will answer any questions to the best of your abilities, and with politeness.'

Jack Simpson nodded in thanks, and continued:
'How long had you worked together as source handlers.'
One said, four years, another three, and the third just

shrugged, and said. 'Fuck knows.'

Jack Simpson stared at the men in turn, and then his manner and voice changed. 'Right you fucking gobshites, I don't like your pissin' attitudes for a start. Sit up properly and start listening. And you will give me the answers that I want, and in the correct manner. A manner befitting the status of the work that you were obviously unfit or fuckin' well unable to do...

Before I ask anything further of you let me spell out a few home truths. You three, and Craig Bell, worked together for seven and a half years. In those years, you paid out, supposedly to touts, the sum of £125,785.'

They looked at him with stunned amazement.

'I have looked at the information you received from Mulvenny and over a period of eighteen months, it is crap, nothing less than utter fucking garbage. When I went back five years on your so called contribution, which is all I have had time for at the moment, the picture gets fucking worse,' he said raising his voice.

'Indeed, I have not found an arrest from the so-called information that you have gathered, from any tout. This is so bad that I wonder if any of you have ever met a fuckin' tout...

You three had been employed, handling touts for a long time, and during that time you must have looked at the regular photofits, or rather mugshots that are distributed, hundreds of times, or, are you going to tell me that this is something that you never did?

You, he pointed to a selected officer. 'Trevor Hann, right?' He didn't await reply.

'In your report you said that you did not recognise anyone involved in the operation, from the mugshots provided.'

'That's right,' snapped Trevor.

'Then tell me why Craig Bell said in his report, that he recognised Pat Maguire. He's a known PIRA bomber and gunman, yet is not in any of your reports, and you've supposedly worked together all these years?'

'I cannot answer for Craig Bell or for who he saw.'

'Is that the answer for you all?' charged Jack Simpson, to the other two. There was no reply, but Jack noticed by their body language, they were visibly shaken. Especially the smallest one...he was trembling.

'Is the man in this picture, Pat Maguire?' He held aloft a photo in front of all three, awaiting answer.

All three remained silent.

'You're Glen Wright, aren't you?' Jack said to the smallest one. 'Yes...yes...yes I...I am,' he stuttered.

'You attended three interviews with Pat Maguire when he was questioned by your Special Branch colleagues, after the operation.' Jack Simpson paused...' Yet now, you are denying by your silence, that you knew or recognise him.'

'It was two years ago and we see a lot of mugshots.'

'Bollocks,' yelled an angry Jack Simpson. 'Don't even think about lying to me.' Jack went right up to Glen's face, glaring into his frightened eyes, not even inches separating them, when he snarled, 'I handled over fifty touts and that was ten years ago, and I would recognise every last one of them today...

Ten years ago I could recognise every PIRA member from mugshots and there were hundreds more then than there were in 1991...

Now, fucking well answer me, and this time, with the truth, because you're not clever enough to deceive me, and that goes for the lot of you.'

He lowered his voice and quietly, but firmly whispered, 'now tell me, Mr Wright. Did you see Pat Maguire during that operation?' Glen Wright was sweating, profusely. 'Yes, yes I did,' he retorted. 'Let me now try again with you all. Was Pat Maguire an active member of that operation, the operation you all admit to having observed?'

They all replied, 'yes.'

'Then why, for god's sake did you not support Craig Bell's report?'

Silence.

Chief Superintendent Ian Walsh moved forward to stand alongside Don, where he could look at all three, face to face.

Jack Simpson said again. 'Why no support? Had he been supported, and there was enough corroboration from you lot on identity, the interrogation of Pat Maguire could have led to the capture of the other members of the active service units, at the very least... Certainly, Pat Maguire would have been locked up for a very long time. He should not have been able to make a fool of the RUC Special Branch investigators as he did. Why, tell me why?'

They still remained silent.

Ian Walsh tried to speak, but Jack stopped him.

'Right you lot... I have the picture and I know what's been

going on and unfortunately it's not something new around here. You have all had an easy life in this land. In Northern Ireland, people trust the likes of you to be honest, to be fair and free of corruption.'

Jack Simpson was stopped in his tracks...

'Now you fucking listen to me Simpson, don't accuse me of corruption. I'm a Chief Inspector, and have served for twenty years,' charged Heslington...

Jack Simpson interrupted, 'not for much longer, Chief Inspector Heslington. I have enough evidence of your malpractice, deceit and fraud, to have you and your fucking cronies kicked out, and with a considerable sentence behind you.'

Jack spelled it out slowly to them.

'You have been on the fiddle for years. Probably since you became handlers, if the truth was known, and it will come out. Tell me, how far up the ladder does this corruption go?'

Chief Inspector Heslington spoke, 'this is just assumption. Cheap speculation against us...You are wrong.'

'We'll see, when I interview Craig Bell next and hear why he was the only one to identify a known terrorist. I will get a little closer to the truth, and the net will tighten on you three...

In the space of half an hour you all admitted that you saw Pat Maguire during the operation, yet it has never been disclosed before by any of you. In fact, what amazes me is that you do not seem to have been quizzed on this point before. This goes deeper than I had imagined.'

He turned to Hann. 'Have you ever spoken with the known terrorist Pat Maguire, at any time in your service?'

There was a long pause, 'I don't believe I need to speak to you and I'm leaving.'

Hann stood up to go, and then Chief Inspector Heslington did the same, followed by Wright.

Jack Simpson also stood up, and said, 'I have been ferreting around all of your records, going back some years. Not just your abysmal work records, but more importantly, your bank and building society accounts, all your investment portfolios, and indeed, all your very healthy assets that you have accumulated over a relatively short time.'

'You cannot do this, and a court of law will jail you, you bloody bastard, 'he screamed. 'I am not tolerating this behaviour. I am a serving police officer and I know the law, and you,' Heslington pointed menacingly at Don, 'are in serious trouble, and I am just the man to sort you out.'

Jack was slightly taken aback, he realised he was out of practice, but he had been bluffing to a certain degree, especially about their accounts and assets. But he must retain control and he did that by thinking on his feet, gathering his thoughts, as he stood, slowly making eye-to-eye contact with each in turn, thinking, then grinning at them, and he went for the weakest.

'There is the door Mr Wright, be my guest, I not only can prove that you are a corrupt officer, but your wife, son and two daughters are also guilty of receiving and aiding and abetting...'

Glen Wright interrupted, 'that's lies my wife and kids knew nothing of what was going on...'

'Really Mr Wright, so please, do tell us all, what was going on...'

'There was fuck all going on, you are just putting words into his mouth,' screamed Heslington. 'And that is final we are all leaving.'

Jack stood his ground, glared at all of them, then quite quietly said, 'at the moment this is an unofficial investigation, which you have been formally requested to attend. This is in compliance with an ongoing operation called Operation Combating Evil, which, as you are all aware, is categorised under the Official Secrets Act.'

Then raising his voice, threateningly, and with sheer audacity, said, 'the moment that you walk out of that door you will be arrested on charges of collusion with the Provisional Irish Republican Army.'

The threat from Jack Simpson shocked them; they were stunned, staring, transfixed at Jack Simpson, this was obviously not going according to their plan...

Jack decided to continue the verbal attack.

He turned to Ian Walsh, and said, 'Chief Superintendent, I would like all three in separate rooms...'

Jack noticed the horror on Glen Wright's face.

'Have you a problem with this, Mr Wright?' Jack queried.

Glen Wright placed his hands over his face, shaking. 'I think I need a solicitor.'

Chief Inspector Heslington shouted at him, 'don't be fucking stupid. The moment he is called, you will be charged.'

Chief Superintendent Ian Walsh nodded in agreement, and said, 'you seem to have got the message.'

Jack immediately knew at that point he had broken them and he would win.

Jack Simpson, said, 'we will have a short break for coffee. Then gentlemen, I will give you the opportunity to tell me the truth, and be warned. I will not tolerate any more stubbornness or difficulties, I demand full and total co-operation or you will be left to hang, I am not wasting any more time.

Is this clearly understood by all?'

They all nodded.

After coffee Jack Simpson got the proceedings underway again, keeping the men in the one interview room; his first question directed at Chief Inspector Heslington.

'Why did you not support Craig Bell on the identification of Pat Maguire?'

Heslington shuffled his feet and looked at the other two, then said, 'will you guarantee us immunity from charges if we talk?'

Jack Simpson looked at him, then at the other two and said, 'I promise you I will bring no charges to bear whatsoever, as long as I have the truth. My sole purpose is to find the terrorists that attacked the two soldiers during that operation.'

Chief Inspector Heslington then spoke with enthusiasm. 'You are right. We have been raking off the tout fund for five or six years. Craig Bell had agreed with all this. We very often made up our reports and dreamed up our long lists of touts. The only ones we spoke to were people who telephoned the confidential hotline but their information was always negative, as they were in general seeking cash payments for nothing in return...

Mulvenny was one of the few that we actually spoke to and it was just unfortunate for the two security forces people to have been there at the same time. We did feel sorry for them, but felt that we could exploit the situation to our benefit. After all, there was nothing that we could do to save them...'

Heslington suddenly had verbal diarrhea; he 'rattled' on seemingly quite pleased with his exploits.

The more he talked, the angrier Chief Superintendent Ian Walsh was getting; seething, listening with sheer disgust and contempt at the evil that was unfurling, and with such blatant nonchalance, in front of him. He viewed these people worse than the terrorists that he had spent his life hunting. He had full admiration for Jack Simpson in the way he was handling these people. No investigating police officer could get away with his methods.

Jack had let Heslington blurt on, incriminating himself and the others. Then at last, he broke the silence, 'going back to Maguire, how did you manage to exploit this situation? No, not you Mr Heslington. Perhaps you can enlighten me, Mr Hann.'

Trevor Hann sat back with a smile, then said, 'Glen Wright and myself approached Pat Maguire. We'd arrested him on charges of murder at his home...

So we sat down with him and dropped hints that we could be bought.'

Ian Walsh cringed at this statement.

Hann then said, 'he offered us £50,000 not to testify or make a statement against him. We realised that he had obviously siphoned a huge amount of funds from the Provo's. So I managed to get that upped to £100,000...

We felt we were ripping the PIRA off, not the Government.'

Jack then said. 'Surely, you must have felt that you did this at the expense of the two security force' members who had been taken by Pat Maguire and his cronies.'

'No, they were dead, and besides, Pat Maguire had nothing to do with the capture of the two security forces members. His team took Mulvenny, who was anyway, just another low life scum.'

'Who took the others, what were their names?'

'We couldn't see them from where we were. Their van had obliterated our view and all we saw in the van was a female in the passenger seat. We had never seen her before, and could not identify her from any of the mugshots.'

'So where does Craig Bell fit in with this?' he asked Glen Wright, who nervously stuttered a reply, 'Craig Bell would have nothing to do with this and said he would retire if we did a deal with Pat Maguire...

Chief Inspector Heslington insisted that to take money from a terrorist was in any case no different to the Government giving money to touts, who after all, are nothing other than terrorists themselves. We all agreed with this, except Craig Bell, who did what he said he would do, and retired.'

'So why did you not try to find out who the other PIRA members were, that is the ones with Pat Maguire and the other team? You could have blackmailed that out of Pat Maguire.'

'We just wanted our pay off, nothing more...

If we had demanded information from Pat Maguire that

would have made him into a tout and probably would have reduced the payments to ourselves.'

'So, what you are saying is, that you were prepared to do a deal with him for your own greed. Accepting £100,000 rather than try to recruit him and extract valuable information that could have saved many lives. Which is what, as source handlers, you were paid to do.'

'Remember by this time we had been moved out of Special Branch because of our other failures in the operation.'

'Which were?' Jack asked, 'no, don't tell me. You went on the operation totally unprepared.'

'Yes, that's right. How did you know that?'

Jack Simpson said, 'I noticed in the reports, no radio, no camera's, no bino's, and now, worse fucking still, no allegiance to the crown, nor to your own force, the Royal Ulster Constabulary, and none to yourselves...

You watched the ambush at 1100 hours yet it was 1145 hours before the first report was made. Why?'

'Well, as you know we hadn't taken a radio with us and that was the time it took us to drive back to base.'

Jack was about ready to explode and hang these cretins out to dry.

'You fucking set of useless bastards, did it not cross your tiny minds that you could have raced to the pub and had every policeman and security force member alerted within minutes of the ambush? Roadblocks could have been established; every chopper available could have been airborne. You could have saved two people from a horrendous death. I hope that when you are locked away that the key is also thrown away.'

Their faces paled. Surely not, they all thought. No...he would not renege on his word, would he!

Jack Simpson looked at Chief Superintendent Ian Walsh, and said, 'I don't like their company any longer. Do what you wish with them.'

'Now hold on here, Simpson, you promised us immunity. We'll deny all of this.'

Chief Superintendent Ian Walsh spoke, 'he is not in a position to give you immunity. He is not even a policeman and never has been. You have spoken with him of your own free will.'

Then, in walked two policemen who had been listening in on

the meeting...

One of them said, 'sir, it's all on tape.'

Heslington screamed. 'You lousy rotten fucking bastards.'

Chief Superintendent Ian Walsh stood up, and said, 'I think you have all you need Don, is that correct?'

'Yes, I must now find our friend Pat Maguire, and that won't be too difficult.'

Chief Inspector Heslington shouted at him. 'Who the fuck are you?'

Jack Simpson smiled at him, 'I'll tell you, when I visit you in prison.'

Ian Walsh then said to the senior of the two officers, read them their rights and commence the interview...

* * *

They were driven the few miles to the nearby barracks where they were staying the night, or rather the morning as it was 2am when they arrived there. It had been a successful interrogation. Though it was an angry and bitter Ian Walsh that said with venom. 'Don, those are the type of people that I could cheerfully kill.'

Jack Simpson was equally as angry, and right when he said, 'Ian, what we have gained in good intelligence is far better than the demise of corrupt police officers. They always get caught in the end, and their just deserts will follow, no matter which force they belong to. One thing I would say Ian, is that I firmly believe in the men and women of the Royal Ulster Constabulary. Take any force in the world, and unfortunately there will always be a corrupt element.

Thank goodness it's always a small minority, and that is due to the high quality in any active police force such as the RUC. The training, and the life style of policing in a terrorist environment makes for severe demands on its members. Just remember Ian, in all previous wars and campaigns, corrupt entrepreneurs and criminal elements made millions out of the sufferings of the people. Scum take every known advantage that will earn profit, whether it be selling arms, ammunition, food, materials, and the new curse, that of drugs.'

He shuddered in disgust.

'All this as you know, has happened in Northern Ireland, it's just more galling when police officers are involved. If I had my way they would be charged with treason, then hung drawn and quartered...

The main constructive fact that we now have, with the corroboration of all three, is that they've placed Pat Maguire at the scene of the ambush. Despite the garbage that supplied this knowledge, we are now in a position to grill Pat Maguire, and believe me, I will extract from him those who had anything to do with the abduction of Jeremy and Heather, either directly or indirectly. Get one, as you know, the rest follow.'

Ian Walsh spoke to the duty RUC officer, William Molloy, and instructed him to trace by whatever means possible, Pat Maguire. Wherever he might be, Willie, find him. It is urgent. You can contact me at the Ashford number at about 8.30am.

Whilst Ian Walsh was doing that Jack contacted the guardroom and organised an early call for Tom Galloway to be woken at 5am ready to move at 5.30am. He also requested three early breakfasts for 5.15am.

They arrived at Ashford at 8.25am.

* * *

Chapter Twenty One

Joe had arrived at Helsinki to be faced with brass monkey conditions. Even the short walk from the aircraft steps to the terminal had taken the wind out of him. There he waited for two hours and then took a connection flight up to Kemi. On arrival there, he just wanted to go back. Cold weather and Joe did not agree. He stayed in the hotel that night preferring the comforts of the bar and the central heating.

Then the next day he hired a car and drove on nearly to the Arctic Circle, stopping at a hotel in Rovaniemi. He bought loads of cold weather clothes and boots, wondering what he would do with them when back home; perhaps better to dump them pre-flight

He hired a snow mobile from the hotel, the next day, and tried it out on the frozen river opposite to his hotel. He mastered the machine and apart from the cold weather, enjoyed it like any big kid.

For a week he did as Kerry had directed: keep yourself to yourself and don't attract any attention. Don't use the room telephone and don't use the reception pay telephone. They're traceable. Use your second passport at all times, your own should only be used in the direst of emergencies...

During his second week, Joe was watching the slalom skiing when a red-hatted blonde came skiing past, tw children ahead of her. Kids or not, very nice he thought, but right now his nuts were frozen, and a sizzling response in a nether region bloody near impossible.

About two minutes later, further over from where he was he could see a group of snowmobiles, all in line astern. They were obviously tourists and travelling at a snails pace, in comparison to the locals. He decided to follow them, and after thirty minutes they stopped. The lead snowmobile had pulled up alongside the woman skier and the two children. As he got closer, he recognised the rider. It was Michael Mulcahy.

Joe grimaced, you fucking evil bastard, Mulcahy. You're a dead man and so will your whore be, he said to himself. If my brother were here now, he would have him screaming in agony. I can wait, but when I get back, I will visit him in the Maze. He can decide how Mulcahy will die: Bernadette would agree with him.

He noticed a large hut set back amongst the trees. It was a picturesque location, the scenery magnificent. Icicles were glistening in the huge pines, the sky a beautiful blue with very little cloud, the sun shining, but Joe was still freezing cold.

He guessed the hut was where they donned their cold weather clothing, where they stored their equipment and it was miles from anywhere, where both would suffer. Mulcahy had made Joe suffer with what he had done to his brother, so he would make her suffer and Bernadette might want to enjoy herself as well.

He watched the comings and goings all week; dogging their tracks. They had a nice chalet in Rovaniemi, where they went to bed quite early. Mulcahy, the bastard, was enjoying life now but soon he and his bitch would die. In days, Sean would leave, knowing their routine, and the snowy conditions could only last for another month or so. Then spring would creep in with the thaw, followed by summer.

There was little more he could learn now, without exposing himself to them. He decided to return home the next day. The only concern for him was the change of season to come. There might not be the time to plan with the necessary care that Kerry and Bernadette would demand. He could go it alone, right now, but that might ruffle the wrong feathers.

He thought of his brother in the Maze, the purgatory that he had gone through during the seventies and early eighties. He had suffered the blanket protests. The long freezing nights when all he had had to sustain his body heat was a thin blanket. This combined with constant heating failure, all deliberate, made him bitterly resentful toward the establishment.

The prisoners, in their attempts to achieve their aims, along with the refusal to wear clothes, had started to deface the cells with their own excrement. They had suffered this ultimate humiliation of self-degradation for years. It had virtually ended when the prison authorities made the prisoners involved, rotate their cells. It was bad enough living in your own excrement, but to live with someone else's shit destroyed at a stroke the long campaign. Yes, he thought, these people would be made to suffer.

It took all his resolve and determination not to take his own revenge, but his turn would come round.

He would wait…

*** * * ***

Joe arrived back two weeks before Sean.

Kerry debriefed him in the normal methodical manner; grilled more like. Nothing was left to chance. If there were an error, any future mission would be aborted.

Bernadette then quizzed him, going through everything including his ideas for the operation itself in the outer edges of the Arctic Circle. Finally, she reluctantly agreed it was best that this operation was put back until the weather changed. This would mean that another recce would have to take place.

'What do you think he does for a living in the summer,' she asked.

'I believe they all take their holidays early, then get back and start the maintenance on their equipment ready for the winter. The summer breaks are so short.'

'Well done, Joe,' Bernadette remarked. 'Go off and have a break with your children. Speak with Kerry and sort out what you want to do, she'll get the money for you.'

Joe liked the girls and admired them, but he and Billie had been divorced for years. They were miraculously still good friends. She very often went on holiday with him, because Joe couldn't handle the children on his own. It had always worked well and Billie had a holiday out of it, but there was no sleeping together, she had insisted on that. He hated there parting and lived in hope that one day she would come back to him.

He knew that whilst he was still active in the organisation she would never have him back. She hated Joe being involved in the violence, but he couldn't change. She did not want her children involved so she had to free herself. Therefore, he knew it was fruitless to talk to her about reconciliation.

*** * * ***

Chapter Twenty Two

Tug and Jock had caused total havoc in the Intelligence Training Block.

Instructors training aids, which had been meticulously prepared for lessons, had been removed or changed. A Major, giving a presentation to senior officers on Security of Classified Documents had had his notes and the documents to be used on the presentation, stolen. It had caused severe embarrassment, the files having disappeared from the Regimental Secure Room.

Only the Adjutant had access to the combination locks and when the strong room door was opened at 6.30am, he was aghast. He immediately reported to the Commanding Officer that three trays of sausages had materialised in place of documents, now missing.

The CO had merely smiled realising what had gone on, and had simply remarked, 'It is obvious Andrew, where the documents are!'

The adjutant replied, totally flummoxed. 'Sir, could you please enlighten me, as Major Dawson is furious. His presentation to the senior officers' course was due to start 15 minutes ago.'

'Andrew, if the men's breakfast is in your secure room, I would have thought it logical that your documents were in the refrigerator in the cookhouse!'

The Adjutant looked even more distraught, then said, 'but of course sir, I never gave that a thought...'

There he found his documents!

He raced to the instruction block and entered the senior officers' course with the documents, 'I am most sorry sir,' he said to the Major, who was adlibbing from memory.

'Thank you Andrew, and pray tell the course and me where you had lost them.'

The Adjutant just looked at the Major in horror, went white, stuttered and faced the audience of high-ranking officers.

'Gentlemen, they were found in the refrigerator in the main kitchen.'

To roars of laughter, a Colonel shouted out, 'I suppose you had bacon and eggs in the secure room, Andrew?'

'No sir, but there were three trays of sausages.'

'Get out,' screamed the Major.

It was nearly 15 minutes before the Major got his presentation underway, the audience relishing his embarrassment.

But before he did, the senior officer stood up and said. 'May I, on behalf of the course, congratulate you Major on your very original introduction to what at most times is a boring subject.'

The Major, then to everyone's surprise doubled up with laughter. It took nearly an hour for the Regiment to get to work that day and there were some nasty accusations of theft and other anomalies, until the Commanding Officer relayed on a special, Regimental Part One Order, that a security exercise had taken place. He further expressed reservations on the gross lack of security in the camp.

* * *

Tug and Jock were delighted at some of the new techniques that they had learned at MI5.

Len had missed the fun, but had meantime organised a flight from Netheravon to Hereford, and took with him the 'equipment' that he had been given by MI5. He had wanted to sort out the weapons and ammo and meet up with the crew that were going to support them over in Northern Ireland. He also arranged a flight back at lunchtime the next day, in a Lynx that belonged to the Regiment.

* * *

At 1100 hours on the Thursday, Ian Walsh received a very welcome call from Pete Daly who was the senior officer in the RUC team in Northern Ireland, Jack Simpson at his side.

Pete had taken over from William Molloy who had done a lot of good solid police work through the night in locating Pat Maguire. He confirmed Maguire had moved three times in the past two years, that his wife had probably left him as she hadn't moved with him, nor had she been seen for some time.

Pete Daly then said. 'Pat Maguire is living in the Andersonstown area of Belfast. His current address is under observation by the Intelligence Company and we had been monitoring his movements away from that location. He spent the night at the Hibernian Club, a drinking hole in the city. He returned home at 0100 hours, looking the worse for drink. He is still in his house and the close observation boys will inform us of any movements.'

'Pete, that's great, could you now organise a system to ensure that he is followed everywhere and we must not lose him. We will be back over there late Sunday evening and will be operational immediately.'

Jack Simpson spent the rest of the day with Tug and Jock briefing them on Pat Maguire. He had already identified another potential target in his intelligence-gathering mission. She would be their first target unless of course, they were able to pick up Pat Maguire in their first week. The she would be easier and would be willing with pressure, where Pat Maguire would be extremely difficult.

Jock inquired, 'how do you lift a known terrorist like Pat Maguire, in his own environment? This is strange territory for Tug and me.'

'Every meet or snatch is an operation, and has to be planned accordingly. Every one will be different, location, personality of the tout, the urgency, but without doubt, every last one will be dangerous. You can never tell whether you are being set up as a target for an ambush, and all you can do is rely on your own organisational ability and certainly, instincts...It is strange territory, and unfortunately, being a handler, you cannot be armed to the teeth.'

Jack grinned, and continued.

'I would be delighted with steel to hand, but it just cannot be done, it is not practical, the tout would run a mile if he saw a weapon. I just don't bother...

I have lists of people who I am going to talk to, and I will need you both on every operation. There may be times that you will have to use your initiative, especially if you see something that affects either my safety or that of the tout.

That is where you will come into your own element...

With reference to the physical act of the lift, we all have our ways. I like to persuade him or her, rather than the heavy hand. Once I have something on him, like for example, "I have your wife and children, locked in my cellar", he'll most likely plead to talk with me no matter the thug and villain he might be.'

Jack looked grim.

'In Pat Maguire's case, we are going to have to follow him for a while, just to get the feel of things. By the time we get there we should be totally familiar with his routine. He is now being followed day and night, in fact, has been for sometime. Tailing is so vitally important on this type of lift. Once I know his routine I can work on how we will lift him. His habits should give me a good clue, but all I have at the moment is he visits the Hibernian drinking club in Belfast...

I would dearly like to find his wife and kids, contrary to RUC opinion; I don't think that she has left him. If he has a hundred grand to splash out on those fuckers I met yesterday, how much has he splashed out on her? I just can't accept that she would up and off. If we can find her, we have got him. That gentleman, is when I come into my element.'

'Well,' Tug said, 'we heard that you were in your element on your last foray in the Province.'

Jack smiled, 'yes Tug, it was a good start and we needed that. Pat Maguire will be a greater challenge, because he will eventually lead us to the bastards that caused David's heartache. They are the ultimate goal.'

Both Tug and Jock patted Jack Simpson on the back. That's what they had wanted to hear.

'I am looking forward to working with you, both. Do you have any questions for me?'

They grinned, then Tug said, 'Don, you are one of us, believe me when I say that, we are just as happy for you to be on board, doing your specialist work, than anyone else.'

They all shook hands, and were ready.

* * *

Much time was spent on individual tasks and getting equipment up together. David Carver gave the updated briefs on both the Thursday and Friday evenings, which had been excellent and both the MI5 and RUC teams were due in shortly.

David was taking everyone for a meal and drinks on the Saturday afternoon. Saturday evening was strictly teetotal for all.

Operation Combating Evil was fully operational...

They all assembled in the briefing room. It was nearly 0800 hours when Sir Peter Wilcox stood up to address the assembled team.

'Gentlemen, we have had an excellent week, and we are all now ready to go. I do have to remind you all of the Official Secrets Act you have all signed, and I have a further declaration involving Operation Combating Evil...

You are all hand picked for this operation, every one of you. We are supporting David Carver in his quest to eliminate the terrorists that destroyed his son...In doing that we intend to take out every known and unknown terrorist that we come across. Then, hopefully we will have given the people of Northern Ireland the peace they deserve...Good luck to each and every one of you, I will now ask David to continue the brief.'

David Carver began his brief.

'Let me first of all summarise where we are now...

We have recce'd and decided on our base in Northern Ireland. We are situated on the eastern coast, in a large farmhouse that has been used by the RUC for a number of years. It lies between Newcastle and Strengford. It is set back about three hundred yards from the beach and lies between two spurs. It is hidden from the road and can only be seen from the sea. You may notice, when driving on the coast road or coming in by chopper, a fishing vessel two hundred yards out. There are friends aboard...

The facilities at the base are excellent. The Reserve Company who is looking after us is billeted in three out houses... May I remind you all, that I want no contact with them and should this necessitate for whatever reason, it should only be done through our own people. We will meet them tomorrow.'

He paused, as though expecting questions: none.

'The man in charge is Warrant Officer Spike Wilson. He's a good man. He and his team are already in location, as is the Reserve Company. Spike will brief us all tomorrow evening on base security, of leaving and entry drills. This is his responsibility and he has absolute autonomy. That is without question by anybody. This makes sense for everyone's security and protection...

His second in command is Sergeant Luke Denton, another great, but ageing SAS soldier. His main duties are looking after our logistics and ensuring we are fed and watered at all times...Also, two loyal friends of us all, from the Regiment, Corporals Jimmy Bartlett, and John Laing will assist him with this...

There are four others from the Regiment who will work with us in our control room. It may be that the guys from the Regiment will inter change, this is something that we will only know once we have been operational for some time...There is ample room for the choppers and I believe that Tom Galloway has this side organised.'

Tom raised a thumb, David continued:

'Finally, on base requirements, your first port of call will either be Spike or Luke. They are geared to deal with any problem.' He then further outlined the aim of the operation. 'For this operation to be successful it is vital that everyone understands what role each and everyone is playing.

In a situation like we have, there is no opportunity to rehearse or practice. We are operational immediately, and each operation is the real thing. We all have the individual skills that are necessary. We just need to integrate them and develop a sound working practice together...

Yes, things will go wrong and if they do there will be no witch-hunt. We just get on with things, learn from any mistakes, and do our best.'

He surveyed his troops, a tentative smile escaping.

'After the meeting please get together and discuss your ideas with the men who may have to implement them. For example both the RUC and MI5 team members must become familiar with the operational team. That is the obvious reason for you all being invited here. I don't want anyone to feel that they are just backroom staff.

Everyone is as important as the other, so let there be no mistake about that...

Information gathering even at this early stage has already brought tremendous results, which Jack Simpson put to excellent use. We all know that Pat Maguire, an active service unit commander, known bomber, and gunman, was present at the ambush two years ago.'

David paused, cleared his throat, and noticeably affected by the last few words that meant so much to him, continued.

'We are building on that information. Pat Maguire is the next stepping-stone. We have found him; we now need to find his wife and family. Then gentlemen, we really are on our way.'

David Carver continued with the technical and communications element of his brief and finalised it with the command and control objectives.

There were no questions and everyone was excited and ready...

* * *

The equipment was moved across to Chelsea Barracks and loaded onto the choppers. At 1600 hours the rotors were spinning and the three aircraft lifted their precious cargo off the tarmac square in the barracks; watched by only two members of the Regimental fire piquet, standing by a fire hydrant.

Tom Galloway reported to Heathrow that they were airborne and heading out of London airspace. They were instructed to climb to 6,000 feet and fly on a course direct to Liverpool, where they would stop to refuel. They would then take the final hop and land at their base in Northern Ireland.

David Carver sat in the front seat of the Gazelle with Tom Galloway, just as he had done on hundreds of other occasions in the past. Sometimes Tom had dual controls on board and David had often kept his hand in as a pilot, flying, which he very much enjoyed. He had attended a Senior Officers flying course at Middle Wallop before his last trip to Vietnam. A hands on course really; six weeks but it quantified him as a helicopter pilot. But more important for him, as a soldier working behind enemy lines, it had given him another extension to his many skills.

Later, much later, they finally landed at their base and it was wet and windy, a typical Northern Ireland February. But there was no despondency; they were on a mission all had volunteered for.

* * *

Jack Simpson, Len, Tug, and Jock spent a week familiarising themselves with the area, both in vehicles and with Tom Galloway in the air. They visited the RUC and MI5 team members and were most impressed with the computer systems at their disposal.

Jack Simpson asked Pete Daly to organise a meeting with three source handlers, Ray Standwick, Benny Benford, and Lee Clarke. He also asked for full details on the information gained from their touts and how much they were paid. He then instructed him to go back a maximum of five years.

* * *

It was the Saturday morning after they had first arrived, the 20 February 1993, when Paul Garfield, one of the RUC team, telephoned to speak with Jack Simpson.

The time was 0530 hours. Paul said to Don, 'Pat Maguire has just left his house with a suitcase and a holdall. He was picked up by taxi.'

Maguire was on the move.

Jack immediately roused Len, Tug, Jock, and Tom Galloway. Within ten minutes they were in the air, and Jack radioed for a location report.

Paul said, 'he's heading for the docks. I've checked and there's a ferry leaving for Stranraer at 0645 hours and one for Liverpool at 0730 hours. Therefore, we assume he is leaving on the earlier one. We have someone at the docks now and will keep you informed.'

'Good man,' Jack Simpson said, and radioed back to base to speak with David Carver.

Within minutes David Carver answered.

'David, we are airborne near the Belfast docks. Pat Maguire is in a taxi heading there with luggage. It is almost certain that he is going to board the first ferry that is to Stranraer. Paul Garfield has a man there and one following the taxi. I have the lads with me and intend to head off to which ever port he moves to, we will then wait for him.'

'Well done Don, please keep me informed?'

'Just one point David, this must be a planned trip.'

'There was no telephone call for a taxi. His number has been scanned twenty-four hours daily since we arrived and not one call to a taxi firm or to the mainland...It wouldn't surprise me if he is to be met by someone on the other side. That's why I feel it necessary to fly on and to be there on his arrival. I will contact you again as soon as we have something positive.'

* * *

Chapter Twenty Three

Sean had been away six weeks now and it was the middle of May. He was due back that night. Both Bernadette and Kerry had missed him. They were leaving shortly for Heathrow, and all Kerry was talking about was what presents he would be bringing her back.

They waited for nearly four hours, the plane delayed, and then he seemed to be in customs for ages; finally appeared, cursing and in a flaming bad temper.

Kerry was immediately disturbed: what the fuck had he done. She was dumbfounded when he said that he had brought 800 cigarettes too many through customs and the Customs and Excise had gone to town on him.

'Which passport were you travelling on?' she asked.

He thought about it and said, 'my second one.'

'Sean are you absolutely sure? It is vital for your future security that you tell me the truth.'

He looked at the receipt the customs had given him and it was his own name. 'Sorry Kerry, I got that wrong.'

Well, we will just have to hope that you're not picked up in the future.

On the way back they talked and talked. He told them all about the massage parlours, the vice dens and all the other seedy places he had visited, and they left other business until the morning when Kerry debriefed him first.

She was very unhappy with Sean, as he had obviously forgotten to apply some of her golden rules on personal security. She snapped at him like a viper for his lax attitude:

'You made gross errors. Totally unprofessional for a man of your experience, and they were not even errors of judgement, but errors of sheer carelessness...

Why Sean?'

He was under pressure; there was no point in lying.

'Kerry, I was elated at my success, I decided to enjoy myself, I was wrong and this would not have happened had I returned earlier. I know that you are furious with me, and it will not happen again.'

'Remember Sean; it can take very little for a professional

investigator to spot the tiniest of clues, which could lead to the ultimate arrest of us all. When you make the mistakes that you did, the whole team is at long-term risk. My recommendation to Bernadette is that we abort this mission for at least a year.'

Bernadette listened to Kerry and admired the skill with which she gleaned information and chided Sean for his stupid errors. Then she spoke to him: 'Sean, Kerry has spoken of your stupidity and I totally agree with her. I am not going to labour that point now...

What I want to do is to evaluate your opinion, your conception of a future operation against the Murphy's. Once we have covered everything then I will balance the outcome with the incorporated risks that have been placed on us.'

Sean's brief was excellent. Without doubt, there was a great opportunity to take these two out and make them suffer for what they had done. With the help of their friends, it could happen very quickly and easily, once the operation was underway.

Although Bernadette was under no pressure from the PIRA Army Council, she would like to show what could be done. She had already decided that the Mulcahy operation would have to be postponed. There were still recce's to be done in Australia, New Zealand and Bermuda, yet still she favoured the Murphy operation going ahead. Sean's main misdemeanour was that he went out on one passport and came back on another, but the risk was manageable.

She spoke in detail and gave sound reasons why she considered the operation should go ahead. Kerry frowned and was very sceptical. 'In all our years together not once have we taken a risk. We have survived because of this policy. We do not need to take any risk, we can wait, there are other things that still have to be done.'

Bernadette listened. 'Kerry I want the operation to go ahead. No matter when the operation takes place there will always be that element of risk. I now feel the sooner we do it, the better.'

Sean listened to all this, then said, 'I here what you both have said, with a very heavy heart. I can't turn the clock back, I have done what I have done and most sincerely regret it. I have to agree with Bernadette, though. The other point, which has not been mentioned, is that they moved to the Royal Cliff Beach Resort nine months ago...

After meeting me only twice, Murphy's bitch was ready to jump into bed with me. I feel that given the opportunity and under the right circumstances, she would dump him and they'd both be on the move again. If that happened we would have an enormous task trying to find them.'

   Kerry said, 'Sean you are a randy bastard, but you've convinced me. I agree Bernadette, the need to go ahead, is greater than the risk.'

   Bernadette smiled.

   'There is a lot of planning to be done. I want this operation to be slick. We go in and out within four days.' Bernadette then looked at her diary. 'The operation will start on the 14 July. Kerry, I want you to have Joe and myself in place, to meet at the bus station car park in Sattahip at 12pm on the fourteenth. Sean, contact your friends and tell them that their part of the operation commences on or about the ninth of July. You will travel out on the sixth and make sure everything is in place and, that the first phase is successful.

   We do not move until hearing from you. I want you to meet us as planned on the fourteenth. We will meet here again on the third to finalise details. Kerry, as soon as Joe is back brief him for me, please.

   Are there any further points or questions?'

   There were no replies.

* * *

They met as planned and finalised all details. Sean was leaving not on the sixth, but earlier at midday on the fourth. He left Heathrow and flew to Singapore where he stayed the night at a small hotel. Before he left, Bernadette had severely warned him to remain in the hotel, and not to do anything stupid. He gave his assurances, knowing if he blew this operation, he would be out, if not dead.

   He arrived at Bangkok at 11am.

   He met his contacts at Sattahip and went through the final details with them. They had been observing the Murphy's for weeks and they knew exactly when they would be in the house together. They were, apparently, off shift from the afternoon of the ninth until the morning of the sixteenth. The lift would therefore take place on the night of the ninth.

   His informers drove him to the hills, nearly forty miles east of Pattaya. They eventually pulled up to face a dense wall of

Jungle; the track had ended and Sean immediately thought this is useless! The female grinned at Sean, as if knowing his thoughts, and prompted him to leave the vehicle. Two of the men leapt out of the back and pulled away some green hessian that had covered an opening behind where the van had stopped. The van was reversed into the opening and was then completely lost to the outside world. At the other side of the track, again concealed by hessian was a small opening that revealed the start of a track that, until recently, had last been used many decades ago. It was then a three-mile foot slog up a narrow winding track deep into the jungle.

On arrival at an old deserted hut, which was once part of a village, Sean was delighted. It was a large hut that was still useable for his purposes. Sean praised them. They had done well. He then went through the plans with them again for the snatch. He was more than satisfied, they understood, and then they wanted the twenty thousand bahts he had promised.

Sean watched the block of flats from about a hundred yards away. The light in the bedroom was switched off an hour ago. From the shadows, he saw three figures slip into the four-storey block of flats. There was nobody else about.

The only sound was that of jungle animals, and in particular the perpetual buzzing noise of insects. The light went on again. This was the crucial point. Anxiety was creeping in, as the minutes crept by. The door then opened. The Murphy's were clothed. Their hands tied behind their backs and they were hooded. The snatchers' instructions were to bring them in their nightclothes. That was the reason for the delay.

The expected van seemed to appear from nowhere with a female driver, and a man sitting in the passenger seat. Sean breathed a sigh of relief, when he saw the Murphy's bundled into it, and then it moved off as quickly and as silently as it had appeared. He waited two or three minutes and when satisfied they were not being followed, he moved off.

The Murphy's were hauled out and marched to the hut. Sean was delirious with excitement; he couldn't wait to get his hands on them. He would now have his own fun. He might even discover the whereabouts of McGurk, which would be the icing on the cake.

They yanked the hoods off the captives. The portable gas lantern cast subdued light making it difficult for the Murphy's to see who their captors were. Sean stood in the doorway. The four men and the woman in front of him all held wicked looking knives.

Patrick and Yvonne were pushed against the back wall, which was about fifteen feet away from Sean. From their position, all that they could see was the group of what they supposed were Thais and the silhouette of a tall man in the doorway.

Patrick was trembling in the semi dark, muttered, 'what do you want? If it's her, you could have had her in our flat, she's nothing but a whore anyway?'

'You fucking bastard,' she yelled at him.

'It's true, I know all the men, and that fucking woman that you have been having it off with, that rich bitch you hoped would get you back home, but you're lumbered with me, bitch.'

Sean thought, how interesting.

The woman in the group then took the lead. She screamed at them in near perfect English, 'fucking shut up.'

Patrick, grinned, 'yes, you can have her too, but let me go.'

She walked up to him and put her knife into his mouth cutting his top lip, as she did so. 'Now Mister, my name is Shari, and I am not like that, so are you going to shut up?' she snarled. He nodded, eyes wide, she had scared him.

She took the knife and slit open his tee shirt. Then cut down the arms and it was off in seconds. He was now standing in his Jeans and flip-flops. She undid his belt, opened the press-stud and eased the zip down.

'Pack it in, you have gone far enough,' he said.

'No I haven't.' She grinned, and pulled his Jeans down to his ankles.

He had obviously been sleeping with nothing on, as he was not wearing any underpants. He was embarrassed, and didn't know what to say for fear of the knife. He was trembling, watching it. She had it resting on his chest, then lowered it. He felt it, lightly, on his penis; she was gently moving his penis with the knife. She looked down and saw that her actions were arousing him. She rolled the sharp blade around it, not cutting though. He was in downright, pure and unadulterated panic. Yet he was unbelievably aroused.

He nevertheless sighed with relief when she lowered the knife.

She moved it down, caressing the inside of his thigh, stroking the skin. Then, all of a sudden, she stuck it straight into his thigh, right through to the bone. He screamed with all his might, drew breath. 'Why,' he screamed at her. 'What the fuck have we done, I done, for you to do that?'

Sean wandered over to them.

'Well, well, look who we have here...

Patrick and Yvonne Murphy...

Would you believe, the most hated pair of parasites that ever fled the catholic ghetto's, and from the people they betrayed.'

They both stared at Sean. Alarm, dread, and absolute terror raced through them. Sean had slipped on his black balaclava, portraying the most fearful sight imaginable. They both knew, at that moment, the IRA had caught up with them. They also knew of the treatment metered out by the nutting squads.

Then Sean said to Patrick, 'you're right about her. She tried to flog herself to me, but unlike you, I have more taste. She was very kind to us though because she supplied me with your telephone number and address. In fact, we couldn't have done without her.'

Patrick, still shaking from the knife attack, shouted at her, 'you fucking stupid fucking whore. I hope you bloody well suffer like me?'

Yvonne stared at him. 'Paddy, it must be you, you've come back, thank god.'

'Shut up, whore.' Sean walked right up to her and said, 'yes Patrick, I will personally guarantee that you both will suffer. Anyway Patrick, as I have come all the way over here again, I think we will all have a little look at her body, shall we.'

She was in despair. 'Please Paddy, no, not here. I will do anything for you, anything to you.'

'Strip her,' he demanded.

With a gleam in their eyes, the snatch squad were on her, her bonds were cut, and her clothes were ripped off. She was now standing, trying to cover herself. Begging, hands clasped to Sean. 'I did nothing, it was him the bastard who dragged me into it, I had no choice it was him.'

Sean walked behind her and pushed her forward. She fell on her face and there looking at him was a tiny bird on her buttock.

'Stand up,' Sean snapped at her. He then turned to Patrick, 'and I suppose you are going to tell me it was all her fucking fault.'

'Yes I am, it was always money with her, still is. The

constant demand, I had to do something.'

'How many of your own friends have you had jailed?'

Silence not a murmur from him.

Sean beckoned to his female companion; she was still holding her knife.

'Cut his tongue out.'

'No,' he screamed.

'Well answer me.'

'I don't know, all of them... I think....'

Sean fumed.

'Cut his other leg.'

'No...no, for gods sake no, please...

Then she walked up to Murphy, grinning, and slowly drew the knife down his body, repeating the same action, and then viciously stabbed Patrick just above the knee. He fell on the floor screaming, 'my legs, my legs, I need a doctor.'

'Get up you filth, get up, now.'

He lay there sobbing.

He tried to stand, and failed.

'For the last time stand up.'

Patrick forced himself to his feet, in agony from the knife. But he knew if he didn't get up, there would be more of the same. He was nearly bent double, his hands covering the wounds on his thighs. He looked at his wife, she was trembling, and he wondered what was going to happen to her.

The bitch, this was her fault.

Sean was now standing in front of her. He was looking at her breasts, not bad he thought nice pointed nipples, her breasts full and rounded. Further down, a nice mop of dark pubic hair. He grabbed her pubic hair and viciously twisted what he held. She yelled, but he smiled and then started tugging, staring, and grinning into her face. 'Yes, both of you,' mark my words, 'you'll suffer.'

She started crying, 'Please, you are hurting me,' and that made him tug even harder. She was rising on her toes.

'Is it, is it really hurting? How fucking sad, Yvonne.' He eased off, she relaxed back on her feet. 'Tell me slut, does this hurt as well.'

He stamped viciously on the toes of her right foot, and when she screamed and lifted her foot up, he did the same with the left foot.

She was hurting and had difficulty in standing, and looked

horrified when he said, 'you can have a choice. You can take all four in the corner, or they can boot the fuck out of you. What is it to be?'

She had just been stamped on and she was in agony.

'Please no, just one, please.'

He nodded to them, 'give her all you've got.'

She started to shake and cry...

Thirty minutes later he left, and they were still there, one man resting, the other three all inside her...

Sean made a telephone call: 'Phase One, completed, and successful.'

'Well done Sean see you in a few days,' Bernadette said.

* * *

Sean returned some twelve hours later. Both of them were in sheer hell, in agony, and suffering, as they should.

Patrick was in the centre of the hut, standing, with his hands tied behind his back; head bowed, legs wide apart, trying to retain his balance. He whimpered when he saw Sean, and in a croaked voice, uttered, 'please, please, you have done enough to me, let me go?'

The cord was taut, stretching down from the roof. It had been secured to the sidewall after being slung over the main crossbeam. At the other end, it was tied around his swollen and bruised testicles. After much kicking, he had been standing there ever since. Each time he dozed his weight went on to his balls and he screamed. He was fighting to stay awake. They had constantly tortured him by loosening the strong cord at the wall. Then he would try to lie down and would end up only a few inches off the floor and it would be secured again. He hadn't been able to get into the prostrate position so was forced to stand. His whole body was mercilessly racked with unending pain. Pain of the beating, the knifing, and the prolonged standing, without sleep, food, or drink.

Sean looked at Yvonne, walked over to her and stood there grinning at her. She was tougher than Patrick, although she was suffering a different kind of pain. She spat straight into his face.

'You fucking bitch, you'll regret that.'

They had humiliated her. She had been wickedly violated. It had gone on for hours and hours, the things that Orientals like to do. She realised very soon, that she had chosen the wrong option. She was standing on her bleeding toes, and like Patrick, in severe pain, tortured with lack of sleep. Hanging from the roof by her wrists, he guessed she would be feeling too sick to be hungry, though very thirsty by now, wishing she hadn't done what she had.

Still fuming and wiping his face in front of her, he said, 'I have some news for you... for you both. In a few days, friends of mine will be visiting us.' He paused to let his comment sink in, then raised his voice and shouted. 'If you think that you are in pain now, you are fuckin' wrong. You are going to suffer more pain that has ever been inflicted on any other touts.'

They both stared at him, filled with horror of what was to come. Sean walked over to his group, who were playing cards at the other end of the building. He asked for the girl's knife, she gave it to him, and followed.

'Spit at me will you, you vile bitch! Well, we'll see if you like this. Hold that leg,' he beckoned to Shari.

He went behind Yvonne, who screamed and yelled at the top of her voice, 'No, no,' as Sean sliced a square around her tattoo. She felt the sharp knife penetrating her skin, cutting, slicing into her buttock. Then he walked round in front of her, held the knife up to her face, it was covered in blood.

'Are you going to spit at me again?'

Shaking her head violently, she cried aloud. 'No, please no, don't cut me again. That hurt, it hurt so much.'

'Did it now.' Sean said, 'I am going to ask you a question, and if you don't give me the answer, my friend here can slowly remove your bird.'

'Where is your friend, McGurk?'

She was horrified, trembling, how did he knew of her lover, but she couldn't stand the pain, and would have to tell, and did, 'he is out here, but left, Patrick knows where he went.'

Patrick yelled, 'you lying fucking bitch. I never knew where he was over here. She was fucking with him. I don't know where he has gone.'

Sean was in front of him now. 'Where is he, where was he working, where was he staying?'

Patrick liked Sam McGurk; they'd had an arrangement!

He took a chance and said, 'I don't know, if I knew I would tell you.'

Sean went back to Yvonne, 'who is telling me lies?'

She looked at him, 'please he is not a tout, why do you want him?'

Sean fumed, 'you lied, you know where he is, and you will fucking tell me.'

He went behind her again. This time two snatchers held her. She yelled out, 'no, please no, I will tell you...'

He ignored her, and the blade of the knife sliced at the top right corner of her tattoo, cutting slowly into the flesh. Her screams were deafening. Sean ignored them, just thinking of his friends in prison.

'He's here, stop, stop,' she gurgled, 'stop,' she hollered, but it was too late, he went on and ever so deliberately and delicately, sliced the tattoo off her buttock.

He walked round and she was gasping for breath, pain etched on her face and she had pissed on the floor. 'So Yvonne, are you now going to answer my question?' He snapped at her, holding the bloody knife to her face.

Stuttering, whimpering, she cried. 'He works in the same hotel.'

Sean turned and looked at Patrick...

'No, no I didn't know, please no,' he screamed, as Sean moved towards him.

'You knew all right,' Sean scowled. 'Have some fun he said to Shari, then handed her the knife.'

She went behind Patrick, smiled at Sean. The men had already moved from the corner and had been watching Sean in action. Their mere presence instilled an enormous fear into both Patrick and Yvonne. They had already experienced their cruelty. Despite frightening screams, screeching and howling, the female snatcher continued cutting. When finished she walked in front of him. 'You both have bare patches,' she said holding up the four-inch square of skin and flesh.

Sean went back to Yvonne and said to her, 'before we cut the other side, I want to know where McGurk, is right now...Answer me?'

'Please let me down,' she begged. 'Please, please.'

'For the last time, answer me?'

'He lives in the hotel, he has a flat in the basement.'

'Please let me down, please.'

Sean nodded to them and she crashed to the floor, crying, sobbing then shrieked aloud. Sean spoke to the men. They picked her up and tied her hands about six inches apart. She hadn't even had time to rub her aching body. They pulled her arms back; thrust the wooden pole between her arms and back. The poles had ropes on each end and they were secured on to the wall, holding her up. She was about a foot off the ground with her shoulders and upper arms bearing her weight. She yelled at Sean, 'I told you what you wanted to know, please let me down, this is worse.'

'Yes Yvonne and it will get worse, terribly more painful, than just standing like you were.'

Then he moved to Patrick who was in turmoil, still wearily standing, the strong cord still tied around his balls. He surprised Sean when he said. 'Please hang me up, anything but this, I cannot stand it any longer, please.'

'Maybe, but first tell me of McGurk's movements. Because my friends,' he said to them both, 'the sooner he is here, the sooner I will let you both down.' He then raised his voice. 'Who is going to tell me first?'

Yvonne pleaded, 'I will, I will, but please let me down, first.' Sean walked over to her, 'you will tell me now.'

'He plays darts in the bar of the Bangkok Hotel in Pattaya on Friday and Saturday nights, but I don't know what time or day it is now.'

Sean grinned; Bernadette and Kerry will love this.

He walked to the door, she screamed at him. 'You said you would let me down.'

'Yes Yvonne, I have let you down, I am a rotten bastard, so you can fucking stay up.'

* * *

It was Saturday night when Sean went into the bar with Shari. She could lure any man from a game of darts, and Sean had spotted McGurk. She soon had him singled out, played around with him, and enticed him out the back. It was dark, it was late, but there was still many people milling around. As Shari and McGurk approached the back of the van the doors were flung open and McGurk felt the point of the blade in his back.

'Get in,' she snapped.

'What the fucks going on,' he yelled as he was heaved in the van.' No answer, he tried again. 'Who the fuck are you, and what do you want?'

Sean watched from the opposite side of the road and he was sure that the lift was successful. He hung around a few minutes and left in his car to follow. They had trussed McGurk up in the back of the van.

When Sean arrived, they were parked and although dark he could see his prey lying on the ground. Sean walked up to him and booted him in the gut. It was too dark for McGurk to see who had attacked him. Then the others started to kick and thump him. They then stripped him and he knew it was more than a mugging; he was scared.

When they arrived at the hut, his feet were bleeding from the lacerations of being dragged, pushed and brutally manhandled. Sam McGurk was shoved into the hut and his worst fears were soon founded...

* * *

Chapter Twenty Four

Pat Maguire boarded the earlier ferry. And so did his watcher. The choppy seas delayed the ferry and it arrived at Stranraer at 12 noon. Jack Simpson and Tug were there, Tug was at the exit point, with Len, and his instructions were to grab the first taxi if Pat Maguire headed in that direction, Jack Simpson was at the other end of the terminal where foot passengers alighted.

He saw Maguire; positive in his movements. The man didn't look in any direction just straight ahead, walking fairly briskly. He stopped outside and placed his luggage down. There were three taxis waiting but he just stood there.

Tug had got in a taxi and it had already pulled forward just out of the parking area. Meanwhile, Jack Simpson was getting impatient, and then he received a tap on his shoulder from behind.

A scruffy bearded individual asked him for a cigarette, then said, 'Operation Combating Evil. I have followed him. He is all yours.'

Jack Simpson nodded in thanks as the operative slipped away.

McGuire was still standing outside the terminal; waiting for someone. Then at last, a red BMW pulled up and a dark haired slim very attractive lady got out. She moved quickly to him and kissed fondly, three children also ran up to him, shouting. 'Daddy, daddy.'

Jack Simpson walked past them and headed for the idling taxi. They hadn't been able to hire a car or van, so Tug got out and thinking on his feet, walked back to the entrance. They couldn't follow for too long in a taxi before it would become blatantly obvious, so someone had to play games.

Pat Maguire had already gotten into the driving seat, so Tug headed for the passenger door knocked and asked if they were going to Glasgow. The woman lowered the window and asked what he had said, 'I am sorry ma'am to disturb you, but my wife hasn't turned up, you wouldn't be going to Glasgow would you?'

'No I am so sorry, we don't have room either, and we are heading down...' Maguire interrupted ... 'Sorry we cannot help, now piss off.'

They pulled away and Tug headed for the taxi. 'Follow that car,' he shouted at the driver. Within a short while they turned right on to the A75. Then Tug said to Don, 'I think I know where he's heading. She said, "...we are heading down," I presume she means south.' Tug then said to the driver, 'let him go and drop us off at the transport café outside town.'

Five minutes later they were airborne and Jack Simpson was speaking to David Carver. 'We are following a red BMW registration number E994MHM, heading towards Dumfries. We believe it will turn south for Carlisle...

Can you get local assistance to follow the car from Dumfries? Tom will need to refuel at Carlisle, can you organise a very quick refuel?'

'That will all be done immediately.'

They were waiting at the fuel point and the turn around was brilliant. Two unmarked cars were waiting. The first was tucked out of the way, just before the roundabout on the east side of the Dumfries bypass. It picked up and followed the BMW down as far as junction 44 north of Carlisle where they handed over to the other car.

They then continued south keeping a safe distance and Tom made contact from the chopper. He was about ten miles behind but catching up. They had turned off at Penrith and were heading for Keswick, when Tom contacted the following car. 'Stay with them I will be with you in two minutes.

'Just entering Threlkeld,'

'Yes I have you, and the BMW, please stay with him.' Tom Galloway watched the two cars. They were now heading for Keswick. 'They have parked in the centre of Keswick, but he's remained in the car. She is heading back with what looks like shopping.'

'Stay with him for as long as you can, we must find their final destination.'

'Moving out now. He's heading east picking up the A66.'

Jack Simpson spoke, 'we have him, drop about a mile back, and let a few cars through. Keep back from him, he's increased his speed he may suspect something.

'We have visual on him and are climbing to 9,000 feet...

He has just pulled in at a lay-bye. Stop as soon as you can.' Jack was using the high-powered bino's that Tom kept on board, they would hardly be able to see him but they were well visible. 'They're moving again, I think he was just being ultra careful. He is now heading off towards Cockermouth.'

Jack Simpson asked Tom to drop back down to 4,000 feet and told the police to close up.

'They're turning left before Cockermouth on to the B5086. Don't take that turning unless I tell you. The BMW is moving quite slowly down this road. He has turned right on to what is little more than a track...He has pulled in and the kids have jumped out. They have gone straight to a play area and just beyond that there is quite a large swimming pool. The car has disappeared. He has obviously driven it straight into a garage. We have him.'

Jack gave his thanks to the police, who turned and headed back to Carlisle, while Tom landed in a field north of Cockermouth. Tug remained with Tom and Jock had his instructions to walk up past the property, without drawing attention.

'When Pat Maguire returns to Northern Ireland, I want to come back here and have a break in, that's what I want you to do Jock, you and Tug, you have to get me inside...Recce as best you can now, for that purpose. I am going to pay the local 'Bobbie' a visit. We will meet back here in two hours, or earlier if you have completed your task. See you soon!'

* * *

Jock enjoyed the swift walk, he had stopped and bought a small pack, and walking boots, in the small town. He thought he might as well look the part. He put his own trainers in the pack with some other odds and ends, which he had bought, and slipped it over his broad shoulders.

Now he was just strolling, slowly, past the house, taking everything in, committing to memory the salient points. It was a very nice house he thought. At least six, maybe seven bedrooms, with a huge conservatory that probably cost as much as the average house. There were large front and back gardens, and a gate, which led into an adjoining field; obviously part of the property. The house was double glazed right through, but he could not detect any signs of any external alarm system.

Yes, Pat Maguire, he thought, you've made yourself a very rich man through your activities.

From the air it had been noted that Maguire hadn't come out of the garage, so there had to be a direct route into the house. He looked hard at the garage doors and grinned, yes fifteen seconds and we are in, no problem. The children were playing outside.

Have fun now Maguire, because it will soon be over!

He then noticed the sign on the double gates that were set back a little and left in the open position. He hadn't dared look when passing before, and now his attention alighted on drawn bedroom curtains, children playing in the garden. Siesta or more? He moved towards the gates read the house sign 'Sangria'.

Duty done he headed back to the waiting chopper. When Jack returned, Jock briefed him on his recce, his confidence of easy access to the house, high. He informed Jack that they would have him inside in less than half a minute, and Jack Simpson believed him.

'Right Tom, get us home across the water, we have much to do…'

* * *

Chapter Twenty Five

Joe had left for Hong Kong on the eighth and stayed there for four days. Then he departed for Bangkok on the thirteenth.

Bernadette and Kerry had travelled separately on the same day but on different flights. Kerry was booked into the hotel in Bangkok and would remain there until Bernadette rejoined her that night. She always remained by a telephone throughout any operation.

On the fourteenth Joe and Bernadette met Sean in the car park as agreed. When they were in the car, Bernadette asked what he had been up to. 'Well,' Sean said, 'keeping comfortable and happy until you arrived!' He grinned, and then said. 'I have a wonderful surprise waiting for you?'

Joe asked, 'what's that then?'

'You'll have to wait and see.'

Bernadette smiled, 'I think I know, and if you've done what I think you have, Sean. I will love you to death.'

He laughed.

When they reached the hut, Sean was beaming with pride. Bernadette stood by the door looking in, and then nodded to Joe, who followed her in.

Three victims were moaning in agony. The first two had been tortured for five days, and he had released them for the first time, during the night. He wanted them fresh for the arrival of Bernadette. They'd had a few hours sleep, and then before fetching Bernadette he had had them strung up again.

He'd bidden farewells to his friends. They had been great and were paid their twenty thousand, with an extra ten thousand bonus. He knew that he couldn't have achieved what he had without them. Shari had said to him on the parting of the ways, 'if you need me again, please call me.' She'd kissed him, and to his surprise, grasped him indecently but sexily nice. 'Anytime, anywhere,' and then she had winked.

McGurk had only suffered for the last two days, but his suffering had been even more intense than that of the other two.

Bernadette went to him first. 'Give me your belt,' she said to Joe.

Sam McGurk screamed, 'no, why, fucking well why,' and then she hit him with all the strength that she could muster. Repeatedly, the fierce strap struck his naked body with such force that he bled, and it hurt, so badly.

He screamed and screamed for her to stop.

She did, eventually, sweating and swearing.

'McGurk,' Bernadette yelled pointing at the other two victims. 'These two are fucking touts...'

He interrupted and shouted as loud as his beaten body would allow, 'I didn't know that. I only fucked her. I have always hated fucking touts. Why do this to me? Why do this to me, and who the fucking hell are you?' he cried in agony.

'McGurk, you fucked with my man, you put him to the torch, you bastard.'

He cringed with fear; realised what this was all about.

'Oh, no, no.' He pleaded, protesting, begging, 'Please. Please, for god's sake, no, no, that was a dreadful mistake. I have suffered ever since.'

'You will, McGurk, I promise you. If you think that Sean has made you suffer, I again promise you, I will see you beg to die. Your fucking suffering is about to start, and it will end with the torch...'

She grabbed his penis and pulled him towards her, he screamed. His hands were tied behind his back. The cord tied to his testicles. He was up on his toes, the cord was tightening, and he was losing his balance; he was being forced forward by her grasping and pulling his penis.

Then she did the unthinkable.

She kicked his feet from under him. He was already very weak. His testicles were stretched, the cord now cutting into them. He hit the floor of the building...

He was screaming, his knees drawn up to his stomach. She laughed at him. Then walked, menacingly, towards the two horrified touts, who had seen exactly what happened.

She still had the bloodied belt in her hands.

She walked round them both; saw the mosquito's that had attacked their bodies, and the bite marks. She saw festering wounds on their buttocks. She saw thighs, swollen and septic.

Then she stopped in front of Patrick.

'No, please no,' he whispered.

She scoffed. 'Wimp, don't plead with me. You haven't been touched yet.'

He closed his eyes.

As she turned away, she spun and flayed him viciously with the belt across his thighs then his balls. He was desperately trying to stay on his feet, had seen what had happened just a few minutes ago.

She beat him across his stomach, fiercely, then scattered the mossies with a horrendous beating on his raw buttock. He was teetering on his feet, fighting against the inevitable, and she smiled, and then kicked his feet from beneath him. He hung there, momentarily, and then went down, screaming. He roared in agony. Then passed out.

Bernadette then walked up to Yvonne, who had just seen two men have their testicles ripped from their bodies. She was white, with fright and in tortuous agony. Both her shoulders and elbows were dislocated. And still, she hung there. Frightened, absolutely mortified as to what was going to happen to her.

'Well fucking female tout,' Bernadette sneered. 'What do you have to say, and what do you want me to say to all the men and women that you have had jailed? Give me a message for them?

...Can you put it into words how you feel about their demise?

How sorry you might be... tell me.'

'I don't know, I don't know, I am so sorry. I am so very sorry.' She sniffled.

'Don't fucking lie to me.' Bernadette screamed.

Yvonne was crying, uncontrollably.

The men pulled her down. Put her on the ground; hold her down. Yvonne screamed with the manhandling of her shoulders, arms, and elbows. Then Bernadette stood over her, facing her, and struck her full force with the belt in the face. The belt was already wet, and bloodied from McGurk and her husband; it rained down until she was hoarse with the screaming.

She was spared no mercy.

Lashing her with all her might, Bernadette yelled. 'Fucking tout, fucking female tout.'

Yvonne fainted, as she had done so many times in the past few days. When she awoke, one of the men was pissing on her. They tied her hands behind her, and then she was placed on the apparatus that their friends had set up, facing the wall, her feet six inches off the ground.

She screamed...

Both her battered companions were strung up again. Their hands had been tied behind their backs; the rope tied to the bonds around their wrists. They were heaved up against their shoulder joints, dislocating them instantly. There they hung, waiting for the next tormenting and repulsive act; incessant nerve penetrating torture. The violence that had been inflicted on their bodies, horrendous, constant, incessant pain, of the worst kind. They were doomed and the end couldn't come quick enough for all.

Bernadette lit the escaping gas. It then roared into a strong blue flame, before she adjusted it to as low as possible without going out. She walked over to a sobbing Sam, who was looking on, and in extreme pain, 'no, please no, no...'

And she took the flame to him, right there, just as he had done with Fred, all those years ago. She ignored the horrifying screams...

* * *

Hours later, they were all at the poolside.

It was a glorious day.

They, in contrast to the painful ordeal of their captives, were enjoying themselves, as if nothing had happened.

Bernadette spoke first, 'Sean, I want you and Joe to finish them off tonight. Kerry and me will head back to Bangkok, stay the night, and fly home tomorrow.'

Kerry then spoke, 'are you both happy with your travel arrangements?'

Joe was pre-routed through Singapore staying one night, then to Sri Lanka for one night, then on to Dusseldorf, in Germany. From there, he would take a train to Ostend, catch a ferry, then finally by train to Bournemouth.

Sean was to catch a flight to Taiwan and from there to New York, stay two days, then fly to Manchester. He would finally, catch a train to London, then on to Bournemouth.

'No problem they had both said,' and Bernadette and Kerry left...

* * *

Sean and Joe, a few hours later, headed up to the hut in the hills. Yvonne had a very slow pulse; the men were gasping in agony, but still very much alive.

Both Sean and Joe had already discussed that they would

not take too long in ridding themselves of garbage.

Joe took the torch.

'Well, Patrick and Yvonne Murphy, your time is nigh. On behalf of my comrades in prison, due entirely to yourselves, you are to die by my hand.'

He walked up to Yvonne and slapped her backside. Then torched it. She screamed. 'Good,' he said, 'I thought you were already dead.' He spun her around, glared into her fear-ridden eyes, and then placed the heat source on her left breast...

Patrick watched the heinous bastards. Nobody would rescue them, and he too would soon be dead. He looked at Joe in front of him; filthy teeth stained with nicotine, grinning.

The lighted torch hissed, then gas burning flesh...

Then it was screaming McGurk's turn. He was raised about six inches above the ground. Sean placed the torch directly under his feet, said it was a present from Fred Short, and then they walked out, laughing...

* * *

Sean dropped Joe off at the hotel outside Pattaya, and then turning as he had done the previous week, headed south! He stopped at Sattahip and called her. An hour later he picked her up at Ban Khlot and drove back to his hotel in the centre of Pattaya.

From Shari, he received the delights of his last extended stop in Bangkok. She stayed with him all the next day, too. He had never had love bestowed on him, such as this, before. She did with him, so he thought, what she wanted to do. All other times in the past, he'd had to pay for this sort of pleasure. Then he had to reluctantly leave for Bangkok Airport.

'Take me with you, she said, let me join your organisation.'

'I can't, not now. But I will speak back home and see if we can send for you.'

'Will you promise me, that? Sean, please promise me. I will be good for you.'

'Yes, yes,' he said, then gave her taxi money to return to Ban Khlot.

The PIRA group all met up in Bournemouth four days later...

* * *

Chapter Twenty Six

When Jack Simpson entered the police station at Cockermouth and gave the codeword, the police sergeant thought he was cracking up. Jack didn't labour the point that there were many other ways of finding out about the occupants of a house.

David Carver then debriefed them on their return; delighted with the initiative that had been shown. It was now a simple police matter. Ian Walsh had passed it on to Dave Bonner and within hours they knew everything that Jack Simpson needed.

The couple had been married since Dorothy Gillespie turned eighteen, and they had three children, who all went to school in Cockermouth. The man of the house was now known as Patrick Gillespie. The DVLC at Swansea revealed that and subsequently everything else had appeared in his new name.

The couple had moved to their house 'Sangria', three years ago. According to the entry in the Land Registry it was bought as a freehold property, with seventeen acres of land, four acres of which outline planning permission had been granted, for redevelopment. They had paid £250,000 for the property and there was no record of a mortgage. The deeds were located in vaults belonging to a security firm in Carlisle. They were not assigned to anyone or any company.

Credit checks revealed that there was no borrowing or loans of any sort. Registry Trust confirmed that there were no judgements against the owners. They banked with two branches of Lloyds and had three building society accounts. From a very humble background it would appear that the master had done very well for himself...

* * *

It was now the middle of March 1993. Jack Simpson was waiting for the return of Pat Maguire and in the meantime he had been busy talking to handlers and touts.

He had an interview arranged for the Wednesday afternoon with two of the source handlers, Benny Benford, and Lee Clarke. Both were RUC and he had studied their backgrounds, and most important of all, their performances.

Benny Benford hadn't been successful as yet. He had been

trying and wasn't getting anywhere. He had two touts, one he recruited and the other who had telephoned in to the confidential number. Jack looked at his tasking sheets, then remarked, 'neither have given you information that you have requested. Why do you think that is?'

'I really don't know, I ask searching questions, they both seem keen to answer and when I task them on the follow ups, they come back with nothing.'

'This tout here, Mally Cork from Derry, fix a meeting up with him, and I will come along. Get him to park in the main car park behind Wellworthy's in Enniskillen at 9pm, tomorrow night...

Tell him you have £500, and you think he could have the information you want. Ring that number in the next twelve hours with confirmation. Your other tout, Billy Hargraves, from the Springfield Road, Belfast, tell me about him, and why you have a problem with someone who telephones you with information and you can't or don't obtain it?'

He shook his head, 'I don't honestly know and if you can help me I would be grateful.'

'Listen to me Benny; you're trying to be too nice. What you have here are two low life, fucking idiots who are taking the piss out of you. They will leave your meeting, head off to the pub, and with the hundred quid, get drunk, have a jump, then wait for the next ton. Well believe me, sunshine; tomorrow your touts are in for the shock of their tiny lives. Arrange Hargraves meeting for 7pm...

That's all, any questions?'

'Yes sir, what if they don't want to come or can't make it?'

'For fucks sake Benny, who is the handler, you or fucking them?' Jack shouted at him. 'Who fucking trained you, the bloody Girl Guides! You will get them there, won't you Benford, because if you don't, you will end up as a fucking traffic warden and not a Special Branch Officer... Now fucking get out!'

About twenty minutes later there was a knock on the door and in walked Lee Clarke.

Bold and brash, a much stronger looking character than Benford, but his record, apart from one tout bitter against an unknown PIRA member, was extremely poor.

'Sit down Lee,' Jack Simpson said.

'What's this all about, Mr Simpson? I'm a busy man and do not have time for crap.'

'Oh Really, and could you tell me what you are busy doing?'

'I have been Source Handling now for five years...'

'No, you have been handling for three years and two months. Now, what is your success rate? How many terrorists have you had imprisoned from your information?'

Lee Clarke was completely taken aback.

'I have always done my best.'

'Your best is next to useless. So how are you going to improve?'

'I have difficulty in recruiting good grade touts.'

'What have you learned about this Sean who beats his girlfriend up so bad she turns into a tout? We don't seem to have a record of this happy chappy. Give me your view on this girl. Tell me all about her and how we can benefit from her? What is her role in the organisation?'

'She seems genuine enough to me. She wants us to uncover him, Sean, for what he is, she meets with known PIRA members, she tells me she is part of an active service unit, and has valuable information that might save lives. I've been nurturing her, bringing her slowly on our side.'

'Lee, are you dreaming this up? There is no record of what you are telling me? If she has told you she is in an active service unit then why have you not got the other members names? Who is this Sean? Where does he operate? What's his role in the organisation, if indeed he is PIRA? Has she a photograph of him...'

'I am not dreaming this up. I have kept it to myself until I can confirm it. I had hoped to get the other names from her, on my next meeting.'

'When is that?'

Oh god, why did he ask me that thought Lee.

'I haven't been able to get hold of her.'

'Why not?'

He paused. 'Because I haven't rung her up.'

'So, its not that you haven't been able to get hold of her, it's because you have been too fucking lazy to contact her. Yet, from what you maintain, she has valuable information that could save lives, is that not correct?'

Waiting for his answer, Jack thought, who the fuck is this Sean bastard.

'Well...Well fucking tell me, Mr Clarke, has she, or has she not got access to valuable information?' Jack Simpson demanded.

'Yes, and I am embarrassed...'

'Too right you're embarrassed. I can plainly see you for what you are, and now you can also see that this woman could be a top grade informant, if she is telling the truth. That I will find out, by you contacting her immediately, and I don't care how you induce her; I want to talk with this woman on Friday, at 6pm. I will be at the eastern end of the promenade at Bangor sea front.

Let me tell you this Mr "fucking" Clarke, this meeting has been recorded. If you value your job, you gutless pathetic specimen, you had better have her at the meeting. If she is not there, I will see you out on the beat. Do you understand?'

Lee Clarke trembling, was gob-smacked, brash and cocky when he came in, and like a "jelly-fish", on his way out.

That night Jack Simpson met with Ian Walsh and spoke to him about the quality of the source handlers that he had met to date. He gave Ian the tape of both meetings and said, 'I am sure that all are not tarred with the same brush, but Ian, I have met with five active source handlers and one that is retired. They are worse than bad. What is happening with training, where is the supervision? Something, somewhere is sadly going very wrong.'

Ian Walsh looked very glum, and said, 'on face value you are right, there is work to be done.'

Jack Simpson realised he had touched a sore point. 'I am sorry to have brought this up at this time Ian but I feel that you should know about it. Perhaps as it seems to have been going on for some time, we should make the best of a bad job and get on with things ourselves. I will see what response I get from these handlers in the next two days, maybe I have scared them into improving their performances.'

Ian Walsh said, 'I would appreciate it if we could leave it for the time being, Don. I do feel it best that you deal direct with the touts from now on. If there are complaints, then I will confront them head on.'

'Ian, I think that I'm out of order here. You have enough on your mind as it is. I have an idea where I can put right the mediocre side that I have come up with. The others, well in time they can bloody well rot in their slime.'

Later that day Jack Simpson spoke with David Carver and Sir Peter Wilcox, bringing them up to date with the tout handling side. As Jack expected David was horrified. Peter wasn't surprised! He said, 'remember me outlining that MI5 were assuming responsibility for all covert operations in Northern Ireland. Well, what you've already grasped in two days is part of the "big picture".'

Then he added. 'Let's get this operation out of the way Don, then I will look very closely at who will head up the new training wing I intend to set up!'

Jack Simpson's face changed, and he walked out of the room with a huge grin.

* * *

Jack Simpson and his backup, Tug and Jock were sitting in the van in the car park. As always he turned up early for his meetings to survey the land. Watch the coming and goings, looking for the unusual.

They had waited an hour; the tout was late. Only five minutes, but this was the first of two danger signals that Jack Simpson had always observed, and would not break. Both for his own safety and that of his team.

He would wait five more minutes; searching, eyes straining, watching for movement.

One more minute, weapons at the ready, he ordered, 'prepare for action.'

The 9mm pistols they were carrying were cocked. Tug had pulled the machine gun out and it was also cocked ready, live rounds ready to scythe into any would be assailants.

A Ford Escort with a driver and passenger was pulling into the car park. It stopped near the second hand shop, that many years previously had been demolished by a 200-pound car bomb. Benny stopped exactly where he had been instructed. If the handler had been under duress, he would have driven straight in. He now moved on towards the bottom of the car park and slipped into a vacant space.

Jack Simpson waited a further five minutes. No one else entered either by car or on foot.

'Jock, nip out and walk towards the car and speak with the driver, giving the codename FIREBRAND. He will or should reply with CRACKER. If he doesn't hit the deck and we will blast the car. After the first blast, race back here and we'll be off. If he acknowledges correctly put your right thumb up.'

Even though Benny had followed the entry drills correctly,

these were still tense moments. Jack saw the thumbs up and instructed Tug to drive round and stop in front of the car.

'Both in the back,' Jack Simpson said. Billy Hargraves was apprehensive and didn't move. Jock walked up to him. Nothing was said, but Billy was plain scared. He got out and clambered into the back of the van.

'Jock, follow us in the car.'

He knew where Jack Simpson was taking the pair.

* * *

The huge gates swung open, the sentry looking at Jack Simpson, who after showing his ID, simply said, 'the Escort behind, is with us.'

He drove to the top end of the camp, where an old mobile home, had many years ago, been modified into an interrogation room. Tug and Jock remained outside, one at each end of the 35-foot trailer.

Jack Simpson sat opposite the tout.

'And you're Billy Hargraves,' Jack Simpson said, with a smile.

'Aye, I'm that, and who the fuck are you?'

Jack ignored his question, and said. 'Why did you phone the confidential hotline two months ago saying that you had important information?'

'I needed the money.'

'You have been paid £300 for three meetings and I cannot see where we have received any information whatsoever.'

Billy just sat there, and grinned. Jack Simpson stared hard at him and the grin slowly dissolved.

'So, Billy, what you have done is to take my money and I presume, piss it up, yes?'

'Yes, I have, and you can't do fuck all about it.' He stood up and said to Benny Benford, 'let's go.'

Benny didn't say anything or even move.

Billy stood there.

Then the silence was broken:

'You, Hargraves are in dire trouble.'

Billy Hargraves, laughed and said, 'I have already told you, you can do fuck all about it. I have been taking money off you lot for years, he boasted. Normally I can get a couple of grand before I am binned, but then I just move elsewhere and you can do fuck all about that either. Loads of us do it. Now clever arse, either let me go or I will report you for kidnapping.'

Jack Simpson remained steadfast; glaring at him, and slowly shook his head. 'No Hargraves, you are going nowhere. You're married with a two month old boy aren't you?'

'Keep them out of it shithead, they're fuck all to do with you...

How do you know that anyway?' Billy said.

It was Jack Simpson's turn to grin now. 'Is Wendy a good fuck, Billy?'

Billy Hargraves shouted, 'I'll kill you, you evil fucking bastard.'

'Really, Billy, that's very unfriendly of you. My men asked me if she gave good head, and I said they could find out.'

'I'm warning you, mister, any more filthy remarks like that and you are dead.'

Jack Simpson continued, a vicious edge to his voice. 'If you think you can take the piss out of me Billy Hargraves then you had better have another think, because you will do exactly as I tell you.'

'No I won't, I know fuck all,' he said grinning, 'pay me now for this meeting and I will not shop you.'

'I know you no fuck all, you miserable little fucking shit...

That is why you are going to do other things for me, and without pay, and you are not going to shop anyone, are you?'

'Bollocks! Fuck off, you can't make me do nothing, you fat four eyed load of shit.'

Jack Simpson shouted, 'Tug, Jock, come in.'

'Yes boss,' they both said.

'This fucker has been ripping us off...

Tape his mouth to stifle his screams, and then strip him.'

'No, you can't do that, you are not allowed. Stop; get off, you pair of bastards.' Hargraves was no match. The brown masking tape was wrapped around his mouth and round the back of his head, sticking to his hair. His eyes were bulging. They were hurting him, and they soon had him standing naked.

Jack Simpson then went right up to him, grabbed his balls, and squeezed. 'You will do as I tell you, you are going to join my gang.' Perspiration was streaming from him and yet it was very cold in the unheated building.

'Are you going to join us, shithead?'

'No, fuck off,' he tried mouthing through the tape; shaking his head.

Jack Simpson then said. 'Cut his balls off and take them to

his wife.'

They were strapping him to the table, laughing at him as he struggled, then Jock swiped him hard across his face with the back of his hand and all resistance ebbed. When Tug drew the blade from its sheath, Billy started shaking his head violently.

Jock slowly ran it down his body. The point of the blade was a fearsome sight, terrifying, giving off awesome power as it stopped at his penis. Then Jock scared the life out of Billy, when he said, 'this pathetic thing as well?' Holding up the tiny limp member.

'Changed our mind, have we Billy?' queried Don.

Billy was by now nodding frantically.

Tug saw that he was broken, and knew exactly what to do next. He moved the knife down and around his right testicle

'Too late,' Jack said, as the point of the knife eased upward, the point ready for decisive action.

Billy was shuddering from head to toe.

Tug moved away, laughing. He hadn't hurt him but the psychology of what he had threatened, sufficient for complete compliance.

Jack Simpson said to Billy, 'when we get back Hargraves, utter one word of opposition to me and my man will slice everything off, and believe me, he will skin them first.'

'Do you understand?'

Billy's eyes were now tightly closed but he was nodding his head, so quickly, it was in danger of dropping off.

They left him bound and taped, crying his eyes out.

* * *

They were back in the car park later than expected. Mally Cork was due in thirty minutes. There were very few cars about and Tug and Jock were told by Jack to take a walk around.

Jack Simpson and Benny were in the front of the van. Then Jack asked Benny, 'what arrangements have you made?'

'The same, just different codewords, the entry drills are the same, too,' he replied, voice shaky, conscious Jack was out to treat like with like.

'Sir, you frightened the life out of me back there.'

Listen to me Benny, 'how many men have you seen killed in Northern Ireland... None I'll bet?'

Benny replied, 'I've seen the bodies after, but not the actual killing.'

'Well let me tell you Benny, when you see a man killed in front of you, when you see the sheer terror in his face, when he knows he is about to die, it will stick with you forever. What is worse, is when you know a man to be a family man, and a colleague, a close friend, a friend trying to bring peace for the future of his children and the children of others, and is then killed trying to do his best. That kind of killing brings into perspective what the likes of you and I have to do, to stop these horrific killings. If I have to frighten the living daylights out of a tout who is ripping us off, then I will gladly do so. I've had close friends tortured to death by the evil perpetrated by turned touts. Most touts have no scruples, and will shit on their own for money, so what will they do with you?'

At that Tug and Jock returned. 'All seems quiet boss.'

There was still ten minutes to wait for Cork when a motorcyclist pulled into the car park.

'That's him,' Benny Benford said.

The biker had stopped as agreed and pulled in at the bottom, also as agreed.

Jack left him there for a few minutes. 'Ok, go and talk with him, and finish off with the correct verification procedures.'

Jack Simpson watched and listened; he had slipped a tiny but very powerful microphone in Billy's pocket, and could hear every word spoken. He heard them going through the verification drills, then Mally Cork said, 'where is the £500?'

'You'll get it, now come up with what my boss wants and it will be a grand.'

'You never said that someone else would be here?'

'That's because you never asked, now belt up and come with me.'

'Fucking hell, you've never spoken like that to me before.' Rallied the biker, dogging Billy's footsteps. 'What's up?'

He was climbing into the back of the van, and then all that could be seen was the soles of his shoes as he disappeared. The lads threw him face down on the floor and the van moved off. They again headed off north. As they neared the barracks, this time they turned left, instead of right, and drove to the far end of the airfield.

Tug and Jock got out. Jack Simpson and Benny got into the back. No one had followed them, but the lads still stood out on guard duty.

'What the hells going on?' shouted the tout.

'We want information,' Jack said, quietly.

'Then why the fucking rough stuff? If I have information for you, you get it and you pay me.'

'Sit up on the seat.' Jack said. 'We have to take precautions ourselves both to protect you and your handler. Now, Mally, tell me what's going on in the Derry area?'

'Nothing that I know about, I came here to pick up five hundred quid that he promised me.'

'What sort of information have you got for me for that kind of money?'

The biker started to get irate, 'I never asked for this meeting. I had some information and was going to get paid for it.'

'Mally who are your contacts, and where can you get information relating to the PIRA? Who is involved with the organisation at the moment that you know of, or your friends know? Why did you offer information to your handler at the beginning, and now reluctant to tell me?'

'Listen, I have not come here for this crap,' the biker stressed, pointing at Billy. 'He wanted information and I've passed it on. Now he wants more and I don't know what he fucking wants, but I want my £500. I turned up, and now you must keep your side of the deal.'

'We will keep our side of the deal when you answer me. I have seen nothing that warrants any payment to you. Yet you have received over a thousand pounds, why?'

'I can't remember everything that I have passed to him, we've met about seven or eight times now.'

'Tell me who you know in Belfast that is involved?'

'Fucking hell, I left Belfast four years ago and nearly every one I knew is either dead or in the Maze.'

'That's all right Mally, but you might be able to tell me something that I don't already know. Have a good hard think.'

There was along pause, then Mally said, 'I don't know anything.'

'Were you a tout when you were in Belfast, Mally?' Jack noticed that he froze. 'Speak to me, now.'

'No, I was never a tout then, and I wouldn't be now, if I wasn't so desperate for money.'

'Why are you desperate for money Mally. You are only twenty eight and you work for Customs and Excise, and are reasonably well paid.'

'How do you know all this about me?'

'Never mind. I know everything about you and you are going to tell me even more. Then I will know if you are lying and if you do, Mally, it will make me very, very angry, I know you know something, that there is something that you want off your chest, I have been doing this job for too long... What is it?'

Silence.

'What is it that you are keeping to yourself? What happened four or five years ago in Belfast? You were a tout and still know something of value, don't you? Tell me your secret, Mally. You will tell me, even if it means staying here all night and tomorrow and the next day.'

He paused.

Silence.

'And when you still haven't spoken with me, then I will take you up to Belfast and we will have a walk around the Bullring in the Ballymurphy, then we will wander down the Whiterock Road, head up to Andersonstown, and that's a nice republican area, is it not. It would be really interesting to see the gathering behind us wouldn't it.'

'You would be killed as well.'

'Oh, no, Mally, it wouldn't be just you and me.' We would have an RUC and army escort... I'm not stupid.'

'You're a bastard, and I think you'd really do that.'

'No Mally, you are wrong. I have always dedicatedly protected my informants. When I become a bastard, Mally, is when informants who accept money from us then do not deliver...When I am cheated, Mally, I am more evil than any PIRA member is...

Believe that Mally. It is almost certain that when a tout cheats, some one dies. That someone is invariably his handler...And when a handler dies, his death is even worse than that of the tout. You have said that if it weren't for the fact that you needed money, you wouldn't be a tout...

Well Mally, you are a tout for whatever reason, and you are here to collect £500. You came of your own free will. I am not going to waste any more time with you. I am going to ask you two questions, and if you do not answer to my satisfaction, tonight you will be chained naked to a lamppost in the centre of Derry. A placard will be placed on you saying: "I am the tout responsible for 100 soldiers rotting in the Maze".

So, Mally, it is payback time.'

Jack Simpson paused, looking at the shocked and shaken figure in front of him.

Billy slumped forward, his head in his hands and started crying.

'Do I call my men in, or are you ready to talk?'

He sat back drying his eyes, looking across at Jack Simpson. 'Give me a moment, and I'll talk.'

Jack waited, and then resumed his forward attack. 'Are you ready?'

'Yes,' replied Billy.

'What was your role in The Provisional Irish Republican Army from leaving school, to leaving Belfast? Take your time, I want every finite detail.'

'I was a member of an active service unit for three years. I hated it. I only joined because three friends of mine joined. We were great mates and it seemed the right thing to do at the time. We spent three weeks training in the south near Dundalk.

Then when we returned to Belfast we were split up between other groups. None of us thought that would happen. I was with a group from the New Lodge area. The leader was Gary Sullivan, his son Billy was a member of another group. I couldn't shoot or bomb anyone and I was given other tasks. I acted as a courier, transporting weapons, money, driving gunmen and bombers about.

Gary Sullivan was a brigade commander, and I was his lackey, nothing more.'

He cleared his throat, feet shuffling.

'One of my mates was killed when his group was ambushed on a bank raid. That hit me very hard. As time went on, we had realised that terrorism was not the answer and we were trapped. Simon Haig was another of my mates. We helped each other. Then we moved in together, and our relationship developed into a bisexual friendship.

We had women enough, from time to time, but were sort of trapped in a situation that had brought us together this way. We were open about it but other members were vicious and callous with us. Then disaster hit us. A large amount of money went missing and Simon and Johnny McGurk were blamed. They were both interviewed by PIRA security. The man that interrogated them was a brigade commander. By coincidence, his own unit had to collect the money from a PIRA safe house where it had been stored ready for movement.'

Jack listened intently, names whirling in his head.

'It was nearly half a million pounds and it had just disappeared. Our flat was pulled apart and it was obviously not there. I knew that Simon would have no part in anything like that. The theft happened when I was in London, delivering documents, so I was not involved in the interrogation.'

Mally Cork then broke down, crying bitterly.

Jack Simpson placed a hand on his upper arm and said, 'Mally you are showing tremendous courage. I know from a number of things that you have said to me that you are telling the truth. I also believe you know who took that money. Or at the very least who betrayed Simon. I believe every word, Mally, and if the name of that person is who I think it is, then trust me, we can destroy him together.'

Jack Simpson looked at Mally; the man devastated, distraught, still crying, and Jack knew that he was on the verge of something big, something very relevant to what had happened two years ago, and he would not let go on this one.

'Mally, please listen to me. Your heartache is the same as a friend of mine... One day I will tell you of this, but right now I need you to talk and to trust me.'

He knew he had to win Mally over, and he also knew he was nearly there. This had grown out of all proportion to what he had expected. So many years he had handled touts, yet, this again was so different. Given his vast experience, he could read the touts like a book. Yet, nevertheless, here again, trusting his instincts, digging deep, he was still cautious, but would get there in the end.

'Mally, calm down. Listen carefully to me. We are nearly there. I need answers, and you have them. I know that I can resolve your money problems. Just trust me.'

Mally Cork's eyes lit up. 'Do you really mean that, and you can honestly sort out my problems?'

'It depends, but you are doing well. We will talk about that in time, as that was obviously going to be my second question...

Now, this question is vitally important to me, but even more so to you...

What was the name of the PIRA internal security commander?'

A long pause reflected Mally's anxiety.

'His name was Pat Maguire.'

Mally broke down again; sobbing his heart out. He

spluttered, trying to talk, crying aloud, but managed to get it out what he wanted to say.

'They brought Simon to the flat. He had been horribly tortured. He was naked. My Simon, and he was dead. He had been whipped. There were other terrible marks on his body, too...'

There was then a very long pause as Mally had totally broken down...

Crying uncontrollably, the nightmare came back, the vision of his male lover, Simon, flashing before him, in front of his eyes, his head, now in his hands, spluttered again, 'it was horrors of all horrors, I hadn't noticed at first, everything was black, then the smell hit me, his private parts had been burned off. I dearly loved him, you know, and we had both been trapped into something we hadn't wanted.

They just slung him on the floor in front of me. I bent down and cradled him in my arms. They scoffed and taunted me. The only person I had ever loved, and they had dreadfully violated his body and I'll never ever forgive that.'

Then the reality hit him, and he screamed aloud, collapsed on the floor of the van in tears.

Jack Simpson nodded to Benny, 'I'll be back in a second, just look after him.'

He went outside.

Listening in, both Tug and Jock were heading to the van.

'Get in the front and drive into the camp. You drive Jock. Tug, you jump out at the guardroom and get Tom here urgently.'

* * *

Jock pulled up at the guardroom, then drove to the end of the camp, and pulled up alongside the converted mobile home and the Ford Escort.

Jack Simpson cut the rope that tied Hargraves's arms and told him to get dressed, then said to him, 'are you now going to do as you are told?'

His mouth still taped, Billy nodded his head furiously.

Jack left Jock with him and went back to the van, just as Tug raced up to him. Jack spoke with Tug outside the van and said, 'you will have to take over and sort this one out...

I am going back to base with Mally. He knows too much, and we have to get everything from him in a better environment...

I think we can put this fucker Hargraves, to better use than being a tout. He knows fuck all, and you can lay it on with him. As you have seen, he does not like the rough stuff...

And this is what I want you to do...'

* * *

Mally Cork had tried to pull himself together, even though he was distressed, and emotionally upset. The memories of his lover, hideously tortured had flooded back to him; a traumatic experience relived, and now, in another frightening predicament.

Jack entered the van and said, 'you have done well Mally. We will collect your bike and you're coming with me.'

'Where are you taking me?'

'Mally, I know this is very difficult for you but remember what I said earlier to you I always protect my informants. That is what I am doing now, for you. There is obviously a lot more that you need to tell us. We stopped because you were dreadfully upset.

I need time with you, and to help you. I cannot do this sitting in the back of a van. Then we can look closely at your financial dilemma and help you there. You have done well to co-operate with me, and not only will you feel better, but also you will gain revenge for Simon. You will never have to testify. No one else will know about you.'

Jack hoped that would be so, but fate could foul any plan.

'What I want you to concentrate on is your time as a courier. Who you met, where you met, especially on the mainland, I want the names of every single person, going back to your earlier days when you were recruited, through training, and then to when you first joined your unit.

I want to know about every operation that you were involved in prior to being used as a courier. Even if you committed a crime I want to know about it, there will be no recriminations against you. You will be making a complete new start, and as I have said, we will help.'

Then Jack heard the Gazelle flying over.

Mally, as if in another world, said, looking up to the roof of the van, 'am I going in a helicopter?'

'Yes,' replied Don, grinning at the expression of amazement on Mally Corks face, 'that's our transport. Just wait here a moment.'

He spoke with Benny Benford. 'I'm taking him with me, and want you to stay with my men for the time being until Billy Hargraves is sorted out. They know what's required, and they will brief you. You are now going to earn your money. For the time being you will work directly for my men...

Have you any questions?'

'No, other than I can't thank you enough. I have learned something this evening, I certainly have.'

'Right get Mally Cork down to the guardroom and I'll meet you there.'

Jack Simpson went back to the interrogation room and there was much strong talking with Billy Hargraves. He said to Billy, 'well are we happy with our new role in life, Billy?'

'As long as you keep paying, it suits me.'

Jack Simpson nodded to his men, and said, 'don't forget the bike; sling it in the back of the van. See you back at base.'

Jack then headed for the guardroom to pick up Mally, and within minutes they were airborne.

As Tom eased the sleek Gazelle on to its landing skids at the base, both David Carver and Sir Peter Wilcox were waiting. Jack told Mally Cork to remain in the Gazelle until the rotors had stopped and that the pilot would bring him out. Jack Simpson leapt out on to the hardstanding and handed the tape to David Carver, and said, 'listen to that, while I sort out my guest.'

They both moved quickly to the operations room.

The time was 0300 hours.

Spike Wilson was also waiting, as he had known something was afoot when the Gazelle had left. He took Mally Cork from Tom and gave him a cuppa, and left him in the room that had been set up for briefings.

The debriefing of Mally Cork would continue after a hearty breakfast on the Friday at about 1100 hours. He had already telephoned in to his work saying that he was sick and would not be in until Monday.

* * *

Chapter Twenty Seven

It was early in 1993 and Bernadette and her group had been extremely busy. They had earned tremendous praise from the new Army Council.

The destruction of the touts in Thailand, the Murphy's, and two in Australia and New Zealand, caused much elation. They now had two operations to complete, one in Bermuda, and the twice-postponed Michael Mulcahy execution, in Rovaniemi, Finnish Lapland.

The reconnaissance had been done and both awaited budgetary clearance. The brutal destruction of the touts was communicated from the Army Council down the PIRA chain of command. The message was clear to all. There will be no place to hide, and death will fit the crime.

Bernadette had also fulfilled her promise with the selective targeting of much larger and more effective bombs. She'd had two planned for the summer of 1992, but unfortunately the explosives were seized on route to her.

What she had said at the recent Army Council meeting had been delivered with zealous fervour and vengeance. The destruction and havoc she would create was to be greater than that caused by anyone else throughout previous campaigns.

In addition to the devastation already initiated, the increased security measures to prevent further attacks had been implemented at great financial cost, insurance companies squirming, so too their underwriters.

* * *

Fred had got bored in his retirement. Months of inactivity were too much, and he was now reinstated within the unit, but had primarily been used as a courier. They were, at the moment, planning their trip to Bermuda. The tout Dermott Black was in for a shock, they had been patiently waiting and now he would feel the punishing tortuous horrors that would be inflicted on him.

Bernadette had told Fred of the demise of his tormentor, Sam McGurk. The man who had nearly tortured Fred Short to death some years earlier, his manhood taken away from him.

Sam McGurk had got the wrong man, had mistakenly thought Fred to be in Pat Maguire's active service unit, the unit that had destroyed Sam's twin brother; four years previous.

Pat Maguire's unit had horrendously tortured Johnny McGurk and Simon Haig, but Fred Short had had nothing to do with it. And even worse, neither Johnny McGurk, nor Simon Haig had committed the crime to which they were accused. The Army Council had decreed that it was a dreadful mistake and Sam McGurk's punishment was nothing more than to be dismissed from the organisation.

But, Fred Short's life had been ruined and Bernadette had promised Fred that she would see to it that McGurk's punishment would be much more severe, and it had been. Fred was pleased, but he would've preferred to wield the torch himself.

* * *

Bernadette and Sean were up near the army base at Larkhill in south Wiltshire. They wanted to hit a military target, perhaps, sometime during 1993. They toured the area and found many camps. But it was a time when increased security measures were been introduced. Where most of the camps had been open plan, now, ten-foot perimeter fences were protecting them. These posed no great problems but did make it more difficult for reconnaissance.

After the drive they decided to look around the nearest reasonably sized town and parked up in the centre of Amesbury. They walked from the centre, back towards the Texaco Garage at the traffic lights. Turning left at Pitts, which was a car sales garage and walked on past the George Hotel, which was a very old, but very large hotel.

They went into the New Inn, which was packed with drinkers and people in the restaurant. It didn't look to be a soldier's pub. Most of the men that were dining were in collar and tie, which suggested that the business fraternity used it, so they went further on after a drink and went into the Queens Arms.

Bernadette saw the vacancy sign requesting a bar person. She looked around and immediately thought the place more of a soldier hangout. When they left they took the telephone number; perhaps, an ideal job for Kerry or Fred!

Bernadette said to Sean. 'This must be a busy little town as The Bell and The Greyhound pubs were also advertising for staff.'

They spent the next two days in and around the town.

The following Monday, Fred started work at the Queens Arms, and Kerry started at The Greyhound.

Bernadette had found a caravan to rent at a local caravan park near Boscombe Down airfield, which was ideal for Kerry, while Fred stayed at a room in the pub.

The airfield could present itself as a possible target. It was a top-secret experimental establishment and also housed a test pilot school. Yes, Bernadette had thought - great potential.

Kerry moved into her caravan on the outskirts of Amesbury in October and settled in as a bar person later that week. It was the first time that she had served in a bar. When she had wanted to in the past Bernadette had stopped her, saying that she didn't want men ogling at her all the time, and in any case, they had sufficient money to last them for life. This was different. Bernadette needed a way into the camps and to find a suitable target.

Bernadette also wanted to recce areas in the big City in readiness for morale boosting blasts that prisoners in the Maze liked to hear about. The bombs previously detonated at the Baltic Exchange and at the motorway intersection had caused total and absolute havoc. What had infuriated Bernadette was the lethargic attitude by the Army Council after these bombings. She'd wanted to pursue her success with ever-bigger bombs, but had been told that while peace negotiations were taking place, though unlikely to become absolute in a long while if ever, she would just have to wait.

Bernadette had her own agenda and would go ahead and complete planned reconnaissance of three potential targets. They were all easy, the headquarters of the major banks, the huge office blocks housing all the major investment brokers, and the London Stock Exchange. Hitting these targets would cause devastation and financial chaos. Take out the equipment, specialised manpower, and this could destabilise the world economy.

She soon realised that little security was in place, it being difficult for police and security forces to enforce without totally disrupting the lives of everyone working the city's financial core. The three attacks were ultimately refused, but she was given the authority to attack the National Westminster Bank headquarters, and duly organised with the South Armagh

Brigade the supply and delivery of semtex.

The NWB operation would go ahead in late April 1993.

* * *

Kerry was finalising the movements of Bernadette, Sean, and Joe out of Bermuda. It would be imperative to get out immediately, after they had sorted out Dermott Black. There would be an enormous outcry in the aftermath, but the team would be well clear.

Their entry had been taken care of, and the operation was due to take place in March 1993.

Finally the Bermuda operation was underway. It was the weekend of Saturday the 13 March. Sean and Joe had arrived separately, as usual, with meticulous forethought to their safety and security. This was going to be much quicker than the other operations. They were getting quite slick at this type of killing.

Kerry went ahead, with Bernadette leaving the following day. They both loved Bermuda and had enjoyed their time on reconnaissance, the place seeming to revitalise love that occasionally waned in the throes of active service. There was nothing wrong within them apart from the fact that Kerry was not a hard and fast lesbian like Bernadette. Kerry, in fact, wanted a child, and this caused great resentment from Bernadette because all she ever wanted was Kerry and not for Kerry to have anyone else but her. In the past Bernadette had given in to Kerry being with a man, but Bernadette hated it and weeks would pass before inner jealousy lessened sufficiently for amicable loving.

Kerry was to be used as the bait to get Dermott Black, or as he was now known, Cornelious McAloon...

They came out of the hotel very late on the Saturday evening. She had used her charms and sexual prowess, inviting him to spend the night under the stars with her; Kerry driving him to the caves, caves both she and Bernadette knew so well. By now she knew that Joe would have broken into the ventilation entrance, both he and Sean awaiting their arrival.

Bernadette was following at a distance in case anything went wrong, and as Kerry pulled into the car park she had to endure Black's probing hands and fingers, and didn't much like it. Her blouse and bra were undone just as soon as she parked up, so were her pants. He was inside them, exploring. Kerry was flustered, wondering where the fuck the others were.

His zip undone, he was aroused, Black grabbed her hand and placed it upon himself. 'Go down, now...' he said, and then the door was opened.

Bernadette was standing there.

Sean and Joe were at the other door.

'What's going on here,' Dermott Black shouted.

He was pulled out of the car and taken to the ventilation entrance, which was about a mile away from the car park.

'Who are you, what the fuck's going on?'

Black had his hands tied behind his back. Sean was belting him with his leather belt. Once inside the entrance they threw him to the ground. He was booted in the face and body, screaming for them to stop. He was stripped, but not gagged; there was no one to hear him.

Sean and Joe dragged him down to the subterranean depths of the huge caverns, and laid into him again. They were at the bottom and by the side of the large pool that they had now twice visited. It was full, indicating the tide was in. Joe had the bag, which had the rope, the strong cord and knives. It also held the blue canister, torch attachment and the portable drill.

The rope, which was weighted, was fed over the rafter and then hauled back with the hook on the end of the bamboo cane. When they rehearsed it the first time, they realised that they needed something to ensure that they caught the rope and got it back to the side of the pool. The hook was ideal.

The strong rafters also held the hidden light that emitted an eerie glow. The dimness that still highlighted the hundreds of natural colours was the attraction that drew tourists to the underground caverns.

It was no attraction to Dermott Black.

He was scared, he was hurt, and he knew why.

What was more, he knew there was more to come. Why, he thought, why had he listened to the evil cow... the bitch. He'd only been out for a blow-job, a jump, and never got further that a quick grope.

Made to sit on the low wall surrounding the pool, he eyed their equipment. No, no way, and he threw himself backward into the pool. It was cold. He kicked free of the hand that grabbed him. Better he drown now, than later.

The water was sucking him down.

He was choking.

Then he felt the hook pull on his bonds; tied behind his back. They pulled him back, and one of the men grabbed him by his arm and he was hauled up again.

Bernadette shouted at him.

'No Black, there's no easy way out for you.'

He was tortured with their knives and other instruments for two very long and pain-filled hours. Then they hung him by his ankles over the pool. His eyes, and then his nose were submerged, and although gruesomely tortured he was still fighting to raise his head above water. He realised what they were at, the tidal water would recede and he would remain in this position until the tide returned to its higher level. He could see the side of the pool; would see the water slowly rising.

Black was now no more than a foot above the water, all the while the level in the pool dropping away. He knew he wouldn't have the strength to keep his head above the water on its return, the original high-tide mark proclaiming doom! The pain from the burning and drilling was getting worse, and to die would be better than this.

They were watching, waiting, but for what... his gurgling last watery breath come high tide?

Then it happened...

With frightening speed a barracuda leapt at him, gripping the side of his face with its fang-like teeth. Black screamed hideously and shook his head, frantically, until he dislodged it, and it fell back into the water with a strip of his face.

Smaller species of barracuda swam in schools, but larger species found in the area from Bermuda to the Gulf of Mexico were solitary and grew to about a foot in length. These species were particularly vicious, though rarely known to attack humans.

The smell of blood would attract more of the damn mini sharks, and Dermott Black knew this. He pleaded for mercy, pleaded to be killed, but his captors ignored him.

They stood for ten minutes watching him shaking off attacking barracuda...

His pain, his agony, and imminent death denied him.

Sean laughed at him, and then said, 'you had no mercy on your friends, and I'll have great delight in telling them how you died, you fucking bastard.'

Bernadette then said. 'Well, Dermott, only about another ten hours to suffer before the next attack, then a further two hours to drown, if you live that long.'

They left him, hung upside down, screaming, hollering, and begging...

* * *

They left on Sunday 14 March, all by different routes.

When the underground caves reopened on the Monday morning, the sight that confronted the young Chinese couple was horrendous. Their own screams were soon drowned by the terrifying screams of others that joined them.

The Royal Bermudan Police were called.

Then senior British police officers had to come out from London. The Bermudans did not have the ability or experience to deal with something of this nature, and there were well-recognised hallmarks of internal executioners at work matching reports of similar incidents involving Irish nationals.

* * *

Chapter Twenty Eight

Mally Cork had sat for hours with Sir Peter Wilcox and David Carver. Although a great deal of information was historic, most of it was still relevant. They had the names of active service units that had operated at that time, and their locations.

Peter had immediately despatched his MI5 team to London to check them out, where they in turn organised watchers and placed 24-hour surveillance on houses that were not previously listed.

Mally's financial problems were severe. Two brothers who operated on the fringes of the organisation had looked for potential business from discarded members such as Mally Cork. They knew what had happened, and had put the knife into him by demanding the return of £50,000. Mally Cork thought they had been acting on behalf of PIRA and an agreement had been drawn up to repay over a long period of time.

Whatever, that Saturday night Len, Tug, and Jock raided offices in Derry. They extracted all the files and Len placed a timed incendiary device. Tug broke into the huge safe and was astounded at the cash stored therein. They quickly bundled it into black sacks, and carted away the files. Two hours later the timing device activated the detonator, and the building disappeared in a massive pall of dense smoke.

Paul Garfield was tasked to unearth what the two brothers had been up to, and subsequently found that they had had a very clever enterprise going. The two racketeers had stolen over three million pounds from the people. They had used every trick in the book including protection, deception, blackmail, and downright theft. All in the name of the organisation, who had never received a penny!

David Carver said to Jack Simpson, 'we can use these two to our advantage. I want you to come up with something to enable the people to get their money back. I also want to use them in the same way as Billy Hargraves.'

Jack Simpson said, 'if we don't take immediate action they'll be straight at the so-called debtors and wringing them for cash. Today's Wednesday, I'll take Len and the lads and sort them out. We're off to Pat Maguire's at Cockermouth on Friday, so there is no time to waste.'

***

They drove straight to Derry and parked between the two properties. The brothers, Nigel and Chunky Murphy, lived next door to each other in large detached houses. Jack was in the front of the van and Len was sitting alongside him in the driver's seat. Tug and Jock were parked about two hundred yards away and both had visual and audio contact.

Jack spoke on his car telephone and said to Nigel Murphy,' go next door and bring your brother Chunky out to the white Transit outside your house.'

As Jack expected, he received a right tirade, then he said, 'I blew your office up on Saturday and your two houses will go up in five minutes unless you do as I have said.'

Jack Simpson then put his phone down.

Nigel's door was opened after a short delay and he went round to Chunky's house. They then walked slowly up the drive and along the path toward the parked vehicle.

Don's phone rang, it was Jock, 'he telephoned a Derry number and told whoever, to get the lads and be at his house in five minutes with shooters.'

'Did he,' Jack said, aware of company closing in. 'That's very interesting.'

'Who the fuck are you and why have you done this?'

'Get in the back,' Jack said.

Len then drove off followed by Tug and Jock.

They headed south passing through Strabane and after a few miles turned right onto one of the many minor roads that headed east towards the border. Shortly after, Len pulled into a wooded area well off the beaten track.

Jack Simpson climbed into the back, then said to the two brothers, 'you and your fucking gang have ripped off the people and the organisation for far too long. It is now your day of reckoning.'

'Who are you, you fat four-eyed grey-headed fucking idiot, and what's all this to do with you,' Chunky Murphy said.

'Shut your mouth and listen.'

'Before we blasted your office to bits we took every document and we emptied your safe. Very interesting reading isn't it, and over three million quid. All of it was stolen on the pretence of helping to fund PIRA and the UVF, two notorious terrorist organisations, who you have ripped off!'

Their faces were now one of total disillusionment.

Then Nigel Murphy said, 'look, we can do a deal here... We will cut you in with a fair split.'

Jack Simpson laughed, 'you have fuck all to split. None of you have anything left. We will take all your houses, and I mean all. Yes, my friends, the two houses that you both own in Miami, the two in the Costa del Sol, and your homes here in Derry. And that applies to your four friends, who you asked to head to your house with shooters...

In the meantime I will be meeting with a PIRA informant to give him the low-down on your activities. Have you heard of The Provisional Irish Republican Army's 'nutting squad' better known as internal security?'

He laughed, a blood-curdling laugh.

'For what you six have done you will all have your nuts burned off, nice and slowly. Then you will be flogged, viciously, and skinned alive.'

'For fucks sake pack it in will yeh. What do you want?' Chunky Murphy stammered. 'You have our money, you have our deeds, so there is nothing left.'

'Yes there is. I have a few jobs for a gang with your creativity, ingenuity, and obvious daring. If you comply and complete the tasks that I give you, we will see what we can let you have back. That's very fair considering everything that you have is stolen.'

'What pissing tasks?'

'You will be briefed in due course. Persuade your men, because there is no alternative? Do you both understand?'

They nodded their heads, and said. 'Yes.'

Jack then said to Len. 'Drive down to the main road, they can get out there.'

Jack Simpson finally said.

'I'll be in touch.'

The two stranded men looked forlorn and dejected as Jack and Len drove away. Worse still, a few minutes later a grinning Tug and Jock waved at them as they drove past.

* * *

Chapter Twenty Nine

Bombs exploded in the north of England, and upon hearing the news of the bombing Bernadette was absolutely furious. She telephoned her mother, who was still in charge of security and demanded to know who had authorised the bombing in Lancashire, when she, Bernadette, was in charge of all active operations on the mainland.

She was furious that two children were killed in the blast, and the movement castigated for such a malicious attack.

'Who and why,' Bernadette demanded?

Her mother was speechless; didn't know.

'These are the kind of attacks that are absolutely fruitless; nothing is gained when kids are killed. More to the point it could prejudice my operation.' Bernadette further said, 'I am not changing my plans though, London is going to be hit and hit in a big way,' and slammed the telephone down.

* * *

Kerry was quite enjoying herself working in the Greyhound in Amesbury, and had made many new friends, something she had never been able to do before.

She loved Bernadette well enough but was totally dominated by her, and Kerry was beginning to realise that she had to seek pastures new if she were ever to achieve her heart's desire; children of her own. But, if she left Bernadette she would be dead. Bernadette would not risk her own security no matter what. They had been together since they were ten. They were now thirty-three.

Kerry had been with two men since she had been in Amesbury, but that was all right in Bernadette's eyes, because she had been planted there to make contact with soldiers. The two having enjoyed themselves with her, and she knew what she wanted from men and how to get it, on top if necessary. She had a job to do, but also wanted to find her true self not what Bernadette wanted her to be.

She was now going out with a quiet Yorkshireman, who was kind and considerate. He had never been married and had always put army life first. He was a Sergeant Major working at

Larkhill. His name was Tony Hey, and had only two years to do to finish his service then he wanted to retire to southern Spain and buy a small bar. Not very ambitious or even glamorous, but she was very fond of him and to go with him to Spain could be a way out of her existing lifestyle of organising trips for PIRA butchery attacks.

Now that they had made love he was besotted with her, insanely jealous, and never out of the pub. He said he had never been loved before with the same passion and feeling that she had bestowed upon him. And, she in turn, would do almost anything for him.

He was now at the end of the bar. It was late in the evening, and she was cleaning the glasses when in walked Bernadette and Sean. Kerry ignored them at first, but the other barman was out in the cellar, stocking up for the morning. This was against their rules: No visits to the caravan, and definitely not to her workplace. They had agreed that they wouldn't break this unless it was a dire emergency, so what was up?

'Good evening,' Kerry said. 'Can I help, we're about to close.' Bernadette whispered to her, 'what time do you finish, we need to talk?'

Kerry replied, nodding toward her soldier lover. 'In about half an hour, but he's driving me home. He's staying the night with me, and he's our way in.'

Bernadette said, 'not tonight, Kerry. I've booked us in at the big hotel between here and Salisbury, so change your plans. We will wait in the car, opposite the fish and chip shop. Try not to be late. Fred is coming along in a few minutes.'

Kerry, normally very solid and unflappable, was left shocked with the abruptness of it all. She walked over to Tony. 'I will be back in a moment Tony, stay here.' She said.

Bernadette had just got to the bottom of the steps outside the pub, when Kerry spoke, 'Bernadette what the hell's going on? If you remember, I am currently on an operation right now and you are as good as compromising me.'

Bernadette said, 'that will have to wait, I want you and Fred back home. We're bringing forward the operation in London and we need you both immediately.'

Kerry said, 'that's it, is it; you want me to stop what I am doing immediately, regardless of progress on the military front? Surely you could have called me to arrange this properly.'

'No, Kerry, you must have heard about the bomb in

Warrington today. Surely you must realise that we have to react quickly ourselves.'

'This is neither the place nor the time to discuss this. We can sit down tomorrow and sort it out. Bernadette, you are over reacting, and I'm surprised at you, and you Sean, for that matter. I'll come for breakfast at the hotel at 9am in the morning. Sean you pick me up. Now, goodnight.'

She walked away from them...

Bernadette was livid.

Kerry had shown her up in front of Sean and she would not have that.

She had been awake all night still expecting Kerry to come to her. She hadn't and her mood was getting worse by the passing hours of sexual frustration. All she was thinking of was Kerry in that man's arms, her Kerry, the only person that she had ever wanted and loved. She knew that she had made a mistake. She had hated being on her own, and now this, Kerry scolding her and not coming to her.

The next morning Bernadette said to Sean and Fred, 'we'll do this one ourselves.'

Sean never argued with Bernadette, but on this occasion he felt she was wrong, 'how can we? Kerry does everything for us.'

'Sean, we will manage. Kerry is getting too big for her boots, and we'll show her that she's not the fucking bees-knees she seems to think she is.'

Sean said, 'I'll go and collect her, then we can sort things out.'

'No, Sean, we will head home. I will contact Kerry in due course.'

Sean noticed an evil glint in Bernadette's eyes; she was in one of her vilest of moods. He shut up.

Fred, his normal self, just kept quiet.

* * *

Days, then weeks went by. Still no contact from Kerry and this was becoming a battle of wills, the active service unit as a whole was suffering. Fred, after a few days went back to work at the "Queens". He wouldn't get involved, as he liked them both.

Bernadette, Sean, and Joe had been up to the safe house in Camden Town. When Kerry had been up with them the first time, she was most upset about using it for their operation. She felt that it had been used for far too long and she had already started the preliminary enquiries to obtain new premises. Bernadette had insisted that this operation would continue from the existing house and that was that.

Bernadette and Sean did not go anywhere near the house on their recce, they walked past the bank, walked around the whole area and Bernadette made her decision.

It would be the Nat West and it will be soon. What she said next absolutely stunned Sean. 'We are not going to do this one ourselves, I am going to brief Ryan Flynn's active service unit and they can do it. I want you and Fred to go to Northern Ireland and visit our friends in South Armagh. They have been preparing the bomb and are arranging for its delivery to the farm at Heathgate Mews. Inform them I require it seven days earlier. I want it there for the morning of Friday, the 23 April. Flynn can move the bomb into position, with the timer set for noon when the building will be at its busiest.

I want you and Fred to bring the detonator and timing device back and deliver it to Flynn at the safe house.' Sean said, 'Bernadette, we have never done this before; we will all be at risk. If any of Flynn's unit is picked up they will blabber as sure as eggs are eggs.'

'No we won't be at risk, just do as I have told you.'

Sean and Fred left the next day for Northern Ireland, travelling together by hired car. That was something that Kerry had never allowed.

Sean asked Fred, 'what do you want to do over the weekend?'

They were in the docks at Belfast and it was Saturday 17 April at about 11am, when Fred said, 'let's get the business over with and stash the goods in the car, that way we can head back whenever we want.'

'Sounds good to me Fred.'

The Saturday they spent in Armagh both ending up 'legless'. On Sunday afternoon they headed for Belfast where they topped-up from the night before. They decided that they would stay the night in Belfast. Fred wanted to go to the Social Club in Andersonstown, to play bingo and this they did.

It was getting late and the club was starting to empty when Sean in a drunken state said, 'I have spotted an old tart of ours Fred. Fancy a thrashing session, old boy?'

They both grinned at each other...

* * *

Chapter Thirty

The MI5 team had been observing Pat Maguire for over a month and he had made no move. He had spent virtually the whole of his time with his family. He received no telephone calls, and made none. His mail was checked daily, nothing to indicate his PIRA lifestyle. The Lancashire bombs had exploded and he was still in his house. It was as if he had done a runner himself from the organisation!

* * *

Jack Simpson was building a dossier on all known active members. He now had a working rapport with two of the source handlers and Billy Hargraves was proving to be an excellent investment in his new role.

Tug, Jock, and Benny Benford kept him on his toes and he was causing the disruption that Jack Simpson wanted.

Len had spent a day teaching him the art of Molotov cocktails. In the past month Benny Benford's skills' were developing nicely. He was using Billy Hargraves to excellent use. If a tout knew nothing of the organisation or had no access to relevant information, then he should be binned or if possible put to use another way. That was Jack Simpson's methods. If the RUC tried that there would be hell to pay.

One of the scourges on the Catholic estates was the men and women who reported the every day activities on the estate. The lives of the people for years were not their own and they lived in fear and trepidation. The mistrust stemmed from the watchers, sometimes known as 'dickers'.

Many times in the past these people reported maliciously just to get even on past grudges and often resulted in both men and women being tarred and feathered, purely because of spite. These people were well known and the local population despised them. In general, with the vast improvement in the Catholics quality of life, all they now wanted was an end to all violence.

Billy Hargraves was spending time firebombing the people who had provided the information to PIRA for years. PIRA did not have the resources to protect them now. Billy was being paid £100 for every one he put out of a home. Jack Simpson knew these people would not be missed within the community. What he was aiming for was a group of useless touts to take over this role. He knew he had many available.

In the first month Billy Hargraves had destroyed fifteen homes belonging to these watchers, dickers, and creeps that infested the Catholic estates. When a house went up, the locals were out cheering and some were known to hinder the firemen racing to the scene.

It was spreading out from the Ballymurphy, Andersonstown, and Turf Lodge areas in West Belfast to Derry and other strong Republican areas, throughout the Province. Jack Simpson was creating havoc and the PIRA command did not know where the attacks had started from, or who was doing them.

Jack Simpson was talking with David Carver and agreement was given for Jack to break in to Pat Maguire's house in Belfast.

There was already a team of observers in a house opposite and they knew that no one had visited the property since Pat Maguire had left. They were informed that the break in would take place the following Saturday at about midnight.

The Tuesday before the break in Jack Simpson had met Mary Hardwick for the third time. She had been providing useful background information for Jack to build on. She had been a tout with Ray Standwick and Jack had handled her since realising that Standwick was ineffective. This time was different; she had concrete information that a bomb was about to be detonated.

She didn't have the location of the target, but she knew the active service unit. The commander was Mick Coombe. He was on the active list and was a specialist bomb maker. Many of the larger bombs, the remote controlled devices were Mick Coombe's work.

This was good information and needed to be acted on immediately. He was being watched.

On the Wednesday morning the watchers reported that he was at that moment working in his workshop at the bottom of his garden. David Carver decided to act. David, Len, Tug, and Jock would call on him. They had all been pressing him for action, even if it was just throwing the odd petrol bomb, but David would have none of it. Now was the time.

Early that night, they visited him. They had been informed

that he was still in his workshop. They were ready. Tug inserted the picking tool into the lock and silently brought the barrels into line, then eased his weight slightly on the door as he moved the lock. He saw Mick Coombe at the far end of the building. He was reaching up, taking something off a cabinet, which was mounted on the far wall. Tug was in, and moved to the right, out of the terrorists' line of sight. David Carver was now watching, the door left open with the tiniest of gaps.

In seconds, the sleeper was applied and Mick Coombe was on the deck. They were all in the building. This was a small bomb factory; there were detonators, timing devices, batteries of all shapes and sizes. There were masses of equipment that made up the improvised explosive devices that the Provo's were renowned for. Jock had noticed the uncovered trap door and slithered through like a fast departing snake.

'Well, well, what do we have here then, Mickey boy,' David Carver said, with a rough Belfast accent.

Mick Coombe's clenched fist had already been inserted in the large vice on the bench. Len was busy at the bench opposite where Mick Coombe was secured. The building itself was made of builder's bricks, similar to breezeblocks. There were two double glazed windows, which were covered. There was two roof lights and plenty of desk mounted lights, sufficient for this type of covert work.

'Who the fuck are you lot,' Mick asked.

'We're friends of yours Mick. Now how about telling me what you are doing?'

'Fuck off.'

'That's no way to talk to friends, now is it Mickey.'

'Who the fuck are you?'

'We're from the Real IRA, Mickey, and we need some help and you are going to help us, aren't you,' David Carver said, as he tightened the vice.

Mick Coombe squealed, 'what do you fucking want?'

'The use of you and your group for two hours and you will be well paid. Like to the tune of two hundred grand.'

'Is Brendan Riley and Alan Flaherty still with you, and what about Billy Sullivan? You will need yourself and at least four to do the job, who's the four going to be?'

'What is the job and who told you about my men?'

'Pat Maguire said you were the man, probably the only one with the capability of doing what we want. He sends his regards by the way.'

'Maguire? Don't give me this shit, he fucked off with PIRA funds. He's a dead man.'

'Pat Maguire recommended you in January, when did he leave?'

'Some time in February, I think.'

'Well, when you help me, I will take you to his mainland address. That, Mickey, will please your masters, will it not?'

Mick Coombe would do anything to get his hands on the fucking traitor who'd tortured one of his men, Johnny McGurk, to death.

Anything to get him, 'what do you want?'

'I want a meeting here in two hours. I need four men and you.'

There was a telephone at the end of the building, and on the wall a set of numbers, all Belfast numbers.

'Whose numbers are these Mickey?'

'Get my hand out of this fucking thing and I'll contact them.'

'You didn't answer me. Whose numbers are these?'

'My men,' yelled Mick, in agony. 'Now, will you release me?'

'I don't trust you, Coombe. Get your men on the move; I want them to arrive here together. I want them here for a meeting to discuss my requirements. I will give you fifty thousand up front and the rest when you deliver, and that will include Pat Maguire's address.'

'Do you agree?'

'Show me the fifty thousand,' Mick Coombe said.

'No, but I will compromise and tell you where Pat Maguire is living. He is with his wife Dorothy living near Cockermouth in Cumbria.'

'How many children has he got?'

David Carver grinned, 'all three are taken by Dorothy in her red BMW to school every morning. Now does that confirm my credibility, dickhead?'

'Give me the telephone.'

Mick Coombe contacted the men.

He was enthusiastic. 'Two jobs,' he said. 'One for us with great reward, and I have found Pat Maguire for the organisation.' He then turned to David. 'As you heard, Brendan Riley, Alan Flaherty, Ginger Smith and Billy Sullivan will all be here at 2245 hours.'

Mick Coombe then informed David Carver that Billy Sullivan

had just taken charge of his own active service unit. David remarked. 'Has he now, that's very interesting!'

'Now will you fucking well release this poxy vice,' snarled Mick.

David Carver walked up to him, stared him in the face and said, 'tell me Mickey, what do you know about the active service unit that took part in the same ambush that Pat Maguire was involved in, two years ago?'

'What ambush, what the fuck you on about now?'

Mick thought a moment or two, then said, 'you're mixed up. That was four years ago. He seized my man, Johnny McGurk and another bloke called Simon Haig. Sam McGurk was the twin brother of my man, Johnny McGurk. He knew that Fred Short was a "nutting squad", member, and thought that he had tortured his brother. Sam had burnt the privates off both Fred and Simon. Fred survived, but Simon died. Fred has never worked for Pat Maguire. He may have been with the other "nutting squad", the one that you're on about.'

This rang a bell with David. Three men had been active in the ambush of Jeremy and Heather, but only two had raped her. Which would answer that part of the puzzle, Fred being incapacitated. David felt that he now knew the first name of one of the active service unit members. Fred Short.

'Tell me all you know about Fred Short.'

'No, you tell me who you are. I've spoken enough, and where is my fifty thousand. Fucking well let me go, now.' Len walked over to him, carrying a box and tightened the vice. There was a loud cracking sound, and Mick Coombe screamed.

'You bastard,' he spluttered, trying to regain breath. 'Why did you do that? You've broken my fucking fingers?'

Len spoke for the first time, 'well, that's sad Mickey because you won't be on any raid now, will you?'

'What the fucking hell's going on here, he's bloody English.'

'Mickey, we all are,' said Len.

'Now just have a look in my little box of tricks that I have made up especially for you. Just look at that Mickey, aren't I clever. An improvised explosive device, or IED, as you would know it by, and made in five minutes.'

'What are you doing? That's dangerous you fucking idiot.'

Len held it against his balls, and grinned.

'Well you can see that with the tiny amount of explosives I have used it will not cause too much harm, will it? Let's just close the box shall we Mickey.' Len secured it with its spring-loaded catch. 'Now, as you know Mickey, all I need to do, is move the catch over and once the lid opens you lose your balls and dick, just the same as your friends did.'

Len then put the box down on the bench, and released the vice and Mick Coombe immediately held his broken fingers with his other hand. Len moved fast and within seconds Mick Coombe's good hand was twisted behind his back and placed into the vice. The quick release spring was activated, forced back with enormous pressure, and the jaws of the vice slammed onto his fingers breaking them all.

'Oh, sorry about that Mickey!' Len said.

He was on his knees, crying aloud, 'please let me go,' whilst sniffling.

'No, you were asked a question, now answer it.'

'I forgot what was asked.'

David Carver spoke. 'Tell me what you know of Fred Short, now, or your balls will go in the vice.'

'Please let my hand out, please, I can hardly breathe with the pain.'

'Tell me about Fred?'

Len turned away and went back to work.

Jock had returned with a large brief case, and at the door were two boxes of what looked like books. He was now speaking with Len

'I am waiting,' said David.

'He's been gone…a long time now,' replied Mick.

'Where has he gone?'

I don't fucking know. His wife disappeared, then he did.'

David Carver went to turn the vice handle again.

'No, no sometimes he is back for a few days, and then he disappears again. He's doing courier work.'

'Don't fuck with me Mick Coombe, both you and I know that a man does not work in the famed "nutting squad" and then end up as a courier.'

David increased the pressure on the vice and they all heard the fingers breaking further.

Mick screamed. 'I don't know, for god's sake I don't know.'

Len cautioned David, 'watch the time.'

Then Len went outside.

Because his hand was also twisted Mick Coombe was bent nearly double in awful pain. David Carver reached for the box and placed it well in front of Mick Coombe. He then forced his right leg forward and his foot was then placed onto the box. He was at full stretch, his weight forward and balancing on the box.

Len brought in a can of petrol, poured some over Mick, and then emptied the rest on the floor. 'The incendiary will only blow your foot off, but the flames will eat you up. All you have to do Mickey is to keep your foot on the box for the next hour, and good luck, you'll need it.' Len smiled, as he released the spring on the box.

'No, you know I cannot stay in this position, please.'

They picked up the boxes that Jock had acquired and then headed to their car.

* * *

Cramp had set in dreadfully to Mick Coombe when the four arrived. He shouted at them. Stop where you are. He then said to Brendan Riley, 'come forward and pick up this fucking box, and don't release the lid.'

He did this.

They were all in near panic as they looked at the box.

'Put the spring catch back in place and secure the lid.'

That was done.

'Come in, come in, and shut the fucking door.'

What they didn't know was that Len had tricked them. When the catch was replaced it triggered a double action timer and in ten seconds a bomb would detonate.

'Now get me out of this fucking vice.' He screamed.

And before they could do that, the box had exploded and the five of them were engulfed in flames, screaming trying to get out. Then there was a secondary explosion, flames instantly gushing out through the smashed windows and doors, swamping the men in the middle.

The five of them were burnt beyond recognition.

The papers the next day announced a PIRA own goal, with five of its members dead, blown up by their own hand. But even more important, these bombers were about to place a bomb with the normal devastation and destruction.

Now they were gone...thanks to a tout...and her information!

* * *

Chapter Thirty One

Mary O'Connor was an experienced PIRA member. Her allegiance to the organisation was for what she could get out of it. She had met Sean for the first time ten years ago, when he was seventeen and she only fifteen.

She'd liked the look of him.

Her friends said that he was the best looking guy around, but that every one was frightened of him. He was rough and ready, and strong and able. She liked his well-muscled, wiry frame, and had flaunted herself at him. Quick to notice he'd then approached her and they'd walked from the Catholic Club to his flat. She'd thought to herself that she'd got him, her, and only fifteen at that.

He'd had his arm around her, and had said, at the entrance to the flat, 'are you sure you want to be here.'

'Yes,' she'd murmured. 'Do you want me here?'

'Only if you do what I want?'

'And what do you want,' she'd said.

'You're a grown up girl, and I reckon you know what us men want.'

He was drunk and she little better.

'Take off your clothes,' he'd said, once they'd stepped inside the flat.

'Do you want a shag?' She naively said.

'When I'm ready, now get naked.'

She'd stood in front of him, unsure, it was different with him. She had always been spoken to nicely, and had felt scared, but every other girl had bragged about being with him. Well, she'd said yes to him, and there was no going back. Anyway she'd felt randy.

He'd sat himself on the settee; she stood in front of him. She'd removed her top, no bra. He'd grinned. Then he'd snapped at her, 'what small tits, now let's see the rest.' She'd felt very uncomfortable, and had said, 'I think I had better go home.'

'Not now, you're not. You had that choice outside. You are staying and will do what I want. Now get those pants off.'

She'd unbuttoned the top of her slacks, dropped the zip, and slid her trousers down.

She was scared, nothing but panties on...and he was letching, staring grotesquely at her body...

'Don't you want to take them off?' he'd asked. 'Shy eh?'

'I'm scared.'

'What of,' he'd said, grinning. 'Take them off.' She'd taken them off, and he'd stared at her mound.

'Very bushy, very nice... Now turn round.'

She had.

Nice bum, he'd said.

Then he'd stood up, massive against her, put his arms around her. Had gripped her right breast between his thumb and forefinger and squeezed, hard. Her small rounded breasts were firm back then and he'd hurt her. With the other hand, his fingers, probing, between her legs, had hurt too, deep inside her. Then he'd let go, and turned her around. Had pulled her down on to her knees.

'Now unzip me, nice and slowly.'

He was aroused.

She was more scared than ever.

But Sean stood there, telling, demanding?

She'd done as she was told.

'Now release the button and pull them down.'

She had done that, too.

He'd been much bigger than the boys she had been with before, yet he only seventeen at that time.

'Take it in,' he'd said.

'Where! In my mouth?'

'No, up your fucking nose, you stupid tart... Of course, where else do you think I want my prick?'

She had done that sort of thing with boys, and it had been fun, because they had also caressed her.

He'd scared her, his tone not nice, and she had known that she was being threatened.

She had done what she was told to do, and he hadn't let her stop, and he'd taken her several times that evening.'

She had met him many more times after that, but as time passed she had unwillingly abided to his demands, and claimed that he'd raped her, and had violated her in despicable ways, abusing her for his own gratification.

She had ended up hating him, and one day, her day would

come for revenge...

When Jack Simpson met Mary O'Connor for the first time, he felt that all she wanted was to see the downfall of Sean Hegatty. She had been treated roughly, but no rougher than some, and despite accusations of sexual depravity by Sean Hegatty, she had gone back for more.

Jack knew some women liked it rough and, those sort of women usually ended up with bastards or ended up dead in a back alley.

Jack Simpson said to Mary O'Connor, 'Mary all good things must come to an end. Unless you have something really concrete for me about Sean or any other member, then your financial gravy train is finished.'

Mary hadn't expected this, besides she now relied on this money. 'Who else do you know that may be involved?'

'I have told you all I know, I just can't think of anything else.'

'When we last spoke I asked if you knew any friends or relations of Sean. You hesitated as if you knew someone. Who is that person?'

Again she hesitated.

'There are some things that you cannot ever talk about and it was only a sexual thing, anyway.'

'What sexual thing? You have already gone through Sean Hegatty's sexual demands and perversions. Most of which were quite sexually healthy, for modern couples. So what is it that you can't or won't talk about?'

She breathed deeply. 'Well, if you insist, it happened the last time that we met. He brought someone else along. He was an older man, rough looking. I immediately said, no way.'

She paused.

'Well, tell me what happened, and more importantly, who was the other man?'

'That was the amazing thing. Nothing happened. That's why I have never mentioned him.'

'Mary you are confusing me. You say, "some things you cannot talk about and it was only a sexual thing, but nothing happened". Am I missing out on something here.'

'When I said, "no way", to Sean, I was saying that I was not going to have sex with his friend. I thought Sean had brought him along for a three in a bed romp and I am not into that.'

'And he hadn't?' Jack queried.

'No, not really, Sean wanted sex and took what he wanted. His friend just sat and watched. I thought then that he was one of those perverts that liked to watch and play with himself. He wasn't, and didn't.'

'So, what happened when Sean finished?'

'Sean just said, come on Fred, let's go.'

'That's the last time that I saw either of them...'

Jack Simpson was delighted, but didn't show it. He said, 'Mary, that's good information, and you are certain that you have not seen or heard of either since then?'

'Yes,' she replied.

'Find out for me, I want to know where both are, and you will be paid very well.'

'How much will you pay me?'

'Are you sure you don't know where they are now, Mary? Do not, I warn you, mess me around?'

'I want to know how much you will pay me for this information?'

'Mary, I cannot give you a figure right now, but it will be substantial, especially if you find out quickly. The longer I have to wait, the less the value of this kind of information.

You have my contact number, I will be waiting.'

* * *

Chapter Thirty Two

Chief Superintendent Ian Walsh was with his team at Lisburn. A mass of information was coming in daily, and Jack Simpson had done incredibly well. He was extracting information at an unbelievable pace.

The documents seized at Mick Coombe's home were still being studied. Initial discovery that he had been ripping off the Provisional Irish Republican Army for a long time, came as no surprise. More importantly, some of the documents brought to light people in the organisation who were previously unknown to the investigating team.

Pat Maguire's home was the next scheduled raid, and would happen within the next few hours.

* * *

Once everything had been collated Jack Simpson spoke with David Carver. 'I would like to break in and search for anything that might further incriminate him to illegal activities against the PIRA. If I were successful in finding something really positive, combined with what we already have, I will turn him. I would confront him over there, tackling him on our patch will be safer for us all… He must be up to something.'

David said, 'when you're ready to go, Don, when you're ready…'

* * *

The MI5 team, with help from both the local force and Carlisle, had been watching Pat Maguire's house round the clock for weeks. Every Friday they went out as a family, sometimes not returning until mid-day on the Saturday. Some of the police watchers were beginning to wonder what the surveillance was all about. The cost against their budget was out of proportion, the operation very expensive, and they seemed to be observing a very happy family.

That Friday night, long after the family had left with overnight bags, the Lynx had landed. Three men had jumped out very swiftly, as the helicopter hovered a few feet above ground. The fourth man hesitated, then at last jumped and landed in a heap at the feet of the others.

'Fucking hell,' he moaned. 'I thought you lot were going to catch me?'

The helicopter climbed and moved off and the men tried to control their laughter at the expense of Jack Simpson, as they headed towards the rear of the property.

Tug broke in within seconds and they searched each room thoroughly. They knew what they were looking for and the black sacks were filling up very quickly. The secure safe posed problems, as Tug and Jock tried for nearly two hours to open it.

They had two alternatives: place a small device and blow the mechanism or, blast the safe from its mounting brackets. Neither was a good option, as it would leave clear evidence of a break in.

Len had to make a decision. 'One more thorough hunt for the numbers, let's say 10 minutes, and failing finding them we'll blow the fucking lock. He left Jock with his task, while he and Jack continued searching the premises.

After a few minutes, they all heard the shout.

'Got it,' yelled Jock, as he opened the safe. 'Fucking hell,' he shouted. 'It's crammed with cash, and more than at Derry. Loads of documents...

Bloody hell, come and see this lot.'

Len was aghast, the cash mountain took his breath away. He also knew that the documents would be just as valuable.

'Tug, call up Tom, and tell him to drop in behind the gate. Let's get this lot stashed into sacks and moved out to the back door. Tug and Jock can then move them from there into the Lynx. Don, we will check that everything is back in place...

Let's go chaps, we'll see you two at the chopper.'

* * *

On there return to base Chief Superintendent Ian Walsh joined in and assisted with the collation and sifting of the material.

Along with the volume of incoming information, Ian Walsh had decided to increase his team by another two. They were now totally inundated with the incoming info from Cockermouth and it had to be dealt with immediately.

Jack Simpson had to get straight back across to confront Pat Maguire, and Ian Walsh decided that the information from Mick Coombe would have to be set aside whilst they all concentrated on Pat Maguire.

They worked through the night and by 1000 hours on the Saturday, Jack Simpson decided that he had enough information to approach Pat Maguire and either shop him or turn him.

David Carver had been monitoring the MI5 team at Cockermouth and Pat Maguire and his family had not returned. What David didn't want to do was to send his specialist team to Cockermouth and wait for hours.

Tom Galloway, Tug, and Jock had been able to get some sleep but Jack Simpson had been up throughout the night, and finally decided that rest was important. He therefore instructed the MI5 team to inform him immediately Pat Maguire's car appeared.

David Carver also instructed the MI5 team to organise local uniformed assistance. He advised that two cars be brought into the area as soon as a sighting was confirmed. What they didn't want was for Pat Maguire to detect a raid had taken place and be off like a scared rabbit.

The surveillance team were still watching and waiting; it was 5pm on the Saturday afternoon. Pat Maguire had never been this late before, and David Carver decided to do an all airports and ports check for the car.

It was found at Manchester Airport. A check back through internal flights showed that he had flown to Heathrow on a return ticket, with his family. He had not returned on the flight he was booked on, so where the fuck was he?

* * *

Chapter Thirty Three

Ian Walsh was called to the telephone. A Chief Superintendent Alan Kirkby wanted to speak with him.

'I understand that you are the senior police officer working on "Operation Combating Evil"?' Said Alan.

'Yes indeed Alan, how can I help?'

'I am not sure that you can, mainly because I have no idea of your terms of reference, but I have information that may be of interest to you. You may of course be able to help me with information that I require....

I recently returned from Bermuda, where, I was assigned to investigate the murder of an American Irishman working on the Island. His name was Cornelious McAloon, at least that was what he called himself there. His real name was Dermott Black...

I got this information from his former wife. She informed me that he was a former PIRA member, turned informer. They had lived together in Chicago, until they separated. I believe he was on the run and his murderers were PIRA, who I know have stepped up their attacks on former touts...'

Alan Kirkby cleared his throat. 'Sorry about that.' And he continued.

'The main problem in the Bermuda case is the manner of his death. Black had been horrifically tortured and an enormous amount of effort had gone into the planning of the attack. I estimate that at least four people must have been involved, probably more. I have checked with Interpol and found two similar incidents in Australia and New Zealand...'

Ian Walsh was dumbfounded, this was a massive breakthrough, and interrupted...

'Alan let me stop you there. I need you urgently over here with all your information. Have you got details from Interpol about the other incidents?'

'Yes, I have.'

'Brilliant Alan, thank you so much for contacting me...when can you leave?'

'I could leave in the morning, but I am unsure of flights as it is Sunday. I will need to get home and collect some overnight gear, then try and get a flight some time tomorrow.'

'Do you live near an airfield or military barracks?'

'Yes, about three miles from Chatham, why?'

'Alan, this is vital information, and I intend to send a Gazelle helicopter to collect you. It is now 1600 hours. I will have the chopper at the barracks for 2300 hours. Can you make it for then?'

'Christ this must be important... I'll be there.'

* * *

Ian Walsh immediately contacted David Carver and briefed him on his talk with Alan Kirkby. David sent for Tom Galloway and passed instructions on to him for the pick up of Kirkby. He then contacted the duty officer at Chatham informing him of the arrival of Chief Superintendent Alan Kirkby and that a Gazelle would be landing to collect him at 2300 hours.

David then sat thinking hard about this new turn of events. Cornelious McAloon, that name rang a bell. He sent for Jack Simpson who was having his first day off since being back out in the Province. When David passed the new information on to Jack he grinned.

Jack Simpson said, 'You must remember Dermott Black, David?'

David was trying hard; like Cornelious McAloon, both names rang bells but he couldn't quite place either. 'Got him, at last,' he said, with a smile. 'How could I forget Dermott Black, Don! He was your tout when you briefed us on our very first mission in the Province. Cor blimey, that takes us back to 1975.'

Jack simply nodded his head.

It was a gesture of true respect and enormous admiration each held for the other. Jack had placed his own life in danger so many, many times, to draw together, good sound intelligence, for others to act upon...

David's thoughts meandered: yes, others had been involved in the operations, thoroughly briefed in all respects and fully armed. Jack had met with some of the most degenerate and depraved thugs imaginable; vicious animals that had tortured, murdered, and maimed their way through life. He, and men like him, were first in the front line of anti terrorism, one tiny slip, or error of judgement, and they were dead.

Yet, Don, armed only with a 9mm pistol, sometimes not even armed, had displayed courage beyond belief. Every time that he'd recruited a new tout, the first ever meeting must have been terrifying, to say the least, he never ever knew if he was walking straight into an ambush. Then it was all guile and wits.

David Carver then said, 'I have met your former tout in his alias, Cornelious McAloon.'

It was Jack Simpson's turn to think, then inquired. 'Where at, David?'

'In the bloody hotel where he worked.'

'Think hard David. When did you first meet him?'

Resting his brow in hand, David said, 'it was after the New Years Eve Ball at the Southampton Princess Hotel, maybe a day or two after. He was a chef. I thought I'd recognised him and said so but he said that he had spent his whole life in Chicago, so I left it at that.'

'You may have got him mixed up with his brother, they looked alike. Remember Seamus Black? He attacked and blew up the UDR patrol in Fermanagh, and was also responsible for the deaths of 10 RUC officers.'

'Dermott Black shopped his brother?'

'That's right David.'

'I know, I paid him, and Seamus is probably still in the Maze.' Jack grinned. 'When I left the Province between tours he refused to work with any other handler, and became an active bomber again, until I returned. This was ideal for him because he was never under suspicion and he was always well placed with ready information from his brother. When I retired, Dermott Black did a runner. It was a stupid move for him, because he was never thought to be a tout. He could have simply fired off a few more rounds or detonated a couple of IED's and then walked away. He didn't, and they found him.'

Jack had David thinking hard, if silent.

'If I remember David, it was your lads that cornered Seamus with his terrorist chums in about 1984. He got life about twenty times over. David, cast your mind back to your hotel in Bermuda. Did you meet any other people of interest? Did you see anything that might not have bothered you at the time, but now, with this new revelation, might just seem relevant?'

'Not really Don... I was totally switched off. I had just retired and Angela and myself were enjoying ourselves.'

Jack Simpson looked at him, 'yes David, and you're still smiling.'

'Sorry Don, she really brought me out of my hell. I'll telephone her tonight, see if she remembers anything.'

'David, if she does, I would like to speak with her, please leave that side to me?'

'Of course, Don, and thanks.'

After their preamble talk, that night David asked Angela to speak with Jack Simpson and to answer any questions that he might have about their trip to Bermuda.

'On what subject,' she teased.

Not answering, he laughed and handed the telephone to Don.

'Angela, how are you? Keeping busy?'

'Yes Don, but I'll be delighted when this is all over. What is it that you wish to know? David said that you needed to speak with me.'

'I do, Angela. David told me about an Irish American that you met at the hotel on your holiday in Bermuda. I would like to hear your take on him, if you can remember the man. Just take your time, and think about it.

'I really don't need to Don, as I never actually met him. I remember David as being deep in thought and I'd asked him what he was thinking about? As I remember, he remarked that he thought he knew the chef, but it turned out that he didn't.'

'Can you remember the name of the chef?'

'Yes, because we laughed about it. Poor fellow, it was Cornelious McAloon.'

'Did David mention his name in any other context, for example to another person, perhaps another couple.'

'No, we didn't involve ourselves with anyone else as we were enjoying our own company.'

'Think Angela, when you were in your hotel, who did you talk with, anyone in a restaurant. Anyone that you may have noticed watching this McAloon chap? Who did you see, maybe more than once? Think very hard Angela, this is vital.'

'I am sorry Don, I have to admit, I was really only aware of David. Might sound childish, or even romantic, but I am sorry, I don't think that I can help you.'

'Angela just promise me this, keep on thinking about your trip, there might just be something that may mean nothing to you now, but keep turning the trip over in your mind. If you think about anything please telephone me, I will hand you back to David. Bye for now.'

Jack Simpson thought about the conversation, knew there had to be more to the trip than David, in her minds eye. Damn it, women were usually far more observant and inquisitive; women's fashion details, suave men, and snipits of gossip, even if obtained by covert eavesdropping...

* * *

Tom Galloway flew into the base at about 0230 hours. Sir Peter Wilcox, David Carver, Jack Simpson, and Ian Walsh, met Alan Kirkby and they thanked him for his thoughtfulness in contacting them.

Over a cup of tea they went over the actual killing in the cave. Alan Kirkby then gave a short but comprehensive account of his investigation. The full details pointed to a nutting type operation.

David Carver thought, as others did, that it might be one and the same who had ambushed Jeremy and Heather.

Ian Walsh said to everyone, 'I have put out a trawl to all agencies world wide, for immediate reports on any unusual deaths over the past two or three years. In particular, any that might indicate attacks on any Irish Citizens. There might just be more that we haven't heard of.'

David Carver liked Alan Kirkby. He was a good officer of strong determination and desperately keen to find the killers of Dermott Black. The Bermudans had never had this type of crime and were obviously eager to allay the fears of their tiny population that a killer was not on the loose.

David said, 'we will retire now and I would like a full brief by Alan at 1100 hours. Don, can you make sure that Len, Tug, Jock, and Tom are here? Also, both RUC and MI5 teams. I think it will be a good time for us to have an update on all matters.'

Alan Kirkby said, 'what on earth is this all about?'

Peter Wilcox answered. 'Alan it may be, that we will need you on the team. If we can meet after an early breakfast I will summarise the current operation. There will be a requirement for you to sign an additional copy of the Official Secrets Act. You will also need to let me know who I need to contact for you to remain with us until the end of this operation or until your input is at an end.

They retired at 0400 hours.

Ian Walsh was woken at 0600 hours by one of the night watchman. 'There's an urgent call from CIA Headquarters.'

Ian slipped on his shorts and slacks, and a jumper and raced through to the operations room. He talked for nearly an hour then thanked Bill Kent. He would get back in touch with him and looked forward to the information to be faxed, direct.

Ian went back to his room, showered and dressed. He then roused David Carver and briefed him of the new developments.

* * *

During breakfast Jack Simpson had a telephone call from Angela. 'Don,' she said, 'I am not sure whether this is relevant or not, but we did meet with an Irish couple. That is, two young ladies. I remember one was Sharon, the taller of the two. I met them the day before David did. Well, bumped into them. The next day they joined us by the poolside and we had drinks.

David had been reading one of his foreign books, I think it was Chinese, and then he went for a dip. Sharon remarked that David must be extraordinarily clever to read a book like that, and I remember agreeing with her and thought at the time here was a man of enormous intelligence, with me, a simple minded Geordie.'

Jack laughed and then scolded her saying, 'stop undermining yourself.'

She paused gathering her thoughts and realising that this must be quite critical to what has been going on.

'When David returned, one of them said that they had been working in Spain for twelve years, I think. So clever clogs Carver spoke in Spanish to them and neither could understand what he'd said. David, embarrassed, had apologised. We then met them by chance, once more, at underground caves on the Island. We had arranged to meet that night but they didn't turn up. And for now Don, that's your lot, because I cannot remember anything else. David might be able to help a bit more, if you jog his memory with what I've told you.'

'Angela that is brilliant, and very helpful, we have a meeting now, so I must go. Thanks again.'

* * *

The fax came in from Bill Kent, and Ian Walsh had become engrossed. Even though it was Sunday, Sir Peter Wilcox was on the phone to the foreign office, which in turn was an open line to the Ambassador.

David Carver was studying everything relevant to present and past happenings, as was Jack Simpson. The atmosphere was tense, everyone on a knife-edge.

Jack spoke to David, outlining his conversation with Angela, David then responded. 'Yes Don, I remember them now, a tall thin girl and a smaller but quite petite one. Helen I think, and the other Sharon. Both spoke with a Dublin accent, but I fail to see any connection or anything relevant to our operation. The only curious point, being that they said that they had worked in Spain for what, twelve or thirteen years, yet couldn't reply to the simplest of questions in Spanish, in fact, hadn't grasped a word I uttered.'

'That's right David, and they were also at the underground caves, where the murder took place, and why did they not turn up to have drinks with you as arranged? Don't forget David, we know for certain that the active service unit we are looking for, has at least one dark haired female member, four points, all of which tell my inquisitive mind that we need to follow up on these two women.'

David poised, rubbing his chin, and grasping Don's reasoning...

'Don, you have it! You once again have it!'

'Yes David, "great minds think alike", we both now know how and when the recce took place for the Dermott Black operation!

* * *

David Carver spoke with Peter for about thirty minutes prior to the briefing. Their strategy was changing with the tide of events.

Decisions were needed.

Sir Peter Wilcox gave a very quick brief to Alan Kirkby and after the brief Alan thanked him and said, 'whatever you want of me, whatever I can do will be a pleasure. My only requirement will be to get home, grab some clothes and to leave the necessary instructions at work.' Alan then offered his hand, 'Sir Peter, this operation will be a success, I can see that by the quality of men around me, and I'm thrilled to be joining the team.'

'You are most welcome, Alan. I'll introduce you to the full team in a short while, and oh, by the way, no one here stands on ceremony, rank or privilege, and my name at all times, is Peter.'

They entered the briefing room, which was full, and the change from a whispering buzz to immediate silence, amplified the growing tension. Sir Peter Wilcox addressed the assembled, 'before David starts I would like to introduce three new members to our team.'

'Chief Superintendent Alan Kirkby is a senior member of the Met, and has just returned from Bermuda, where he has been investigating the horrific murder of what now appears to be a former PIRA tout. I would also like to introduce Chief Inspectors Bob Gordon a specialist collator, and Peter Williams, the Head of RUC Computer Studies and Strategies. As with the rest of the MI5 team, they are here on the personal recommendation of Chief Superintendent Ian Walsh...

Gentlemen, you are very welcome to our team, and without further ado, David will now give a much shorter brief than was expected, but I am sure he will tell you why.'

David Carver started by thanking everyone for the long hours of work that had already been contributed; the immense amount of digging and delving for information, the cold nights out in the field for Peter's team, watching, following, always concentrating in the dangerous twilight world of undercover operatives. He praised his lads, Len, Tug and Jock, who had worked with him for nearly thirty years, still as ever, dedicated, loyal, and always there, in at the deep end. And of course, not forgetting the huge input from our taxi driver,' he added, a broad grin. 'Tom Galloway, having amassed a year's flying time over the past three months.'

The odd clap and comment reverberated around the room, then David continued:

'I can't help but single the next man out for special praise. I know of no one else who has his uncanny ability, by fair means or foul, to ferret out the necessary information... Jack Simpson...

There was much shuffling of feet and good humoured comments, like from Jock, 'fat bastard...' but then silence soon descended.

'Gentlemen, it seems an eternity ago when we met up at Ashford. It was my intention to go through everything that has been achieved today by your efforts. However, with the information that Alan Kirkby has brought, the result of which prompted Ian to trawl other agencies worldwide, and has subsequently brought in further dramatic information. This has now limited us with time, or lack of it.

Alan Kirkby was called in to investigate a particularly horrific murder on the Island of Bermuda. The victim as Alan discovered, was Dermott Black, a former terrorist, turned informant. During the 70's and early 80's Black was actually handled by our very own, Jack Simpson. If I am right, I believe that Jack actually recruited him.'

Jack simply nodded at David.

'During the course of his investigations, Alan discovered two more deaths very similar to that of Dermott Black. One occurred in Australia and the other in New Zealand. The close timing of these murders gives rise to the belief that it is the same PIRA squad that committed the attacks...

When Ian Walsh first spoke with Alan Kirkby and was given this information he activated a channel of enquiry that alerted every major investigation agency worldwide...

At 0600 hours this morning, Ian's remarkable instincts and experience brought a sensational report from a CIA agent. Nearing the end of a three-year tour in the Far East, the local police in Bangkok had requested the agent's presence at the scene of a murder. At the time, the MI6 agent responsible for the area was fully employed dealing with drug elements in the north of Thailand, so Bill Kent and his replacement, Michele Peers, dealt with it.'

A couple of corny remarks about Langley were voiced, but David's scowl silenced Jock, immediately.

'Bill Kent was duty officer at Langley, CIA Headquarters, and last night he contacted Ian Walsh, informing him of an incident that he had attended in July last year. That incident resulted in the deaths of three Europeans. As we now know, Northern Ireland subjects working in Pattaya. The very nature of their deaths was especially sadistic...

The Thai authorities wanted to keep the incident quiet, as they felt that they had enough on their plate with drug problems and were sure that this incident was drug and sex related...They discovered that all three victims, on occasions, had shared the same bed and that was enough for them, and were more concerned with their tourist revenue, as indeed are the Bermudans.'

David expected comments about inadequately trained colonial policemen, but his team remained quiet.

'Peter has spoken with his counter part in Thailand and they are affording, through our embassy, rights for investigation with their full co-operation. They are now somewhat embarrassed at the way their earlier investigations were carried out. Their only request, is that it is kept out of the media...we can live with that...the current situation is that PIRA mounted four operations, in four different Countries. The organisation required for the planning and execution of these operations to be of military proportions...

These people are professionals, as we have found, to enormous cost...'

'I firmly believe that we can add one other operation to this PIRA team's name.'

David's jaw suddenly set, firmly, teeth clenched, his mind whirling with memories of Jeremy's battered body. He drew breath, then said, 'at the moment we know of two members by implication that they work together, in this active service unit...

A Sean Hegatty, and Fred Short...these, gentlemen, are our targets... Find them and we will eventually destroy the most despicable, evil set of murdering bastards that ever walked this earth...'

He brushed a hand across his face, hoping no one had spotted a tear tumbling down his cheek.

'We know that the unit consists of at least three men and one female. There's also the possibility that there is a second female. It is almost certain that two females were involved in the recce of Blacks' death, and this will be investigated...

Our achievements so far are excellent. We have eliminated five known terrorists. We are tracing one senior PIRA member who left for Heathrow yesterday with his family. Most of you know him, and if you don't, his name is Pat Maguire...

Our tout, Billy Hargraves has destroyed the homes of thirty-two PIRA sympathisers in Republican estates throughout the Province, and Jack Simpson has turned six criminals who are coming on board, and through our new policy we expect to destroy at least twelve prominent bombers and gunmen hiding in both Dundalk and Sligo.

Although these are strong Republican areas, once we effect our operations, the people there will be singing in the streets...Believe me, the public in the south are as fed up of the "troubles", as the Republicans are in the north...'

He paused, took a deep breath.

'Our aim in the next two weeks is as follows:

1. Get Pat Maguire under our control...
2. Drive out 10 more families who cause severe problems in the Republican estates...
3. Eliminate 12 more terrorists that are based in the south...
4. Investigate the incidents in Thailand and Bermuda, and if necessary the two in Australia and New Zealand.

These investigations should link in the full active service unit that we are looking for...'

He looked directly at Don:

We have done exceptionally well in a short period of time, but it is now time for us to advance and attack our enemy...

In order to catch this active "nutting squad" we need to positively identify them. We therefore start in Bermuda... We get what we can from there and move to Bangkok. Then we will return here, hopefully, with the evidence that will show who has been committing these offences...

You may well ask, how are we going to do this? Right...

Who wants to go to Bermuda?'

All hands shot up.

David grinned, 'I am not saying who is going yet. You can work it out for yourselves. What we have to decide is what has to be done here to achieve the aims that we have set. Len, Tug, and Jock will run our band of criminals, also assisting Jack where necessary.

Billy Hargraves will continue to be controlled by Benny Benford, and I would like Pete Daly to supervise and liase with him...

When your team report back tomorrow Peter, I would like to see Rupert Willet. He will be the understudy in your absence...

Now, gentlemen, you all know who is going to Bermuda...'

David paused, then said, 'you'll probably need to leave instructions for Rupert, depending on the departure time of your aircraft. Your team will work alongside the RUC team...

I want them to fully research the new evidence on PIRA finance. It will mean a visit to your opposite numbers in Germany. It sounds very interesting. I think that Dave Bonner and Harry McFee, one from each agency, would be ideal...

Finally, for those who have not been mentioned, your work continues here, apart from, Alan Kirkby, Ian Walsh, and one of our newer members from the RUC, Peter Williams.'

Everyone turned and looked at Pete, sat at the back, radiating the broadest grin of the day, as David continued:

'Most of the work in both Bermuda and Thailand is going to be computer orientated. And as you all know Pete is acknowledged as one of the best computer programmers and strategists in the RUC. Therefore Pete will be taking the lead in that direction. I will brief the four of you later. We are being loaned a VC10 aircraft from the RAF. It arrives at Aldergrove tomorrow morning at about 1130 hours and I expect you will leave for the eight-hour flight to Bermuda at about 1300 hours...'

Alan Kirkby was over-awed; in the last twelve hours he had provided for him a Gazelle helicopter, and now he was part of a team that had the dedicated use of a VC10 aircraft!

'Before I start on individual briefs are there any questions overall?'

There were none.

'We are on our way chaps. Success is there for us. Maximum effort as we have produced up till now, will bring in the results. It is now only a matter of time. However, a very strong word of warning, these people have obviously worked together for a long, long time. Until now, not even their names were known. Some are still unknown.

They are immensely capable. Pulling off operations as they have done makes them probably the most skilled and experienced terrorists in the world...

These are the people that we are up against. Should they find out about our organisation it could be that they may attempt to attack us...

Be on your guard at all times, not just those in the field, but also the backroom staff. Yes, everyone. It is unfortunate, and I have to say it, even your families must take extra precautions...'

He looked around, the enormity of his warning ringing metaphorical alarm bells throughout the assembled team.

'The horrific atrocities that have already been committed by these people must be firmly established in your minds. We are not dealing with ordinary criminals or murderers, we are not even dealing with average terrorists, we are dealing with people who not only kill for the sake of killing, but torture and execute for the sheer pleasure of it...

I believe they are responsible for the huge bombs that

caused havoc and destruction in London last year...

Furthermore, Ian Walsh is convinced that further destruction is imminent, and that huge loss of life could take place...

Lives rest with us, and upon our covert actions...should our cover be blown...it could be unthinkable.'

David instantly thought about Angela, alone, unprotected, and their brief encounter with two Irish girls in Bermuda.

'There has been an enormous risk taken in establishing a unit such as ours. For twenty-four years, thousands of innocents have lost their lives. We now have autonomy to seek, find, and destroy the perpetrators that freely roam our streets...

The outright destruction of these terrorists is my pledge.'

The meeting ended, all had lunch, and then David started outlining the tasks on separate briefs.

'...And finally, you must obtain flight details of everyone, who has flown into and out of Bangkok via Bermuda or from wherever, over the designated periods that we have established. We must have the names of everyone that has booked into hotels, most data will be computerised. Everyone that has stayed in hotels at both these locations must be checked. It is a tremendous and arduous task, but we can find them. Locate where they stayed, check the telephones; who they called, who called them and so on. Find people who would have spoken with them, like chambermaids, barmen, and waiters. Anyone who might be able to build up a picture. For the rest of today and in the morning, you will need to go through the mountain of paperwork and fax from Bill Kent. Alan, I will give you cash to get whatever re-supplies you need rather than dashing off home now...

Good luck and keep in touch.'

David then briefed Len, Tug, and Jock.

'This task is right up your street...

I want these fucking arseholes used to decimate the PIRA in Dundalk, Monaghan, Sligo, and Donegal. I have a list since we last spoke, which has been increased by the assistance of the Garda. There are five known bomb-makers, and over twenty others who have been related to bombing offences and twelve known gunmen...

With the terrorists we have already disposed of and this lot taken out, we will have the Provisional Irish Republican Army screaming for peace talks...

Their negotiating powers virtually smashed beyond repair.'

David was on form, his son's demise and Heather's disability the driving force behind the whole operation

'Len, I want you to plan these operations. Get the RUC team digging deep on each individual target. Find their habits. Talk to the Garda, for they want the scourge removed just as much as we do. Keep in mind, they are not aware of our remit. Look to take out as many as you can in each operation...

Our six new recruits will receive their initial instructions from Don, and I only wish that I could be there. We have devised a wonderful 'plan of action' for them. Tug and Jock will need to be there at the brief, because even with Don's enormous powers of persuasion, they may not be too happy.'

David sensed his own eagerness for ultimate revenge.

'Once we have achieved harmony in the ranks, then I want Tug and Jock to take the six of them for weapons training...The brief will take place Tuesday, at 1000 hours at Holywood Barracks, Belfast. After the briefing, a Lynx will take you all to a Territorial Unit in Lancashire. Do not return until you have them reasonably proficient in the art of killing...

That shouldn't be too difficult with this lot.'

* * *

David Carver sat back, after all the briefings and reading further reports, he thought, yes, we are now on our way, my son. We will administer absolute justice in your name.

Everything was planned; the atmosphere electric, confidence and enthusiasm was very high. Most were huddled under desk lights studying, examining documents, searching for anything previously missed, anything pertinent to achieving their own objectives.

Then, later that night, just when everyone was settling down for the night they received a telephone call that alerted the whole team...

* * *

Chapter Thirty Four

Pete Daly, a member of the RUC team took the telephone call from Mary O'Connor at 10pm on the Sunday evening. She gave the codeword for Jack Simpson and demanded to speak with him.

'Stay on the line I'll get him for you.'

'No', she shouted, 'I'll ring back in ten minutes. Tell him I have what he wants, and I want ten grand.'

Pete Daly contacted Jack Simpson and relayed Mary's message.

Jack said, 'when she rings back, patch her straight through.' She rang spot on the ten-minute mark, and spoke with Don; a mixture of excitement and panic in her voice. 'I have the information that you asked me for. I want ten grand, and I hope you know my life is at risk here?'

Jack asked, 'do you know where the subjects are?'

'Yes, yes I do, both of them,' she replied.

'For fuck's sake tell me.'

'Ten grand,' she insisted.

'I will pay you two thousand pounds as long as we can get to them now.'

'I want ten thousand. It must be worth it to you, and as I said, my life is at risk.'

'Wait a second.'

'She won't accept two,' he said, turning to David. 'It has to be ten.'

David Carver immediately said, 'agreed, but I cannot get hold of that amount immediately. I'll bring what I can now and the rest as soon as possible.'

Jack passed that on to Mary O'Connor.

'No, you cannot come in here. I will get it off you next week. They are both here, at the Social Club in Andersonstown...They're in black leather jackets, jeans and the elder one has glasses and hardly any hair. Got to go now...'

The line went dead.

Jack Simpson said, 'I'll get Len and the lads, and will also get Tom Galloway ready in case we need him. See you in the operations room.'

Minutes later the men raced into the operations room. 'Where are they?'

'They're at the Social Club in Andersonstown.'

Meanwhile David Carver contacted Ian Walsh at Lisburn, and explained the situation. 'Ian, I need watchers on them now, they could be gone by the time we get there.'

'David this is fantastic news, leave it with me, I will try and get someone in there now, and at the very least I will have the Social Club and the surrounding area watched within twenty minutes. When is the MI5 team due back?'

'Unfortunately, not until tomorrow, if you can cover until then that would be great.'

* * *

Sean was well over the top: drunk. He had spotted Mary O'Connor in the club earlier on, had seen her twice go to the phone.

He went up to her and said, 'well now, if it isn't one of my old flames, Mary O'Connor. I haven't seen you for years. What are you getting up to theses days?'

Mary froze; she didn't want him in her life. 'Hullo Sean,' she said. 'And where have you been. I've been here all the time?'

'Abroad for two years Mary, and it's lovely to see you again. Can we get together again, maybe tonight, talk about old times?'

'No Sean, I'm seeing someone regular now.' She'd lied. 'I'm surprised you're not hitched by now. A good-looking guy like yourself?'

'I saved myself for you, and now you tell me you're spoken for? Where's he at, then?'

'He isn't here tonight...He's at work,' she said, walking away from him.

Mary realised she had made a mistake, lying never easy for her.

At kicking out time he and Fred followed her, nearly at the Falls Road she stopped and turned. 'Sean,' she said, 'I have told you I cannot see you any more... I am soon to be married... Now please leave me alone.'

'Come on Mary I won't hurt you... We'll just have some fun.'

'No, I don't want to.' She turned right into where she lived, but he hadn't taken any notice, and was only a few feet behind her when she opened the door. Before she could shut it he was inside, Fred closing the door behind them.

'They've entered her flat,' a female watcher said, over the radio.

'Get as close in as you can,' Ian Walsh, said.

Sean meanwhile grabbed Mary from behind, holding her breasts. 'Come on now Mary, you know you like to please me, and it'll be much easier for you if you don't fight me off.'

She gave in, and they took her into her bedroom, where Sean told her to take her clothes off...

When she was naked he threw her down on the bed.

'No Sean, please, no rough stuff.'

Fred found the cellotape, and then he stuffed her panties into her mouth, wrapping the cellotape around, tight. They then turned her over and tied her to the bed, spread-eagled. She tried to struggle but she was no match for them. They had done this the last time and it had taken her weeks to get over the pain.

Sean then took his clothes off and she saw him taking his belt from his trousers. He leathered her buttocks with all the force he could. Again and again the blows rained down on her, Mary all the while shaking her head, pleading silently with him to stop. She knew it was a forlorn gesture.

'I am at the front of the flat, with the letter box lid lifted and I can hear them beating her,' said the female watcher. 'We need assistance here.'

Ian Walsh said 'no, we need to follow them, not arrest them, keep observing.'

The beating stopped.

Now Mary knew what Sean would do.

She writhed in agony.

Then it was over.

The other man, she remembered was Fred, who pulled the tape off her and yanked her wet panties out of her mouth. They undid her bonds turned her over on her back and tied her again. There was no resistance at all, just sobbing, and then loud crying.

The beating was enough; let alone the brutalising of her in such a degrading manner, now this, Sean kneeling over her face, just inches from her mouth...

After a while Sean paused, grinning, and eased away...

'Now Mary, tell me who you telephoned, twice, from the club?' he asked, a snarl of sheer venom.

Spluttering, gasping for breath, she was now terrified.

'Sean for gods sake, please, please… I was telephoning for my man to come to the club to pick me up, but he couldn't…

Please, please, just leave me alone.'

'What, the man that was supposedly at work?'
Sean produced a blade, a terrifying sight. 'No, Sean, no, no please, no…'

Fred thrust the panties back in to her mouth, fastened the tape around again. He'd already hurt her when he'd ripped it off. Tied, spread-eagled, already in severe pain, the point of the knife gently, and painfully broke the skin between her breasts. Sean then drew it slowly down her body; blood seeping both sides of the blade. She shook her head, violently, the pain, the horror, and then she started peeing, a wet patch developing on the bed, the blade still moving down her body, and getting deeper…

He couldn't stop himself, he had developed Bernadette's evil desire to inflict horrendous pain, but he hadn't cultivated her technical expertise, in prolonging life to the final moment…

Sean snarled, 'talk you bitch…

You're going to, eventually.'

The tape was yanked from her face.

'Tell me everything, now, or else…'

But then Fred looked into her lifeless staring eyes, and said, fuckin' hell Sean, we'll get nothing out of her, she's pissin' dead!

* * *

Tug and Jock pulled into the car park at the club. There were two cars parked, one an old banger and the other a hire car. The Peugeot 405 they quickly discovered, had been hired in London, and that had to be the one they wanted.

Jock was inside it in a minute. He pulled the bonnet catch, and removed the front nearside headlamp bulb. Tug did the same with the rear nearside light and also shorted out the rear offside fog light. It would now be very easy to follow and observe, whether in front or tailing, and Tom would have no difficulty identifying it from the air, either. They also fitted a magnetic homing device, which would beam out a continuous signal for up to 15 days.

* * *

An hour later the watcher reported, 'they are leaving the

house...Now heading back to the club.'

There were now another three watchers available to Ian Walsh, two in cars and, one on foot supposedly throwing-up his evenings drink over a garden fence...

As Sean walked past he shouted at him, 'get it up,' then laughed as he followed up with, 'silly bugger.'

'Heading into the club car park,' said the Sergeant, leaning heavily against his chosen garden fence.

David Carver said to Ian Walsh, 'we're too thin on the ground...

We need more men.'

'We'll manage David. As soon as he gets in a car, if that's how they are going to move, we will have them.'

'I don't want them lifted...

We must follow them.'

'That's no problem, David...Once he is in his car then we will have all mobiles in Belfast alerted, and if necessary, all in the Province. Lets just wait and see.'

Then horror struck...

The female watcher sounded distressed; in a state of shock, as she yelled, 'I told you so... I told you I needed help. I have entered the flat. It's terrible, really terrible... She's dead, I think... I need help...she has been mutilated.'

* * *

Tom Galloway was hovering in the Lynx at 6000 feet, David Carver and Jack Simpson with him, armed to the proverbial hilt.

Tom was wearing his night scope, David and Jack with similar hand held devices. They had seen Tug and Jock doing their 'thing' with the car, had heard over the radio that they were on the move, and David asked Tom to come round to port side a little.

The slightest touch by Tom brought the Lynx perfectly in to position, as Hegatty and Short walked in to the club car park and went straight up to a car. They then moved out on to the road, turned right, and headed south.

David Carver instructed Tug and Jock to remain where they were. He also instructed the RUC back up to do the same. The rear side fog light of the terrorist' car was like a beacon, and visible for miles.

They were heading south, on a 'B' road, and very little traffic when they entered the small town of Ballynahinch. They then turned right for Dromore, and that was when David called his mobile units forward... He gauged that they were heading to Armagh, but ensuring that they were not being followed.

Before the two terrorists reached Armagh, Tug and Jock were parked in the centre, two back up cars parked in lay-bys, one just outside Armagh on the A3 and the other on the B51. The one parked on the B51 reported a car approaching with only a single headlight, then passed by, a single rear fog light dazzlingly bright.

David Carver again instructed them to remain where they were, as the terrorist' vehicle drove straight past Tug and Jock. Tom Galloway swung slightly north, anticipating that they were going to head south again. Although he knew he was out of their vision, it did no harm to be cautious, and he would still have them in the night scope.

The terrorists picked up the B31, still sticking with side roads and headed towards Newtownhamilton. Tug and Jock were instructed to catch up with them and the other two cars to follow but to keep about one mile back from the lead vehicle.

Tom had moved quickly from Armagh to Newtownhamilton. Still flying at 6000 feet, he called all units: 'Target vehicle now heading on the B30 towards Crossmaglen.'

A few minutes later, Tug and Jock had turned right at the same junction and were closing fast on the terrorists when David Carver said. 'Pull up Jock, they've stopped two miles ahead.'

The two killers were outside Crossmaglen and one of them had got out and opened a gate to allow the vehicle through. The passenger then got back in and they drove about three hundred yards, pulling up at a large farmhouse. No one came to the door, and they let themselves in.

David Carver immediately contacted Ian Walsh with a description of where they had gone.

Tom Galloway was hovering and watching the house. Lights had come on immediately the terrorists entered and after about five minutes they were extinguished and upstairs lights came on. They were obviously settling down for the night. This was confirmed a few minutes later when the whole house fell dark.

With a quick recce, a lay-by was found about two miles from the farmhouse, a superb spot for a surveillance car, from where the terrorist car could be seen. David then instructed one of the RUC teams to remain and watch for any movement. They would be relieved at 0800 hours. The remainder were instructed to return to respective bases, and Tom headed back to base arriving within about eight minutes.

* * *

Ian Walsh had both police and an ambulance at the flat belonging to Mary O'Connor. The ambulance immediately took the female watcher to hospital, the girl suffering severe shock.

And Mary would leave for the last time, eventually, in a black bag.

The police and the paramedics thought the dreadful carnage beyond belief. All had seen the darker, gruesome side of life in the Province, and it didn't get any easier. But, this killing was more in line with a slaughterhouse. A hideous, grisly murder at its worst, leaving others to pick up the pieces of this depraved atrocity.

* * *

On the Monday morning, the Chief Superintendent, investigating the case, contacted Ian Walsh, and demanded to know why the perpetrators had not been arrested if under surveillance.

Ian explained. 'The unfortunate victim was a tout and had got caught up in an undercover operation; the operation was called "Combating Evil", which you must be aware of by now. It was a dreadful crime and they will be brought to justice, but they were only part of the process, and to this end they needed to be followed not arrested. Furthermore, the victim had informed her handler, many times, that she had been beaten up by one of these men, though we had no proof.'

The Chief Superintendent said, 'I am most unhappy with that explanation, and have assumed command of this operation. I have ordered my men to remain on watch, and I intend to lift the two killers in the next hour...

So Walsh, just keep out of my way.'

The phone went dead, and Ian cursed.

Sir Peter Wilcox, having heard the exchange immediately contacted the Chief Constable and told him what had happened.

'He will be suspended from duty, immediately,' returned the Chief Constable.

* * *

The Chief Constable contacted the chief superintendent and told him to back off from his intended operation.

'Why sir, we have the terrorists trapped.'
'No, you don't have them trapped...
Another agency has done that and it is their operation...
Now, do as I have instructed...
You are temporarily suspended.'

The chief superintendent would not accept this. He was sure that public opinion would be on his side and the Chief Constable would be proved wrong. He picked up his radio and said. 'Unit One move now to effect arrest of suspects, Unit Two will be with you shortly.'

The police inspector at the control centre said, 'sir, these are two very inexperienced policemen and you are defying the orders of the Chief Constable.'

'Shut up,' said the Chief Superintendent.

The constables in Unit One looked at each other. What had been ordered was utter madness. There were two terrorists in the house, almost certainly armed, and they as lightly armed officers had been ordered to approach in a police car! The senior of the two constables radioed back querying their instructions.

'Get on with it, or your backup will be there first.'

They headed straight for the house.

* * *

It was only 8am when they heard the doorbell ring. Both Sean and Fred dived for their weapons, at the sight of two policemen standing at the door, and neither apparently armed.

Sean opened the door.

'What the fuck do you two want at this time of the morning?'

The senior of the two pulled out his warrant and said, 'I am arresting you on suspicion of murder... Inform your colleague to come forward.'

Fred did. Only he had an armalite in his hand.

'Both of you inside, now,' he said.

The two officers were led down into the cellar, where Sean said, 'on your knees.'

He then pulled a pistol, and with a bullet to the back of the head, he executed the police officers. Sean and Fred raced up the steps and grabbed their holdalls.

Sean said, 'put the police car in the barn.'

Within five minutes they were across the border at

Crossmaglen. Sean mimicked the arresting officer: 'I am arresting you for murder,' then started laughing.

Both giggled like school children, and Fred then said, 'Jesus, they were a right pair of wallies.'

A further twenty minutes later, their hire car was in a garage at Drogheda and a BMW 320 was heading south. Fortune was on their side. They duly parked at the long stay car park at Dublin Airport with a flight to Heathrow soon to leave.

They were at Heathrow just before 1pm, where they picked up a hire car, dropped off the detonators and other devices that they had collected, and were in the New Forest base by 5pm.

* * *

David Carver had thought the two terrorists would be up and about at the crack of dawn, and surprised that he hadn't heard anything from the RUC, he'd said to Jack Simpson, 'go and get Tom, and have a trip round.'

Later, Jack Simpson's voice crackled over the VHF radio, 'something is very strange here. There's the police car parked at the lay-by where we left them last night. There is no car at the farmhouse and no sign of activity. I cannot raise the officers' in the police car... They are obviously on a different frequency. And there's no response from the tracking device.'

David Carver shouted to Len, 'get the lads, and get moving. Go straight to that police car and find out what the hell is going on.

Meanwhile, Ian Walsh contacted the control centre. The Inspector answered.

'I need to speak with the chief superintendent, urgently.'

'He's unavailable at the moment, can I help?'

'Yes, this is Chief Superintendent Ian Walsh... I am the senior police officer dealing with Operation Combating Evil. This morning your chief superintendent attempted to take his own action against two terrorists holed up at a farmhouse. He was prevented from doing so by the Chief Constable... I want to know what is happening, as we cannot contact the police car at the scene?'

'I...I am not sure I can help you at the moment. The chief superintendent has just walked out.'

'What is the frequency of the police car observing the farmhouse, or can you patch me through?'

'I can do neither, I have been trying to contact our first unit but we seem to have lost them, too.'

'Where are they likely to be, right now?'

'I just don't know... We have been trying to make contact, but no one is answering the radio. Our other car searched the area for them and couldn't find them. It could be that they have gone off for coffee.'

'What, before they were relieved?'

The Inspector was noticeably flustered.

'Inspector, go and find your chief superintendent, now, and I want some answers immediately.'

The Inspector could no longer protect his boss, 'sir, the chief superintendent ordered our Unit One to go and arrest the two suspects, and we have not heard from them since...

This was after he was suspended. I pleaded with him not to send the car in, as both constables were very young and inexperienced.'

'Oh my god, you had better find him, because the Chief Constable will want to speak with your absent boss in about two minutes.'

* * *

Ian Walsh had contacted Len, and after hearing what had happened had gone straight to the farmhouse. They looked in the garage and saw the police car, and now knew the police officers' fate. Tug had broken in through the window and had let the others in through the front door. Jock had looked for a cellar whilst Len had searched the ground floor, then Tug had raced up the stairs with his Heckler & Kock at the ready, where the two bedrooms had been used.

He heard Jocks booming voice. 'Down here, lads.'

The two policemen were very dead.

The police car with the second crew that had been observing pulled up at the house as Len appeared at the front door. They both pulled out their weapons and pointed them at Len.

Then they moved forward.

Len was angry, 'put them away before I wrap them round your fucking necks. Your colleagues are dead, murdered in the cellar... How long have you two arseholes been watching this place?'

'We heard the chief superintendent ordering our Unit One to arrest the terrorists and we were in support. We were still in

Belfast then, and when we got here, there was no one about so we went to the lay-by to await instructions.'

'Why the hell were you in Belfast when you were supposedly in support?'

'We were just coming on duty so we decided to have breakfast first. Then we were going to return and take over from Unit One so they could then have breakfast.'

'I don't believe this, breakfast, in the middle of an operation.' Len had screamed. Who briefed you? Were you not told about what had happened?'

The two officers looked on in stunned silence.

'Get down into the cellar. See what your breakfast has done to your colleagues. Now!'

* * *

They were now all back at the base, Ian Walsh inconsolable. 'Why, fucking hell, why? How can things have got so lax? Every time we hit an obstacle it has been either the fault of, or created by the RUC.'

'It's not your fault Ian,' said David Carver.

'We had every thing covered to follow those blood-thirsty thugs, and now they've crossed the border and somewhere in hiding. They could be anywhere. We'll monitor the tracking device until it expires, but I hold little faith in their being stupid enough to be moving around in the 405, after two RUC officers knocked them up.'

* * *

David Carver called a briefing for 1000 hours.

'Gentlemen, we had them. They could have taken us to the rest of the active service unit. Instead, two policemen are dead. I feel that I have let you all down, and I cannot apologise enough. It was a grave error of judgement to leave two inexperienced police officers watching two highly experienced terrorists. The buck stops with me, not with the RUC. I should have known better, and...'

Sir Peter Wilcox stopped David in his tracks, 'hold on now David, remember your first brief back at Ashford. Errors will be made and there will be no witch-hunts or recriminations. Hindsight is a wonderful thing. Last night, when the decision was made to leave the RUC watching, was a sound one. Two men, who were very drunk and had obviously gone to bed, needed no more watching than as detailed. Indeed, some other incident could have compromised the operation just as easily.'

David nodded in partial agreement, as Peter continued.

'No one queried or had reason to query the decision. Unfortunately the fault was a dreadful decision by a RUC chief superintendent suspended from duty, who chose to ignore his Chief Constable. He also ignored the advice of his own Inspector. How the RUC will deal with him is up to them...

It is, as far as I am concerned, an internal matter. We will just get on with our own business. After all, that was your own advice David, and it also applies to you, and I am confident that everyone here will agree with that.'

And everyone did.

David Carver then took the floor again. 'Thank you, gentlemen; we are trying everything to trace these characters, however it will take time. In the meantime, everything as planned goes ahead. Peter and his team will leave from Aldergrove shortly and all other operations go ahead as scheduled.'

* * *

Chapter Thirty Five

Bernadette was beside herself with frustration and temper. It was nearly six weeks since she and Kerry had fallen out. Neither had contacted the other, and the bomb was due to explode in five days.

It would hopefully devastate the city and create the largest death toll since the campaign had begun. Even so, she felt that for this campaign, without Kerry involved, she herself might be at risk, but Bernadette would never admit this to the men. She preferred someone else to be at risk other than her or her active service unit.

She was also unhappy at what Sean and Fred had done, the two now wanted men on the open police front. There were still too many irregularities in their story, and she felt sure she had not been told all there was to know. It took her three hours to debrief them for the bombing run, whereas Kerry was much better at logistics. She made a decision that she would be the one to give in and telephone Kerry.

* * *

Kerry had meanwhile fallen in love with Tony Hey, and treasured his loving and caring attitude. She hadn't been able to believe her good fortune in finding someone as placid and kind as Tony. Life had suddenly become so good, her obvious nationality and accent irrelevant to him, and she herself slipping away from the past.

She desperately wanted Tony's baby, and they would often lie together after making wonderful love. He would whisper to her, his thoughts for their child, a little boy, naturally. Their love was real, and physical, yet passionately intense and fulfilling; both giving, both satisfying and enjoying the delights of the other. This was so very different to her past, and something she had long yearned for, but in truth, Bernadette could never have given Kerry the one thing she wanted above all else. A child.

Bernadette had needed to inflict pain, and tortuous death to become sexually aroused, and Kerry knew that if Bernadette saw her in a pregnant state both she and Tony would be dead.

Although he had been a soldier for years, she thought him no match for her ex lover.

Bernadette would crush him, and then destroy Kerry, bit by bit.

So many times recently, when Tony lay silently alongside her, a tear channelled its way slowly down her cheek. Then she would look at him; cherish what they had. A future together could work, if it were allowed to. Why had she been so easily led by a selfish, jealous, sadistic, evil woman?

It was now Monday 19 April, and Kerry had just started her evening shift at the pub at 6.30pm. The phone rang, and she picked it up. 'Hullo Kerry,' whispered Bernadette. 'I still love you, want you, and we need to get together.'

Kerry paused, sighed, and thought, oh no, please no. Let me live my life. Go away, leave me alone, I only love Tony.

'Kerry are you there?'

'Yes, I'm here, Bernadette, but I'm terribly busy at the moment. I've just started a shift.'

'Kerry, we have problems that I cannot discuss over the telephone...

We all need you.'

'Bernadette, you haven't needed me this last six or seven weeks and have got by... I'll try and get down in the next week or two, but I can't promise a day or specific time.'

There was stunned silence, because Kerry had never treated Bernadette like this before, then her ex lover asked:

'Kerry are you still with that man I last saw you with?'

'Yes Bernadette, I am... I told you he was our way in to hit a military target.'

Kerry immediately regretted every word said.

'Kerry you tell him you're mine, and forget about military targets... We have to concentrate on something else.'

'Bernadette, I just cannot stop what I am doing. I'm a working girl, and it won't be easy to get time off. Please be patient. I will make every effort to be down on Saturday.'

Bernadette turned nasty, 'Kerry, I have tried to be pleasant because I love you, but you've forced my hand. I am sending Sean and Joe for you in the morning. They will pick you up at the caravan at 9am... Be there.'

Then Bernadette crashed the telephone down.

Kerry was shattered. She now felt hate for the person that she had once devoted her life to. She could not discuss this with Tony, as it would almost certainly end their relationship. There was only one way; she would have to continue a ridiculous charade with Bernadette. It would be difficult, and patient, she would have to be. She had everything to live for with Tony, and devious she could be, if pushed, and she would get back to him, as soon as possible...

Kerry had told Tony that she had to visit her mother in Dublin and would be away for about two weeks. She had felt guilty when telling her employers at The Greyhound Pub the same lie, as they had been very good to her. Nevertheless, she had convinced herself that she would be able to solve a very tiresome problem, given time.

Bernadette looked white and drawn when the car pulled up at the house. The atmosphere between them would be tense, but there in the New Forest the birds were singing, the April sun was shining, and Kerry was on her own mission.

Bernadette walked up to the car as Kerry jumped out, her embrace overtly sexual. 'I love you, and have missed you, Bernadette.'

'I love you too,' rallied Bernadette, hand caressing Kerry's breasts. 'I've hated this loneliness without you, more than anything else in my life. Please say that you will never leave me again?'

'Bernadette, I have never left you. Just remember that I am on an operation we agreed to simply ages ago. Why don't you trust me instead of putting me at risk?'

'Kerry my love, I have been through hell. I want us to bathe and caress for hours, and you'll prove to me that you still love me, won't you? Then we will get down to business.'

Kerry thought immediately, how bloody selfish Bernadette was, but a mission was a mission. And hell, if it meant getting it off with Bernadette, then so be it.

As Sean and Joe got on with their own business, and Bernadette ran a bath, Kerry asked. 'Where's Fred?'

'Oh, he's with his wife at the moment.'

'Bernadette, What is the problem that you had me come down here for? Tell me what has been going on.'

They then sat in the huge bath and Bernadette explained what had happened. 'For god's sake Bernadette, you have been unbelievably naïve. What on earth is getting into you? We are all at severe risk, now. You must cancel the bombing, and you must get Fred back here now, so that I can grill him. I need to talk to Sean as well.'

At that she climbed out of the bath and went to the sauna.

Bernadette followed her, pleaded, 'Kerry cuddle me please, I desperately need you?'

Kerry responded, and loathed every minute. Then, drying herself in front of Bernadette, Kerry said very firmly, though lying through her teeth in the first instance, 'as much as I need you, our very survival is more important than anything else. There are so many questions that need answering. Someone, for the first time since we started operating together, has latched onto us. We need to find who this is. We need to know how they have found us.' She slipped on a towelled robe and headed for the bathroom door, stopped, turned, and remarked. 'Then we need to destroy them, and we must move out of here today!'

Within two hours they were in a small conference room at a hotel in Southampton.

Kerry said to both Sean and Fred. 'What I want to know is every minute detail of what you did from the moment you left Bernadette and headed off to Northern Ireland.'

Sean immediately said, 'Kerry, we have already gone through everything with Bernadette. There is no need to expand on this.'

'Is there not Sean? Then please tell me how two policemen located you at our property within hours of leaving Belfast. What was the murder charge? Was it related to the murder you committed that night? Or could it have been related to our past? Who was the woman on that night, and who else can identify you? How did you pay for your hire car? What identification did you use? How long was the contract for? Where is the car now? When is it due to be returned? Was there a close circuit television camera at the rental premises? Which weapon did you use on the policemen? Was it clean? Where did you get it? Where is it now? Did you check the car for bugs before you left? Where is the second hire car?

Sean, how many of those questions can you answer? Tell me; assure me that you maintained security at all times? Are we all safe from arrest? I want to know everything so that we can react in the correct manner.'

Sean and Fred looked shocked, and Kerry knew then that they had compromised the whole team.

They started explaining in detail, and Kerry continued

querying everything that was said, digging, searching for the right answers. As the grilling went on, the tension and stress grew in both Bernadette and Kerry. The horrendous errors that these two had committed totally belied their experience as skilled and professional PIRA soldiers.

'You are both absolutely adamant that you weren't followed that night. If that is true, then the policemen were there to arrest you on previous charges. The property, I assume, could have been observed for months, and they were waiting for you.'

'I agree,' Sean said.

'Then tell me Sean, why would two very inexperienced policemen turn up at 8am to arrest two experienced PIRA members, alleged killers? Why would that property be under observation? It hasn't been used for nearly three years, other than to be cleaned.'

'It could have been a police fuck-up.'

'Yes,' Kerry said, 'but that would mean that it would have been an extraordinary coincidence that you were there at the time of a fuck-up, especially as you had only just committed a murder.'

'I believe you must have been followed. Either a bugging device, or a helicopter, was used, or more probably, both. Did you stop to check whether there was a helicopter in the vicinity?'

'No,' said Fred. 'We were pissed.'

'If my assumption that you were followed is correct, then why were you followed? It seems to me that we could all be under observation... I cannot pinpoint a time when you would have been identified and followed. Surely it couldn't have been for the murder that night... How would they have found out so quickly? There are too many imponderables here and I don't like it.'

Kerry continued. 'If you had been followed since arriving in Northern Ireland, everything that you did would be known. You would have been seen to enter that woman's flat. Also you would have been seen to enter the safe house in South Armagh, and come away again with a canvas satchel. If that scenario is correct then they will link you to our active service unit.'

Sean said, 'that's a load of rubbish Kerry, how can you justify that?'

'Two very sound reasons. Very simply Sean, tell me what you did, in detail, to that woman?'

257

Sean hesitated and then looked at Fred.

'I take your point.' Sean said sheepishly.

'No, Sean, its not as simple as that. I need to know everything that both you and Fred got up to, now give me the details.'

They were again stunned by Kerry's hard-line questions and sheer determination to unravel the truth. Sean started by stammering and stuttering...

After he finished, Bernadette and Kerry just glared at them both.

Then Kerry said, 'the other reason Sean, is why would you travel to Northern Ireland, collect goods from a house near Armagh, then return to the mainland?'

'They don't know that we have returned to the mainland, we could still be in Northern Ireland as far as they know. Our trail was lost immediately we killed the two policemen. We headed south and there was nobody following then.'

Kerry thought about this.

'If we assume that they entered the flat, immediately after you left, and found that you had committed the murder, and you were not arrested immediately, that means only one thing.'

'Fucking hell,' said Bernadette.

'Exactly,' said Kerry. 'We're facing fucking hell, perhaps around the very next corner.'

'Someone risked losing you, in the hope of arresting all of us, and in the meantime, the RUC somehow interfered and fucked up. There must be a team operating against us and they have obviously got a great deal of power not to arrest when a murder such as yours has taken place. The obvious objective of the unknown hunters is the arrest of all members of our active service unit. What I cannot understand, is how they have identified Sean or Fred in the first place.'

Bernadette said, 'what on earth are we going to do?'

'We must cancel the bombing on Friday. The security forces must know that something is about to happen and will be on full alert.'

'We can't do that,' Bernadette said. 'All arrangements are in place... Ryan Flynn's active service unit is executing the operation. There is no link between them and us. I briefed Ryan through a contact in Northern Ireland. All we have done is dropped off the detonators and timing devices. Sean and Fred did that on Monday morning.'

'That New Forest house still worries me,' posed Kerry. 'It is probably under observation, and that will have implicated Sean and Fred.'

Bernadette said, 'no, if that were the case they would have been picked up yesterday, or we all would have been by now.'

'I think we are still perfectly secure in the New Forest.'

'I still believe that it is wrong to go ahead with the bombing... However, we do not have the risk that Ryan Flynn's active service unit have, so that is their problem.'

Kerry left it at that. Then all of a sudden, she became excited, 'I have an idea,' she said, beaming. 'We draw out the team that is on our case, and kill them...'

* * *

Chapter Thirty Six

Jack Simpson was standing in front of the six recruits; thuggish, awesome, an overpowering sight for anyone. These particular villains had also had the gall to cheat both the Republican and Loyalist communities. Worse still they had done it in the name of both the PIRA and the Loyalist organisations. To do that without being caught had required many skills and guts, and it was time to exploit them.

'As I point to you, give me your name.' Jack Simpson commanded.

'Chunky Murphy...'
'Nigel Murphy...'
'Stu Sweet...'
'Tony Sweet...'
'Titch Young...'
'Patrick Tyrell,' they replied.

'Thank you, my name is Jaffa...

That's all you need to know about me. I understand that you have all volunteered to work for us in order that you can regain that which is not rightfully yours.

Is this correct?'

Chunky spoke up, 'it all depends on the work involved.'

'No it doesn't, by being here you have already agreed. There is no turning back.'

Jack Simpson smiled.

'Then why fucking ask, if it seems we have no choice. What do we have to do?'

'You are all going animal hunting and we are even going to teach you how to shoot.'

Nigel Murphy snapped, 'what fucking animals and none of us here needs to be taught how to shoot. So how about you stop pissing us about and get on with it.'

'Excellent,' Jack said. 'Confidence and enthusiasm is exactly what I want to hear. There are at least three hundred animals that have murdered innocent people in your beautiful country. They have bombed and shot with total disregard, even to the killing of women and children. Your task, with our guidance is to eliminate selected targets, causing panic, and fear within the PIRA and the UVF.

Consider yourselves the chosen ones...

You all are, for once going to do the community a wonderful service.'

'No we are fucking not, Jaffa, and bollocks to you.' Yelled Chunky.

He was not called Chunky for nothing; five foot five, and nineteen stone of muscle, but now with an added paunch, or beer belly, that still made him an awesome and frightening sight.

They were all on there feet screaming at a grinning Jack Simpson.

Patrick Tyrell then said, 'I have never killed anyone, and I am not about to start now.'

'And neither am I,' chirped in Titch Young.

They were all in unison.

Jack Simpson intervened. 'In about thirty minutes, we are leaving by helicopter for a secret base in England, where your training will begin. You will not be charged for this privilege and you will also receive free food and accommodation as part of our formidable generosity.'

Chunky, shaking with both nerves and outrage interrupted Jack Simpson. 'Now listen here, Jaffa or whatever you call yourself, we are not and I repeat not, doing this and that is the end of the matter. We are fuckin' leaving, so go to fuckin' hell.'

'Gentlemen, you were all photographed entering these barracks. We also have photocopies of all of your misdemeanours. We have included your wives' names so that they are also implicated in your racketeering, blackmail and other scams.

We will also spread the news right across the Province that you have all given information to the Security Forces, here at Holywood Barracks. Otherwise why would you be here? When you kill the men I want rid of, you will be well paid. If you don't I will hold you here until we have a crowd of at least a thousand waiting for you all to leave. Your homes within the hour will be surrounded.'

Jack had their attention.

'At the very least, you will all be tortured to death, and I can arrange that, also the method. The previous chappy, who didn't agree with me was very brave, he took his chances saying that he didn't believe me and that we would not be allowed to do such a thing. He had a lot of guts then...but after he was picked up...he had none!'

'What, what do you mean', said Titch Young.

'The PIRA nutting squad secured a cage holding two very hungry rats onto his naked stomach...'

'You have two minutes to make your decision.'

Jack Simpson walked out.

Someone yelled, 'you fucking bastard, you lousy rotten swine, you will not get away with this.'

Jack Simpson, after a few minutes wandered back in, and their faces were grim. Jack knew he would be a dead man if they had the chance.

'Well, Chunky, I presume you will speak for all. I take it that you totally agree with my directives, and for no other reason that you want to rid the earth of this scum?'

Tug and Jock, sitting at the back of the room, were no doubt enjoying the uncanny supremacy that Jack held over the dispirited, devastated six men.

Chunky scowled. 'You may think you have got us at the moment, but we have been around a long time and our turn will come.'

'I don't think so Chunky...

We will not leave any loose ends that may point at our organisation and, I also think that once underway there will be benefits for you. The six of you are the founder members of the "Combined Freedom Fighters of Ulster".

You are a joint force of Catholics and Protestants, from both north and south of the border. Your objectives are the destruction of all known paramilitary organisations, both in Ulster and south of the border. You will be hailed no doubt as the ultimate saviours or heroes of Ireland.'

They were listening, but equally seething...

'We have drawn up Articles of War, Schedules of Operations, Organisation, Administration, and Planning. And of course, to show your commitment to the organisation we have drawn up a document outlining your individual dedication to the defeat of terrorism throughout Ireland. All new recruits will sign this document commencing with yourselves.'

It reads as follows:

Combined Freedom Fighters of Ulster

I, ...of
....
....
....

Membership Number   0001

- **I am dedicated to the defeat of terrorism in Northern Ireland.**
- **I am dedicated to the defeat of terrorism in the Republic of Ireland.**
- **I am not a member of any other organisation.**
- **I do not receive instructions, nor do I commit acts of terrorism, on behalf of any other organisation.**
- **I will display total loyalty and dedication to this organisation.**
- **I will fulfil any given task to the best of my ability.**
- **I will abide by the rules and disciplines of the organisation, at all times.**

Signed   ....
Date   ....

The documents were produced for them to sign and then, they all knew they were dragged inextricably into something that none of them wanted.

* * *

They had climbed discontentedly into the Lynx, and upon arrival the training was completed very quickly. Tug and Jock, with the assistance of two SAS backup teams, had spent three very intensive days training the six.

The men all knew that these men were not ordinary soldiers; highly skilled, their methods ruthless, and this had reflected on how quickly they had all assimilated, not new found skills, but polished old ones to a higher degree.

Jack Simpson had spoken to them again on their return. He congratulated them on the results of the weapons training. He said that they would be immediately put into action and that they would be controlled at all times by the elder of the team that had trained them.

He was simply known as boss.

No one, not least Jack Simpson had ever thought that this operation could have been so successful, but it was, more than anyone could have contemplated...

Len, Tug, and Jock, truly in their element, aided and abetted every attack, and every killing. What had become clear, amazingly, was that the six were operating as skilfully as regular soldiers, but without their hands tied. They also conveyed to their leaders that they were enjoying the tasks, and were now requesting payment.

David Carver hadn't expected this, because in all honesty he had thought they wouldn't be as successful as, indeed, they were proving to be.

Chunky was with Jack Simpson, and angry. 'Jaffa, you are not keeping to your word. I have got my men doing the business and we want payment. I know that you have got us over a barrel but enough is enough.'

'You are right Chunky, you have been doing well, I will sort this out today and make a payment tomorrow. I want tonight's operation over and done with. Then we will discuss this again.'

'Give me an interim payment now of £10,000, for work completed.'

'How many have you disposed of?'

'Six up till now but after tonight it will be twelve. And Mr "fucking big", I might add, that we are starting to get our own targets together from, lets say, past associations. So, we are responding not only to your targets, but to some of our own as well, shites that we know have killed, and only for money. We want back what you have taken, but I have to say, we also agree with the principle of what we are doing, strange as that may seem.'

'Ok, Chunky, I agree.' Jack said. 'One word of warning...If you are organising your own targets I want their names and address first, I am not having just anyone floating around shooting at anybody. There has been too much of that in the past. We also are in contact with friends in the south who are looking after your safety during an operation. Is this clear?'

'Yes, it certainly is, we did not know that we had guardian angels looking after us.'

'Let's just say that we want this operation to succeed for sometime to come and assistance to keep it going is more than welcome.'

'You will get your money tomorrow, and fortnightly thereafter.'

A beaming Chunky left the lay by where they had met.

* * *

Chapter Thirty Seven

Ian Walsh, in Bermuda, was extremely suspicious. No females on their own. No two females together with the first names of Sharon and Helen had appeared on any hotel register. Not only that, they were not registered on any airline, or ship, into or out of Bermuda. Maybe they were on a yacht. That was something he would also have to check.

Pete Williams had obtained on disks, everyone who had entered Bermuda since December 1992 up to the end of March 1993. He reasoned that whoever had committed this crime was listed on his computer. He was confident that he would find them.

Peter Wilcox and Alan Kirkby were following the same line of enquiry as Alan had, previously. They had visited the scene of the crime. Peter had shaken his head a number of times. This crime would take some organising and planning. The execution of Dermott Black had been incredibly well planned...

The killers had made him suffer, and how...

They must have left some evidence, but where?

All car rental offices were visited; names of virtually every one who had hired a car in the past 17 months obtained, also motorbikes; another popular form of transport. After three days their joint efforts were in effect, fruitless, but they had an enormous amount of information, and when combined with other bits of information would start to make sense, surely?

They decided to move on, checked out, and left for RAF Brize Norton, in England. There they refuelled and had two further stops, before reaching Bangkok. The resident MI6 officer met them. His name was Christopher Tyrell. He had already done an immense amount of spadework since Sir Peter Wilcox had contacted the Embassy just a few days beforehand.

He had collated on ten disks the details of everyone that had flown into and out of Thailand, throughout 1992. He also had the names and home addresses of every one who had stayed in Bangkok hotels over the same period.

Putting all that together, along with the information collected from Bermuda, some pattern was bound to manifest itself. Corroboration of evidence was what they were after. It would happen.

* * *

Kerry said, 'we can draw these bastards out. The car is still sitting in our garage at Drogheda. We can assume that both Fred and Sean are now on the mugshots. Therefore either one can go across and drive the car back into Northern Ireland. Assume that it will be followed in a very short time.'

Kerry was in her element; she must do this well to throw the others off her true intent...

'Yes, this can work and we'll demoralise them and throw them in a state of total confusion.'

Bernadette asked, 'Kerry what are you trying to say?'

'Sean and Fred can travel separately to Dublin. Sean can pick up the car from Dublin Airport and collect Fred from the docks, meeting the incoming ferry. They can drive to our house in Drogheda. Fred can pick up the hire car and head north. Sean can put our car back into the garage and make his way back to the airport and head back here. Fred can then be the decoy.'

'What do you mean Kerry?' Fred asked.

'You head north up into the Province, Fred, drive around until you see that you are being followed.'

'How do you know I will be followed?' Fred asked.

'Because you have already been followed in that car.'

'Right now that car will be the most wanted vehicle in Northern Ireland. I doubt you will be stopped, though. They will renew their attempts to follow you and trap us all. Only this time, we will identify and kill the followers, and that will give their team something to think about.'

Bernadette said, 'now Kerry, you can see why we needed you. This is a brilliant plan. If we can take out the watchers just before the bomb is detonated, that would be a tremendous coupe.'

Kerry hadn't wanted to get back into her old ways, but these fools had forced her hand. She was now as much at risk as them, when before she might have been able to fade away without an unknown entity on her tail. 'We must delay the bombing by twenty-four hours to be able to effect both operations in the time scale that you want. That would also allow the bomb operation a greater degree of success, as the security will not be as intense on a Saturday as it would be on a

Friday.'

Bernadette exploded, dramatically. 'No, I do not want to do that. We have one thousand pounds of semtex, and by changing the day to a Saturday we would only create maximum destruction to buildings, which is what we achieved last year, but I want maximum loss of human life.'

Kerry insisted, 'we will all be at far greater risk without having the extra twenty-four hours to plan and prepare our phase of the Irish decoy operation, and a delay on the bombing phase will afford it greater security. The very fact that the Security Forces have traced part of our team makes the successful combination of these two operations even more vital. The value of success for both operations will be enormous. The risk is far less for two operations on a Saturday than a single operation on the Friday. Furthermore, there would be a tremendous backlash of blowing up a building with thousands of workers and passers by killed. Our terms of reference were to destroy the economic structure and force the Government to the peace table. Killing thousands of people would certainly not achieve our goals in comparison to taking out either a MI5 or SAS team.'

The three men nodded in agreement.

Bernadette, dismayed, knew she was losing control.

Kerry continued. 'We have to admit, very bad mistakes have been made, and the bungles have seriously coloured future operations with a need for a high standard of logistical planning as achieved in the past. We can start with this operation, and to accomplish this by Saturday morning will be no mean feat.'

Bernadette was seething deep inside, but said, 'it seems I am defeated...

We do as Kerry has suggested.'

Kerry was back in command, though Bernadette wouldn't see it that way, anymore than she had before. 'Bernadette, it is not about being defeated. Common sense rather than gungho mentality must prevail at all times. We need this operation out of the way, and then we can look to the future. You already know that I have been planning something that will fulfil your ambition of taking out a major military establishment. Believe me, Bernadette; there will be over three hundred deaths of senior military servicemen, who are the enemy, and have probably all served in Northern Ireland, at some time or other. I will outline this to you all shortly.'

Bernadette smiled, then said, 'That sounds interesting, and with that in mind, we'll run this operation exactly as you have suggested...'

***

Pete Williams had been working at his laptop for twelve hours. He had the database filled with all available information to date.

'Gentlemen, I have information on our man Sean Hegatty.'

The kingpin operators gathered around Pete and his laptop. It was late and they had all been at the Embassy for detailed briefs about the scene of the crimes, and were scheduled to visit the place the next day.

Pete Williams felt delighted with himself; ecstatic more like.

Peter Wilcox said, 'Calm down Peter... What have we got?'

'I'll go through what I have, but not how I have got there. If you have a query on any point please stop me?'

'Will do,' assured Peter Wilcox.

'Sean Hegatty came from nowhere, and no trace of his travel movements. On the 12 March 1992, he booked in at the Royal Cliff Beach Resort, which is a popular tourist and business hotel, situated a few miles south of Pattaya. There is no further sign of him until six days later when he made a telephone call to a little Thai village or town, or whatever they are called over here.

It lies on the southern coast about twenty miles south of Pattaya. The call was listed at 1406 hours. Hegatty then booked out after making that call, and that same number was called from a room in the Royal Orchid in Bangkok at 2045 hours. The occupant of the room had registered as Mr Alan Smithson, a businessman from Belfast, who had flown into Bangkok that same morning.'

Pete, rubbed his hands together, and then scrolled down the vast database before them.

'The next information that I can trace of Sean Hegatty, is his leaving Bangkok on the 15 May. He did not book into any hotel accommodation before leaving Thailand. We could assume that he moved and stayed with someone at Ban Khlot. However, I think not!

Meanwhile, Alan Smithson booked out of the Royal Orchid on the 15 May, but there is no trace of him leaving the country. So gentlemen, everything points to Alan Smithson and Sean Hegatty as one and the same man. Sean Hegatty has two passports and that would imply his active service unit are operational under pseudonyms.'

'Pretty much as expected,' remarked Peter Wilcox. 'Bloody fools if they were not.'

'Moving on, gentlemen. Alan Smithson mysteriously arrived back in Bangkok on the 6 July, flying in from Singapore. He had left Heathrow on the fourth. He called the Ban Khlot number from a hotel in Pattaya, and then flew to Taiwan on the fifteenth. That was the last I can trace of him. Tracing back, he now appeared again on the 5 March 1993 on a flight to Bermuda. He booked into the Hamilton Princess hotel on the Friday and left on the Sunday, flying via Washington. He flew from there to Paris, and that is where his trail goes dead. That being said, we now have a pattern of his movements to coincide with the murders, and without doubt, committed either in part or whole by Sean Hegatty alias Alan Smithson.'

There was much straightening of backs, thoughtful expressions, as Peter Wilcox said, 'and...'

'I then spent time searching for people who travelled to both Thailand and Bermuda within specific times that are relevant to our investigations. There are two women who travelled out on the 13 July on separate flights, and stayed at two separate hotels. Can you imagine anyone flying to Thailand, arriving there at 10am one day, staying the night and then flying back the next morning? Most unusual, but it happened. I also traced three other men on similar trips. Two I have dismissed, because they were diplomatic couriers. The third, I believe, is our man...

He arrived in Bangkok from Hong Kong, having stayed there a few days. He then stays for one night at the Royal Cliff Beach Resort, about seventy miles or so from Bangkok Airport, and heads back to Heathrow the next day. Mighty strange, to say the least, if he was going to have a stop over he could have stayed at the airport or even gone into Bangkok. This all corroborates with the same four who appeared in Bermuda at the time of Dermott Black's death.'

Pete was in his element in the world of data absorbency, his software package working overtime in finding and linking with specific keywords.

'I hope you realise we all feel suitably inadequate,' remarked Peter Wilcox, a hand to Pete's shoulder. 'On the computer front you're a genius, my boy, an absolute genius.'

Pete beamed and continued. 'More information can be

obtained by following up the telephone number in Ban Khlot, and from visiting the respective hotels. These are the names that they are travelling under...

Alan Smithson we know is Sean Hegatty...

Gerry Croft is the other male...

Deborah Webster is one of the females...

Karen Wilson is the other...

I also believe that the two females posing as Sharon and Helen in Bermuda, when David and Angela were there, are the aliases of Deborah and Karen, presupposing they are working only two passports.

Both these females were in Bermuda on previous occasions. The first, as I said, coincided with the time that David and Angela were there. I would suggest that the second time was a final recce for a kill, and prior to the ambush. So, unfortunately for David, without doubt he actually spoke with the murderers of his son!'

Peter Wilcox said, 'you have done a great job, Pete. Let's all get some sleep, then we will start the follow ups tomorrow.'

Chapter Thirty Eight

Sean took a flight from Hurn Airport near Bournemouth to Dublin. There, he picked up the car that they had left at the airport on Monday and drove to the docks to collect Fred, and from there, they went on to the house in Drogheda. They stayed the night and went over everything that Bernadette and Kerry had instructed.

The next morning Fred dropped Sean off at Dublin Airport and headed north to Donegal on the western coast of Ireland. He then headed northeast heading for Letterkenny, where he turned right for Derry.

He crossed into Northern Ireland and could see in his wing mirrors that he had company, a RUC officer on his radio.

Within minutes David Carver was informed that a suspect car had been spotted in Derry. With every available unmarked police car on standby, David alerted Tom Galloway and they were airborne within minutes. Another sighting placed Fred on the Derry to Belfast road and a number of unmarked cars were now being placed in position.

He would not get away this time...

Fred Short, meanwhile, drove to the docks in Belfast, where walking around he spotted a helicopter, and grinned to himself.

* * *

David Carver was with Rupert Willet observing, and he guessed Fred to be heading over to the mainland, and knew they needed manpower over there. David desperately tried to contact Len, Tug, and Jock, who were involved in an operation with the team now known as the Combined Freedom Fighters of Ulster and were temporarily out of contact...

Instead, David contacted the local RUC Special Branch who already had men on the ground at the docks, and confirmed also that the driver of the suspect vehicle was in a local bar.

David Carver decided to get back on the terra firma. He couldn't control this operation from the air. He wanted his men on that ferry...

They landed and Rupert Willet raced to the control room

and got the only MI5 officer available to go with him. Before they left he contacted London and explained that they needed men on standby to intercept and help follow the car.

It was 2 pm when Fred staggered out of the pub and returned to his car at the docks. He didn't have too long to wait before boarding the car deck. Rupert Willet and Craig Denton followed him on board.

Fred arrived at Liverpool, where there were two MI5 teams waiting. He was seen to saunter around for a while, and then at 1.20 am he drove out of the docks and headed for the motorway.

David Carver had failed to make contact with his crack squad and had decided to leave for Liverpool in the Gazelle, with Jack Simpson.

Rupert Willet was keeping them informed: Fred Short was boxed in, which was standard strategy, whether mobile or on foot. The roads at this time of morning were virtually deserted, and he was heading south for London, so close up tailing was a no-no.

He'd stopped at the service station at Cannock and used the toilets, bought a cup of coffee, and then seen to be cat-napping in the car. Fred awakened with a start, warily looked around, and was surprised that there was no 'chopper' in sight or distant drone of one hovering at a discreet distance.

He wasn't to know that it was being refuelled.

After a couple of hours more sleep, he continued on his way and drove to High Wycombe, where he again headed south, eventually pulling into the British Rail car park at Woking.

David Carver was desperately trying to fathom out where in hell Fred would be going to next. Rupert Willet, meanwhile, had managed to contact the plainclothes officers who were already arriving at Woking station.

Fred was overheard ordering a single ticket to Andover.

Rupert Willet eventually met them. Rupert instructed Craig Denton to get back to the car and head off to Andover station. He also gave the same instructions for the driver of the other MI5 team. He then had three officers to assist him to watch Fred Short on the journey.

The train was due in five minutes...

Fred was sitting, drinking coffee, as the train trundled slowly into the station. There were very few people waiting for the train and fewer on it, and he felt reassured in knowing that

Bernadette, Kerry, Sean, and Joe, were indeed on board as backup; a trap well set and hopefully about to be sprung...

Fred got up, walked to the platform, and slowly strolled towards the front of the eight-carriage train. Bernadette watched several departing passengers for obvious signs of a suspicious presence. Sean and Joe were equally alert at the front end of the train, as Kerry too got off and walked across the platform to stand by a seat.

She had full vision of the comings and goings of station personnel and the general public; a man dressed as if he were a businessman was holding a copy of the times, noticeably watching Fred's movement along the platform. As soon as Fred boarded the train, the Times man stepped aboard, and stood by the window four carriages back from Fred's. She also noticed a labourer carrying a tool bag who boarded nearer to the engine.

She assumed Sean must have seen a man sat on the bench near the front of the station, who had seemingly watched Fred, before he too boarded one carriage ahead. And, Bernadette couldn't have failed to pick up on a woman standing by the coffee machine. The woman who had watched Fred, and then had turned to face the machine, coffee beaker still in hand, upon his approach. After Fred had passed by, the woman had moved across the platform, had then boarded the train and had stayed at the window watching him.

The guard was now walking the train, closing the doors, and when Fred stepped off the train and walked to a bin to dispose of his empty coffee cup, Kerry noticed all four suspects leave the train. Then all four turned and re-boarded when they saw Fred move back onto the train. Kerry re-boarded and moved towards the rear end. She assumed the team tailing Fred's ass were in radio contact...

Well' so were they...

As soon as the train moved off Sean and Joe moved to the rear of the train, where Kerry confirmed each target as positive suspects. Fred was doing exactly as told, pretending to be asleep. Therefore attack would take place immediately the train entered Basingstoke station. It was a good place, in that it was unlikely that all the watchers would leave their seats just in case Fred did another hop-off hop-on routine at Basingstoke.

Bernadette, Kerry, and Joe were directly behind their targets. Sean's more difficult. The female watcher was sitting behind and to the right of Fred, two more passengers directly behind her. As the train neared the station Sean stood up, moved level with her, looked at her. She was noticeably alert to his presence without looking up; hand on the back of the seat, steadying himself as the train miraculously lurched, only slight, but enough to fake loss of balance.

He had to be quick, and stumbled onto the seat beside her, glad to be rid of the deadly substance, concealed behind the palm of his gloved hand.

She never saw the needle; only felt the tiny prick. In three seconds she was dead, and likewise, her companions.

All five terrorists left the train at Basingstoke.

The train pulled in to Andover station; watched by the two MI5 drivers that had raced forward at breakneck speed to meet the train on its arrival. Only three passengers alighted and about ten boarded. The train pulled away heading towards Salisbury.

Craig Denton contacted David Carver and relayed the information. David guessed that something had gone wrong, very wrong. He instructed Tom to get as near to the Salisbury rail station as possible and land…

Tom hovered about two hundred feet above the front of the station and noticed the car park to the left was virtually empty. He landed there and David and Jack Simpson and an accompanying RUC officer jumped out and raced towards the station.

David scoured the platform looking for someone who might well be awaiting the terrorist. There were very few people about for a Saturday morning and it was now 11.30 am; no one looking to the incoming train.

He watched the train slowly enter the station; Rupert Willet was onboard, his head turned away as though asleep. David immediately instructed the RUC officer to move to the front of the train and Jack to the centre where he had seen Rupert Willet. He himself would enter the rear and work to the front. Instinctively he knew there would be no terrorists on the train.

Jack Simpson found Rupert, apparently asleep, enraged he said, 'what the hell,' as he shook him, then followed with, 'damn.'

He then heard a piecing sound that went right through him; it was the guard's whistle!

He jumped off the train; the door left wide open.

The RUC officer leapt off too; he had found a dead woman. The guard alighted and yelled, 'what the hell is going on?'

and headed towards them.

David re-appeared on the platform, rushed up to his men, and asked, 'bad, is it?' voice lowered.

Jack Simpson nodded and said, 'Rupert and a female...Both dead!'

'Don, we're out of here, now, just in case one of the shite's who did this are watching our every move.' He addressed the RUC officer. 'Paul, you'll have to deal with the situation. Call the police, show your warrant to the guard and tell him to get everyone off the train. Then get the train into a siding. I will get back to you as soon as I can.'

'No problem David, and Paul then advanced toward the guard; with his warrant in hand.

David walked off at a fast pace, while Jack strolled from the station platform hoping to hell they hadn't blown their own cover. Outside the station both men hurried to the car park where Tom Galloway had the rotors still spinning, and within minutes they were airborne.

Both David and Jack were in a state of shock; a fucking set-up, would you believe it, they'd been out-witted, out-thought, out-foxed, by a cleverly planned deceptive trap.

'Fucking hell, how on earth could this have happened?' David, forlorn in his thoughts, pondered, 'how, for crying out loud, how?'

Yet again, their ingenuity had prevailed, another successful operation, all down to this PIRA "nutting squad". How David thought, how could this happen, especially against a man of his experience

What now? Thought David. Who to contact? Two dead officers, two more families to be told the loss of loved ones.

Basingstoke had to have been the jump off point for the PIRA squad.

'Tom,' he said, 'move to Netheravon and refuel, while I try to unravel what has happened. This is turning into a nightmare. These people have to be stopped.'

David and Jack moved from the landing area by Land-Rover, and went into the Headquarters of the Army Air Corps Regiment. As soon as he mentioned the codeword the Commanding Officer and his Adjutant offered full co-operation, and a temporary office to use.

David contacted the senior police officer at Salisbury; half hoping Paul Garfield might have already arrived there. He hadn't but David spoke with a very irate senior police officer who demanded to know what in hell was going on in his patch. David Carver cooled the ether, then asked the senior officer for an update of the deaths on the train.

'Three men and one female, dead, no immediate means of ascertaining cause of death. Speculation is running at lethal administrating by hypodermic syringe.'

David was stunned. Four people dead, where was this going to end?

'Thank you. Please get Paul to ring me, ASAP...'

And still holding on to the telephone, there was a tap on the door and the Commanding Officer entered; David still on the telephone pressed the mute button.

'Sorry, but our alert state has just been increased to the highest level. Any idea what is going on?' queried the CO.

Then the Adjutant hurried in and spoke with both the CO and David Carver, 'a massive bomb has just devastated the centre of London.'

David immediately reinstated communication with the Salisbury police officer. 'I must go, could you please send my RUC officer to Airfield Camp at Netheravon. I would like the train pulled into a siding if this has not already been done. I do not want media attention, and I'll arrange the removal of the bodies...

Your help would be greatly appreciated...'

The police officer went to speak and David Carver cut him short with, 'I am acting on the authority at the highest level, under "Operation Combating Evil" and at this moment, there are more lives at risk. You already know what has happened today.'

'Yes, sir,' replied the senior police officer, 'I was only going on to ask, would it be any advantage to you if I came along with your RUC chap?'

'No, I'd prefer for you to remain there for the time being and ensure the instructions I have given you are implemented. You'll need to come here at some time so that I can brief you further, and I will as soon as possible.'

David handed the CO a number. 'Colonel, could you please ring this number for me and ask for Sir Peter Wilcox.'

Whilst that was being done David Carver contacted Len, and briefly explained what had happened, then said. 'Prepare to move Len, I am sending Tom over to you. Come back to Netheravon in the Lynx, with as much kit as possible. Inform

Spike Wilson to leave the Reserve Company in place, and he and his men are to return here as soon as we can organise it. In fact, I can do that now...'

David then turned to the CO. 'Have you two Lynx available to move immediately with Tom Galloway to Northern Ireland, and an extra pilot to bring our Gazelle back?'

The CO nodded, and David confirmed that to Len waiting on line.

'We will set up on Airfield Camp as a temporary base.'

The CO had got through to Sir Peter Wilcox, silently indicated that he had him on the other line.

'Len, I must go,' said David. 'Get a move on, I need you and the lads here as a matter of urgency.'

Len said, 'we have another operation tomorrow night, can this still go ahead?'

'Only if you feel that it can be accomplished without the presence of you three. That is your decision, Len. Sorry but I have Peter on the other line, I must go...'

'Hullo Peter, David said. 'We caught up with our friend yesterday, and several officers ended up in an ambush. We have lost four, unfortunately all of yours, and I have just heard that a massive bomb has been detonated in the centre of London...

I am presently located at Airfield Camp, Netheravon and I am moving our base here today. I need you back here, urgently.

Can you give me a quick summary on your progress?'

Peter Wilcox informed David Carver of the progress that had been made and said that he would leave Ian Walsh and Alan Kirkby to finish the investigation, and confirmed he would leave within the hour.

'At least you have some good news Peter. Inform Ian Walsh, and Alan Kirkby, that I want the investigations completed within twenty-four hours. We need everyone back here now.'

David wanted all his manpower and equipment moved from Northern Ireland to Netheravon, by 1800 hours the next day...

* * *

Chapter Thirty Nine

The active service unit had dispersed from Basingstoke in different directions; Kerry had organised this to perfection!

Sean and Joe had returned to London on the next train. Kerry had taken a bus to Andover. Bernadette had driven back to the house in the New Forest. Fred had meanwhile walked around Basingstoke, bought a change of clothes, before booking into a family guesthouse, and settled inside, just as a news flash announced the huge blast at the Nat West bank.

All arrived back at the New Forest base on the Monday morning; elated about the bombing, but totally dismayed that nothing had been mentioned about the slaying of the MI5 officers.

Bernadette said, 'we'll have to split up now. There's bound to be a massive search throughout the south. Fred, Sean, and Joe, you can go back as best you can to family life and we'll all meet up again here on the first of June.'

Joe said, 'Bernadette, why haven't we hit Michael Mulcahy in Finland, yet? My brother is still rotting in the Maze, and it's time that Mulcahy's good life was taken from him. Can we make that a priority when we get back?'

'Yes we will, but you'll need to do another recce and then we'll hit him as soon as we can. Let's just let the current situation die down first, alright?'

'Thanks Bernadette,' Joe said.

The men left, and Bernadette put her arm around Kerry, her response less than desirable. 'That was a great operation. We did well. Now tell me all about this man of yours, and what your intentions are for our next big operation. In fact, Kerry, tell me in the bath.'

Kerry was undressing, aware of Bernadette already relaxing in the bath; eyes on female contours, wanting their relationship back where it belonged, under her control, at any expense.

Kerry explained about a conference that would be taking place in the barracks at Larkhill in June. It all sounded a very easy target and a bomb could be planted and exploded at any time by using a timing device.

Bernadette then said, 'that's a brilliant idea, how did you find that out?'

Kerry hesitated, not having expected in-depth questions.

'I asked Tony if we should take June off and have a holiday. He initially agreed, then remembered about this conference. It's scheduled for two days. The dates are 10 and 11 June. He's in charge of the conference centre, and, as one of the organisers, he wouldn't be able to take the time off.'

Bernadette was noticeably furious. 'Kerry, we go on holiday together, not with other people. In fact I thought we could go to Bermuda tomorrow!'

Bernadette had compromised for Kerry and knew she wouldn't be able to refuse, but Kerry went with the flow and changed tactic mid stream.

'What a great idea, Bernadette, but only for a week... I am determined that the military target will go ahead.'

They remained in the bath for an hour and for Bernadette it may have been bliss, but not for Kerry. Yes, she knew how to satisfy a woman, and when she said, 'I am getting out now,' and kissed Bernadette, the now unfit, rotund, unpleasant bitch rallied to the offensive

'What are you doing Kerry, there's no need to go rushing off any where?'

'Yes there is, Bernadette. I have to book tickets to Bermuda and, I also need to prepare for getting back to work. I told you, I need to get back to Amesbury.'

'I don't want you to return there. Sod the military operation... We've done enough with the bombing and the four killings. I'm in charge of mainland operations Kerry, not you, and the military operation is temporarily off the agenda.'

'Bernadette, I never thought to hear you talk like this. You have always said that the organisation must come first. We have both grown up with that belief.'

Bernadette climbed out of the sunken bath, Kerry looking on, disgusted at having had to perform sexual favours merely to keep the peace, hopefully long enough to finally escape Bernadette's oppressive clutches.

At thirty-three and no longer lean like a young stud she was totally unattractive to Kerry, and combined with some of the loathsome things she was prone to do had made Kerry feel quite nauseous. Kerry had accepted her own bisexual tendencies as youthful sexual exploration, her relationship with Tony far more fulfilling in every sense of the word. Bernadette was a full-blown dyke, and a sadistic one at that.

Bernadette pleaded with Kerry. 'We have been together all our lives Kerry...You're mine, and I am yours, and always will be. Forget Tony... We'll have a wonderful long break from the organisation, be together again. Never in my life, as you know, have I begged anyone for anything. I am now begging you. Please Kerry; let's try again...

I love and want you so much... Please, please, Kerry.'

Kerry drew breath. 'No Bernadette.. You're getting everything out of perspective. I have already said that I have never left you...

The cause and the organisation must always come first. After the military operation I will be back here, with you. All we have to do is plant the bomb and leave. We have excellent timing devices. It could be planted at any time. Then we can have a break away, which is what you want. After that we can go to Helsinki and complete Joe's revenge operation. Surely that makes sense?'

Kerry paused, looking somewhat thoughtful, continued.

'Let me just say this Bernadette, and this outlines your lack of judgement at the moment. We have just finished two very successful operations, and one, that was not intended or planned. We were fortunate that it went well, but who knows what will come out of it? There have been no reports about the deaths on the train, not from any media source. Now think about this...

What will the Army Council think? All they know at this stage is that Ryan Flynn's active service unit exploded a one-ton bomb in Bishopsgate, London. They know nothing about our planning, or our efforts in that operation. Ryan Flynn gets full credit. As far as our masters are concerned, we have accomplished nothing.'

Kerry was thinking on her feet, desperate to get back to Tony.

'Tell me Bernadette, why has there been nothing about the four watchers that Fred lured into our trap? The incident should be major news by now, like the bomb?

Furthermore, we still do not know how Sean and Fred were discovered. Someone somewhere might well know all our names and, our false names. The only thing that they obviously don't know is where we are!'

Bernadette looked gobsmacked by Kerry's forthright onslaught.

'Bernadette, if you think about it, after Saturday's events, every port, airport, rail station, and even bus station is now being watched. And, what have you done? You have sent our team away without warning them where to keep away from...

You have seen and also partly caused the errors of Sean and Fred. I can guarantee that the first one to attempt to leave the country will be arrested. Then it will be just a matter of time for the rest of us. As far as I am concerned we should not go to Bermuda. You should also contact the rest of the team and stop them from leaving the country until I can get new passports. Makes sense, does it not?'

Bernadette looked gutted and very agitated; knew that what Kerry had said was all true. 'Kerry let me think about this... I hear what you are saying, but I need to decide the correct action to take.'

'Bernadette, there is nothing to think about...

There is only one thing to do and that is to get the others back. You know how to contact them. I will get in touch with our mole in the passport office. We could have new passports in days. I will go up to Amesbury and see how quickly I can get this operation moved ahead. We have to show the Army Council that we mean business and must recover some credence from a cock-up. Let's waste no more time, and get on with putting things right, like protecting our backs.'

'You are right Kerry. I will get the men back, and you organise the passports?'

'I'll do that now, but will need £5,000 in cash for the passports and a grand for myself. Which account shall I use?'

'Use the building society in Bournemouth and draw money for the men as well... I forgot about that. How soon can you get the passports?'

'It's Monday today, so I'll offer our girl an extra grand to deliver them to me, and hopefully we should have them at the latest by Friday. If you can also organise the explosives, timing devices, and detonators, then, with a bit of luck, we could all be out of the country sometime next week.'

Bernadette grinned, 'I would like that very much, Kerry.'

'Have I at long last made you happy, Bernadette?'

'Yes, as long as you stay with me tonight.'

Kerry saw the logistics of Bournemouth closer to where they

were at present, as opposed to travelling from Amesbury to the building society for a cash haul. 'Agreed, but I have much planning to do first before pleasure games.'

With luck she could have Bernadette yawning, bored, and asleep before retiring to bed herself...

* * *

Kerry was out of the New Forest house before breakfast, standing at a cashier till at the building society by 9.30 am.

She had planned ten thousand pounds each for the men and the rest to cover the passports and money for her and Bernadette, and requested a cash payment of £40,000.

The account needed to be checked to be sure of sufficient funds, and she was immediately invited into the manager's office, who offered her coffee while the money was being counted.

'I sincerely hope that this is not the end of our business Ms McKeefe?'

'No, of course not. Our German account will be transferring funds to the account here, in due course.'

Kerry immediately thought that she had better arrange that as soon as possible, as their UK funds were now almost drained bar for a miniscule float. She also knew that she needed a large amount of cash stashed away for her own purposes.

'Could I instigate the German transaction from here?' Kerry asked the manager.

'Yes, of course,' he said. 'If you write down the name and address of your German bank and account, we can draft the request by telex and provide sort code details. The money should be in your account by this time tomorrow. How much would you like to transfer?'

Kerry thought a moment, and said, 'could you request the transfer of two million pounds, as I wish to purchase a new property.'

The draft was telexed within minutes, much to the delight of the branch manager. A few moments later a cashier arrived with the formerly requested cash in twenty bundles of £2,000 in fifty-pound notes. Kerry thanked both the manager and cashier, and left immediately.

En route to Amesbury she made a telephone call; like teenagers kept apart, they giggled and joked, teasing each other. Bernadette was the last thing on her mind...

Neither Kerry nor Tony could have imagined the dreadful circumstances, that they would be in, when they next met...

* * *

Chapter Forty

The unexpected happened at 11.30 on the Monday morning, when a duty operator reported...

'Pat Maguire is on the move...Pat Maguire and his family have just booked in at Heathrow for a flight to Manchester.'

Tom Galloway heard this and raced out to the Land-Rover, shouted for one of the backup team to drive him up to the takeoff area. As soon as he reached the landing pad he sent the vehicle back to collect the lads. The ground crew had already refuelled the Lynx and Gazelle, and both helicopters had been serviced since he had landed for the final time on the Sunday morning.

David Carver called Don, Len, Tug, and Jock. 'Come on lads, ready to move in five minutes. Tom's already warming up.'

They heard the Lynx, and knew Tom would be ready to lift three minutes from the commencement of the rotors moving. They were running full pace, bent almost double to keep below the rotor blades; now at maximum rotation for takeoff. When they reached the Lynx, he was ready.

Tom had his right thumb up indicating that they could board the aircraft. Len, Tug, and Jock were on board strapping themselves in when they noticed Jack Simpson just reaching the outer area of the blades.

'Come on, you old bugger,' yelled Jock, and they were all laughing at him trying to clamber into the aircraft. Tug and Jock yanked him in, and virtually threw him into his seat.

'No need for that chaps, I was right behind you.'

When they flew over Maguire's property there was no sign of the family. Tug shouted over the noise of the aircraft, 'always the fucking same...

The army never changes, rush like hell, to wait...!'

They all grinned, all aware of the task ahead; everything in perspective.

Tom Galloway kept the machine hovering at the far end of Maguire's land, as Jack Simpson yelled, 'I am not getting out until the skids are on the deck...

No...you pair of bastards...No...' he screamed, and that was all he had a chance to yell, as Tug and Jock picked him up and they all jumped out together.

Upon landing in a heap, he growled, 'You pair of fucking bastards, I'll get you both for that,' whilst trying to scramble to his feet. 'Oh, my bloody back,' he groaned, as he re-adjusted his dislodged spectacles.

Len was grinning, 'Come on you fat old bugger, we're picking him up today, not tomorrow.'

They settled down behind the hedge near to a field gate and waited, and not for very long before Maguire's BMW turned into the drive at the front of the house.

Jack Simpson and Len had left instructions for Tug and Jock, emergency instructions to be implemented if something went wrong.

Moments later Jack rang the doorbell, turned, and smiled at Len whose stomach was churning.

Pat Maguire answered and just stood looking at the two men.

'Yes, what can I do for you?'

'We need to talk with you Mr Maguire.' Jack Simpson said, and then smiled at him.

'My name is Gillespie, who are you?'

'Maguire, we can make this very easy for you...

Look up to the tree line, and you'll see we have friends there who will blast this house to bits, and all in it. This is the last time that I will repeat myself...

We need to talk, or we will just walk away and blow your fucking house up, wife, kids and all...

You have five seconds to make your mind up?'

He immediately said. 'What the fuck do you want to talk about?'

'You will come with us; the length of time we take will depend on your co-operation...

Are you ready to co-operate?'

'No I must speak with my wife.'

He went to move inside but Jack Simpson stopped him. 'Call her, now.'

She had obviously been listening, as she appeared ashen-faced to stand alongside him. 'Why don't you lot just fuck off and leave us in peace. We are happy here and harming no one?'

'Dorothy, life isn't as easy as that; especially with the amount of men he has killed, and even more so, when you have earned in excess of five million pounds in cheating the movement. This is the approximate amount, that has been stolen by you both, from the organisation.'

Dorothy Maguire snapped viciously at Jack Simpson, 'Bollocks, we have no money and no assets... We have a mortgage on this property, now piss off the pair of you or I will call the police.'

Jack kept his cool throughout her tirade, then quietly said, 'that's not very charming language from a wealthy and travelled lady like yourself. It's time you listened to me, especially as I agree with two of your comments.'

They both looked at one another, then paused, Pat Maguire eventually asked, 'agree, what do you mean, what two comments?'

'You have no money and you have no assets. If you want to call the police we are both wired to radio communications, to the helicopter, which is sitting in our field...We can have the police here in two minutes...

Now Pat Maguire, fuckin' answer me, are you going to co-operate?'

'No he is not, and it is not your field.' She snapped.

'Alright bitch, let me spell it out to you...'

Pat Maguire yelled, 'don't fucking talk to my missus like that or I'll take your head off your fucking shoulders, any other time you would have been dead by now.'

Jack angrily pointed at her, 'tell that fucking bitch to go and check your security fucking safe, because, as I was about to say...

We have fucking raided it...

It is empty.'

They were dumbfounded.

'No, no, no...' she screamed.

'Shut up and listen bitch. There's more, all the property deeds that you had, the one's that you sent for, two weeks ago. Well they are with me now, and we are in the process of transferring the properties to other names.

Lets face it "Dotty", or do you prefer that stupid fucking name, Dorothy, darling, get real, you stole them, and we have stolen them back.'

Jack laughed, heartily...

'So, "Dotty", you are correct, you have no money and you have no assets. I have them...

Therefore "Patty and Dotty", you are going to listen and listen well, then you will both do exactly as you are fucking told and, do you know why?'

'No,' they both said in unison.

'Because if you don't, I will hand you both over to PIRA in the centre of Armagh, today, now, yes...I will even give you a free ride in my helicopter. You will both be stripped naked. You will have placards around your necks showing how you and your active service units have ripped off the organisation and the people.

There will be copies of everything that you have done, and of course, circulated before we chain you to the lampposts...

As a long-standing member of a PIRA internal security squad, Patrick, your fate amongst the people will be even worse. Indeed, we can even say that you were both members. We both know that a female led another "nutting squad", don't we Patrick?'

There was terror in both their eyes.

Jack Simpson then said. 'Of course, you both know what happens to the children of people like you, don't you?'

She screamed hysterically. 'Stop, stop, not my bairns, no, no, no!'

'Stop, stop, what do you mean stop, I haven't fucking started yet,' Jack Simpson shouted.

'You've said enough, now what do you want?'

'Well I thought for starters that "Dotty" would invite us in for a cup of tea. Then we can sort things out.

'Stop calling me "Dotty", you rotten fucking English pig.'

'Now, now, "Dotty", such language, and in front of your children.'

She turned and yelled at her three children, 'get up them stairs, you little buggers.' She turned once more to Don. 'Come in and sit down and you are not getting any tea...

I want my money back, it is not his, it is mine.'

Pat Maguire chirped in, 'if you've raided the safe and got the documents and money there's nothing to tell. So, what are you after?'

'Quite a few things Pat, we know that Fred Short and Sean Hegatty are members of the other internal security ASU that you were working with when you captured and tortured Mulvenny. The other ASU captured two soldiers, one a male, the other a female. Who were the other members of that ASU and who were the members of your ASU?'

Jack eyed him at close quarters.

'Now before you answer me Pat, let me tell you something...

You had thirty runners collecting subscriptions from businesses and private citizens. This at one stage was shown to be bringing in as much as £85,000 a week. Now, both you and I know that at most times you were collecting nearly treble that amount. But you were only declaring an average of around £85,000.'

Maguire didn't like Jack one iota; if eye contact could kill, Jack was a dead man, only he wasn't, and continued...

'You had an arrangement with the PIRA Chief Paymaster, codename BALLISTIC, we got this from a friend of yours. You retained 33% of your total and he kept 33%. Then PIRA funds received the other 34%. Your receipts to the paymaster always showed the grand total of 34%. Therefore, just to keep things simple, if you collected £100,000, you would retain £33,000, you would send him £33,000, which he would pocket and also the other £34,000, with receipts for that amount, which he would put into PIRA accounts. This you have had going for twelve years...Self-enterprise has made you and "Dotty" very wealthy.

Well, it did, until I nicked it from you, which is very sad. In fact, this property is a great investment, and I am looking to take over the development of the land that I have parked my helicopter on.'

'Will you fucking get on with it,' Pat Maguire shouted.

'Oh, I am so sorry Pat, I was going to tell you of my new plans to develop the land... I'll not be telling you now! So Pat, now that you know what I know, you're now going to tell me what I don't know...

Who is BALLISTIC? I also want the names and contact telephone numbers of the active service unit members I have already asked for.'

Pat Maguire said. 'The only answer that I can give you is, I don't know.'

Jack Simpson replied, 'following your wife's fine understanding of the English language, I would say to you... Bollocks!'

'The Provisional Irish Republican Army is very strict with its security,' snarled Maguire. 'We all know the member's names beneath us but not above. As regards to BALLISTIC he is an Army Council member and that's all I know.'

'You are fucking lying and I am not wasting my time here, any longer. You will come with us... She can stay here, but your house will remain under surveillance. Say your goodbyes now, I don't think you will be coming back.'

'No, please no, don't take him, give me my money back and I will tell you,' yelled his wife.

'Indeed not, I will take him; he obviously knows and prefers to act the hero. We will see what type of hero he is when hanging upside down thirty feet below our helicopter. Especially when our pilot likes flying at forty feet! Gosh! All the way to Northern Ireland, upside down, 10 feet off the deck, at 150 miles an hour... We could have a wager on whether you would die of hypothermia, shock, or if you survive the trip, the people of Armagh.'

Dorothy looked aghast, as Jack continued.

'Then we will come back, and you "Dotty" will tell us all we want to know, or you will go for the same helicopter ride. You want to protect not only yourself but also your children, so you will tell us in the end.'

He,' Jack said, pointing at a furious Maguire, 'doesn't give two monkeys about any of you.'

'That's not true.'

'Then save us the hassle of getting you tortured and slaughtered, and answer my questions.'

'Please Pat, please, tell them what you know.'

'Seems I have no fucking choice, BALLISTIC is...'

'Wait,' Jack Simpson said, 'Len, take her outside and get the answers from her, and then we'll compare notes.'

Jack grinned...

Upon the conclusion, they were allowed back together, Jack said, 'you've saved yourselves a horrendous death, you know. Your house though, will remain under surveillance and you will remain here until we decide what is going to happen to you, eventually. Is that understood?'

They both nodded, knowing that they were totally defeated.

'In the meantime we have one little job to do before we go, I suggest that you go upstairs.'

'Why, what else can you do to us? Fuck all, so piss off and leave us alone.'

'I am very concerned that you might attempt to drive away, and that would mean that we would have to start all over again looking for you, now you wouldn't want that would you?'

Pat Maguire said, 'don't damage our car, it is all we have left, please?'
Then they all heard a small explosion and shattering of glass.
'So sorry,' Jack Simpson said, with a smile. 'You have just lost the steering column and all the windows! We'll be in touch.'

* * *

Back at Netheravon, they were elated, as David Carver met them on arrival. It was nearly midnight, but he wanted a brief outline and then a debriefing at 1000 hours in the morning. And he then explained that the VC10 bringing both Peter Wilcox and Peter Williams back had been delayed because of engine problems. They were now not expected until Wednesday morning.

Len was beaming with the success that they had achieved, and he said, 'that's sad boss, but we have really cracked Maguire, or rather this old geezer here,' gesturing to Don, 'was on top form today. We now have all the names we require.'

'Great Len, Pete Williams has also cracked names of the PIRA squad, though not all...It is going to be very interesting once they are back and we can begin to collate and analyse the information.

There is also some very interesting information from Dave Bonner and Harry McFee on PIRA finances. If their information ties in with what you have obtained, and Peter's team, we should bring this to a conclusive ending. How we expedite the end is our main problem, and we'll deal with that in due course.'

David rubbed his hands together, a sense of achievement all around him. 'Grab yourselves some food and I'll see you at 1000 hours.'

* * *

The VC10 landed at RAF Boscombe Down, at 1120 hours on the Wednesday morning. Tom Galloway was there to meet them and they were in the operations room at Netheravon within minutes.

Later that same day, Tom Galloway met Ian Walsh and Alan Kirkby at Heathrow. Their news was good... They had followed up information that Pete Williams had provided and had come up with the answers. Like the others they were elated.

David Carver met them at Netheravon at about 0100 hours

on the Thursday morning. They gave him a brief sitrep and David confirmed to them that a conference had been set for 1200 hours.

From early Thursday morning the activity among the group had been intense. There were finishing touches to be added to enable David Carver to give a full and comprehensive brief, and collation continued right up until David Carver called everyone together.

Sir Peter Wilcox would normally have introduced the brief. As it was, he was still resolving the problems of the death of his deputy and the other three MI5 officers.

Meanwhile the team assembled in the regimental conference room. It was a very old and cold wooden building, but sufficed with a large oval mahogany table in the centre. At the front of the room was a dais, blackboard, and an overhead projector. Outside, at the entrance to the building were Spike Wilson and Jimmy Bartlett, two of the SAS team that had been with the team from the outset.

David Carver then started by covering all that had happened over the past ten days, seemingly a lifetime since their last, present and correct, meeting for all concerned:

'At our last briefing, we were all shocked and dismayed to have lost two members of a PIRA unit that we had been seeking...An RUC officer on that occasion reacted badly and the PIRA unit turned the tables on us and subsequently, we were completely outfoxed with the further loss of four MI5 officers. This emphasises the skill and professionalism of the unit we are trying to expose. We take nothing for granted from now on, absolutely nothing.'

He'd made his point, nodding heads and grim faces in full agreement.

'We are getting nearer to them. The mission to both Bermuda and Thailand has been extremely successful, as you will hear, later. The documents seized on raids at Pat Maguire and Mick Coombe's homes have provided invaluable information.

As you know, Mick Coombe and his active service unit met with an unfortunate accident and, we now have full control of Pat Maguire...Our active touts operating in their new roles have been great and are still hammering the PIRA sympathisers. It is my intentions to place these touts under command of our offshoot organisation, the Combined Freedom Fighters of Ulster, which have now disposed of nearly thirty-five terrorists. I intend that both these operations continue and I am also hoping that Jack Simpson will be able to convince Pat Maguire to lead these operations. He is a most skilled terrorist and would fit the bill quite nicely.'

David paused, as though expecting Jack to respond. He didn't.

'Len, I want you and the lads to continue a leading role in these operations. It will obviously mean a lot of flitting back and forth over to Northern Ireland, but this will be necessary to keep things in control and for supplying the necessary finance...

Let me now get into the meat of the information gathered and how best to use it...

Firstly, I will deal with the information from Peter's team. It appears that two recce's were completed by two females, prior to the operation which took place on 12 March 1993, in Bermuda...Two men and the same two females accomplished the operation. The same group of people were also involved in executions in both Australia and New Zealand and, the horrendous murders of the Murphy's, and Sam McGurk in Thailand.'

Legs changed position; knee to knee, and chairs creaked.

'The murder of McGurk is of particular interest. He was not a known tout. However he does fit into the equation. Mally Cork gave his name to us. McGurk was the PIRA soldier who murdered Simon Haig, a very close friend of Mally Cork. McGurk had tortured Haig to death. He had also tortured Fred Short destroying his manhood. Fred Short as we all know is part of the PIRA ASU we are looking for. It is safe to assume that Sam McGurk was tortured to death because of what he did to Fred Short.'

Known facts on Fred's incapacity caused the odd grimace.

'From what Mick Coombe told us, we knew that Fred Short disappeared off the scene for some time, he then reappeared again in a minor role. We know he did not take part in the Thailand operation because Pete found that he had left for Miami with his family. He did not return until after that operation.

Therefore it could be assumed that Gerry Croft was our missing man. Fred Short was not involved in any of the tout hunts, but he was most certainly involved in the death of my son, and also that of Mary O'Connor...Pete Williams, through his computer systems gave us the names of the group.'

David handed a pile of printed sheets to Len, and the pile passed man to man to the last sheet, his men puzzling the content therein.

'As you will see gentlemen...

Alan Smithson is Sean Hegatty.
Gerry Croft, not yet known.
Karen Wilson, not yet known.
Helen Webster, not yet known.
Fred Short - not yet known.

...At this stage we now have Sean Hegatty and Fred Short, with three others whose names are aliases.'

David allowed the men to absorb the names, and then resumed with the brief:

'Ian and Alan followed up the telephone calls to Ban Khlot and, lo and behold, we have an aggrieved female who Sean Hegatty had let down. She was present throughout at the initial torture of the three former PIRA members...

What is curious is how she became involved in the first place? The story is quite intriguing to say the least. Without going into detail at this stage, let's just say that a group of Cambodian refugees had been helped years before by a PIRA godfather and, he called in the debt.

Reg Pink, an MI6 officer was tasked with obtaining this vital name. Shari, Sean's eastern filly couldn't remember, but we'll get it in due course, in fact very soon...'

'Convenient amnesia,' said a voice from the floor. 'Yeh, right.'

David smiled:

'Pat Maguire has been exceptionally kind to us, not only with money and assets, but also with names! To remind you all, Pat Maguire was a brigade commander who for years ripped off PIRA funds for his own benefit. He was also in charge of the active service unit that captured Mulvenny at the same time that Jeremy was taken. He has given us real names, or so we believe, of the other nutting squad...They are Bernadette McGough, who is the leader, Kerry McKeefe, Sean Hegatty, Joe Hagan, and Fred Short. Therefore we should now be able to confirm Pete Williams's findings.'

David held up a sheet of paper matching those in the hands

of his team:

'You can see gentlemen, that Alan Smithson is Sean Hegatty... Gerry Croft is Joe Hagan...Karen Wilson and Helen Webster, we are about to find out which is which.

Fred Short as yet, has no alias...Memorise those names and appropriate alias.'

He glanced at Don.

'Now we come to another interesting saga. That of PIRA finances... Dave Bonner and Harry McFee have burnt the midnight oil in achieving their results...

An organised raid by the RUC and the army took place in May 1992. It was the largest combined operation to take place throughout the Northern Ireland campaign. Every known republican business in Northern Ireland had their offices raided and all documents seized. It was a brilliant operation, but sadly the majority of the information was not disseminated.

It has only come to light with the initiative of our two men, who have indeed uncovered a massive amount of fraud by certain PIRA members. The documents that we seized from Mick Coombe and Pat Maguire corroborate most of what has being going on. That is, individual theft at most levels in the PIRA structure.'

He paused, sipped at a glass of water.

'It was found that PIRA used accounts in both the north and the south. The banks that they used were involved in money laundering, and other scams, which ended up with large sums of money, legally transferred, to a small independent bank in Germany. The German Police have been excellent.

They, like us, are fed up with terrorism from the PIRA, on their doorstep. The co-operation has been unprecedented. The independent bank, which has six branches, had operated illegally for years holding private funds for a PIRA Army Council member who has for years remained unknown to us. He, his wife, and daughter, have now been exposed to us.'

David beamed:

'Their names are Seamus and Brenda McGough and their daughter is none other than... Bernadette McGough... Pat Maguire named Seamus McGough as the PIRA paymaster, whose codename was BALLISTIC. We also received from Reg Pink, the MI6 officer in Thailand, the name of the PIRA godfather that had helped the Cambodian refugees in the early eighties. It was Seamus McGough!'

'William Molloy has searched Bernadette McGough's background and it is very revealing. She along with Kerry McKeefe was expelled from a very expensive private school in Dublin in 1976. Previous to their expulsion they were instrumental in three teachers being dismissed and at least ten other pupils expelled. They had covertly terrorised the school from age eleven until sixteen, and proven themselves to be absolute brutes, until one day when a tough-minded teacher bravely shopped them. A catalogue of sexual perversions committed against all who had opposed them.

The Garda seized videos and photographs of their activities, but somehow, Seamus and Brenda McGough convinced the school to accept a huge sum of money to hush up the incidents. The Garda accepted this, probably substantial back handers as well to the officers involved, the generalised excuse being, that too many youngsters would have been exposed to the media in a nightmare of a trial.'

David took another sip of water:

'Since they were expelled, they had as good, disappeared, but we now know what they have been up to. They, probably along with the three men in the active service unit, are the most evil and notorious of terrorists, in the world...

A German independent banker, Herr Hofferman, stated to the German police, that Bernadette brought Seamus McGough to his office in Munich. She literally ordered him to transfer all their funds into new accounts in her's and Kerry McKeefe's names.

This personifies her evilness... She robbed her own parents, despite their having bailed her out in her earlier years... Between them, these two women are worth over one hundred million pounds. This is the money that Seamus McGough stole from the organisation over a period of about sixteen years. Last Friday, all the funds in the German accounts were frozen.'

There was much shuffling, and covert whispering.

'The bankers in both Ulster and the Republic of Ireland are presently being investigated. It does appear that Seamus McGough blackmailed them all, at some time or other. It is now our turn to turn the tables on him...

It is fairly obvious that the PIRA active service unit will have gone to ground and vanished. They will not turn up again until they recce their next operation. Or alternatively, that may have been done, therefore we have to try and assess what the next target is likely to be? Somehow, we have to try and find them.

Since our operation began they have taken the lives of six security force members. We must not lose anyone else. Their reign of terrorism must be brought to an end...

Immigration are covering every exit point in the country and have all their names that we have collated, Kosha and false. The moment any one of them attempts to leave we will be alerted.'

'Presupposing immigration doesn't have too many Irish stable hands,' said a deep voice, 'and doors closed after horse has bolted.'

'Pray not,' said David. 'We have contacted Land Registry throughout the UK to see if anyone of these names is listed against house purchase, anywhere in the UK, during the past three years. We have also informed banks or building societies to search their records for major deposits or withdrawals in any of these names, too...

What we cannot do though is sit back and wait. We will approach Seamus McGough and he should be able to tell us where his evil fucking daughter is.'

David looked to his key interrogator.

'Don, this is going to be the most important and dangerous meeting of your life. This is one very clever man that you have to turn. I suggest you spend some time going over all the relevant information regarding both Seamus and Brenda McGough. Please let me know when you are ready to move?'

Jack Simpson grinned, then said, 'I'm ready.'

David Carver smiled. 'Good man, Don,' and at that Tom Galloway, Len, Tug, and Jock stood up and started making their way out.

They were also ready!

David said to Dave Bonner and Harry McFee, 'I think you both had better go as well.'

Within ten minutes of the Lynx having left Netheravon, Spike Wilson knocked on the door, and interrupted David's thought patterns:

'Sorry boss, we have just received a message... A Ms McKeefe on Monday afternoon drew £40,000 on the account of Kerry McKeefe and Bernadette McGough at a building society in Bournemouth.'

'Fucking hell, I do not believe it!' screamed David. 'Ian, Alan, get down there as quickly as possible, see what you can get...

297

CCTV pics, signatures, descriptions, address'...
Do your best, and get back as soon as you can...'

* * *

Alan Kirkby produced his warrant card at the building society, and after preliminaries, ascertained; the CCTV had been out of order, the address for the account was a PO box in Northern Ireland and all correspondence received forwarded there.

The manager had no telephone number for the account holders, though someone had rung in today demanding a transfer of funds; a Northern Ireland number. Having been unavailable at the time he had tried to ring the caller back, but an automatic device had transferred him to another number and he was told to wait. Throughout clicking sounds, probably relay systems, he said he had then met with another recorded message and that had passed onto yet another device.

He scratched his head, as confused as his inquisitors, then said:

'Only then did the other lady account holder answer my call. Like Ms Mckeefe, she was Irish. When I told her of the £2,000,000 being refused, she demanded that I recheck and informed me that there was more than enough funds in the account.'

'When I tried to contact her again all I got was a dead line. I am afraid I cannot be of any further assistance.'

Alan Kirkby then spoke with the cashier that had been working the front counter at the time of Kerry's withdrawal, but she had nothing for them.

Here we go again, thought, Alan. These women are too bloody clever by half. Who knows, they may be based in Northern Ireland or even Inverness!

He took every document that he could get a hold of and left.

* * *

David Carver felt extreme frustration building. He knew they were not far off finding the PIRA nutting squad, and had every faith in the men who had already returned to Northern Ireland.

It was now early evening on the Thursday and he decided to stretch his legs and walk around the perimeter of the lower area of Airfield Camp. He walked slowly, listening to the sound of artillery shells being fired from what he thought could be the new AS 90 guns, which he had heard were shortly going to be tested in this area...

Then a huge blast shattered the calm; about six weapons, he guessed. The single shots he had initially heard were the 'gunners' adjusting the shells onto their targets. He remembered from way back when at Larkhill, how an officer would be observing the target area and would see the first shell land. He would then give radio commands to the gun position, would get the shell on line by adjusting either, 'left or right', and then by giving the command 'add or drop', and the next shell would then end up smack on the target.

As David walked on round the perimeter fence, he approached the camp entrance, spoke to the guard, who was sitting in his tiny guard post box. Then a thunderous roar of the guns again shattered the pleasant still of evening.

The guard said, 'that's music to my ears, sir. I spent twenty-five years in the gunners. It must have been horrendous in the Gulf, sitting in a hole with that lot coming down on you!'

David Carver responded with, 'yes, I think you are dead right,' and thought, and thought, yes...

* * *

Chapter Forty One

Kerry arrived at the farmhouse about 5pm as previously promised, having decided that it would be a stupid move to return to Amesbury first. To make up an excuse about having to return to the pub or lose her job just wouldn't have washed with Bernadette. She had become too suspicious, and as jealous as ever about Tony.

'No problem,' she said to Bernadette. 'I have the men's money. Have you been able to contact them?'

'Yes,' said Bernadette, 'Fred and Joe will be here shortly, and Sean an hour later.'

Kerry then said, 'I have sent a telex for funds to cover everything I envisage as necessary over the next few months. Our account was well depleted, and I think Bernadette, that you have forgotten that we pay Fred £5,000 every month, along with our other expenses?'

Bernadette stood in front of Kerry and changed the subject entirely. 'I love you, but your love for me has gone. Why, Kerry?'

Kerry was dumbfounded and had to think on her feet: 'Bernadette, everything is going as planned, and I can stay with you tonight. I rang my boss, and they're not so busy that I need return to Amesbury before tomorrow.'

'No Kerry, you are not going to Amesbury tomorrow. Your days with Tony are over. You are nothing other than a fucking rotten nasty cow. You have turned against me because of him.'

Kerry saw the vicious evil look that she knew so well, and then cringed when Bernadette gloated, 'tonight, when we have him back here, he'll be dead meat.'

'No Bernadette, no, what are you talking about?'

'Your favourite building society manager telephoned me to check about the £40,000 withdrawal from our account, and then remarked that the £2,000,000 you requested had been refused from Hofferman's bank. What the fuck have you been up to, you cheating bitch?'

Kerry was stunned. 'How could it be refused, you know that we have millions in that account?'

'I think between the pair of you the money has been siphoned away. Tell me, Kerry, why the fuck have you drawn £40,000 today, and requested a transfer of £2,000,000, without saying anything to me. What the fucking hell have you been doing? You better have some answers for me.'

Kerry just stood there, unable to respond; what had Bernadette meant about Tony? When he's here?

'So Kerry, for once in your life you do not know what to say, do you?'

There was a knock on the door and it was Fred and Joe. When they entered the large sitting room, neither looked at Kerry. She guessed Bernadette had already spoken to them, evil intent in mind.

'Bernadette,' Kerry said, inwardly scared to hell. 'You are not thinking properly and you are being stupid. Now give me a chance to explain.'

Bernadette just stood staring at her. 'You, Kerry, are worse than a fucking tout. You were about to raid our account and fuck off with your soldier boy. This money is not just ours, you common thief. It is Sean's, Fred's, Joe's, and their families, and you intended fucking off with their money.'

'No,' Kerry screamed, 'that is not true, Bernadette, stop talking to me like this!'

Kerry knew she was in dire trouble. She knew Bernadette too well. Then to her horror, Bernadette shouted at her.

'Strip you bitch...

Get your clothes off, now.'

'Bernadette, no! Not in front of the men, please, Bernadette no.' Bernadette walked up to her, a knife in hand. 'Kerry, you mean fuck all to me now. Ever since you went to Amesbury you have turned against me. She placed the knife at her throat. Now take your blouse off.'

Kerry was trembling. 'Please Bernadette; my body is yours, not Joe's or Fred's. No one else', but yours, please, Bernadette, do not do this to me.'

'Strip, Kerry or this knife will rip you apart.'

Kerry started to cry and Bernadette smacked her as hard as she could across the face. 'For the last time, take off your clothes, now!'

Kerry reeled, undid the buttons on her blouse, her cheek stinging...

She rubbed it, to ease the pain, eyes pleading with

Bernadette. She took off her blouse, unbuttoned her jeans, slipped the zip down, and dropped them to her ankles.

Standing there, petrified in red bra and skimpy red panties that Bernadette had bought her, she knew what Bernadette was capable of...She also knew how the men could treat others when told to do so by their vicious commander.

'Anything Bernadette, I'll do anything for you, please.'

With callous vicious intent and pure malice, Bernadette slipped her hand inside the bra and grabbed a breast and squeezed until Kerry screamed in pain. She stepped back, yelling, 'take it off.'

Kerry, crying, removed the bra. Her right breast was already red, and Bernadette saw that, then said, 'now get rid of them.'

Standing utterly naked, her superb slim body displayed for all, Kerry looked at Joe, and to her horror, saw that he was excited, erect. Bernadette grinned.

'No Bernadette, please no.'

Bernadette was at her most menacing, brutal best, when she said, 'Joe, fuck her, front first...then spread her arse... then...'

* * *

Kerry was lying on the floor; sobbing her heart out. A brute had attacked her, goaded on by the most evil of evil bitches. The same woman that she had spent her entire young life with.

'Sling her over the settee,'

'No,' Kerry cried, begging for mercy. 'Please, not again, no more, I am hurt inside, please Bernadette, please and then she screamed and howled, as Bernadette hit her with a leather belt. Again and again, without mercy she suffered beneath the onslaught.

Then Bernadette paused:

'Tell me Kerry, who is Tony? Has he children, an ex-wife, mother, father...

Tell me, you must know all about him.'

Kerry remained silent, apart from crying.

Then the belt came crashing down again.

'No more Bernadette, please.'

'Then tell me all about him, and I want the truth.'

Kerry just carried on sobbing, hysterically.

'Fred, your turn,' said Bernadette.

With a sadistic grin, he was now in his element; Kerry's

buttocks raw, his knowing she couldn't take much more punishment. He hit her. Kerry screamed, but he continued until Bernadette stopped him.

Kerry was in agony, never before had she been subjected to such savage behaviour. The cheeks of her bum were flayed; bleeding.

'Now Kerry, save yourself from any further beatings, and tell us about your boyfriend, everything...

We want to know absolutely everything, don't we boys?'

Kerry, as best she could, her voice a mere tremor, her whole body trembling, in whispers, told them everything that she knew about Tony Hey. Then she was made to describe everything that they had done together, in bed!

Bernadette's face twisted, her lips quivering with rage. 'You fucking horrible little beast. Fred, let's make her feel better... Go and get the salt and vinegar.'

Kerry soon passed out with the pain.

Bernadette said to the men. 'Throw her in the coalbunker and lock it up. As soon as Sean arrives I want you all to go to Amesbury and bring this fucking Tony back here. I want to know what has been going on, and where they were going with the money?'

* * *

Sean was sitting in the bar of the Greyhound pub; a false moustache and beard. He asked a grey haired old man if he knew an army lad called Tony, who used the pub a lot.

'Yes, young fella... Tony Hey is at the end of the bar... He's love sick at the moment, missing his Irish lassie, he is.'

Sean grinned, walked up to Tony. 'Hullo young man, are you waiting for a young Irish colleen? My sister Kerry, that I have just brought back from Dublin?'

Tony Hey's eyes beamed as he shook hands with the big man. 'Yes, yes I am, where is she?'

'In the car, parked behind the medical centre. She's waiting for you, so you had better hurry, hadn't you.'

Tony was out like a shot, running across the road. He hurried past a block of flats, and just before the entrance to the car park he noticed two men, leaning against a car. He ran around their car searching for Kerry, but there was no other car in the car park.

He stopped and turned. Both men were on him. Then Sean

joined in and he was dragged and thrown into the boot of their car...

* * *

They pulled in to the farmhouse, and Bernadette immediately came out to see the snatched victim.

'Fetch him in.'

'What the fucking hell is going on here?' demanded Tony, aware of Irish accents all around him. 'Who the hell are you, and where is Kerry?'

Bernadette said. 'Shut up, you have too much to say for yourself. You work in the camp at Larkhill, don't you?'

'Yes I do, so?'

'You don't ask anything, you answer my questions.'

Tony Hey said, 'bollocks to you, where's Kerry?'

Bernadette's face was the epitome of jealous rage. 'Do you love Kerry, and what have you two been up to.'

'That's none of your business, and I will ask again, where is Kerry? What is going on, and why the fuck have you dragged me here in the boot of a car.'

'Kerry has just had a good hiding, she's hurt, and shall I tell you why. It's because you and her have attempted to rob us. She arranged to draw £2,000,000 from our account and I want to know, why?'

'I know nothing about any money... I retire from the army next year and I have enough for my requirements. Never in a million years did I know that Kerry had access to that sort of money. I want nothing to do with it, and I would tell Kerry just that. I do love her, and I believe she loves me.'

Bernadette was furious, and Tony sensed he had said the wrong thing. He felt very threatened, and had sussed the bully female to be a dyke. Shit, he was in it, deep.

'Do you still want Kerry?'

'At least let me speak with her... I am sure this is all a misunderstanding.'

'You can have Kerry.' Bernadette sniggered. 'When I am ready to let her go, you need to do something for me, for my group.'

'What's that?' Tony demanded.

'You are going to tell me all about this conference at Larkhill, then you are going to take Sean and Joe up there and then come back here. You and Kerry can fuck off anywhere you like after that.'

The shock waves of what was happening stunned Tony. He had worked enough times in Northern Ireland to know that these were most likely IRA thugs. In a trembling voice, he said, 'you're IRA, right? I can't tell you anything. I don't know bugger all about the conference.'

Bernadette snapped at him. 'You fucking liar Hey, you know all there is to know, and if you don't agree to work with us, the first thing you'll see is your precious Kerry skinned alive.'

'You wouldn't?' He was shocked all the same, by the venom in the dyke's tone.

'You don't believe us. Well, well,' Bernadette said. 'Go and get her.'

Kerry was dragged before him, naked, filthy, and hideously beaten around the buttocks, and thrown at his feet. He felt sick as Kerry came to, and saw him standing there, whimpered, 'I am so sorry,' and started to cry.

'Well soldier boy, do you believe me now?'

'Yes, you heathen bitch... I believe you would do exactly as you said, and I am very sorry for Kerry, but cannot do what you ask.' He knew he was a dead man, escape and survival uppermost, but how? 'Anyway, to me she is just IRA scum, not the girl I knew.'

'Is she now! Your love has soon died a death, hasn't it? So, you won't mind a bit of butchery, at her expense. Cut her Sean, like the Murphy's, but on the front.'

Kerry screamed, 'no Bernadette, for god's sake, no.'

Fred and Joe turned her over; Tony utterly stunned, looking at the wretched naked figure before him, his only true love.

Then Sean moved forward, offensive weapon in hand.

Tony Hey yelled, 'please stop this. Be reasonable, you know I cannot do what you've asked.'

'Kerry put your hands above your head,' demanded Bernadette.

Joe and Fred pulled Kerry's legs apart and Sean stepped between them, looking down.

'Do it, Sean,' yelled Bernadette, and he dropped on his knees.

'No Sean,' Kerry pleaded, 'no, not this, Bernadette please stop this.'

The knife twirled her pubic hair, prodding, pricking, and then it was eased inside her. Kerry shuddered, still pleading, as blood poured forth. Tony remained steadfast, hoping, praying for a miracle.

Bernadette grinned. 'Last chance Hey, what is it going to be...?'

* * *

Chapter Forty Two

Tom Galloway landed at their old base at about 1800 hours. The six-man team spent the rest of the day discussing how they would penetrate and then break an Army Council member. Such had never been done before. Jack Simpson was in a quandary. Len saw that and understood why. The main problem that Jack had was which hook to use to try and turn both Seamus and Brenda McGough.

Then Jack suddenly seemed full of inspiration, said, 'I know, I'll offer them their German accounts back!'

Open mouthed, Len said, 'what do you mean, Don, the German bank accounts are frozen by the courts. The money is untouchable…'

'Yes,' said a grinning Jack Simpson, 'but they don't know that, do they?'

* * *

Seamus and Brenda McGough had just left the meeting in Dublin. It was 11.30 pm on Thursday 29 April. They were driving home to Belfast, tormented by both the organisations present position and also their own.

The Army Council was frantic in trying to find out what was happening to their organisation. Seamus had outlined a serious drop in PIRA funds, and businesses had suffered with the raids of 1992. The income from the republicans had dropped drastically and the Noraid funds were drying up altogether. All support from Libya was over, as was the income from other terrorist organisations.

On top of the financial disasters, the manpower was being decimated. In only a few months they had lost over forty trained terrorists. Dozens of their dedicated supporters had been hounded and burned out of their homes. And there was no indication as to who was responsible. Bernadette's tout hunting had been successful but now the council had stopped all external funding.

Seamus said, 'it is time that we got out Brenda. We are sixty, we have done our share.'

'Seamus we cannot just leave, we don't have enough money. We must speak with Bernadette and recover some retirement money.'

Seamus and Brenda were driving slowly down their driveway. It had turned midnight, and they were fed up. They had spent a lifetime working for their retirement, albeit having cheated and robbed to get funding, only to have lost it, and to whom, their bloody daughter. The movement was falling to pieces, and desperately needed new blood.

Now, here they were, about to go down on their knees and grovel to Bernadette. Bitterness always crept in, especially seeing as they could have retired more than comfortably so.

They parked alongside the mansion, Seamus not bothering to put the Range-Rover in the huge three-car garage. As Brenda placed a key in the house lock, Jack Simpson said, 'good morning.'

They both turned in unison, in utter consternation.

They could see him standing a few yards back, and Seamus's hand moved quickly to the inside of his blazer. He immediately froze when he heard the sharp metallic sound of three armalite's being 'cocked'.

'Who are you, what do you want?' Brenda said.

Jack Simpson said, 'we need to talk, my friends, and I would like to speak with you both. Can we come in?'

'And if we say no?' Seamus challenged.

'Sadly,' Jack said, 'there will be three armalite magazines emptied into both of you. Take your pick?'

'Call that choice?' remarked Seamus.

'Let's be civilised about this,' mooted Don. 'What I have to discuss with you is to our mutual benefit, I suggest you let us in, it is quite cold standing out here.'

Brenda said. 'You have five minutes, then we will activate our alarm systems, and you'll be dead.'

Jack shrugged, and the alarm control box was thrown out of the bushes towards them. 'Believe me, we are not messing about. We would like to leave within minutes, when we have what we want!'

The lounge was very large and warm; beautifully decorated with antiques, no doubt worth a fortune. 'I will come straight to the point,' Jack said. 'We know of your daughter, Bernadette. We know everything about her, except one piece of information, which probably only you can provide. She has been a PIRA hard core terrorist for years and we need to end her vile activities.'

Seamus interrupted. 'You are off your fuckin' rocker... Do you really think that we would discuss our daughter with you? Anyway, who are you?'

'I have told you; we know everything about your daughter, and both of you for that matter. Does BALLISTIC ring a bell?'

They both stared at Jack Simpson, and the other man, who hadn't as yet, spoken, 'what do you want?' Seamus said.

'Where is your daughter, Sean Hegatty, Fred Short, Joe Hagan, and Kerry McKeefe?'

Seamus laughed, then said, 'where she should be, bombing and blasting you fuckin' bastards. You'll not be getting anything out of us, so just fuck off out of here.' Seamus then walked to the door, opened it.

'Now get out.'

'That's a nasty attitude Seamus, especially when we want to help you. It must have destroyed you both when Bernadette robbed you. What will you do, Seamus, when you retire? Sell this beautiful home and all its contents?'

Brenda intervened and said, 'how can you help? What do you mean?'

'Say nothing more Brenda, we are not betraying anyone.'

'You will Seamus. Let me say this to you only once...

You were betrayed by Bernadette, she stole everything that you had in your German accounts. And, you are in serious bother with the current investigations going on in the Province and south of the border. You must be really pissed off, because with the information I have, not only will you be financially ruined, you will go to prison for a long time.

You in the Maze, Seamus, and Brenda in the women's section of the Magilligan prison, and it will not be pleasant for either of you. More so when I send copies of your earlier correspondence with Hofferman, to your PIRA godfathers. Then sixteen years accounts will follow. I think you may have a tortuous retirement.

Now Seamus, close that fuckin' door.'

Seamus, trembling; did just that, and stood staring at Jack Simpson.

Brenda spoke nervously, 'I will repeat myself, what help can you give us?'

'Tell me where Bernadette and her active service unit is?

You cannot owe her any loyalty, and no one will ever know how we found her?'

Seamus said, 'what do we get out of this?'

Jack Simpson smiled. He had them.

'Seamus, you and Brenda, will be sole beneficiaries of her Will. You will inherit all her ill-gotten gains, which she stole from you, which you robbed from the organisation.'

'Can my wife and me discuss this privately?'

'No, we do not know what other alarm devices you have here, and there is nothing further to discuss.'

They looked at one another, in horrible turmoil, indecisive, they hated their daughter for what she did to them, but to betray her to the Brits, well that was unacceptable to them....

'Well, one of you make a decision, we haven't all night...

It is now 3 am, so what is it to be?'

'How do you know she will die, and leave a Will? Furthermore, Bernadette wouldn't leave anything to us, it would be left to that little bitch, Kerry.'

'Your daughter and the rest of the active service unit will be dead immediately we find them. Our organisation will draft her Will leaving you both as sole beneficiaries and that will be with you by Monday. All we would want now, is a copy of her signature.'

'We'll do as you ask, once we receive the Will,' said Seamus.

'No, we need her location now... You can trust us, implicitly; we have nothing to gain by not complying. You will not even see a Will, because our own probate department will prove the Will immediately. You would have access to everything she owns, including trusts, properties, and accounts by Tuesday.

Think about it, she has done nothing for either of you and you can move within days to your house in Miami or the south of France. Even PIRA would wish you well. You would have no one chasing you. We will ensure that all investigations that are on-going at the moment are dropped. There would be no evidence of your misdemeanours... So, for the last time of asking, where are they?'

Seamus looked at his wife, who nodded, and then told Jack Simpson everything he needed to know.

Jack Simpson said to Seamus and Brenda, before departure, 'thank you, but a word of warning. If this is false or they have been warned, PIRA will pick you up before you can do anything. You will be watched.'

Brenda said, 'we have decided, and there will be no problem from us...Now please, get out!'

* * *

Chapter Forty Three

Tony Hey said, 'what you do to Kerry is up to you. I had not realised that I had fallen in love with a PIRA member.'

Bernadette interrupted. 'PIRA member, PIRA member, how fucking dare you, a few moments ago you were saying, PIRA scum. You're getting on my nerves. We'll cut this PIRA scum that you profess to love, and then we'll start on you!'

This horrified Tony. He too, was going to be tortured. He sensed that he hadn't got a cat in hell chance of getting out of there alive. 'Why, why start on me?'

Bernadette laughed, she saw the fright in his face. 'You will watch and you will hear her screams. Then she will return the compliment when we make her slowly slice your balls off.' She walked up to him. 'We will see how clever you are in dealing with pain. Now, bastard watch and listen.'

Kerry's scream was terrible, long, and hideous. She mercifully fainted.

'Your turn Hey,' Bernadette's evil glare, put horrendous fear into him, followed by terror when she demanded, 'now strip!'

'You cannot do this,' he said trembling, shaking in disbelief, at what he had just seen.

'Strip, lets see what you have that she fell in love with.'

Tony Hey just stood there, frozen, shocked and now terrified.

She nodded at the men, and he was naked, on the ground in front of her, in seconds.

'Get up, now,' she screamed. 'What a fuckin' miserable sight you are.'

'Your mother, Tony, lives only up the road at Swindon, does she not?'

He was gutted, trying to cover himself, appalled. No, he thought. Then yes, they would!

'What has my mother to do with this?'

'Because we will bring her here tonight, strip her naked, just like you are, and the PIRA scum here, with you watching, can have some fun, and then you can watch her slowly die.'

She waited, Tony's silence infuriating her.

He was in a trance as she approached him, grabbing him,

wielding the knife...
'Your answer now?' She yelled.

* * *

Fred and Joe had met the PIRA man from Armagh, at Pont Abraham, the pull-in service station near Swansea. They knew him from the past. Not a word was said, and the container was placed in the boot of Fred's car.

* * *

The next morning Bernadette was shouting at a female at the other end of the telephone. 'I need them now, and when I say that, I mean precisely that. You deliver them tonight, do you understand that?'

'You don't understand. I have to phase them in over a few days otherwise I will be exposed. They will be delivered to you Friday afternoon, and only after I have received £10,000 in cash. That, or the deal is off?'

'The agreed figure was £6,000?'

'Yes, but now it is £10,000 because of your attitude. Do you still want them?'

Bernadette screeched in frustration, 'just get them as I have said, or else, bitch.'

* * *

Tony Hey spent the night locked in a cupboard. He had given in, and they had made him telephone to the duty officer that he was sick and would not be in work until Monday.

He had cried throughout the night. He was not a traitor, damn it. However, he could never ever put his mum through what he had seen these animals do to Kerry. He had had to agree with their requests and would alert someone, somehow, even if he died doing it. He was freezing cold, still naked, and then, all of a sudden, he heard the sound of a bolt moving.

'Get out, we have work to do.' Bernadette shouted. ' If this goes wrong, you will be dead and so will members of your family especially your mother... Is that understood?'

Tony Hey nodded, then asked. 'Where is Kerry, and can I speak with her?'

'When the job is successfully completed you can do what the fucking hell you like with her. Now get a wash and tidy up, your togs are in there, and get a move on,' she said, pointing to what looked like the bathroom.... 'The men are waiting.'

They drove through Amesbury and Tony glanced over to the right and saw the Greyhound pub, and thought, twenty-one years service and now this. They turned right into the camp and the guard standing there recognised him and waved them through. After entering the camp they drove for a short while and then pulled up at the building on the right.

Tony Hey rang the bell and a cleaner came and opened the door. 'I am just finishing Tony,' she said. 'That's alright Polly, you go, I have a few jobs to do, then I will hand the keys in for you.'

She left, and the two men were inside immediately. They set the timing device; a very simple video recorder timing unit, set for 11.30 am on 10 June. It was planted at the far end of the cleaning cupboard. They then screwed a container underneath the seating area of the conference centre; very low down and difficult to get at. It was then covered with a multitude of rubbish that always accumulates in areas such as this.

They all departed and Tony handed the key in. Watched every step by the two thugs that accompanied him, they were soon back at the farmhouse, where he was put straight back into the cupboard for a second night.

* * *

'Now, maybe they will listen to me.' Bernadette was ecstatic, and turned to Sean. 'You didn't fuck her. Go and get Kerry, throw her in the bath and scrub her, then have some fun. You deserve it!'

Kerry, meanwhile, locked in the dark and filthy coalbunker, was crying and frightened out of her wits. Sean had cut a small patch out of her inner thigh, and it was hurting like hell.

Bernadette had decided what to do with Kerry and Tony. She had discussed it with the three men and they had spent the day preparing for the grand finale.

Hopefully, Bernadette thought, the passports would arrive on Friday lunchtime and they could then be off with new identities. The last few days had been very frustrating. Bernadette wanted to be away. She now hated this place. She needed to find out what had happened to the German accounts, so that was going to be her first visit. Hofferman was in trouble with her. He would regret this stupidity.

Sean appeared, said, 'it is done, are you ready?'

Yes, Sean, let's get on with it. I am fed up with this wait.'

She followed him into the outhouse. The men had hard-grafted all morning, digging the hole large enough to take a wooden crate. It was a foreboding sight, like a coffin, awaiting a body.

'Where is she, I thought you had her here?'

Fred and Joe then brought Kerry in. She had her clothes on and was clean and tidy, but limping very badly.

Bernadette snapped. 'What the fuck's going on here? Get her rags off, she has to have one more beating before she goes in the box...'

Kerry smiled, then shouted. 'No Bernadette, take your fucking clothes off, now! You're a fucking evil, vile, bitch, and I'll make you regret doing to me what you have done, it is now my turn.'

Bernadette's eyes bulged as she turned her head, only to find herself looking down the barrel of an armalite. Fred had the weapon, and a sinister grin.

'Sean, Fred, Joe, what the fuck is happening here? Kill this bitch...

She was robbing us, you arseholes.'

Bernadette glared at them. Then Sean hit her with a full-blooded, vicious punch, straight into her midriff. Bernadette sank to the floor. He picked her up and threw her to the other end of the building, and for the first time in her life she was panic stricken.

'Get up Bernadette. You over did my punishment and turned the men against you. You told me to draw the cash for the men, £10,000 each. That was for now. Did you not?'

Bernadette frowned. 'Yes I did.'

'Of course you did, and I do not know why you turned on me.' Kerry was on the offensive. 'The men were then to get the balance after the £2,000,000 cleared and we were all to have a five way split when we returned. You were the one that reneged on the deal and blamed me. They know that they will be paid in full from me. The £2,000,000 was from my account and I have shown them my statement. You have cheated on us all. We have found your statements showing over £100,000,000.'

Bernadette yelled, 'no, you have twisted all this way out of proportion...'

The boot connected between her legs and she dropped like

a sack...

'Now I know how much you want to have your first man, don't I, Bernadette? Well, you can double that because you are going to have two. Sean and Joe.'

'Kerry please, forgive me.'

'No, strip her... Now.'

And they did.

She was standing naked in front of them, a sight, that apart from Kerry, hadn't been seen before. Sean and Joe started groping her, hurting her. Then out of the blue, Fred said, 'look what I have found.'

It was a horsewhip, and Bernadette screamed, 'No Fred, you wouldn't, please, no!'

He hit her, and the lash and bite of the whip drew blood immediately.

She screamed, and Kerry laughed.

'Again Fred, again, harder, harder.'

Kerry screamed with delight and after a short while said, 'stop, that's enough. I don't want her to bleed to death. Take off your belts.'

Bernadette was crying hysterically, as others had in sufferance of her sadistic nature. Then the first of the belts hit her and yet again she screamed. Then they were all venting their anger at her, and the beating went on and on for a very long time.

They then turned a hosepipe on her.

Sean and Joe took their trousers off, and terribly hurt and aching badly, Bernadette screamed, 'no,' pleading, 'no, no...not this!'

They spent the rest of the day at her, and then rested while Fred had fun with his knife, then another beating with belts, and then Sean and Joe again.

Finally Kerry said, 'that's it, put the hosepipe on her again. Tie her hands behind her back, then put her in the box...'

She had never been violated like this before, and she was in the box meant for Kerry. She couldn't stretch out. It was tight at her shoulders.

She had conjured up Kerry's demise, and now, she herself was the victim, and in dreadful pain. 'Please,' she whispered, from her imminent tomb. 'Show mercy... We have been together for a long time.'

They laughed and waved at her. 'Bye bye, Bernadette,'

Kerry said, as the lid was shut tight.

Bernadette screamed as the box was slid into the large hole. They then fed a pipe into a pre-drilled hole, level with her mouth. She drew it between her lips, air, she had air as planned beforehand, so that Kerry would suffer a long lingering death. The pipe would just reach the surface. She could hear them filling in the hole, surplus soil raked level. No trace would be seen that there had been a hole dug. The final indignity was both Sean and Joe pissing into the air pipe and then yelling more abuse down at her.

She was doomed...

* * *

Chapter Forty Four

Jack Simpson had thought long and hard on the journey back to Netheravon; and still thinking: Why should Seamus and Brenda McGough get their evil money back?

Sir Peter Wilcox could get it all transferred into something much more important, like the Combined Freedom Fighters of Ulster. What a good idea, he thought!

The British Government had indirectly funded the Provisional Irish Republican Army for years. Now PIRA can fund the 'Freedom Fighters,' and promote their own demise.

Tom Galloway lowered the Lynx on to its skids, and David Carver was standing there, grinning, with his thumbs up. Len had already told him before they had left Ireland that the mission was a great success. For security reasons, nothing more was said.

As they all walked down the central road in the camp, heading for the operations room, it was 0730 hours and there was a huge bang. The artillery battery had opened fire. The first salvo was sent hurtling through the air towards the impact area, seven miles away. They all smiled. The firing would continue throughout the day, but they would not be here to hear it for too long...

* * *

David Carver had called in a Puma. It was fitted with a heat-seeking device. They circled high above the farmhouse, the Lynx a few miles away.

Tom had already landed with Len, Tug, and Jock, and was fully armed and ready. The rotor blades were spinning and he could lift off immediately if necessary.

The monitor showed that there were four people inside the main room. Two other heat sources, one in what looked like a small room in the house, and the other a very small glimmer in a different building. The one in the separate building could have been an animal, David thought!

The Puma moments later landed alongside the Lynx. David Carver briefed his team, as they checked their weapons, grins all round.

'Right, let's go,' David said, and they leapt aboard the Lynx.

Tom swooped in fast and low. Len was out first and at the front door, covered by Tug and Jock, who were both wearing respirators. David raced around the back, to cover the back door. Tom, as soon as the men were out, lifted off and hovered at about three hundred feet, awaiting a signal to descend and land.

It was all over before it started...

Len slipped a new-type of stun grenade under the front door and command detonated it. David had done the same at the rear. As soon as both grenades exploded, Tug ran to the rear and Jock to the front door and both doors were booted in at about the same time.

Tug and Jock entered the house, with Len and David covering the doors; giving running commentaries on what they could see and what they were doing.

'Four terrorists cuffed and room secured... A fifth member cuffed and removed from a cupboard... Continuing search.'

Minutes later...coming out with five terrorists...one a female.'

They were individually handcuffed and dragged out bodily. They had been knocked out with the stun grenades and it would be some time before their senses would return.

Tom Galloway had landed as they were trying to revive the terrorists, and David said, 'something's wrong. Where is the second female and why the hell four men?'

They all just looked at each other.

'Fucking hell David, for god's sake...surely not...no, we haven't been tricked again, have we? No, no...no,' shaking his head, 'we just cannot have the wrong people here,' Len said.

Jock immediately saw the funny side, and laughing, said, 'hell's fucking bell's I'm in the shit again.'

David, ignoring Jock, shouted, 'Len put your respirator on and have a quick rummage...Go.'

Tension was rising, as the group on the ground began to stir. The one found in the cupboard looked around at the others, then grinned, and simply said, 'thank god,' tears of relief in his eyes.

David said, 'what's your name?' pointing the weapon at him.

I am Sergeant Major Tony Hey. These bastards have forced me to assist in planting a bomb at the Royal School of Artillery at Larkhill. I don't know when it is timed to detonate but I believe it is set for 10th June.

David and the others gave a great sigh of relief.

'Where is it, tell me?'

'In the conference centre at the school, go through the main door, turn right, and there's a door on the right. That door is the cleaner's cupboard, and it's also the door, which leads underneath the seating area. The bomb is at the far end, well camouflaged with rubbish...'

David immediately radioed this information back to base...

David left the handcuffs on him until they were absolutely sure he was not one of the terrorists. 'Were there not two women?' he asked.

'Yes,' replied Tony, looking around. 'That one there is Kerry, the end one is Sean, he's Fred, and the last one is Joe, but I don't know where Bernadette is. She was still here when they locked me in the cupboard, and she was most definitely in charge.'

'Tug, Jock, search the area, and be careful, she's dangerous.'

Len appeared. 'No problem David, there's an arsenal in there, also a large amount of cash and documents. They're ours now!'

'We are missing one, Len. Bernadette is not here, although she was yesterday.'

The others were now coming to, and were very quick to realise their predicament. David Carver said, 'where is Bernadette...One of you had better tell me.'

There was silence.

David pointed a pistol to Sean's head. 'Where is she?'

Sean's response was as David expected, 'fuck off.'

'Get them in the chopper.'

Tug and Jock returned. 'No sign of anyone else.'

David Carver and Len checked the outbuilding, and then Len noticed the pipe slightly protruding above disturbed ground. They both put their ears to it. Then Len shouted. Is that Bernadette down there?

They heard a muffled, 'yes, help me, help me, please.'

Len said, 'seems to me they have had a major row, best leave her there David. Maybe we can give her some water to prolong her agony...'

'Sounds good to me, Len, the hosepipe is over there...

Just what I have planned for the others, well, we'll recce that tomorrow.'

Len looked at David and saw tears forming. 'We got 'em.'

'We are nearly there Len, and I cannot thank you all enough.'

They approached the Lynx, and David said to Tom, you had better call the Puma, or some of us will have to walk.

* * *

They landed at Netheravon about 1400 hours.

Sir Peter Wilcox was there to meet them, and had been totally involved in the problems of the deceased MI5 officers. His problem had been retaining silence amongst those in the know, but had eventually achieved D notice status, with a lot of money from the 'kitty' changing hands, plus the threat of severe action under the Official Secrets Act, if anyone breached the documents that they had signed.

The terrorists were now locked in the squash courts, where they remained handcuffed. Sean said, 'I am speaking for us all, here... We have done nothing and demand to speak with our solicitors.'

Jock said, 'bollocks, Sean Hegatty, there's no legal requirement needed. We are not taking you to court. So you can be pleased with that.'

Tug grinned.

'What will happen then? As I have said, we have done nothing.'

'Of course you haven't, Sean. When we dig up Bernadette and she tells us everything that you have done, your fate will be decided. Me! Well, I am in favour of taking you up to 10,000 feet, tipping you out, and when you hit the deck, if you have done nothing, then the good lord will protect you!'

Kerry said, 'take no notice, they can do nothing, they wouldn't dare.'

Tug and Jock went up the stairs to the viewing area of the squash court. 'We don't have the time for that, so we have decided just to shoot you.'

They both raised their weapons...

'No, no,' their captives screamed.

Then Tug and Jock 'cocked' their weapons, and the terrorists saw the safety catches removed. In the closed confines of the squash court, the sound itself was destructive. Tug and Jock emptied both their magazines, and the terrorists dropped to the ground...

* * *

David Carver and Len had returned; a special recce at 1500 hours completed, roughly within or around an hour. The firing had finished for the day on the ranges, peace all around them, as they strolled toward the squash court.

They had no reason to hurry, the smell bloody awful once inside.

'What the fuck's gone on here?' demanded David.

'Jesus,' said Jock. 'It's unbelievable, two of them have shite, David, and they've all pissed themselves, god knows why.'

David could smell the cordite lingering on the stale air, as he looked at the front wall, and then turned to see both his men grinning. The wall was nearly ripped apart, and it would be a long time before anyone played squash in that court.

David felt no compassion for the thugs before him, his voice cold as he said, 'remove their clothes, and get a fire hose and clean them up, then bin their rags, they won't need them anymore.

Be ready to move half an hour before first light, say 0530 hours. We meet here with Tom and his Lynx. Get that shower up and aboard before I arrive.'

Tom had the Lynx ticking over, as the naked, gagged and trussed bodies were bundled on board.

David and Len arrived, as Jock said, 'what the hell's this kit?'

'You'll see,' said David. Then he handed them a roll of brown, very adhesive, box sealing tape. Wrap that round their eyes.

They were airborne for only a few minutes, and Tom was in hover mode as handcuffs connecting the terrorists together were taken off, one by one, as they departed the aircraft. The first to be shoved toward the door was Fred.

'Throw him out,' shouted David.

Fred screamed as he flew forward, the others noticeably shaken, guessing they must be high up.

Tom knew different, he was hovering at 10 feet.

Len, Tug, and Jock leapt out and threw Fred into an old armoured personnel carrier. Len took the kit out of the back of the Lynx and after a while, used it to weld the rear door.

Fred was now sealed in one of the targets that the gunners would be firing at on Monday. The terrorists didn't know that, and David had selected the targets with great forethought, all on the outer edge of the impact area.

Sean was next; after Tom had eased the chopper about fifty yards to the left. Tug and Jock picked up a kicking Sean, inwardly yelling his head off, as he was dragged to the door. He was picked up, dazed, and then thrown into an old tank. Still handcuffed, eyes taped, he hadn't a clue where he was. Not even the sound of the welding kit gave him any inclination.

The same procedure happened for Joe and finally Kerry. She was unfortunate; she broke her leg when she was thrown out of the helicopter.

No mercy was afforded the terrorists; they had all been tied by their hands, to the roof of their tombs. They would stand till they were either killed, or died. And that meant Kerry as well, and her agony was reflected in her screams and pleadings, all to no avail.

David had played his part in the operation, too, with pre-placed five-gallon water containers in each target, and had delighted in fastening a tube securely into each container, feeding the tube up through the handcuffs and back down in front of their mouths.

'Have a drink anytime,' David had said, so that their suffering would be prolonged.

The terrorists still did not know what their fate was to be. They would come Monday!

* * *

At 0600 hours David Carver arrived with Jack Simpson, Len, Tug, and Jock. They searched the range with binoculars and identified the targets where the terrorists were placed.

The targets, about thirty of them, comprised, old tanks and tracked guns, APC's, vehicles and many other discarded military hardware. The impact area was out of bounds at all times. The range was closed down every two years to destroy unexploded bombs and missiles, also to paint the targets.

They wouldn't stay too long. If the bombardments and aircraft attacks didn't kill the bastards, then they could die of thirst, hunger, shock, or hypothermia. Whatever, David didn't care. Operation Combating Evil was now over.

The Harriers soon screamed over and attacked the targets. Some of the targets received direct hits, others being hit by shrapnel. The Harriers were followed by Tornado's and just the sound of its Gatlin guns, let alone its own engines, could put the fear of satan into the hardest of men.

Artillery weapons, infantry weapons, the Fleet Air Arm Harriers, and the RAF Tornado's fired throughout the day. The four targets which housed the terrorists, were hit by the smaller infantry weapons, nothing big enough to kill them though. The headaches from these weapons would suffice for now. Their mental state would deteriorate and then eventually they would be destroyed.

Their suffering would be enormous.

And it was!

David had sworn that to his son, Jeremy...

* * *

Epilogue

David and his team walked away from the observation post overlooking the impact area.

Nothing could ever bring Jeremy back.

No, but there was an enormous sense of relief, and tremendous satisfaction in what they had achieved. The removal off the streets, of known terrorists, and their sympathisers, for at least a few years, would give stability to the people of Northern Ireland.

* * *

Jack Simpson, Len, Tug, and Jock were set to continue working with the Combined Freedom Fighters of Ulster. They selected the targets, organised attacks, and ensured that funds were always available.

Jack recruited Pat Maguire, who was given back his house at Cockermouth and now had to earn the rest. The freedom fighters respected Pat Maguire. Well, they did exactly what he said! They knew that if they didn't they were dead, and preferred to be looked after and keep their properties, and like Pat Maguire they had to earn the rest back...

* * *

Tug and Jock had returned to the New Forest farmhouse where they dug down about three feet to saw off the air pipe, leaving no trace of a burial ground. They also monitored the rest of the active service unit who were residing in the firing range impact area. They had all survived the first week. The second week was different. It was the only week in the year, when the Army, Navy, and RAF all demonstrated their maximum firepower. Quite remarkable, considering these same terrorists had killed members of all three services.

It was as if a combined effort was underway to share in there destruction, but the truth would never be known as to how many lives would be saved by the destruction of Bernadette's active service unit.

* * *

The Combined Freedom Fighters of Ulster disbanded on the 31 August 1994, when the Provisional Irish Republican Army declared a cease-fire.

Peace talks continued, but Sinn Fein was not achieving their objectives. Their ultimate goal of a United Ireland was drifting even further.

PIRA wanted an end to the talks and returned to the bomb and bullet. On the 9 February 1996, PIRA detonated a 1,000-pound bomb in London's Docklands. This marked the end of the cease-fire agreement of 31 August 1994.

* * *

In early 1998 the Provisional Irish Republican Army was virtually extinct. Their negotiators at the Good Friday Agreement, Sinn Fein, had their hands tied behind their backs. They had lost all their negotiating power.

So they must have been absolutely delirious to have a whole army back on the streets, for giving virtually nothing back in return. In 1998 not a single weapon or bullet was handed in. Yet at the same time, terrorists were released during 1998 and 1999, and it was to be the greatest folly ever by a British Government.

It was the politicians that had put them on the streets. It had always been a joke in the Maze; one terrorist with multiple life sentences against him, had said to a visiting politician, 'you have given in to all our previous demands, so you may as well appease us all, and just release us. That will save us time and effort in having to cause trouble to get our way. So unbelievably, over 500 hard-core terrorists were released.

The government having done as the prisoners told them!

A moment of utter madness, would eventually turn the streets of Belfast and Derry into rivers of blood again.

* * *

The vicious years of the early 70's would return, and this time with a vengeance. A vengeance that far exceeded the atrocities of earlier years, as the men and women who had been incarcerated, full of venomous hate, wanted revenge. Some were seeking this from society, some from the security forces. But wreak their revenge, they would.

Summary deaths and severe beatings were taking place throughout 1998 and 1999. Eventually leading to full scale bombing both in Northern Ireland and back on the mainland.

David Carver and his team would eventually be recruited again to attack all paramilitaries, republican, and loyalist alike, in a manner that the security forces would be forbidden to do.

Operation Combating Evil was an enormous success but a few years later the team would re-emerge to deal with the further horrors of terrorism and the new Operation was to be called:

"Operation Freedom Fighters"

Authors Note:

In May 1997 a change of government brought in fresh ideas and attitudes to end the long and vicious conflict in the Province. One of these changes specified that military intelligence operators that had not acted within the laws of the land, would be brought to justice, and prosecuted.

This was built into the Good Friday Agreement.

Although this is a work of fiction, the very idea of the men and women that work in the raw environment of intelligence gathering, and can then subsequently face criminal prosecution, is abhorrent.

The war against terrorism needs Human Intelligence. Without it terrorism cannot be defeated. Terrorism is a cancer that propagates itself worldwide. Groups will get larger; their tentacles will stretch into every corner of the globe. If Human Intelligence sources are depleted for whatever reason, the terrorist targets will get bigger and more outrageous.

Neglect or abandonment of the use of Human Intelligence can only be to the detriment of the people; let any government do that at their peril!